THE RIGHT WAY TO BE CRIPPLED & NAKED

THE RIGHT WAY TO BE CRIPPLED & NAKED

THE FICTION OF DISABILITY

EDITED BY

Sheila Black

Michael Northen

Annabelle Hayse

CINCO PUNTOS PRESS

Printed in the U.S.

First Edition
10 9 8 7 6 5 4 3 2 1

Library of Congress Cataloging-in-Publication Data

Names: Hayse, Annabelle, editor. | Black, Sheila (Sheila Fiona), editor. | Northen, Michael, 1946- editor.
Title: The right way to be crippled & naked : the fiction of disability: an anthology / edited by Sheila Black, Michael Northen, & Annabelle Hayse.
Description: First edition. | El Paso : Cinco Puntos Press, [2017]
Identifiers: LCCN 2016014303 (print) | LCCN 2016028162 (ebook) | ISBN 978-1-941026-35-9 (paperback) | ISBN 978-1-941026-36-6
Subjects: LCSH: People with disabilities—Fiction. | Short stories, American—21st century. | BISAC: FICTION / Anthologies (multiple authors). FICTION / Literary. | SOCIAL SCIENCE / People with Disabilities. | LITERARY CRITICISM / American / General.
Classification: LCC PS509.P58 R54 2017 (print) | LCC PS509.P58 (ebook) | DDC 813/.01083561—dc23
LC record available at https://lccn.loc.gov/2016014303

Cover image of David Toole by Nick Knight / Trunk Archive. The image was shot for a fashion story celebrating beauty and grace with disabled models, 'Acess-able,' in the magazine *Dazed and Confused*, 1998.

Book and cover design by erstwhile curmudgeon
JB Bryan of La Alameda Press.
Final touches executed by Michelle Lange and Johnny B. Byrd

This is a fiercely unsentimental, deeply moving, sometimes thrilling, and utterly necessary book. These stories use the lens of physical and mental disability to enlarge and complicate our sense of the world. Characters who are too often invisible to the eye of mainstream culture shine in these pages, sharing pain, wisdom, and humor. This is a book we've needed for a long time. A great collection, too, for anyone who teaches fiction writing.

—**Jane McCafferty**, author of *First You Try Everything*

For those already familiar with disability literature to those new to the genre, there are stories to delight and challenge all readers here. *The Right Way to be Crippled & Naked* brings together a diverse chorus of voices who explore the joys and pains of the human experience with humour, compassion, anger, and unflinching honesty. Quite simply, an outstanding and memorable anthology.

—**Kathryn Allan**, author of *Accessing the Future*

Here are stories of lust and sex, news of work-arounds and strange sensations, tales of mythic patience and pissed-off patients, flash fictions of protest and red-glitter keyboards. These stories arrive full-blooded and bloody, and difference leaves its trail on form and content. Highly recommended.

—**Petra Kuppers**, author of *Studying Disability Arts and Culture*

In memory of

ROBERT FAGAN

LAURA HERSHEY

THOM JONES

CONTENTS

INTRODUCTION

The Right Way to Be Crippled & Naked is a labor of love and something of an experiment. As strange as it may seem, over a decade into the twenty-first century, there have been no previous anthologies of short fiction by writers with disabilities that feature disabled characters. There have been a handful of single-author collections by writers like Ann Finger, Floyd Skloot and Noria Jablonki that feature some disability content, and some admirable collections like John Lee Clark's *Deaf Lit Extravaganza* that highlight one particular disability. Yet no previous collection has provided a survey of the field. As in *Beauty is a Verb: The New Poetry of Disability*, we have attempted to unpack—or open up—rather than resolve the question of what is encompassed or contained within the term "disability." To this end, *The Right Way to Be Crippled & Naked* presents twenty-seven stories by as many authors—some well-known, some published here for the first time. The stories they present range widely through physical, cognitive and psychological disability and various social and physical environments. Each is followed by a short commentary giving some insight into the story's genesis, the writer's relationship and/or interest in disability and what conception of disability most animates his or her work.

We lead off these stories with Laura Hershey's "Getting Comfortable," a meditation we think sets the mood for the stories that follow. At the end of this anthology, we have added an *Afterword* by Michael Northen. It provides a brief historical and literary context for the stories included here and helps place them within the framework of disability literature. Beyond such critical concerns, however, all these stories were ones that moved or challenged us, unsettled and upended us—stories in which we felt the slight shock one feels when experiences hitherto unexpressed come into words. We hope you will enjoy reading this volume as much as we enjoyed putting it together.

Sheila Black
Michael Northen
Annabelle Hayse

Laura Hershey

GETTING COMFORTABLE

I just spent the past twenty minutes getting comfortable. "Move the head pillow down and a little to the right," I told Ruth, my attendant. "Push my shoulders up and to the right...a little more. Now push the pillow down again. Straighten out my hips, please."

What I really wanted to do was write. First, though, I had to get comfortable. "Now could you pull my right knee to the left. More." It will be a while before another attendant comes—which is a good thing, offering promise of some quiet time, with just my partner Robin, without my having to instruct, advise, respond or wonder whether an aide is hearing and/or seeing the private words I dictate to my computer. But that precious time undisturbed is also time unaided. "Shift my hips a little more to the right. Then pull my feet down. Also, can you move my hands up a little." For a while at least, my body will have to stay in whatever position Ruth leaves it.

"Move my shoulders up and to the right," I said. "Hmm. Okay, now pull my hips down just a little...Now shoulders up again. No, straight up."

This went on for a while.

"My back still doesn't feel quite right," I said. "I think we need to start over. Sorry." I said "sorry" even though Ruth had shown no sign of annoyance. "Could you lower the head of the bed. Take out the pillow for now...Okay, now, pull me up straighter by my arms, pretty far up...even further. Now scoot my hips to the right again. All right, let's raise the head of the bed again...There, stop. No, maybe a little higher. Good. Now will you put the pillow back under my head. Move it down and to the right. Pull my chin up, up and a little to the left. Now pull it straight up. And pull my right knee to the left."

I stopped to assess my position. "All right?" Ruth asked. "You comfortable?"

"Yeah," I answered. "So could you set up my lap table and my computer?"

"You sure?"

"*Yes*," I said, a little impatiently. I was anxious to write.

For a long time, and still sometimes, I have hidden the part of my life that involved the services of another woman's strong hands, arms, legs, back.

I saw no literary potential in scenes like the one above. They were merely background music to my story, I thought, not the story itself. My simple, seemingly straightforward, first-person sentences conceal the truth of the help I need in order to carry out my daily actions. I say, "I went to the bookstore and looked through a dozen books and finally bought this book of poetry by Adrienne Rich"—(not, "Carmen drove me to the bookstore and held a dozen books up for me to look at, turned the pages for me, put all of them back onto the shelf except for one by Adrienne Rich. Then Carmen got my wallet out of my purse for me and handed my credit card to the cashier, who rang up the sale.") My grammar gave no ground to the idea of dependency, for that's what I've heard it called in fundraising appeals and theoretical discussion. Instead, I spoke of my actions the way I feel them, as self-determined events filling my days. To people my scenes with a supporting cast might conjure me, the main actor, as a tragic figure, as a body with need but no will.

Readers, I feared, may not be able to read such a writer, may not relax enough to follow me on the paths I choose to chart. A reader must trust her writer, even if that means meeting only the physical writer, a floating intellect. So I deleted the dance of *turn, shift, lift, pull, push.*

Why now, then? Why reveal the tedious process involved in getting comfortable? Why not just forget about all that and write?

"Just a minute," I say to Ruth. "Before you go, I need my knees straightened out. And pull my elbows outward and up a little bit. Also, could you scratch between my eyebrows…Good, thanks."

Why write about this? Why divulge the esoteric secrets of this craft of getting comfortable?

I could, and usually do, write without telling what it takes to get ready to write. I could disembody my writing, let my words *stand* alone, *march* across the page, a straight line of characters on paper, of ideas soaring through the ether. Text without context, at least without the physical context of its creation. A pretext of text, sexy or sexless. Text extracted from existence, text that excludes distress. I could write mind-over-matter text. Text expressing the best of the story; text repressing the rest of the story. (Or is it the other way around?)

Now my joints rest in comfortable positions. Each tissue-inch holds its proper share of weight and pressure. I'm breathing easily, my head well supported and turned to just the right angle, my back as straight as it's going to get. Ruth is gone. Robin is in the next room. I sit in a silent space that awaits my words.

Now that I'm comfortable, I can start making choices. Do I start the story *here*, with my focused concentration and blank screen? Or do I start the story *there*, with the concentrated effort needed to assemble a body capable of thinking and writing? Do I write as disembodied mind, or discombobulated body?

I could try to write in the voice of a body easily arranged, a body requiring only a thoughtless stretch of limb or a self-controlled fidget to achieve comfort. Since that simple, graceful body is not my own, that would be the same as writing without a body.

If I leave behind my body to write, what (how) does the reader read? Can a reader read a mind without having a body to read?

On the other hand, when I write from, of, about a discombobulated body, how (what) does the reader read? Can a reader read a mind while worrying about a body?

And what about the writer? If I write about my body, will I disappear into the shadow of the taller, stronger, more mobile body of the woman working on my body? Will her quick, easy movements draw the reader's attention away from my main points? As I highlight my attendants' contribution to the plot, do I make myself irrelevant?

That sometimes happens in real life. A store clerk will listen to my question and then turn to face my attendant, replying, "The elevator is at the back. You can take her this way, through the magazine section—there's plenty of room for the wheelchair—and then turn right and go all the way back." Some strangers must see my attendants as keepers, as wardens wholly responsible for me, serving alternately as nurse, as guardian, as conduit to the world of the normal.

If these strangers knew about the extent to which I depend on these helpers for the smallest maneuver, for relief from discomfort, and for readying myself for any productive activity, would this not deepen their sense of my utter helplessness?

So why should I be the one to script that stereotype? Why describe the bodily ministrations performed by other people for my benefit? Why not concentrate on my own heroic journeys?

This *is* my journey, from chaos to order. I locate the stress points and iron them out, shuttling like a diplomat among my brain, my voice, my attendant and my body. My quest carries me to far shores, elbow to toe, neck to tailbone. I do battle with inertia and pressure. No: I negotiate a dynamic peace.

This is also my narrative: I envision an aesthetic of comfort, the parts of my body that do function—eyes and windpipe, tongue and imagination, nerves and ears and judgment—working together to optimum effect. I begin to tell that story, assembling sentences, then rearranging them. My discombobulated body the conflict, my attendant the instrument of resolution. Who is the protagonist? Perhaps we both are. A narrative not linear, but circular.

The process of getting comfortable demands a certain style, both explicatory and poetic: *You see, this is the way I want it. This is what I mean. Not quite that far. Left, not right. Pull a little further. Push again.* A careful calculation of timing, tune and tempo. This is my language: explication, correction, repetition.

I've decided that I needn't leave my disabled body behind in order to fool and comfort my reader. Instead I'll violate what Nancy Mairs, that chronicler of her own discombobulated body, calls "the conventions of polite silence," in order to write, as she puts it, "as plainly and truthfully as the squirms and wriggles of the human psyche will permit" (p.xi).

One day, one reader, or perhaps many readers, will be reading this after—or while—going through a similar process of request, instruction, adjustment, to get comfortable. Such a reader may peer into the page and see herself reflected, at last. This reader may weep with relief, or may snort with relieved impatience—what took you so long? For this reader was way ahead of me, always already knowing that there is no authentic thought that is not born in the thinker's body's cells, nerves, secretions, in its kinetic and/or sensate experience.

No real journey can happen without a foot on some piece of ground (or a bottom in some seat) and the wind's kiss on skin. There is no philosophy in the absence of a sweating fear; no humor without hiccups; no love without blood in a beating heart.

So get yourself comfortable, and let's begin.

—LAURA HERSHEY—

I only met Laura Hershey once though I corresponded with her because we were both writing about disability. This was back in 2010 before Mike Northen and I became involved in editing *Beauty is a Verb*, an anthology of poetry by disabled poets. Laura's work and this essay, which she wrote for the book, are memorable and integral parts of that volume. We met her at the Denver AWP conference when she circled her wheelchair around me and said she thought we had a lot to talk about and would I like to go hiking the next day with her and her partner Robin Stevens and their adopted daughter.

Laura was so comfortable in her own skin she made you comfortable, too. She was funny and forthright and smart and loving, though she had a disability that most popular culture would view as *overwhelming* or *tragic* or *hopeless*. Yet Laura so quietly and calmly and sensibly—and yes, joyfully—refused to view her life that way, that once you were with her for five minutes, you stopped thinking that way too. She knew how to get comfortable and how to live fully and uniquely, with courage and love.

I regret I didn't go hiking with Laura Hershey that day. I chose instead to hang around and go to a bunch of poetry panels because I was sure that I was coming back through Denver, and I would hike with her and talk with her all night long sometime very soon. That sometime never happened. Laura Hershey died suddenly that November of a lung infection. She was forty-eight, a year older than I was, but I had thought of her as much older—simply because she seemed to know all the things I was just learning: how to be a disability activist; how to live and fight for the rights of people with disabilities; what it would take to remake the notion of disability in the public imagination.

"Getting Comfortable" is the perfect way to open this book. It tells us the first thing we need to know—how to get inside the non-normative body without drama, without undue sentimentality, but with a fierce regard for truth, the kind of truth we refer to when we speak of "truth and beauty."

—*Sheila Black*

Kobus Moolman

THE SWIMMING LESSON

to Julia

24º C

Her name was Maggie. She smelled of cigarettes not perfume. She held me in her arms. And I floated.

Lap 1

I would have never dared call her by her name. Though she insisted. I was brought up properly. I called all women older than myself Tannie. And all older men Oom. She was nobody's Tannie though. So we settled on Auntie. Auntie Maggie.

Lap 3

They lived next door. Auntie Maggie and Uncle John, who had been stricken with polio as a young man and played the drums in a jazz band in his spare time, and their two daughters, Rayne, who was the same age as my older sister and teased her mercilessly, and Janine, who was two years younger than me. There was also a relative of Aunt Maggie's who stayed over with them, although an infrequent visitor. I never knew his name. His real name that is. I only ever called him by his stage name. I was allowed to. It would have been strange calling him Oom. Oom Tickey the Clown.

Lap 5

Tickey was a midget. I think I only met him once. When he visited next door. And I was about to have my lesson. He was sitting on the low wall of the veranda. A cigar in his one hand and a quart of beer in the other. He was staring off into the distance and only nodded when Auntie Maggie introduced me. I saw him more frequently in his shows though. When the Big Top visited town. The Boswell-Wilkie circus with its lions and its elephants and its white horses with plumed headdresses and coiffed tails and its trapeze artists swinging through the air in shiny gold costumes. And the ubiquitous smell of popcorn and sawdust and animal shit.

Lap 7

My costume was black. It was tight. It squeezed my testicles. It had a white drawstring that I tied in the front in a bow. The way I did on my boots. I would put my costume on at home. And then walk next door. Up the long gravel driveway just in my small costume and my big black boots and with a towel around my shoulders. And no matter how carefully or slowly I walked, the gravel always made a loud noise beneath my big boots. And made me feel as if all the eyes in the world were watching me.

Lap 9

I also had water-wings. That I carried in my hand. They were made of very thin plastic. Mine were blue. My sister's were red. Although she did not use hers anymore. She did not need them. You put your arms through them and then pushed them right up to the top of your arm, around your biceps, and then Auntie Maggie would blow through the small clear valve and they would puff up quickly and become tight. Your arms would stick out like a scarecrow then. But it was better than drowning Auntie Maggie said, so I must just shaddup. Auntie Maggie used to say shaddup quite a lot. Especially to the two girls. And even to Uncle John. My mother would have never said that to my father. I don't know what would have happened if she had.

Lap 11

Some kids also wore a plastic inflatable ring around their middle. Together with their water-wings. I didn't have one. I thought they were for sissies. But I had seen children got up in this way somewhere. I can't be certain where though. It can't have been at the public pool in Pine Street because I'd only ever gone there years later as an adult. When I watched the boys jumping off the high-diving board. (I couldn't even bring myself to use the small one.) *Check me! Check me! Check me!* they always shouted. Before plummeting through the air like bright red stones. And there was an older woman who walked around in a bikini unaware that her pubic hair was sticking out of the side of her costume. I wasn't sure whether to look or to look away. But I was glad that for once at least somebody else was being stared at.

Lap 13

I was forever losing my water-wings. That's what my mother said. You are forever losing your wings, you nincompoop. I swear you'd lose your head if it wasn't attached to your body. That made me laugh. The thought of me walking around without a head. Bumping into things and falling over. More so than usual.

Lap 15
Auntie Maggie wore an old black one-piece costume. It was rough and smelled of mothballs. Even in the water. She wore this when she gave me my lessons. But one day when I was looking over the concrete wall that separated our two yards (I think I was practising spying) I saw her and the two girls. They were all wearing bikinis. Brightly coloured tops and bottoms. My father said it was shameful for women to walk around like that. They may as well be in their underwear. That's what my father said. My sister had a blue one-piece costume with little daisies up the side. And a little white skirt sewn around the bottom.

Lap 17
It was a circular plastic pool, reinforced with a wire frame. The pool was sunk into the ground except for the last foot or so which was bordered in bricks. The water was cold always. And green. Not from neglect. But from the reflections of the shrubs and the bushes that grew close and overhung the water in some places. Like an exotic island advert at the cinema. Complete with cigarettes. And everybody walking about barefoot in brightly coloured costumes. Laughing.

Lap 19
Auntie Maggie smoked cigarillos. I can't remember what brand they were. I think it sounded foreign. Like the name of an imported car. But perhaps I'm getting confused with the green Chevy El Camino that Uncle John owned. (I don't think that car was imported though.) It had a white canopy at the back. And once I drove in the back with my sister and with Rayne and Janine. I can't remember where we were going. Maybe to town. To the library or to King's Sports to buy a set of tennis balls or a cricket bat. It would definitely not have been to Sunday School. My mother said that although they were nice people, Auntie Maggie and Uncle John were not saved. They took the name of the Lord in vain. And they drank alcohol. So we shouldn't spend too much time with them. But I didn't know what she meant by saved. Auntie Maggie certainly saved me by teaching me to swim. I remember you had to climb over the tail-gate of their car because it could

not open. Maybe it was broken. Maybe it was just stuck. I can't remember. But if it was stuck Uncle John could have opened it because he had very strong hands. So I don't know. Uncle John played the drums so maybe that made his hands strong. Also maybe because he walked with crutches.

Lap 21

I didn't need to use crutches all the time. Like Uncle John. I only used them after an operation. To my ankle or my knee. When my leg was in plaster-of-paris and I was not allowed to put any pressure on it. I hated the wooden ones that came under your arms and made you walk like a penguin. The best ones were the silver aluminium ones that clipped around your biceps. They were very light. Which was good. But they made a metallic clicking noise when you walked. So that when you walked down the school corridor you knew that everyone knew you were coming.

Lap 23

In biology they taught us that about seventy percent of the human body is water. In geography we learned that the earth is actually more liquid than solid. That all the planets and the stars and the asteroids and the moons float about in space as if on a dark tide. Carried away further and further from our tiny beginnings. I liked all these ideas though I didn't understand them. I liked to think that I wasn't walking. That I wasn't even ever falling. But that all the time I was floating. Suspended really. Like one of those trapeze artists in their gold costumes who came on after Tickey the Clown had tripped over his shoes. And fallen flat on his white face.

Lap 25

Auntie Maggie's skin gave off the smell of tobacco. The way other women's skin smelled of soap. Or onions. Or sour milk. Or Johnson & Johnson's baby powder. The way my mother did. Because my father got hay-fever from all perfumes and scented soaps. Except Lifebuoy. Which my mother refused point-blank to use. That's soap for poor people she said. Who live in the square railways houses in Prestbury. Or in Oribi Village. Where her parents lived.

Lap 27

There are a whole lot of different types of cigarette smell. There's the smell on your shirt after you've been in a busy bar all night. There's the smell of the ashtray in your car after you've been to the beach for a weekend with your friends. Then there's the smell of your grandparents' house. They drank tea and smoked cigarettes and played cards all day. So the smell was part of the house itself. Part of the wallpaper. Part of the linoleum floor. In Oribi Village. But then there's also another type of cigarette smell. A smell you sometimes remember very clearly. And sometimes forget. The smell of smoky hair. Long dark hair tied up in a bun. Or loose at night falling down the back of a long white gown. A thin gown that slides up eagerly over long strong legs. Up. Up. Up.

Lap 29
Kick! Kick! Kick! Kick! Kick! Auntie Maggie shouted in her gruff smoky voice. *Lift your head up. Up! Up! Up!* As I floated in her arms. On the green water. In her strong, bare arms. Up and down.

Lap 31
Up and down on the dark green waves. Up and down. Up and…

Lap 33
Below me the water is clear. I can see the white rectangular tiles on the bottom. The sun slides bright yellow discs rapidly across the bottom. Like a game. My arms are strong. They pull me through the water. They are doing all the work. My legs drag behind me. *Kick, kick, kick,* Maggie used to say. In her gruff voice. But my legs were stronger then. They're worn out now. Forty years later. It's all I can do to keep them straight out behind me. To stop them sinking and slowing me down.

Lap 35
Operations are meant to fix you. But after thirteen operations I think I'm actually worse off. I can't run as I used to be able to do when I was a child. I can't jump. Never mind hop. I remember Rayne once telling me (this was before Maggie got cancer and died, before John re-married and they moved away) that her father was fine before he went into the hospital. He went in to have some very minor surgery. Appendix or tonsils or something equally inconsequential. And he came home paralysed from the waist down with polio. I don't know how that happens. Just one of those things, my mother always used to say when she was trying to explain the inexplicable. Just one of those things. Like why some children are born normal and others

are born with cleft palates or with holes in their heart or with water on the brain. Which isn't really water at all but actually cerebrospinal fluid — the clear fluid that surrounds the brain and the spinal cord.

Lap 37

I'm coming up to the end now. Just four more laps to go. Strange the kinds of things that go through your head when you're swimming up and down, up and down, in a public pool. When you were at school, and it came to the swimming lesson, you always had to ask permission to get out ten minutes before everyone else so that you had enough time to put on your boots. 'Please Miss…Please Sir…' Rushing, rushing. And then the lace snaps because you pulled it too hard. Or it comes out of one of the eyelets and you can't push it back because the plastic seal at the end has broken and the lace has frayed. Panic stations, your mother always called it. And then after John and the girls moved away, if you wanted to swim, you had to go across the road to the Dewar's. They were an elderly couple who had erected a circular plastic pool behind their house. The pool was not sunk into the ground, like Maggie's pool (I call it Maggie's pool for convenience, because of course it did not belong to her but to the whole family). There was a long ladder that you had to climb in order to get into the pool. The ladder was aluminium. In summer it got so hot that it burned your hands and the soles of your feet. Do you remember, there was a strip of black slasto paving around Maggie's pool? The paving got very hot in summer too. But you usually took off your boots sitting on the grass and then only had two or three steps on the hot slasto before you got to the pool. Where Maggie was already waiting for you. Smelling of cigarettes not perfume.

Lap 39

Auntie Maggie got cancer. Cancer was a swear word in our house. Because my mother's parents both succumbed to it. It was like saying shaddup. Auntie Maggie got thin. She stopped smoking. I stopped going over to her house for swimming lessons. When I saw her I wanted to shout at the top of my voice *Shaddup! Shaddup! Shaddup!* Just so that she would hear me above the noise of the disease that was eating through the tissue and the nerves in her liver and in her pancreas.

Lap 40

Maggie saved me. By teaching me to swim. Although nothing could save her from what was in her bloodstream. When I swam then I no longer walked lopsided. I no longer dragged my right foot. My right knee no longer buckled at every step. I no longer fell over. Flat on my face. Because I floated instead.

Finish.

—KOBUS MOOLMAN—

There is a poem on my laptop I started ten years ago. And have not been able to complete. It is a poem about water and about death. About a very good friend, a poet and musician, who drowned himself in the ocean. It is a poem about my own relationship with water, a medium which allows me a grace and strength and speed in my body which I have not been able to achieve elsewhere.

Because I have not been able to write that poem (and may never, I suspect), because I find swimming easier than walking, and because I seek to speak more closely in the language of my own arhythmic body, I decided to write a story instead that would somehow draw all of these ideas together.

But with the added element of memory. Not memory as the recovery of fact or memory as mechanism for releasing actuality. But memory as what Michael Hamburger, the German poet and translator, called "the darkroom for the development of fictions."

In this way, "The Swimming Lesson" is more evocation than autobiography, more a kind of conjuring or calling up than an act of mimesis. The story works with what we usually term real-life characters (including myself), but it is not interested in what really happened. It is interested instead in how the past (childhood) intersects with the present, swims alongside the present, and also how the present (the adult swimming his daily lengths in the pool) makes the past understandable and even bearable.

Tantra Bensko

VIRUS ON FIRE

The most beautiful man you have seen is part tree. He lifts his arms slowly in front of the crowd around him. He can barely hold them up, but doing so keeps him trim. His finely formed cheeks, square, with nice rounded edges, catch all the sun they can. His eyes are deep but you know he couldn't feel you if he reaches out. His hands extend into grey cutaneous horns, waste material of warts that just keep growing.

He lifts his feet, with their roots, while people cheer. That gives him strong leg muscles, but he's not muscle-bound, as he can't do much work around the place. He keeps to himself, and you want to tell him stories in the corner. Everyone else is busy. Everyone else has felt many women. You walk up to a tree and hug it, petting its bark, and glance at him. You love trees.

You wonder if anyone has ever put her arms around him. His waist is fine. People stand back, so they don't catch his virus.

You hear someone say it's because his mother must have made love with his father in a tree. But his father left when he saw the branches coming in. And his mother won't talk. Only the man's brother pours his bath, and sews special clothes he dresses him in, and gives him a hand-rolled cigarette stuck in a stick he hollowed out. He places the contrivance between the tight branches in between the tree-fingers.

One of the other freaks performing moves his head back and forth lugubriously, making his nose, which flops down below his chin, wave squishily. Another one balances a ball on his head like a seal, and claps his malformed flippers. Tree-man can only perform with them once a month and you can see why. After he curls into a ball, uncrouching slowly, raising his giant hands to the sky, and standing on his toe roots, looking up, he becomes a little more tree. He can barely move afterwards. His sap is running downward, but you want to make it rise for you. If he could just get better, he would have so much more life to live. You would cook for him. You would clean him.

You look in the mirror at the trading circle and make faces while you dance to the drums. You like to make people laugh. One time you drew an outline of your face on the mirror. It was easy to draw it to make it look just like you. But you shouldn't call that cheating. Sometimes the sunshine feels so mellow on your face you can hardly stand it. You barely sneak open an eye to look at tree man to see if he notices the angle of the sun on your sensuous face.

His brother is giving him a cigarette in a hollowed out stick to revive him. The cigarette catches his hand branches on fire. His eyes are closed as he takes a drag, meaning he can't see your dramatic look of horror, and he doesn't feel the horns at all on fire. Until the heat informs his face. His eyes get big and he screeches and rolls on the ground. But the smoldering has gone deep. Like peat moss under the ground, his brother says it will never really be put out.

You watch, and you wait.

Some of the limbs grow brittle and break off, some harden. His brother tries making one into charcoal but it doesn't work at all. He thinks of eating it powdered to settle his stomach but the thought upsets it instead.

A fire inside makes the tree man more poetic. More smoldering. He looks at you, as his hand becomes closer to being able to feel you. As perhaps his self confidence grows, as he can wave now, relatively smoothly. The fire in his hand would leave an imprint on your body if he touched you long. Your naked body. Your long, narrow back. Your low-riding hips.

It would say you are his. Only he could leave a mark that shape. His hand grows smaller and more beautiful, the other one still tree. The small one looks like a pine cone that went mad. You make sure he can smell you. You stand close to him, as you are fertile.

Your mother always told you it's important to plant trees. You give him a look you hope he understands: you want him to plant a baby tree inside you. You want it to grow and take you over. It is already made of fire.

I wrote "Virus on Fire" after watching a documentary about a man who had a rare wart overgrowth virus, giving him the appearance of a tree. His hands and feet looked like heavy grey branches. His countenance and demeanor were gentle.

I've always felt compassion for people who struggled with isolating bodily symptoms, especially when the cause mystified them. When I grew into my own disability, my empathy became even more informed by the difficulty of doing tasks healthy people take for granted. I imagined his life, wondering if anyone has fallen in love with him. I hope so.

I don't mind being alone. I can't expect anyone to voluntarily take on a romance with someone so damaged. I could imagine someone doing so, though, with the kind, patient tree man. I wrote the story from the point of view of that person who could embrace and celebrate that man's unique beauty.

Raymond Luczak

WINTER EYES

Bright autumn days are what I miss the most, but I hadn't cared for those trees back when I could see. The way a dozen hues of orange and gold could wave leafy hands in a breeze seemed like fires trembling with happiness. I didn't know how much I'd ignored color until I started to notice patches of blankness float across the horizon of my vision. I thought they were only temporary, but the floating patches grew bigger and lingered. I couldn't always see everything directly in front of me. It was as if parts of my vision had been erased, and not always in the same spots every day. But I realize now that my eyes had been like those brilliant leaves in full knowledge of what must come next, and that was the barrenness of winter.

As a photographer, I had always found winter the most vexing of seasons to shoot. When snow coats everything like thick slabs of paint, it can overwhelm the film. There's too much white, which means refraction of light from all directions. If I don't adjust its exposure levels, I lose so much detail in the blank canvas in front of me, so, like a painter with very little oil left on her palette, I must choose the half-hidden details I want to showcase. Sometimes my pictures had the same stark qualities of Andrew Wyeth's paintings made in Maine. I was proud of not needing to retouch these images in my computer.

Like my idol Robert Mapplethorpe, who'd obsessively pursued lighting the white Calla lilies and staging them just so before capturing the blackest black background possible on film, I wanted the whitest possible with a mere ghost of details, as if everything had been bleached, and outside where I couldn't control the elements. I couldn't wait for winter to return. Spring, summer, and fall were too full of color, and they nearly hurt my eyes even back when I could see normally. I didn't want to feel overwhelmed when I took out my camera. Where should I focus? What was the most important detail right there in front of me? I wanted the landscape to be stripped away of ornamentation because the few remaining details were powerful figments of something larger than what could be captured. Suggestion is far more resonant, and gives us fuel for dreams on cold nights when we are alone in our beds.

My husband Paul loved to hunt deer. He couldn't wait for the first day of hunting season. He cleaned his rifles and knives, applied for his yearly license, and brushed the dust off his neon orange vest while awaiting his buddies from his construction job to show up at our cabin. When he and his buddies brought the dead animal into the chill of our garage, they cleaned out the deer and divided up our share of the venison for our freezer. I couldn't bear to look at it in the garage; it had eyes!

Paul loved the woods more than anyone I knew. He didn't mind the solitude, and I married him for that reason. He liked pulling at his bushy beard as if he wanted it to grow longer faster, and he was fond of smoking his pipe, which was his daily pleasure after working around the cabin. He liked to be kept busy when we drove up north on weekends, and there was always something to do. Wood needed to be chopped and stacked for the next winter. Unruly brush overtaking the path to our cabin had to be trimmed. Leaks had to be inspected and caulked. He always told me that if I weren't busy taking pictures, I should be keeping warm inside with a quilt and a book. "You're way smarter than me anyways," he always said with a smile. I had two college degrees; he never went to college. He worked nonstop in construction from spring to fall, and winter was his time off.

Our marriage hit a rough patch a few years back when he found out why I couldn't get pregnant. His sperm count was too low. He fell under a dark cloud, and not even the prospect of another hunting season cheered him up. He stared off into space even when I suggested that we adopt a baby, perhaps from among the Somali and Hmong refugees who lived in St. Paul. His buddies tried to cajole him with invites to nab a deer together, but it was something that we had to ride out. When spring came, it was time to start building new houses again. He worked for a corporation that assembled prefabricated pieces into houses that looked more or less the same in any subdivision and they were sold at a nice markup.

His job was why he loved our cabin so much. His grandfather had built it with his own hands, and none of it was prefab. Here in Minnesota, most people head south from their cabins in winter, but not us. We liked weathering the drops in temperature and appreciating the bone-tingling warmth that came from our sturdy fireplace.

That winter I noticed that I was tripping a lot more.

He was the first to say, "What's going on?"

I tried to focus on him in the dimness.

"You can't see me, can you?"

He stepped into the glow that came from the fireplace and held me.

When Dr. Rasmussen said it was only a question of time before I became truly blind, I focused on the ends of his waxed mustache curling upward as he frowned gently. He stopped talking for a moment. By then I couldn't see all of his face in a single glance. Later I would remember a budding liver spot was hiding in the shadow of his mustache.

He held my hand for a long moment on the table. Paul, who was sitting next to me, didn't say anything, but I heard his sharp intakes of breath, which meant he was trying not to cry, and he never cried. I squinted, trying to sharpen my vision a bit more to see the thin hairs coating the back of Dr. Rasmussen's thick fingers, but all I saw was the fuzzy outline of his hand against the gray tabletop. Once he withdrew his hand, Paul's hand took his place.

There was nothing new to add. We had gotten our fifth opinion, which was identical to everyone else's. We couldn't afford any more opinions.

That was also the day I realized that I had to stop wasting my time taking pictures. I took my camera and aimed it at my face one last time while I stood in front of a mirror. It was something that I'd always done when it wasn't winter. I had been well known for taking one self-portrait after another, charting the subtle changes in my face as I aged. I had quite a few shows done of my work, and I sold a few prints over the years.

When I looked at my last self-portrait after importing it into my computer, I was startled. I hadn't realized that there had been the start of a tear's dribble leaking out of my left eye as I glanced downward in the moment of pressing the shutter button. I was smiling, as I always did in the face of hard times, but my countenance told the truth. I stared at the computer monitor for a long time, memorizing the atlas of lines sketched across the globe of my face. It eventually became one of my most popular prints once the story behind it became public. I refused all invitations to attend gallery openings for my work. I had gotten tired of the strain of pity in their voices when they expressed sorrow over my vision. Paul had never cared for gallery openings; in fact, he never felt comfortable mingling with people who talked above his head.

I asked my sister Fiona to take over. It was overwhelming for her to deal with these galleries and museums at first, but she understood why I had to let go even when I could still see some. I also said no more writing abstracts for exhibition catalogs and introductions to retrospective books by photographers. I didn't want any more reminders of my old life. I also didn't want to burden Paul.

As my vision expanded and contracted hourly, I snapshot everything mentally and left the undeveloped prints in the darkroom of my brain so that one day, when I couldn't see anymore, I could turn on that red light and swirl the photographs in water until details became clearer than crystal. I watched movies on my iPod because it was small enough for me to see in a single glance, and later, when I couldn't see anymore, I listened to these movies and remembered their facial expressions, the very bounty of my old life.

In time I forgot what my own work looked like. All I remembered were the hours I'd spent behind the camera, learning to love the challenge of winter: the squinting through the viewfinder, the light meter checks, the aperture changes. It was my real eye, and it was a perfect one.

Each time I saw Paul's face in bits and pieces, he looked sadder and older. Wisps of white stuck out like twigs from his beard. He didn't say much.

"We'll get through this, Paul."

He tried to smile. He didn't do a good job of it, but I understood.

Then came the day when I knew I had to stop praying for my vision to return. I could still see blobs moving about on the periphery of my vision, but they told me nothing of substance. Just movement. I didn't have the heart to tell him that my vision wasn't coming back. I went through weeks of mobility and orientation training. It was so frustrating, but I was always careful not to tell Paul just how much. I didn't want him to worry.

When he drove me to appointments, I asked him to describe what he saw while driving. He wasn't shy with his bawdy opinions, so he made me laugh. Listening to him gave me a great deal of comfort. It meant I hadn't lost my way.

By then I'd convinced him how much we needed to continue as before. We'd still spend winters up in our cabin. I had all the time in the world to learn every contour of our cabin, and I would still cook. My cane would map out the safest route on the terrain outside.

Each time I touched Paul when he returned to the cabin, I reached out for his beard. This always made him chuckle. He made me feel strong even though I felt like a wren in his arms.

*

Each time—when my eyes had healed enough from yet another surgical procedure—the gauze was removed with my silent prayer that I would catch the unholy sight of Paul's disembodied voice. Instead I saw only the perfect blend of black and white hanging like a window shade on the wall of my eyelids. I ached to see his beard in all its gnarliness and his unabashed beams of teeth whenever he broke out in laughter. But he touched me far more than he had since the early days of our courtship. Depending on the pressure and location of our fingers, we developed a shorthand code of touch.

It was a matter of time before I stopped thinking in color. All I cared about was detail, and it had nothing to do with sight. The most important detail was him coming back from the woods—the clumps of snow still trapped in his beard, the drip of his runny nose, and the clammy moisture from inside his union suit underwear. When he and his buddies brought in their first kill of the season, I insisted on touching the deer in the garage. My request surprised them. Before when I could see, I couldn't look at a dead creature up close, but my fingertips told me a very different story. Its fur was soft. Its antlers had splintered off in one place. Its nose was surprisingly coarse. The garage reeked of guts and sweat. One loses, and one gains.

—RAYMOND LUCZAK—

The tall tales surrounding the giant lumberjack Paul Bunyan (he could
swing a huge ax across clusters of old-growth trees in a single blow,
his footprints became lakes, he had a blue ox named Babe) had always
fascinated me growing up, but it wasn't until I moved to Minnesota that
I saw how much the state had embraced Paul Bunyan. I had also noticed
the paucity of realistic portrayals of disabled characters in fiction—they
were usually heroic and saint-like in "conquering" their disability, or to be
pitied because they couldn't participate fully in the able-bodied world. That
they could lead ordinary lives like anyone else seemed out of the question.
Given how inspiration porn has often made disabled people seem "heroic"
beyond their means, I wondered how they would live in the shadow of a
character so extraordinary in strength and size. Could they be heroes not
because they tried to be able-bodied but because they sought strength in
their own limitations? That was how I came to explore the lives of disabled
Minnesotans through the kaleidoscope of the Paul Bunyan legends.
"Winter Eyes" comes from my forthcoming short story collection *Paul
Bunyan Doesn't Live Here Anymore.*

Noria Jablonski

SOLO IN THE SPOTLIGHT

Mother crocheted and John the Gambler, he whittled. Animals mostly, potbellied old men, lined up single file on the mantel. When he wasn't whittling, he flipped the pages of catalogues that came to the house—Sears & Roebuck, ladies' clothing, Mother's magazines of yarn and crochet designs. John the Gambler wore a pair of crocheted slippers with rosettes on the toes. I, naturally, had no use for slippers.

John the Gambler was Mother's friend. He lived with us the summer I was eight. She called him John all that summer, and when he was gone he became John the Gambler.

This was back when I was collecting mermaids. I hadn't intended on collecting them. I saw one I liked, a china figurine, then Mother bought me another, and Mother's friend before John the Gambler added another. Three little mermaids on my vanity. I soon amassed a school of mermaids. This is what happens when people see that you have two or three of something.

On some nights, Mother put Arthur Murray on the hi-fi and practiced the cha-cha with John the Gambler. I watched and wished. Her sassy kicks, the click and scrape of her heels on the living room linoleum, made me wish I could give up my tongue for a set of legs, like the mermaid in the fairy tale. Though that one doesn't get the prince in the end. I did, I got mine, legs or no.

Days while Mother worked, John the Gambler took me to the Boardwalk. He liked the shows, he liked the rides. I think he liked me okay too. On account of my chair, we got to go right to the front of every line. He always smoked a little grass before we headed in. I didn't mind, and I didn't tell. Some days we'd go to the track, just the two of us. I liked to watch the horses run. I liked eating chocolate milk that John the Gambler fed to me from a wooden spoon.

SEE THE REAL MERMAID! is what the sign said at Neptune's Kingdom.

I was excited and breathing hard, and John the Gambler couldn't wheel me fast enough through the crowd. At the tank, people jumped aside, pulling their small children away from me by the shoulders. Don't stare, they mouthed. The mermaid was not a mermaid at all, it was a manatee, a sea cow. The placard above the tank said that sailors delirious with fever and starvation would see the manatees and hallucinate beautiful women. Mermaids. Many sailors leapt to watery graves chasing after manatees, apparently. I was crushed. I thought, I am a real mermaid. A fat brown beady-eye sea cow, that's me.

That evening, John the Gambler whittled me a manatee. He didn't mean to be unkind.

Another night he brought home a TV set. For two weeks, before he had to return it, Mother crocheted, John the Gambler whittled the Seven Dwarves, and I watched television. During the *Mickey Mouse Club*, they showed a commercial for a new doll, three of them on a stage, turning slow and shining under the lights like cars on a showroom floor. I want her, I said.

You have dolls already, said Mother. John the Gambler hollowed out Dopey's ear with his Swiss army knife.

It was true, I did have dolls, baby dolls. They didn't have fur-trimmed capes slung over evening gowns, bubble hairdos, mean sidelong eyes. They didn't have breasts.

The TV went away, and, for a time, John the Gambler was glum. I didn't care so much about the TV set, I only wanted that doll. Then, on one of his up days, John the Gambler took me to a toy store, said I could have anything I wanted. I picked the one in a black sparkly dress, strapless and molded to her body with a netting flounce at the ankles. Solo in the Spotlight, she was called. In her dress she looked like the pretty kind of mermaid, not the real kind.

When mother saw it, she looked pained, and all the blood went out of her face like it did the time I asked her to paint my toenails (I've got *toes*, just not feet exactly). Oh for God's sake, said John the Gambler, slapping his thigh with a catalogue folded in half.

Eventually the sparkles wore off the front of the dress where my doll's chest stuck out.

John the Gambler went away, and Mother slid his carved figures off the mantel into a cardboard box. That manatee he made for me, I didn't keep with the rest of my mermaid collection. I kept it on my nightstand where I could reach it with my head. I chewed it at night before falling asleep. My teeth loved the soft wood. When I asked Mom if I could have that box full of wood, she sighed, drew her lower lip in and let it go.

I still do it, collect odd wooden figures and chew them. I gnaw off the faces and limbs. Joe, my husband, he said what I do is art, so I became an artist. We're all some kind of artist. Mother crocheted, John the Gambler whittled, and Joe's art is fixing toasters. He put a motor on my chair, rigged it with a stick so I can drive it with my teeth. My *chair*iot. I get around on my own now, I do my sculptures, and I play music. With my tongue, of course. On the Boardwalk come summertime, me with my red-glitter electric keyboard, I'm practically famous.

—NORIA JABLONSKI—

"Solo in the Spotlight" was written during a summer workshop I took with Elizabeth McCracken, author of *The Giant's House*. I had clipped an obituary from the newspaper, knowing there was something in that short description of a remarkable life that could become a story: Celestine Tate Harrington, a quadriplegic woman known for performing on a keyboard that she played with her tongue, had died in a car accident. More than twenty years earlier she won the right to raise her own daughter when she demonstrated to a judge how she could change the baby's diaper with her teeth. The story I wrote is an imagined version of her childhood told from her point of view—a story of an ordinary girl with ordinary longings—a kind of antidote to the so-called "true life" pamphlets that sensationalized the lives of people with extraordinary bodies.

Bobbi Lurie

THE PROTECTIVE EFFECTS OF SEX

That morning he woke before her.

She walked into the living room where he was sitting, staring into the television set.

"I've been sitting here, reading the ticker tape," he said, in response to her questioning him about the war. "I've been reading about some of the people who died today. I wish I were one of them."

"I'll bring you back a coffee," she said, grabbing her purse, her clothes thrown on in a fit of rage. She pressed her feet into her flip-flops, anxious to leave.

"Don't bother," he called back to her.

She walked out into the safety of the street.

The night before they held each other in bed for over an hour.

It had been two years since they had had sex.

He stroked her hair gently as she lay stiff beneath the sheet, embarrassed by her body, thinking of the chemo and the anti-depressants which took away their previous intimacy and any drive she once had for sex.

Her husband had been patient and respectful throughout the entire ordeal of cancer. They tried many times to have sex. But she'd end up crying, having lost any semblance of a sensual self, all too aware of the screaming scar making a mockery of her once-beautiful body.

She stripped naked.

She climbed back into bed, covering her naked body with the sheet. He lay beside her, completely clothed.

A minute earlier, when she was clothed as well, she was caressing his face, kissing his lips, hoping the kisses would deepen.

They didn't.

She lay still, unmoving, unmoved by the way he kissed her cheek, got up, and left.

The door stayed open.

Because eight American oncologists said they did not know how to treat my cancer, I went in search of treatments unavailable in the U.S. I met hundreds of people from around the world who had truly horrifying cancers. For a while I connected with many of these people. Unfortunately, everyone I got close to died.

When I first sent this story in for publication, I wrote about surviving ten years longer than what I called "my due date for death." Since then, however, I've had a recurrence and things feel quite different.

This vignette was written partly from my own experience and partly from the experiences of my friend, Melanie, who died of breast cancer.

Melanie and I became close not so much because of cancer but because we both had sons diagnosed with autism. I do not know what happened to Melanie's son, but my son almost died from a severe drug reaction, Stevens Johnson TEN, which affects the skin, the mucous membranes and the eyes. He lost one of his eyes from this devastating condition and he is always in danger of going completely blind.

The most important lesson I've learned in life, which I try to teach my son, is how important it is not to compare ourselves to others, especially if that "other" is ourself in a previous time.

Jonathan Mack

THE RIGHT WAY TO BE CRIPPLED & NAKED

Dear family and friends,

I recognize that many of those dear to me—my beleaguered relatives most especially—are confounded by my recent decision to become a Jain monk of the Digambara (or "sky-clad") sect. Accustomed by force of habit to my eccentricities and indiscretions, many of you are nonetheless dismayed by this latest decision, which, please understand, is not in any way negotiable. I hope you will allow me this opportunity to provide some explanations, the reasons why I feel this is the only way forward for me, i.e., completely naked.

I understand, too, that the Jain community, which is generally closed to conversions, may have significant misgivings about taking on a convert who is white, American, middle-aged, homosexual, crippled, promiscuous, and whose life has been rife with the sort of regrettable incidents which ought not be discussed on television before 11 P.M.

Nonetheless, I aim to gain your approval, as well as that of the worldwide Jain community. I hope that your support—perhaps tentative at first—may in time bloom into full-fledged understanding and sympathy. I recognize that my choice places me upon a path of many difficulties. It is reasonable to expect that my situation will be dire from the moment I strip down.

Digambara Jainism, in its naked monastic aspect, is generally practiced within a cloistered community. As I have not been granted admittance to such, I have no recourse but to be naked in public. As a promiscuous homosexual, I have spent a considerable amount of time naked in public already. Thus I recognize that such total self-disclosure is not always well received.

Once a course is determined, once it is found to be essential, any difficulties found therein become, in a sense, inconsequential. Such is the depth of my determination, spurred as it is by the desire to:

a. Do no more harm
b. Acknowledge the harm that I do
c. Discover the right way to be crippled & naked

In the holy *Sarvarthasiddhi* it is written, "Enjoy the company of the holy and better qualified, be merciful to afflicted souls, and tolerate the perversely inclined."

For this toleration, I give my ardent and humble thanks.

The *tirthankaras*, those great liberated souls who deign to teach, have revealed that everything arises based on causes and conditions. Certainly my decision is no exception. In what follows—I apologize for its length—I will do my best to point toward the seeds of my decision to follow the path of renunciation. I will presume to trace the hidden roots of the recognition that has grown within me, put forth green shoots in this fresh determination, and which I hope will bloom, sometime in the unimaginable future, in my total liberation. Only a *jiva*, one who has been liberated, can see the full functioning of karma. Nonetheless, I'll do my best.

The first seeds were planted years ago, when, as a queer backpacker adrift in India, I first arrived in Sravanabelagola, that blessed village sacred to all Jains, and stood at the base of the long and steep stone stairway that climbs to the summit of Indragiri Hill, to the austere monolith built a thousand years ago by order of the Rama kings: the image of the austere, sky-clad Lord Bahubali.

It is no exaggeration to call myself a lost soul. My ignorance was vast and comprehensive, my anger venomous, my lust that of a globe-gobbling demon. And yet! It is said that one glimpse of Lord Bahubali is enough to start the process of liberation. Now, verily, I can say that is the truth.

Like any deluded human—I grant that I am among the worst of that deluded breed—I had to wander for many years through that bitter signless swamp of falsity and self-deception which we call "ordinary human life" before I could open my heart at last to the possibility that there might be another way.

The way in which this came about may seem peculiar. My understanding received a crucial prod from a story in the *Guardian* about one Stephen Gough. Perhaps you have already heard of him. Mr. Gough, a British man, had the tremendous misfortune one day at the age of forty to realize that he was basically good. Essentially, intrinsically good. Like every other living thing. From that, Mr. Gough extrapolated, his body must *also* be basically good. Ablaze with this realization, he stripped down, mortified the in-laws, and took off walking toward John o'Groats in Scotland. Apprehended by the police and found guilty of indecency, he has spent much of the last decade in prison. In solitary confinement. Naked.

It occurs to me that Mr. Gough would do well to consider Digambara Jainism.

Extensive psychological evaluations have repeatedly shown that Stephen Gough is sane. Unfortunately there are no practical means of administering these tests to the society of which he is a part.

I acknowledge that my own sanity is—a hit-or-miss affair. Like a juggler who always drops an egg. Like a surgically augmented celebrity in a dress that cannot possibly cover everything at once. Nonetheless, I remain one hundred percent confident in my decision, which, I remind you, is not in any way negotiable, a decision which has persisted through my nervous hours, my Sloughs of Despond, my delusions of grandeur as they follow, hurriedly, one upon another. Crazy people can still make decisions. Crazy people have been making decisions for years.

The sight of Lord Bahubali, the fate of Stephen Gough—and this as well. Several weeks ago at the gym, while toweling off and attempting to use a nearby mirror to spy on the naked muscle hunk around the corner, I happened to catch a glimpse, instead, of my crippled leg. The angle was odd, the sight unexpected, so that it seemed I saw my leg as I had not seen it before.

There it was, my crippled leg, which I always try not to look at. My left leg, from birth crippled below the knee, that hairy stick which ends in a withered hoof. That repulsive peg, speckled in an angry red rash because it is almost always encased inside a plastic brace in which the skin cannot breathe.

The leg looked to me like half a dried wishbone. Like a thing designed to snap. I could not imagine how I'd managed to spend my life standing on so flimsy a thing. I was startled by its ugliness, but even more by how unfamiliar it seemed, how unexpected and out of place. As if I'd suddenly discovered I had a tail or a tentacle. As if I'd looked at my body and, rather than seeing the outside, had seen the inside instead.

When the reporter from the *Guardian* visited Mr. Gough in his cell, one thing he noted was that Mr. Gough "doesn't move like a naked man." This observation interested me exceedingly much. I knew exactly what he meant. Almost no one moves naturally when they are naked. Not when they know they are observed. Naked people tiptoe or cower, they scamper or strut. *Self-conscious* is not nearly a strong enough term. Naked people are usually catastrophically aware of themselves. I sure am.

I ought to have a real advantage. I have spent drastically more of my life naked than most people. At the age of twenty I embraced the baths as my life's work. I've hardly missed a week in the twenty years since. When I was young and broke, I even worked at the baths, two nights a week, so I could get in the other nights for free. I used to dream I had my mail delivered to the baths. It is no exaggeration to say that I am a benchmark in the history of promiscuity, the standard by which sluts are measured.

Night after night at the baths I circled the halls, I knelt in the steam, but mostly I had my special designated corner. The corner where I could watch the porn and see the guys going past, and I think it would be really nice if, when I am dead, somebody puts up a plaque there, in my memory, the same way old birdwatching ladies are given plaques on benches in parks, in memoriam.

As a young man, queer in a considerable number of ways, with no pretty face and no horse cock—and with a crippled leg besides—I figured that I had better have *something*. And so I set about upholstering myself.

I think I've done all right. No one can say I haven't been disciplined. I built myself a porn-star chest, with big erotic arms. I invested in dermatology. There are shrubs in imperial gardens that do not receive as much attention as my rugged beard. Yet always there is this hairy stick leg, this knotted and clawed hoof. This bird leg, which mocks my best attempts. This crippled foot, as non-negotiable as sickness, old age, and death.

I intended once to write a memoir titled *My Life at the Baths*. I even attended a workshop to learn about *creating a likeable narrator*, and the necessity of appealing to the *broadest possible audience* and avoiding, at all costs, that deplorable thing, the *niche*. Oh the kiss of the niche of death!

I gave up the memoir. It's hard to find much plot in stumbling around in the dark sucking strangers off. Penises are notoriously difficult to describe memorably—particularly after the first several dozen. These are some of the reasons why there has not yet been great literature of the gay baths. A central challenge: no one ever has a name, it's just the same pronoun again and again—*he he he*—and there's no telling who's doing what and to whom. Actually it's even hard to tell while it's all going on.

As compelling as it seemed at the time, in retrospect the baths seem quite horrendously repetitive. Thus, I am choosing to emerge, once and for all, from the steam, untug my towel, and escape from the suffering-saturated coils of cyclic existence.

It is my deep wish that what I am writing now will resonate not only

44

with my friends and family, but also within the larger homosexual disabled Jain community. Only Digambara Jains presumably. Svetambara Jains (who wear white) may well not see the point.

As I write, I imagine my Aunt Lavinia, so lively despite advanced age. My dear Aunt Lavinia, who persists in visiting even those most hopelessly out of favor with the family. Staunchly traditional, my aunt is also unimpeachably correct. She will no doubt wish to know the proper etiquette when visiting a Jain monk.

In response, I say—please, we're family. The finer points need not concern us. Expect a strictly vegetarian lunch. If a fly flits past, don't swat it. If you would like to be particularly sensitive, please (please!) don't lump Jains in with some other faith and then presume to know us. A Jain is not a Hindu. A Jain is not a Buddhist. A Jain is a Jain is a Jain.

Aunt Lavinia, please keep in mind: if you drop by—I will be completely naked.

Karma, for example. Although the same word is used, karma, according to the Jains, is very different from the concept promulgated by Hindus or Buddhists. Karma, by the Jain teaching, is *a complex of very fine matter*, imperceptible to man or machine, perceived only by the jiva. Karma is not an inaccessible force, or merciless accountant. Karma is a *substance*, which interacts with the soul, its quantity and intensity in proportion to the thoughts, speech and actions made under the influence of hatred, ignorance and craving. Karma is actual stuff. I've got tons of it.

This crippled leg, itself the result of karma, seems to me horrible— though it is quite un-American to say so. I am from the country of militant self-esteem, where negative thoughts are stamped out like small recalcitrant nations, where every quadruple amputee is expected to write a book about how jim-dandy life is.

Whereas I am from the Frida Kahlo School of Self-Love, she who said of her own crippled leg, "Every year I hate it more," and painted her portrait with monkeys, and went to bed with Trotsky.

If I were a proper American, I'd tape my leg round (not much tape would be needed, my thumb and my forefinger completely encircle it) and hang a Post-It note: *Perfect in every way!* Or maybe I'd get a tattoo: *I adore myself! Learn how! On six CDs for $89.95—call now!*

I could have a thousand hours of therapy—ten thousand would be better—and learn how to embrace the leg, et cetera. I could simply wait until the rest of the body decays enough that I have too many problems to bother with it. Seriously, I'm nearly forty. This *COLT* calendar shtick cannot possibly go on much longer.

As I believe I mentioned, I spent only one night in Sravanabelagola, at the holy and immense stone feet of Lord Bahubali. (I was in a hurry. Of course I was. I had to get to the next place, and the next place, and the one after that. I have been at all times, and in all ways, an insatiable person.)

I remember the great stone monolith, still scaffolded from the *mahamastakabhiksheka*, the head-anointing ceremony, held once every twelve years, when Lord Bahubali is doused with milk and sugarcane juice, with saffron paste and sandalwood, with turmeric and vermilion, with flower petals and gold and silver coins, with precious stones.

I remember staring into the Lord's stone eyes. They did not seem in any way disapproving. Or compassionate.

Lord Bahubali seemed…infinitely removed. Jains believe that, when you are enlightened, you are completely finished. Done. Finished. Extinct. There's not a thing that hangs around. Gone beyond is really gone.

Sign me up for that. I've circled round these halls quite long enough.

Digambara Jain monks are permitted only two possessions. A hollowed-out dried gourd for carrying water. A "fly-whisk," a feather broom for sweeping the earth before them so that they may avoid crushing even the tiniest insect.

I think I learned this first when I was a boy, reading *Ripley's Believe or Not*. It seemed to me quite finicky, particular to the point of madness. Now, however, the process of my awakening has begun—even if it takes a trillion years. It does not seem finicky to me anymore. If there is one truth to which I can attest, it's this one: *small harms add up.*

Think, for example, of all the small harms accumulated from a night at the baths. The countless small hurts given and received. The brush-offs, the groping, the glares, the squabbles over visiting servicemen. The awkwardness when meeting a man who was my lover in 2009, or last month, or five minutes before—but now it's time for the next. The way I stare through those I do not desire, the way I am stared through. Or someone grabs my dick through my towel, considers it, then pats me on the shoulder and walks away. Damn. But I have done it too. Then, when the night is finally over, you go home and do your best to kill all the crabs.

Jainism is above all *sensible.* It's a science. Jains developed the doctrine of *syādvāda*, or "conditioned predication," which is based upon the recognition that every possible proposition is only relatively true. Basically, no matter your opinion, you really ought to keep in mind that there are always seven ways at least to look at something.

Syādvāda has seven parts, summarized as follows:
In some ways it is.
In some ways it is not.
In some ways it is and it is not.
In some ways it is and it is indescribable.
In some ways it is not and it is indescribable.
In some ways it is, it is not, and it is indescribable.
In some ways it is indescribable.

I remember I believed all my problems would be solved, if only I were beautiful. Then I was beautiful. Sorry you missed it. Actually, I sort of missed it, too.

I was beautiful just once, in Montreal, at the age of thirty-four. I'd been going to gym a lot, was having spectacular/terrifying amounts of sex. Mostly, however, I think my beauty was because of poppers. One huff from the little brown bottle and I'm an instant, perfect, ravenous, cock-crazed motherfucker. For approximately twenty seconds. God—it's fantastic. Have you ever tried the first-class British kind? A whiff of that shit and a doorknob is hot enough to be my perfect lover.

My apologies to Aunt Lavinia.

I was in Montreal about a week. I don't think I removed the poppers from my nose. I remember beer for breakfast. I don't remember oxygen.

That was beauty. It did not solve all my problems.

Unlike Stephen Gough, I move like a man who is *naked*. N. A. K. E. D. Naked, hurrying slouched across the wet area of the baths, I move like a man escaping naked across a floodlit yard, the prison ground, surrounded by watchtowers, men with guns. This is how I move in my own skin.

Where is that prison yard? Who built the watchtowers? Who put the guards there? Who armed them? Is there no other option then, but to live in that prison till I die?

Karmas. Causes and conditions. Seeds. Although it can be said that there is no effect without its cause, and that hatred cannot by hatred cease, and that ordinary hunger leads only to more of the same, it is also necessary to admit that every event is the result of countless seeds and that most of the time, just peering at seeds, there is no way to guess what extravagant and unlikely flowers may be produced.

Lord Bahubali taught the end of "me" and "mine." Why do I hate the leg? I hate it because it is *mine.* I always adore *other* crippled men. Recently I fucked a French dwarf, just barely three feet tall. The dwarf rocked. His dick was only normal but it looked HUGE.

I wouldn't hate myself if I were a dog. What's more adorable than an easygoing, adoring, gimp-legged dog?

All these years in this body, which has never once left me behind, no matter where I dragged it, no matter how I insulted, neglected, or beat it. My life, neurotic fuckfest marathon, conducted at all times in close proximity to the body. The body which I do not know, and do not occupy, and do not always even recognize.

I am like an anxious, self-important businessman, hurrying about, considering himself essential, living all his life in a city he has never visited. He has not been to the zoo, he has not walked in the park, he has not sat all through the afternoon in a café looking out at the rain. Perhaps he has been to the city's tallest skyscraper—but only on business and only as far as the lobby. He thinks it is ridiculous that people pay five dollars just to ride the elevator all the way up.

How does one learn to be naked? How does one relearn? What is the way to be crippled & naked? Not mended, not corrected, not disguised. Crippled and whole. Like a pious beggar in a holy town, a beggar who believes the way he crawls along the road has been ordained by God.

Or like the old man I saw once at the public bath in Hakone, floating in a pool of water that reflected snow-capped Mount Fuji. He was a hundred and one years old, he announced to me proudly. As he used both hands to push himself out of the water, his nut-brown body resembled the gnarled roots of the mangrove. He was neither ugly nor beautiful. He was amazing.

I stayed one night in Sravanabelagola and, in the morning, before I left town, returned to Indragiri Hill. Lord Bahubali does not look down upon the village. He gazes directly into the air, which is not empty but full of microscopic and invisible beings. So full that if you are a Digambara monk, you must learn to move very gently, so as not to harm them.

To get to the feet of the Lord you must climb an ancient stone staircase with more than a thousand steps. That morning a group of Svetembara monks arrived, the monks who swathe themselves in white. They were carrying a pallet on which lay an emaciated old man. He was dying and had come to pay his last respects. The monks were about to carry him up all those stone steps.

How foreign and exotic it all seemed to me then. Not anymore. I am ready to climb the steps, though I may climb forever. I would like to carry others with me if I can. I cannot wait until I am old. I am delivering myself now.

Lord Bahubali. Poppers. Beggars. Ardent dwarf. Stephen Gough. Hakone. Then there was this seed as well, this green shoot, which appeared in my mind without warning.

One night, arriving at the baths, after approximately twenty years, after several thousand lovers, between fumbling with my locker and tugging off my socks, I suddenly noticed that every night at the baths begins with the same thought.

Tonight I'll really let go.

Tonight I'll stomp around naked and be fully and gloriously depraved. Tonight tonight tonight.

Incidentally, I have a theory of depravity: depravity is nothing other than making yourself crazy enough to let go. For some folks, a beer's enough. Others require a pipe packed full of meth. Many people have to be just about vegetables, before they'll let go, and letting go happens for thirty seconds—then they pass out.

I do not let go. Instead I cower. The wet area at the baths is as broad and brightly lit as a football stadium at night. I scurry. I duck down my head and scuttle. It appears that I believe that I can render myself invisible by pulling my eyebrows down closer to my nose. Above all, I hope someone will choose me, and choose me soon, before they look too closely. Look at the chest! Not at the leg! Look at the chest. Et cetera.

I have decided that I would like to learn how to let go for real.

To my family and friends, I wish to say: thank you so much for everything. Seriously. I apologize for any harm I've done, intentional or not. I'm sorry, too, for being—so endlessly embarrassing, so apt to proclaim what anyone in their right mind would hide or cover up. "Candor ends paranoia" said Mr. Allen Ginsberg. To which I'd add: *This offer not valid within the family.* Wherein candor just makes people freak.

Anyway, so long. I apologize if there's media attention. You won't hear from me much anymore. If the Jains won't take me in, the cops will. Honestly, I do not mind. Do you understand now—how once you finally make up your mind, nothing else much matters?

I'll devote myself to the sacred scriptures, I'll meditate and pray— even though, according to the Jains, no one is listening. If I walk across the room, I'll brush the earth in front of me, to make sure no beings are harmed, not even invisible ones. Maybe Stephen Gough will be my pen pal. Because for me there is no other option. I've got to stop doing harm. I've got to acknowledge the harm that I do. I've got to find the right way to be crippled & naked.

OK, that's enough out of me. It's time to say goodbye for good. Thank you again. And sorry.

I am entirely naked now. In a little while I'll go out for a walk.

—JONATHAN MACK—

As a teenaged boy with a disability, I couldn't have cared less about mobility, or pain, or even health. I was only upset because I was pretty sure that I would never, ever get laid. But it turns out that a crippled leg is no bar to a life of promiscuous wandering. In fact, I suspect it has served as a goad. Fascinated by the story of Stephen Gough, the writing of William Dalrymple, and a long-ago trip to Sravanabelagola, I started thinking about how an obsession with feeling physically defective had fueled an endless mad craving.

Stephen Kuusisto

PLATO, AGAIN

It was spring in the college town where Caroline Moore was wasting her day. Caroline had been wasting dozens of days. She watched young girls and boys on the college lawns and saw how they danced without knowledge like Plato's figures—people in the dark since their childhoods. That's what she thought. Young people…and not one of them was ill…

Everything is easy, she thought. The doctors had been easy, the cancer had been quick to come: chemo, radiation, surgery—all of it had been a dark season but strangely beyond her control and now, eight months "in," it was mostly behind her. *Easy enough.*

She set a cup of Starbuck's coffee on her knee and cradled it as she pulled her rolling briefcase closer to the bench. A girl with a blonde pony tail that swayed from the back of her red baseball hat stopped abruptly and caught a Frisbee, turned, thrust out her left hip and sailed it back to a stand of boys who were rapt with attention.

Things are easy in the Platonic shade, Caroline thought. *Easy in the shadows, in health or illness, until you want to keep your job…* She thought that Plato in fact didn't mention jobs in his allegory of the cave. Just votive objects, the easy things… Now here she was: fifty two years old, a black woman with a master's in computer programming: post-irradiation, post-chemo, post surgery—votive, upright, half in darkness, and most likely a victim of sexual harassment and disability discrimination. And good work she thought, all she'd had to do was "show up." All she'd had to do was stand behind a closed door with Bill Densk, the Chief Information Technology officer of Grandville College. He'd asked her into his office. She'd gone in. Easy…Now she sipped her coffee. Watched two college boys: one black and wearing a T-shirt that said "Corporation T-shirt" who was playing keep- away with a football, dodging around his friend, a cheerful looking boy who might be Korean, athletic, fast, but laughing too hard to succeed. She watched as they fell to the ground, each gripping the ball, laughing in breathless spasms. A home video…

She'd gone into Densk's office her first morning back. She'd had the first mastectomy. She'd had the full course of chemo. She was back at work.

She remembered being euphoric: they'd given her steroids, she was happily wound up. She'd been ready to work on course management software, a thing she hadn't much cared for before her illness. But she was back and ready. And she thought Densk was going to outline the project, tell her how important it was, put her in charge after her hard months on medical leave.

She'd never really looked at him before that moment. She remembered now how surprised she'd been to see that Densk was so round-faced and hairless. He looked like that band leader on the David Letterman Show, a smiling, smirking, little white guy who thought he knew a good joke. He'd looked her up and down, there behind his office door, appraising her body in that exaggerated, grinning examination that certain men employ to make you feel small. She remembered how fast things went just then.

"Does it hurt?" he asked. He was looking askance, his head tilted, still with the smile. He was staring from her face to her chest. She knew this wasn't the right question. It was that jaunty grin. And her mind had been moving fast. Compassionate people, she'd thought, don't ask this question first thing. It was the pronoun "it" that was the giveaway." She remembered that she'd sensed this. She'd been alert but things were running too fast for evasion.

"No, it doesn't hurt," ahe said. She remembered pulling at the bottom of her blouse.

She recalled how he repeated her answer. How he smiled.

"So it doesn't hurt?"

And she remembered how he touched her just there, where her breast had been. With his index finger. Tapped at the loose fabric. A tentative touch as if he was touching a bird's nest. She recalled how he kept smiling.

And then she'd had presence of mind. She'd said he shouldn't do that. She had stared into his vulgar face.

In turn he'd shown no sign that her reproof had bothered him: he made a courtly sweeping gesture with his arm—suggested that she sit down on his office couch. She'd sat then.

He took a chair to her right: one of those black alumni association chairs with the gold seal of the college displayed for status. Harvard had them. Grandville had them. She remembered thinking that the chair had no status of its own. She remembered her heartbeat and the odd way that Densk was still appraising her blouse. He looked both smug and coiled, as if he might touch her again where her breast used to be. Then he plunged into his speech. He was smiling as he talked. He kept his eyes on her blouse.

"We are pleased to have you back after your medical leave," he said, "and we recognize that you will soon be having another procedure."

She couldn't believe that he was staring at her remaining breast. He was staring unguardedly. She noticed that his eyes were small and gray. They seemed ill matched to the pinkness of his skin. She had been taking steroids and her thoughts were quick. She decided that Densk was really Pinkerton, the womanizing naval officer in Madame Butterfly. All he needed was a little white naval uniform.

"You will be back with us for about two months, is that right?"

She saw he was asking her a question. She thought that the question was unnecessary. She was coming back to work. There would be another mastectomy soon. It might come in about two months. She didn't know. She leaned forward just slightly, the engaged and professional shift of position and said that she was back full time. Said she would likely need another medical leave soon. Repeated that she was back full time…ready to work…prepared for something new…

Densk had waved his hand then. A sideways gesture.

"We are bringing you back but with a new assignment," he said. "You will be working for Lori on the payroll system. You will of course continue in a full-time position. Continue with benefits…"

His smile was like molasses. She remembered how her grandmother had used that expression. And now she understood it. The man had the slow, sweet smile of power.

"You will of course see this as a step down," he said. "But Lori Gustafson needs emergency help with the new payroll software and we're of course hopeful that once this situation is straightened out we can re-examine your old position."

He was telling her they'd taken her job away while she was undergoing surgery. She was being demoted. The words were rolling across the floor like beads from a broken necklace. She wanted to reach down and gather them up.

In Plato's allegory of the cave, all the men are chained in place. They see only a small glimpse of the world. As a college student she'd thought this had been about aesthetics. Caroline had left Densk's office speechless but clearer about the Republic. And things got clearer after that. Time on the job began to speed up. Where formerly she had enjoyed her co-workers there was now an unmistakable look in their eyes. People were in a hurry to get past her. Sandra at the front desk actually looked at her wrist as if she'd been wearing a watch. Then she'd smiled sheepishly and grabbed a stack of mail and run away.

Lori Gustafson with whom Caroline had always had a good rapport was also either diffident or critical. A soft-spoken woman from Minnesota, Lori was a friendly but reserved number cruncher. But now she was clearly troubled by Caroline's every piece of work.

Caroline was the one with the master's in computer science and the undergraduate degree in literature. Lori was a high school graduate and a junior college accountant. On their first day together, she'd actually said, "We are pleased to have you back after your medical procedure." Densk's words.

After that, almost all of Caroline's work was wrong. It wasn't that she got the numbers wrong. But according to Lori her reports weren't centered on the page in the right way, she used staples where she should have affixed a paper clip, had used the wrong colors for highlighting figures for review. She'd been back in the office for about two weeks when her oncologist called. She'd be going back in for more surgery in ten days if her blood counts stayed good.

She knew she shouldn't tell anybody. She figured it would be best to wait and make the announcement a few days before the hospitalization. She thought of the word "tenor"—the tenor of the office was wrong. Where formerly she had been employed at a managerial level, she was now an administrative assistant. Her work was being devalued as well. Densk had returned her federal withholding report because she'd used a blue paper clip when he'd specifically said that red was the color for federal reports. He had conveyed this through Lori who hadn't even looked apologetic. There was a new and stern look about Lori Gustafson. She'd actually said, "You better get it right."

Then time had collapsed like a star. The second round of surgery and chemo and radiation had been harder. She would always remember the lights of examination rooms: fluorescent strobes had been everywhere. Nausea. And brutal headaches. One afternoon she'd thought her entire body could hear. She'd been unable to stand. She remembered the unanticipated compassion of a nurse who brought a damp cloth for her head. Her legs had felt like there were insects walking just beneath her skin. Then she'd had the strange sensation that her internal organs had been rearranged so that her heart was down by her kidneys and beating there like a caught bird.

Then came her first steps out into the late winter light. She had felt a kinship with the trees. Nothing was budding yet.

Then it happened: back at work she saw that Densk had filled her old job as co-director of information technology. No one spoke to her about it. Lori Gustafson brought a clip board to Caroline's desk. First day back.

"We'll have to work out your hours," Lori said. She said it without inflection. There wasn't a hint of embarrassment or the whispered half tone of apology that happens when shy honesty is called for. Nothing. Just the de facto part time hours marked on a chart.

She thought of her paper trail then. Her work had been exemplary. It couldn't be that cancer was the problem. It couldn't be Densk's desire to touch her blouse. Caroline had imagined the Republic was a more evolved arrangement. She'd walked out the door then. She saw Lori Gustafson standing with the clipboard and she could see two or three other women holding in place like shaded figures standing back from the mouth of a cave.

The story "Plato, Again" got its incitement from a tale I heard about a woman who lost her job as she was recovering from cancer surgery. Having experienced disability discrimination on my own, I knew a good deal about how civil rights violations occur. Accordingly, my aim in writing this was to show how ableism, sexism, racism are utilized—put into play—as workaday tools. The protagonist never has a chance because her humanity is stigmatized as a matter of course. In turn the apparatchiks of the human resources crowd, having labeled her as sub-resourceful, can willfully strip her of dignity and whatever we mean by value these days.

A superior scolded me twenty years ago when I was an adjunct professor at a small college. He confronted me behind closed doors. He told me if I wanted to keep my provisional faculty appointment I'd have to also take on a summer job, one which involved driving a golf cart around campus and hand-delivering towels to teenagers in summer sports camps. When I told him I was blind and couldn't drive a cart, he told me I wasn't competitive enough for continued employment.

Such things happen to people with disabilities, more often than many would like to believe.

Liesl Jobson

STILL LIFE IN THE ART ROOM

Dalila paces about the art room like a plover, with jerky steps. When she stops moving, her head is cocked, as if listening to some half-heard thing.

"Mafudu is restless today," says Sikelela, an eleventh grader, under his breath. He rinses a sable brush in a jar of water.

"Mafudu indeed!" The scissors grumble on the shelf. "Why don't these children call their teacher 'ma'am'?"

"She's probably dieting," says a girl.

"These children show no respect," murmurs a charcoal drawing-stick.

"Go awaaay!" cries a loerie in the tree outside the classroom, startling Dalila.

"Silence," she says.

Shortly after her return from compassionate leave nearly a year ago, Sikelela had noticed the scraps of paper filled with tortoises on the teacher's desk. Dalila had passed the time doodling serried ranks of the ancient creatures marching eastward toward an imaginary shoreline beyond the page.

"You really like tortoises, Ma'am?"

"Mmm," she'd nodded, flipping the pad closed.

Dalila did not point out that what she drew were turtles, not tortoises. No Zulu word exists for the former, only an extension that approximates: *ufudu-lwaso-lwandle* or the tortoise-of-the-water. The nickname Mafudu stuck. Miss Tortoise.

Dalila had been unperturbed by the nickname. She recognized that it fit her heavy tread and fixed gaze, but had no desire to change either. She was relieved that her students had noticed only her eccentric drawings. They hadn't heard, it seemed, the rattling palette boxes in the cabinet or the shuffling of the sketch boards. Perhaps these sounds were lost against the scraping chairs and the grinding of the old-fashioned pencil sharpener on her desk. A few days before Sikelela's observation, she'd presented an easy lesson, saying, "Today we're doing 'Take-a-line-for-a-walk.' Who knows which artists developed this style?" She nodded towards the girl with unruly dreads whose hand was raised while the question was being asked.

"Klee, Ma'am," said Refiloe.

"Yes. Another artist?"

"Miro," answered Salmaan.

Dalila switched on the overhead projector to demonstrate. "This way you let an abstract line take shape, as it curves, zigzags, makes corners—let it wander freely over the page." Her hand whizzed over the screen. "Now shift the page until you see something recognisable." She swivelled the transparency around. "Maybe you'll see an eye or a claw. Look, here I've got the skeleton of a tree." She pointed with one hand. With the other, she made rapid gestures filling in leaves like eyelashes, twigs like feathery bones and beaks. "Keep going until the whole page is covered in detail." It was the last time her hand moved swiftly, unselfconsciously for many months.

"The other way of performing this task requires some planning to create a specific image. It is more controlled and presents a bigger challenge." She put another transparency on the projector and drew the tail of a turtle, raised the hump, formed the head, the flippers and lower carapace. Without lifting her pen, she entered the shell cavity, interweaving three rows of scales. Lastly, she created a diminishing spiral in the head cavity to form the eye out of negative white space.

"Try a waterfall, a skyline, or a garden. Whatever you do, keep your pen on the paper."

The class had already begun while she talked. The exercise was a favorite. She switched off the projector and drew another turtle, this one on a piece of paper, and then another beside it before returning to check her students' progress. She stopped a boy about to erase his work, "Keep going," she said over his shoulder. Pointing to an empty space on his page she said, "Keep it loose and free; don't think too hard."

The bell rang. The students gathered their books and pencils and sauntered out. Once they'd gone, Dalila completed an entire sheet of inch-long turtles. She put the page in the bottom drawer of her desk, the first page of identical scribbles that would accumulate over a year. Soon hundreds of miniature beasts were crammed into her desk, scraping their flippers, yearning for release. An erratic fluttering sound, barely audible, caught her attention. It sounded like the overhead projector's fan slowing after being switched off. But it was under its cover, unused, in the storeroom. She opened the drawer. The noise stopped.

Today is the first anniversary of her mother's passing.

"No cartoons today," hisses a flat pencil.

"Draw us a turtle, Mafudu," taunts a coloured pencil.

Dalila drums her fingers on her desk fifteen minutes before the final bell of the day. She chivvies the daydreaming Refiloe and complains at Salmaan's dithering. Ten minutes early she says, "Finish up. Don't start another colour. Put your folios away." The students look up. Surprised, they comply.

As the last one leaves, Dalila flips over an empty bucket placing it upside down, in front of the window. The label stuck to the bottom reads Powder Tempera: light green. The colour of hospital walls. Residues of poster paint ingrained in the plastic release a faint odour of sour dust. Usually she constructs still-life compositions on a plinth in the centre of the room. Today she needs a different perspective.

She removes a faded kikoi from her tog-bag and holds it to her face, inhaling deeply.

Her mother brought it back from Nairobi, a few weeks before getting ill. The open suitcase had released the fragrance of grassy plains, Kenyan shillings and Watamu Beach, where Dalila lived as a child. She had walked beside the waves holding her grandmother's hand. They found a strange depression in the sand.

"Look, a green turtle nest," said Bibi. "Turtles lay their eggs, then leave them to hatch."

"Does their mother not stay with them?" Dalila asked.

"No. The hatchlings must dash toward the surf before the gulls catch them. Only the lucky ones make it into the sea."

"They go in search of their mama and papa?" asked Dalila.

"They go to continue the cycle of life."

"Do they ever find them?"

"Turtles don't think that way, but they return here throughout their life."

"Return to Watamu?"

"The females will return to lay their eggs here when they are forty years old."

"They return looking for their parents," said the girl.

"Hmmm."

"Bibi?"

"Green turtles live to be ninety."

"Do the babies find their parents?" Dalila tugged on Bibi's skirt.

"Hmmm."

Dalila had already learned that, when Bibi said, "Hmmm" in that mournful tone, she would not reply, and it served no point to ask again. There were many questions for which Bibi had no answers, including why Dalila's parents had been gone so long. Bibi didn't know where they were. Perhaps they were attending a congress in Dar es Salaam or a conference in Botswana, or were sneaking in and out of South Africa. They never told her. It was safer that way.

That night Dalila dreamed of late hatchlings, flopping in vain against the outgoing tide. They were almost at the shore when hovering gulls plucked them from the sand, their flippers swimming in midair. Dangled low over the water, the babies could see their parents. Then the gulls swooped to the beach where they cracked open the shells and gorged on the rich meat. Dalila woke sobbing.

Bibi cradled her, rocking her back to sleep, crooning, "*Harambee, harambee, tuimbe pamoja. Tujenge serikali. Harambee.*"

She sang slowly, in the key of blackness. It sounded like a song for harvesting serpents. The next morning the news came that Dalila's father had opened a letter bomb in Lusaka.

Dalila pinches her nostrils and blows hard. Her ears pop. Her sinuses feel as if she has swum a mile underwater. She wonders if she developed an allergy to paint. The theme of today's lesson is identifying environmental and historical factors that influence visual artists.

Sikelela has brought a mbira, the traditional herd boy's piano. Salmaan's flag provides the backdrop and Refiloe's leggy strelitzias add colour. An exhibition of the work is planned for the Heritage Day celebration, and the president of the country is scheduled to visit the school that his grandchildren attended.

"Here we go again," sighs the bucket.

"Another plastic snake, ja?" mutters a thin yellow stripe woven into the kikoi.

"Be quiet," says Dalila, sniffing. She will not tolerate the voices today. Like her students, they pay her little attention.

"You should stick to porcelain dolls," says the bucket, "in gingham frocks and lacy petticoats."

"We haven't seen dolly for a while," says a cerise stripe.

Dalila's grandmother had sewn her party dresses, Western-style, in pastel shades, with matching dresses for the dolls from leftover fabric scraps. Peering through her bifocals, Bibi formed delicate stitches. Then she braided Dalila's hair in satin ribbons of the same shade. Dalila tried to braid her dolls' straight blonde hair, but it slipped from her fingers, refusing to hold the weave.

"Does porcelain ever come in shades of brown?"

"Hmmm," said Bibi.

Dalila drapes the kikoi, which has softened with washing, over the bucket, letting the stripes fall in a gentle curve. Once there were traces of her mother's scent in the cotton, a faint whiff of crisp herbal beer even, the brand her father had allowed her to sip when she sat on his knee that last time.

"No, Mandla," her mother had scolded. He had laughed at his daughter smacking her lips, but had whisked the bottle away.

After her father died, her mother walked along the beach with a kikoi wrapped around her thin hips. She had always been a round comfortable figure. She stopped eating until clothes hung on her angular form. She'd sit alone in the sand, staring at the horizon for hours. Dalila would watch her from afar. The following breeding season, a record low number of eggs were documented by Turtlewatch Kenya. Her grief scared the females away. They refused to lay.

The shushing in Dalila's ears is like waves inside a seashell. She tries to depressurize her nasal chambers again, but there is no relief. The turtles scuttle in the drawer. She places the potted plant on top of the bucket. Sunlight reflects off the finely demarcated green and white leaves.

Dalila had taken a slip of the hen-and-chickens plant from her mother's balcony garden when the flat was sold to cover the doctor's bills. She left the cutting in a bottle of water. When it developed roots, she transplanted it into a large ukhamba, a traditional Zulu beer pot she bought at the Rosebank market.

"Those shocking shades will quite outdo me." The pot plant glares at the bold kikoi. "My delicate stripes will be utterly lost."

"Hen lady, relax your sphincter," says the bucket.

"How uncouth," says the plant.

Dalila runs her fingers over the elaborate patterns, Iron Age motifs, incised into the dark clay. She wishes she had a banana frond to frame her composition, but Johannesburg's winter frost burns the tropical plants. There were banana groves around Gogo's kraal. Dalila recalls visiting her paternal grandmother in Gingindlovu before her father fled into exile.

Gogo showed her how to twist sticky coils of clay over bunches of rolled grass to make an ukhamba. Dalila was about six years old. Her cousin Zodwa terrified her at bedtime with stories about green mambas.

When they walked along the muddy path to the long-drop toilet, Zodwa screamed, pointing into the grass beside Dalila's feet: "Snake! Be careful!" The first time it happened, Dalila wet her pants and ran to her father. The sniggering Zodwa disappeared into the long stalks of sugar cane with the other village girls. The second time it happened, her father comforted her: "Gogo's mean stick will talk to that naughty Zodwa." Dalila was not comforted.

This morning before school as Dalila sipped her coffee, an article in *The Star* grabbed her attention:

> *GABORONE—The remains of Thami Mnyele were exhumed on Wednesday from Gaborone's New Stands Cemetery for reburial at home. Mnyele, a gifted graphic artist, was one of twelve ANC cadres killed by the South African Defence Force in a cross-border raid on 14 June 1985. His artwork had been deliberately destroyed in the attack. This soft-spoken gentleman, who had a passion for poetry and music, will be buried in Tembisa after a memorial service at the Mehlareng Stadium.*

Dalila took the newspaper in shaking hands into her tiny garden to gather herself. On the wooden bench beside the lemon tree, she recalled her indebtedness to Thami Mnyele, the kind uncle she had met once at Beitbridge with her father.

They had just fled South Africa in a hot, gritty train, and were both tired and thirsty from the long journey. A stranger arrived with two cans of cold Coca-Cola. Her father gave her a pen and an empty envelope to keep her busy while they had an important meeting.

"Draw me a picture of Mama," he said.

Dalila drew a tiny train chugging around the edge of the envelope. In the centre was a little house. Her mother waved from its window where she had remained to cover for her husband and to sell their few belongings.

Uncle Thami noticed the girl's picture and reached into his briefcase. He brought out a pad of paper and some pencil crayons. At the time, she thought he was trying to keep her from disturbing the adults. But he had taken the drawings she offered him. He admired them, praised her, and remembered.

A few weeks later, Uncle Thami sent her her first set of paints. When the slip for the parcel had arrived bearing her name, she waited with Bibi in a long queue at the post office. When the post-office clerk eventually placed the mysterious parcel in her hands, she itched to open it right there at the counter. Bibi stopped her. The clerk gave Dalila a toffee to reward her patience.

That was when the rustling of brown paper was still sweet, when string and sealing wax meant only that one had been remembered.

A few weeks later her mother appeared unexpectedly, and Dalila tried to piece together the whispered fragments she overheard while pretending to sleep.

"Is this Mandla's child?" asked Bibi.

Dalila couldn't see in the dark whether her mother nodded or shook her head.

"Does he know?"

"He must not," said her mother.

"How often?"

"Every night for two weeks."

"And what else?

Stifled sobs were the only answer.

"Is Mama very sick?" asked Dalila the following morning.

"Don't worry," said Bibi. "Your mother will be all right. These are old screams your mother is passing. They will go. When a woman's screams get stuck inside, her sisters have ways to set them free…"

An old woman from the village arrived with herbs and oils. She rubbed Dalila's mother's belly and pressed cool cloths against her forehead. Later she bled into the long-drop. When Dalila went to relieve herself, she stared in horror at the livery chunks that caught the sunlight through the cracked tin roof.

This morning the deep purple irises growing beneath the lemon tree reminded her of the previous winter. On her mother's last day, she'd taken a bunch of the flowers in a Heinz bottle. It was a make-do arrangement since her mother's favourite vase had been stolen in the hospital. Perhaps a nurse recognised the fine crystal that had been a wedding present.

In the ward, she had wiped her mother's face with a warm cloth and brushed her thin grey hair. Her mother whispered in the oxygen mask. Dalila couldn't hear.

"Pardon, Mama, what was that?" she asked, bending close. Her mother's rapid breath smelled fruity.

"You are my blessing," said her mother.

Dalila reached beneath the lemon tree to pick a single stem with a bud, an unfurling bloom and a fully opened flower. Back in her kitchen, she placed it in a moistened blob of cotton wool, twisting silver foil around it. A sudden yearning to paint its yellow tongue pecked at the inside of her heart. She remembered the tiny beak of a green turtle poking through the last egg at the bottom of the nest.

An angry gull had hovered overhead as it struggled free. She had chased the bird away and urged the baby on. The gull swooped and dived above. Dalila shouted at it, flapping her arms. "Hurry, little one." She faced her grandmother, crying. She wanted to pick it up, to carry it to the sea.

"If you carry that baby, it cannot develop strong flippers for swimming. It will be too weak for the ocean," said Bibi.

"But it will never get there." Dalila chased the gulls away, over and over, until the tiny turtle slipped into the waves.

Beyond the wrought-iron school gates, a queue of children waits at the bus stop. A lemon rolls off the table. Dalila catches it.

"Your roots smell off," says a stripe in the kikoi.

"Too much water," say the leaves curling over the edge of the ukhamba. Dalila blows her nose.

"School out?" asks another stripe.

"No peace unto the wicked," says the lemon.

Sikelela and Refiloe disappear into a rickety taxi headed for Soweto.

Dalila had shown her mother the striated throat of the iris. The old woman lifted a frail arm to touch its indigo petal, and then removed her oxygen mask.

"Put it against my cheek."

Dalila had neither words nor tears. No question lingered in the folds of the hospital curtains. Not a tear fell onto the pale green linen. Dalila readjusted her mother's mask.

That evening, she had tried to paint her mother's hand holding hers, but all she had to show hours later was a blank sheet of paper. That night, and every night since then, her paint box remained still silent. Nothing else let up: the chatter of desks, the prattle of chairs, the mumbling of the classroom blinds. Even the kiln in the corner sighed periodically. In her drawer, the turtles waved their flippers in agitation. But neither the pastels nor the oil paints made a murmur. The blues: phthalo, cerulean and sapphire all remained silent. Ultramarine, turquoise and Madonna blue lay like miniature coffins in her paint box. The flat and round sablette brushes lingered, soundless.

Dalila unclasps the long string of pearls her mother wore and drapes them over the lemons.

"Beats a plastic snake, I guess," says the yellow stripe.

"Pearls," says a lemon in an irritable tone. "Not very good quality."

"Hush," says Dalila. The pearls slip and clatter on the tiled floor. She picks them up and curls them around the base of a tomato sauce bottle containing the irises.

"Why can't we be juxtaposed against a simple urn?" asks the plant, glaring at the shabby bottle. Dalila chews a hangnail and rearranges a lemon. She removes a little package wrapped in paper towel from her tog-bag. She places it, unopened, beside the composition. The pearls glint in the sunlight.

Her mother had pulled the plastic mask off and said, "Take this away." Dalila tried to slip the mask back over her face, but it separated from the oxygen tube, bubbling loudly. The papery skin of her mother's cheeks was grayish against her dark-blue lips. Her mother turned away. "I don't want it any more. It's killing me."

Dalila opens the package, removes the oxygen mask and sets it beside the largest lemon. The mask, shaped like a ghoulish nostril, has a faint green tinge. She tries to identify the exact sheen: copper resinate, viridian, verdigris, cobalt green. Turning it in the light, she recalls the many-hued shells of the baby turtles.

"What next?" ask the pearls.

"Who can tell?" answers a stripe.

Very softly, the kikoi starts to hum, "Harambee, harambee..."

Dalila's ears are finally clear. The loerie in the tree outside calls "Go awaaay."

Her mother, trying to get out of the bed, had gasped, "Take me home. I don't want to die here."

"Okay, Mama," said Dalila, cradling her. With her free arm, she pressed the button that called the nurse. She wanted to ask whether home meant Watamu Beach or the little flat in Yeoville.

"I want to lie beside Mandla again. It's been too long."

"Shhh, Mama, shhh," she stroked her mother's hand.

"Where will you bury me?"

"Watamu," she said to soothe her mother. She still believed, even then, that she'd improve enough to be taken back to her ancestral village, but the hospital bills had precluded that.

Dalila buried her mother in the alien soil of Westpark Cemetery, which lies at the base of the Melville Koppie, under a scraggly oleander that drops toxic pink blossoms onto her grave all year long.

Dalila wipes the textured paper with a damp sponge. Her movement across the easel is swift and focused. She blends the under-wash in a palette cup with a wide hake brush, forming a streak of colour, and another. When she looks up again, the loerie is perched on a branch. Its crown fans out. The large grey bird lifts into the air and flies off. The only sound is the wind in the leaves.

—LIESL JOBSON—

"Still Life in the Art Room" was first imagined in the art studio one parent-teacher evening. We waited in vain as parents sailed past the open door with nary a glance at the bright walls, interested in their offspring's mathematical progress but not their musicianship, acting or pottery.

The different environment enabled me to look at the creative urge from the vantage point of the frustrated art teacher. The furious invisibility I felt enlivened the voice of the inanimate objects.

This story reflects on the lingering and disabling effects of trauma, silence and displacement, and the compulsive work-arounds that help one to pass for normal in the wake of devastating life events.

Living in a mad and violent world it remains unclear when a response is normal (and elegant) adjustment or whether it is pathological. The desire to make art is a healing and hopeful urge, commencing the fusion where the psyche has ruptured. I never take it for granted and am always grateful when it returns.

Joe Vastano

TWINNING

January

I sit on Rae's front porch and watch another shiny black scuttlebug make its way to the sea. I call them scuttlebugs for the sounds they make—deep bass clacks and a scritch against the concrete. This particular kind of invertebrate has been nicknamed whip scorpion for its resemblance to same and its long spindly tail, but its proper name is vinegaroon, after the pungent scent it sprays on predators. I guess its armored body isn't enough to protect it and could easily be crunched in the jaws of a coyote, which would swallow it wriggling. I bring three of them to my sister from Arizona once a month. Every morning of the weekend she takes a pair of salad tongs and picks one out of the terrarium on her kitchen counter and sets it down on the porch.

The scuttlebug leaves the edge of the concrete flopping over like a tank. Its legs get traction and it cuts a gash through the sand, raising its claws into the hiss and fizz of whitewater. It tosses in the surf and glides over the water to be deposited again on the sand, where it regains its feet and stumbles in a circle and then back toward the sea. Invariably they walk to the sea. The water catches it again and again until it comes up dead on shore. Rae rushes out of the house wearing a nightgown. She gathers three palm-sized rocks along the way and places them so that they triangulate the scuttlebug to keep it pinned when the tide fingers back up. After a minute she gathers up the gown and hurries to the house and into her room to change into work clothes.

Rae lucks into places like this beach house. She'll get a job as a horse masseuse for a rich client and they'll let her stay while they're on vacation and board her four horses on top of it. She doesn't believe in luck, though. She says it's God taking care of her. Her favorite passage in the Bible is 2nd Corinthians 12:7-10, where Paul asks God to remove the thorn from his flesh—some undisclosed habit or affliction—and God refuses, saying only "My grace is sufficient for thee." She says it's God's way of keeping you as dependent as a child, and invokes the verse to excuse herself for turning the occasional trick when funds get low.

She's been here six months and has made herself at home, so much so that she has devoted half the living room space to what looks like an art project. Opposite the big window that faces the sea she has mounted a grid of several pairs of animal horns in X-shapes on the wall. The horns are dazzling white to dark orange and in various stages of decay—some as solid as teeth and others brittle with sea rot. She prizes the rare white ones and so they run in two upswept diagonal lines from the middle, one going right and the other left. This is so her eyes can focus as she moves them back and forth to the click-clack of a metronome. The rest of the horns are arranged around them from darkest to lightest. In front of the wall is a shrine to her son, Shad, a collection of three photographs on a table. The large school picture in the center has him at six years old, smiling through two missing teeth. On the left is a teenaged Shad with Rae and our father at a beach. On the right he's a young man with a red baseball cap flipped backward on his head and his eyes fluttered at the camera—the last picture taken of him before he hanged himself nine years ago.

Rae had a therapist for a while who was helping her deal with Shad's suicide. The sessions lasted three months, until her fourth divorce went through and she lost the health insurance benefits that had come with the marriage. It was one of those Cadillac plans that paid for controversial trauma therapies like EMDR. "It stands for Eye Movement Desensitization and Reprocessing," she told me. "The shrink puts a metronome on and it clicks back and forth and you follow it with your eyes like you're being hypnotized. And then she brings up bad stuff that happened to you when you were a kid or whatever. And you know how your eyes naturally go up at an angle when you think of certain things? It's a way to force you to do that when you think about the past."

"What's the point?"

"Somehow or other it makes you relive the events. Emotionally, I mean. But at the same time it's like you're watching a movie. I did it with her enough times I know how to set it up for myself. As soon as I get all the horns up I'll have everything I need."

"Everything but the shrink."

"I can take care of myself." Among the many things Rae and I share is stupidly fierce Italian pride.

She discovered the first two pairs of horns while she and her therapist were on the shoreline engaged in play therapy. Rae had dug several interconnecting tunnels through the sand and her fingers hit something hard and she exposed not only the horns but the skull they were attached to. The next one was a few yards away and each was buried at an approximate depth of two feet. There are dozens of buried skulls and they all face northeast, as though a migrating herd of different kinds of animals was frozen by a sudden cataclysm. She has no use for the skulls though, and revels in leaving them in the ground with their horns cut off—her joke on archeologists. She believes all that Creationism stuff—that the world is only twelve thousand years old and that God planted dinosaur fossils here to test our faith. "It's obvious," she says. "God wouldn't make anything as stupid looking as T-Rex, with those tiny arms." She has no use for geological time, the eons it takes for mountains to buck out of the earth. She believes that after the Apocalypse the surface of the earth will consist of fused glass.

Rae comes out of her bedroom dressed in old Levis, a T-shirt and a pair of rubber boots with a small army spade hanging from a tool belt fastened around her waist. She picks up a shovel leaning against the house and goes out and stabs right through the dead scuttlebug. She wiggles the shovel and jumps with both feet on its shelves until it's submerged and then bends and lifts a slab of wet sand and heaves it into a growing hill around the hole, digging a three-foot- wide circle until she hits a horn. She taps on it and then bends to work with the small spade. The horns emerge caked with sand. She removes a stiff paintbrush from her tool belt and dusts them off. Once she has them exposed, she waits for the tide to overcome the sand barrier and pool into the hole. She pulls a Leatherman tool from her pocket and works its branch saw at the base of each horn until it twists off, then sets the horns aside and lets them tumble in the surf. She files the mounds where they came off and smoothes the edges with fine wet sandpaper until the file marks are gone.

She walks over to me with the horns in hand and turns around to stare at the gray plane of the ocean. Her eyes go from sad to serene, as though she's looking over a shattered house in the aftermath of a hurricane and has spotted a safe. She turns toward me and puts her arms around my waist and draws from me the easiest, most natural smile I'm capable of. Her hair is kinked like a used Brillo pad. I part it and lean over to kiss her forehead —sloped and furrowed like mine, like our Dad's—a jungle throwback on a classically beautiful face. She gives me a calloused hand and leads me into her bedroom. It's dark and syrupy inside and dust particles swirl across the nickel-thick ray of light from the window, that one laser streak that comes from a hole in the sheet she has tacked over it. The room smells of uncleaned fish tank and is dominated by a king-sized bed.

"I want you to go to the store and get us some yogurt," she says.

"Why not just snort it this time?"

"Because I don't put anything up my nose. You have some to lose but I don't." She tweaks hers back and forth. "This is my granny's Cherokee nose. It's my best feature."

"You have her cheekbones too." I never knew her grandmother but I've seen pictures.

She grabs the flab under her arm and wiggles it. "This came from Dad."

"My nose is all Dad." I survey the bedroom. "This is perfect, you know. It's everything a person could want."

"A womb with a view."

I wave my hand in and out of the light beam. "Not much of one."

When I get back with two small yogurt containers, I chop six 30 mg time-release Oxycodone pills into grit with a razor blade and then go over the pile with a rolling pin. I figure sixty for me and ninety for her, since my tolerance dips during the weeks I'm away. I open both yogurts and split the mound of crushed pills and sprinkle a 60/40 amount into both containers, sopping up dust with a wet finger. I stir each with a plastic spoon and sit across from her on the bed. "Why don't you sit up and I'll feed it to you." She obeys and I feed her the yogurt, scraping globs from her lower lip into her mouth. A few minutes later she slides down the wall and into a fetal position. I watch her for a while before starting in on my own. I'm licking the inner walls of the container when the rush hits.

I settle in next to her and close my eyes and watch a sexy female cartoon rabbit sashay across my mind. The rabbit sprays herself with perfume that drifts off her in a cloud the shape of an enticing finger. A male rabbit corkscrews around when the finger tickles his chin. He stamps the ground and then his feet hinge up and he floats horizontally over to her with a ring of hearts swirling around his face. The female rabbit does a genie dance to a song I remember from childhood:

There's a place in France
where the naked ladies dance
There's a hole in the wall
where the men can see it all.

I hum the melody while Rae hums one of her own and the two

incompatible songs find each other. I spider-walk fingers to her wrist and feel around for a pulse, noting its slow regularity, then place two fingers of my other hand on my neck and press the carotid artery. The two sets of beats work off each other in a galloping rhythm.

The Oxy makes me not care about the dankness of this room. I accept the funk as if it were the very gravy of life. "You know who Dad sounded like?" I say. "He sounded just like Fred Flintstone on downers."

She giggles.

"Did he ever tell you why he wasn't around for you?" I say. "Did he ever give you an excuse?"

"Yes."

"What was it?"

"I'll tell you all I can remember sometime. I just want to be with you now." She presses her head against mine.

"Come on, Sis. Give me the short version."

She rolls onto her back and crosses her arms corpse-like. "Before he died he said he went to Vegas when I was a kid to hit the Big One and shower me with gifts. But he never hit it big and was too ashamed to come back. He called me his Little Princess. Whatever, man."

"He always had a trunkload of presents for me when he hit the ponies."

"Fuck you." She slugs my shoulder; a glancing blow intended to produce a charlie horse. "He did take me to the beach once," she says. "No, twice. One time was with Shad. The other time was with my friend Sandy when we were teenagers. He stayed up in the bar and sent a waiter down to see if we wanted anything. Sandy thought it was strange, but I didn't."

"He took me once."

"Don't try to make me feel special by lying."

"Serious."

She curls her feet in toward each other and then points them straight down. "Then when I was all growed up we went to the racetrack and placed some bets. I was pretty jazzed, but he said we couldn't stay to watch because of his ol' ticker. He couldn't handle the excitement, he said."

"That was him all right."

She leans her head on her hand. "One time we went out drinking 'cause he wanted to show me how it was done. We went to different bars and then he took me to my apartment in Long Beach. I told him I hung out with him all day and did his thing, so now we could smoke some dope. He said he didn't really do that, but he'd make an exception for me. Special, huh?

Well he smoked me under the table and I passed out and he left. I didn't see him again for a few years."

"He had no business having kids."

"My mom never really talked about him. Just said he never hit her."

"He didn't need to hit anyone."

She scratches at her arm and I take her hand in mine to make her stop. "My granny told me he was a bookie, always hocking his mother's furniture."

I get up and go into the kitchen and make us each a rum and Coke. I hand her a glass and she gulps it down. I lie on my back and sip mine. "Why didn't he tell us about each other until I was twenty?" I say.

She kisses my neck. "Maybe he was afraid of this."

"What, that we need each other? I guess needing other human beings was something he did try to train us out of."

"Some people don't need anyone. Like hermits."

I steady the drink on my chest. "Maybe we could be hermits together."

"You and me in a cabin in the middle of nowhere."

"Like the Big Rock Candy Mountain—only pills grow from the trees instead of cigarettes and booze flows like rivers instead of lemonade."

"Or some weird version of Willy Wonka's chocolate factory."

I take up the glass and tip an ice cube into my mouth and crunch it. "I always thought someday I'd be as lucky as Charlie. You know, how he got his golden ticket after he bought only two candy bars while all the rich brats bought fifty thousand of em and Charlie still ended up winning it all."

"Dad would've laughed at you and called you crazy. He had a pretty elaborate system at the track. He tried to explain it to me once but it was too complicated."

"Well, he obviously wasn't a genius at it. He did end up in a trailer park." I'm starting to itch, but resist the urge to scratch. "Why did he always drive an LTD, anyway?"

"Poor man's Cadillac," she says. "He wanted to feel like a big shot."

"My friends and I used to buy LTDs just to trash em. We all pitched in a hundred dollars and tried like hell to roll em over."

"He sold me his LTD before he moved back east. Five hundred bucks. I figured it was a pretty good deal but I thought about it later. Most dads give their daughters a car for graduation. Most dads do that, right? God, I was a sucker."

I cross three deserts on the way to Rae's: the Sonora, the Colorado and my beloved Mojave. I usually go the back way—jumping on Route 66 in Seligman and winding up and over the Oatman Grade. At one time this was the most feared section of Route 66, the bloodiest part of Blood Alley. The narrow road contours through a mountain range studded with saguaro and barrel cacti and there are numerous hairpin turns and stretches of deep gully and the cars at the bottom look like sun-blanched aluminum cans. It takes me over six hours to get to her house this way—four-and-a-half if I stay on Interstate 40 and swoop down to the 10 near Indio. I have a load of firewood in the back of my truck and three scuttlebugs in individual Tupperware containers on the seat next to me.

I drive a Power Ram with dual gas tanks and tool compartments on both sides for my arsenal of chainsaws and rigging equipment. Like Rae, I've done a million things—EMT, logger, blaster—but finally settled on my own tree-trimming business. The firewood is a fringe benefit and I bring her a cord every month.

She's of the sea and I'm of the desert. I need craggy mountains and ego-zapping space. I need to be surrounded by other intensely self-protective life forms: cacti, horned lizards, rattlesnakes and vinegaroons. Above all I need sun. The ocean is therapy of a different kind for her, dissolving her barriers like water lapping against caked sand. It's moody and cool but mostly I think it's the salt air that helps her—lithium without the toxicity.

She and I have no one else to talk to about our dead father, from whom we inherited bipolar disorder and a tendency to quit on ourselves. I was luckier than Rae, though. At least he tried to buy my love with a 10-speed bike and a rocking horse and a cowboy suit and about a dozen other things. Maybe one day I'll be able to tell her that he was there in the hospital after my tonsillectomy when I was eight, and that he showed up at my high school graduation, too. If that works out, maybe I'll let her read the long letter he wrote to me before he went back east for good, a narrative of his romance with my mother and how she died young and how that destroyed him. I can't say I love the guy but I hate him more for Rae's sake than for mine.

When I was growing up in the foster home with Mary, he came to visit on birthdays and such wearing a golf hat and corduroy slippers. He'd hug me and I'd disappear into that huge body with his chin gristle against my face and he'd actually kiss me on the cheek. He always smelled like the

Old Spice Mary gave him every Father's day—the token gift she always claimed was from me. We'd sit in the air-conditioned bubble of his LTD and he always had a Muzak station on—elevator music—and he'd promise me trips to Disneyland and Knotts Berry Farm and New York and always qualify it by saying, "…if I'm still alive then." Sometimes in the movies they play the "Battle Hymn of the Republic" or "Star-Spangled Banner" behind a speech for dramatic effect, but Muzak was the perfect background music for the kinds of things he said.

Rae is a product of the family prior to mine, but Dad didn't tell us about each other until I was twenty and she was thirty. She was just starting to strip then—bikini dancing before she got sucked all the way in. Shad was around eight, I guess. But Rae loved cocaine more than me, and I loved adventure more than anything and so we lost each other for eighteen years. Now we try to make up for that with weird rituals:

One Saturday morning we dressed in pajamas to eat cereal and watch cartoons together and ended up fighting over the toy in the cereal box. It was a box of Trix and the prize was a lick-on tattoo, the kind you wet with your tongue and slap on your skin for a minute and hold it there and when it comes off you get a blurry greenish-blue Trix Rabbit. The cereal spilled and we wrestled for the tattoo until we tore it apart, then we rolled all over the kitchen laughing. We left the red and yellow corn balls on the floor and switched to Cocoa Puffs and watched Pebbles & Bam-Bam.

Once we made a blood brother-and-sister pact and talked about slicing our palms open with a razor blade and joining them together so that our blood could intermingle—the way I used to do with the kids in my neighborhood. But I got worried about her sexual history so we did it another way. We went to a Plasma Clinic and I arranged it so we could lie side by side on cots and have them draw the two pints of blood from each of us at the same time. We held our free hands between the tables while the bags filled up.

"Next our blood goes into that machine over there," I said. "They separate the white cells from the red ones and give you the red ones back. That's the best part because the blood is ice cold when it comes back in."

She dug her nails into my palm. "Why didn't you tell me that?"

"It's not bad at all. It's kind of cool actually."

She jerked her hand out of mine. "Asshole."

"Seriously, you feel the cold for just a second, even less than a second. You're gonna be surprised at how fast it moves through your body."

"But it's going to touch all of me!"

She refused the blood when it came back and they had to get the head nurse. When he told her that they couldn't legally let her go without putting it back in, she worked him for 20 mgs of Valium—which she refused to share with me. She called it Asshole Tax.

When I arrive at Rae's the ocean sky is cumulus black and gray, like a CT scan of a human brain. Water bubbles in like so much stomach acid and deposits a chaos of burrowing sand crabs. Seagulls dive-bomb a scuttlebug carcass. Their blunt beaks peck at the shell in search of meat underneath. I get out of the truck with the three stacked Tupperware containers and find the house empty except for two scuttlebugs in the terrarium. They duel from one side to the other, arched into s-curls with claws up high and their shells clacking glass. If I didn't know so much about them, I'd think that they were two males fighting over territory, but they are actually male and female and this is part of their courting ritual. They slice each other up and then they do it.

I set the containers on the kitchen counter and go look at the horn wall. There's an empty space at the junction where the white ones soar off. Only one pair to go but it has to be white, and those are the hardest to find. Five scuttlebugs might not be enough to do it. I figure Rae's in the back pasture with the horses so I grab a few carrots from the refrigerator and head out. Rae's four horses are roaming around the large corral and the two that belong to the owners are in their stalls. Rae is a moving black dot in front of a tall stack of hay bales. I walk toward her while she cuts a bale into fourths and drops the flakes into a wheelbarrow. Her pregnant mare Annie Oakley walks alongside her and for a moment they resemble a couple of drunks staggering home from a bar. Annie spots me and lopes over for a carrot. She stops a few feet short and leans her head in and pushes out her teeth and takes the carrot out of my hand. She bites it in half and the other half falls to the ground. Her belly is huge and it won't be long. Rae dumps the hay next to a water trough and wipes her hands on her jeans and comes over to me. Her hazel eyes are bright and cheerful. She is happiest out here with her horses.

I put my arms around her and then drop and lean all of my weight against her. "I get so depressed on cloudy days." I say.

She rubs my back. "Really, Brother? I love the gray and wet."

"I don't understand that. Your brain is no more a serotonin factory than mine."

"Don't even start about the meds, fucker." She pushes me off her and turns and wheels back to the hay bales.

"I brought you some firewood. I'll go stack it."

"I'll get spaghetti going when I'm done here," she says without looking back.

We get high after dinner and I take my shirt off so she can massage my back. "It's just funny somehow, you know, how we fit," I say. "I have all these kinks and sore spots and you have magic fingers that know just where to go." She digs into my neck and then kneads the muscles all the way down my back and then touches me lightly on the spine and it makes my muscles clench. "What have we here?" she says, and touches me down the length of my spine. My nerves jump.

"You could do that all day long."

"It's like I have a snake in my bed." She laughs and touches random places on my back and neck and I keep squirming until she gets bored and lies next to me.

"Who was your biggest hero growing up?" she says.

"Evel Knievel, of course." I put my hands out as though they're on handlebars and twist an imaginary throttle. "We stuck playing cards on the spokes of our bikes so they sounded like motorcycles and set up ramps and jumped Tonka toys. Nobody ever heard of a bike helmet back then."

"Parents really protect their kids nowadays."

"No shit. They start em playing T-ball and they get ribbons for just showing up and trying no matter how much they suck. It's anti-evolution."

"You know what couples do nowadays when the chick gets pregnant? Providing the fucker stays with her, that is." She laughs and tosses her head back and scratches her nose with the heel of her hand. "The guy puts his face down between her legs and sings lullabies into her pussy."

"I'd rather not think about my foster mom and her grizzled old husband doing that. I bet she smoked cigarettes when she walked the floor with me. I bet my crib was covered with lead paint and I chewed on it."

"That's why you're not a genius." Her eyes go from serene to sad. "I could have been a lot more protective with Shad."

I change the subject so Shad won't ruin another high. "Well, I think the Trix Rabbit should be on the Cocoa Puffs box."

"What the hell are you talking about?"

"Cocoa Puffs are the shape and color of rabbit turds. The Trix rabbit gives kids the impression that if they eat Trix they'll end up shitting rainbows."

"You seriously think that."

"Well, if bleeding heart liberals can ban books like The Little Engine That Could because it presents an unrealistic idea that hope and persistence might actually get you somewhere, I figure something like that wouldn't be too far behind."

"You actually have time to think about this stuff."

We're both cranky in the morning, hung over from the drugs. I make coffee and bring Rae a cup and set it on the edge of the bed and steam my sinuses over mine. "Know what I was thinking yesterday?" I say. "I was thinking you could tweak the ritual a little bit with the scuttlebugs and get more bang for the buck. You could just dig where the seagulls drop em, then you'd get three or four digs off the same one."

"They need to be freshly dead."

"Why?"

"They just do."

"Well, you've got five of em now." I take a sip of my coffee. "Maybe you'll get lucky and find some white horns."

She looks into her cup. "Honestly, Brother, you can take them all back with you. I'm re-evaluating things. Annie's gonna pop in another couple of weeks and then I'll have a colt to hang out with. Spring is almost here."

"What the hell are you talking about? You have one space left on the wall." I get up off the bed and face her from the middle of the room. "It's so fucking typical of you to quit something just when you're getting somewhere with it."

"Brother, what's the use of looking back? There's stuff to look forward to, you know. There's joy in the present. Besides, '…by His stripes I am healed.'"

"Which means you've been going to that stupid church. It's going to be like always, Sis. You'll just put a band-aid over it and when Shad's birthday comes around you'll get suicidal."

"Well, that's bullshit too. Depression comes from Satan. I've got some Bible verses memorized: 'I have not been given a spirit of fear, but of power, and of love, and of a sound mind.' 'Greater is He that is in me than he that is in the world.'"

"I don't care what those unevolved idiots at the church say about depression. You and I have an illness."

"Well, don't worry about me and suicide. I'm not that much of a chickenshit."

"Really. Like it doesn't take balls to just hurl yourself into the unknown."

She turns her head away from me as though I've slapped her. I get dressed as noisily as I can. I'll say a casual goodbye without hugging her and storm out and give her the usual two weeks to choose between me and the church.

She keeps her face turned away. "There's a hundred dollars there on the counter to cover your expenses," she says.

"What expenses?"

"Driving all the way out here and putting up with me."

"Shut the fuck up."

"Well, it wasn't easy to come by and you should take it."

"What are you telling me, Sis? Did you trick for that money?"

She presses her head into her pillow.

"You told me you were done with that. What is this? Once a whore, always a whore? You do this because you like it, not because you need to."

"I haven't been giving many massages lately."

"And you can't just ask me for some money. Way to make me feel totally useless."

"Well, you should take it."

"I don't want it."

I get in my truck and leave. On the long drive home I think of how I might have used that hundred dollars.

March

Usually it's me who calls and only to tell her I'm on my way, but this morning she calls and she's hysterical. She sobs and then draws herself up as with an elastic string around a bag and she says "Sorry," in a clipped monotone. "Sorry, sorry," and then she bursts and spills again. "Who the fuck is God?" she says. Her voice is slurred.

"What happened, honey?" I've been expecting the call but the timing isn't right. Shad's birthday isn't until next month.

"Everything I love dies on me." She puts the phone down but I hear her crying in the background. She yells, "Stupid! Stupid!" and picks the phone back up and says, "Whatever, man. Sorry I bothered you."

"Stay with me, babe."

She gathers her composure and speaks evenly. "There was a problem with the colt. It was coming out wrong and I knew Annie was in trouble, so I pulled on its legs and pulled and goddamn pulled as hard as I could. Then all the blood and the colt's legs stopped moving and I knew it was dead. I had to put Annie down, Brother."

I grab my wallet and keys and head out to my truck.

"Can you get here today?" she says.

"I'm getting in the truck now and I'll jump on the 40. You got any pills?"

"I've got half a bottle of Oxy."

"Don't take them with booze."

"You promise you'll come?"

"How many mgs?"

"Forty."

"Time release or not?"

"Not."

"Okay, can you do me a favor? Don't take more than two."

"I already took three."

"Goddammit, don't take any more. And stay away from the Xanax."

"Okay."

"Did they take Annie away?"

"No."

"Don't go look at her."

I start my truck, then step back outside and open the hood and hold the phone up to the engine. "Hear that? That's me on the way. Four hours at most."

"I'll stay in my room." She says it with a catch in her voice.

"I'll keep my phone on."

I fill both gas tanks and call her a few times on the way, but there's no answer and it's all I can do to stay just ten miles over the speed limit. I go all Zen and try to detach. A fatal overdose only looks bad from the outside, I tell myself. On the inside it must hit like an unexpected shot to the back of the head while you're playing with a kitten.

Rae's in bed when I get there. I snap my fingers next to her left ear and she lolls her head up at me—jerkily, as if it's on an engine hoist. Her face is pale and she's blank in the eyes. The inside of her left forearm has a huge spot of pink and purple welts with beads of blood on the surface. "Damn, Sis. How much did you take?"

Her eyes drift over me with faint recognition and she lets her head drop back on the pillow and looks at me askance. There's white goo in the corners of her mouth. She holds her arms out and I ease them down and take her wrist and feel her pulse. It's what they call "thready" in the books and it's slow—about sixty beats a minute. Her respirations are also slow. I take a pitcher of cool water out of the refrigerator and add some ice cubes to it, then I go out back looking for an oil pan. Annie's lying out in the dirt the way horses did when ambushed men on the Plains laid them down as shields.

I grab a ball of twine off a shelf and slip a clove hitch over Rae's wrists and join them together on top of the oil pan. I tip the pitcher so that the stream is about the thickness of a quarter and pour cold water over her hands. She startles and turns her head with dim curiosity. She does this over and over while I pour the water. "I want you to try to sit up," I say. She groans and struggles up against the headboard and I untie her hands. In her right mind she'd be cursing me for going to this kind of trouble, but she does what I ask without complaint. She scratches at her arm and I pull the hand away and look at the ugly blotch. "Do you have any calamine lotion?"

She laughs. An encouraging sign. "There's no poison oak at the beach, stupid."

"Where are the pills, Sis?"

She reaches underneath her and brings up the bottle and shakes it like a rattle. I take it and feel her pulse and give her small sips and stop her from scratching herself by tying her right arm to the bedpost. "Don't struggle with that or it'll get tight."

"Asshole."

I doctor her arm as best I can with aloe vera. Color comes back to her over the next two hours and her pulse and respirations return to near-normal. She goes to sleep and I untie her hand and push her onto her side with the basin on the floor beneath her. Soon she's snoring. Another encouraging sign.

I go out back to deal with Annie and stare at her, at the little legs sticking out. There's a small red bullet hole from Rae's Colt 45 in her forehead, a trickle of dried blood matting the hair on her nose. I grab a fifty foot length of rope and two blocks and tackle from my truck and set them on the ground. I take up Rae's shovel and start digging a hole in front of Annie, but at two feet I hit one of those skulls. I grab hold of the horns and pull and twist but there's no give, so I hook the blocks and tackle up to a corral post and slip a noose over the skull. I pull on the rope and the skull begins to rise. Dirt collars around it and the rest of the skeleton begins to emerge, its shoulders and then its ribs. I reposition the grappling hook around its mid-spinal column and go back to pulling and finally have the full skeleton of what looks like a gazelle on the ground, clotted with dirt and bent from the torque. I roll the skeleton over to the side and smooth out the hole and hit another skull but this one pries off. I stand back and lean on the shovel, sweating from the work. I throw the shovel to the side and go and get firewood and build a shallow pyramid of it in the center of the pit, careful to leave a large space in the middle for the chimney effect I want. I slip the rope around Annie's neck and pull but she doesn't budge. The corral post bends to the point of breaking. I stop and look at her.

I'm not good at this stuff. Once I saw a fawn kicking beside a road from a hit-and-run and all I could do was cradle its head and watch its eyes glaze because I couldn't bear to slit its throat. But I need to make Annie disappear before Rae wakes up, so I go back to my tool box and pull out my most powerful chainsaw—a Husqvarna with a three-foot bar. I gas and oil it and run the chain around the bar, pulling out a quarter-inch of slack. I file the rakers down and the teeth at a severe angle, then bring the saw outside and set it next to Annie. I take two pry bars from my truck and position them over the hole to act as rails. As an afterthought, I grab a set of earmuffs and go inside and slip them over Rae's head. Then I go back outside and fire up the saw.

My first dig is into Annie's throat, and blood spills out as thick and wide as a sheaf of paper. I make another incision in her belly and shut off the saw and watch the blood glug out. It forks on the ground and spills into the hole and pools around the wood. After she's bled I take off her legs, then her head. The saw is so sharp that it doesn't even make clacking noises on bone. I seesaw the last cut through her midsection and let the chain spin in the dirt until the two halves of her slump apart. I shut the saw off and ease it out—the chain clotted with gore—and set it down and try the rope again. The front half of her moves with relative ease and I drag it over the pit on top of the pry bars. I drag the other half and then throw the head and legs in and light a fire with gasoline. I pile more wood on to make her go up as fast as possible.

Neither of the skulls I've unearthed are the cherished white ones, but one is a dark bone color with solid horns so I go into my truck for a can of flat white spray paint, the kind I use to mark doomed trees for forest-thinning jobs. I spray the horns and let them dry in the garage and go in and check on Rae again. Pulse and respirations normal. I sweep the inside of her mouth with an index finger. No vomit. I pick the two scuttlebugs out of the terrarium, put them in one of the Tupperware containers and loose all five in the back yard. They burrow in the ground like they're supposed to.

I go back in the house and take two well-deserved Oxys and get into the shower and weep. Toweling dry and beginning to feel the glow, I cut off the painted horns and mount them in the vacant space on the wall. I stand back to admire them, moving my eyes along the chevron of white horns from one pole to the other like Rae said to do. I glance at her through her bedroom door—dead to the world—then step over to the table and turn the pictures of Shad face down. I track back and forth and after a minute or so my eyes feel like pulleys on a steel cable.

The first mental images to come are black-and-white photos of our father. In one he's leaning on an elbow on a beach towel and plucking a ukulele with a cigarette in his mouth and a Frank Sinatra-style hat on his head. In another, he's sitting on the hood of a Studebaker flashing a movie star smile. Finally he's in a wife-beater shirt and sunglasses, helping a three- or four-year old Rae climb to the top of a playground swing. She has a cautious look on her face. Gradually the photos take on the blanched color quality of Kodak prints from the sixties and seventies. In one I'm hoisted up on his shoulders and smiling at the camera. In another I'm standing next to his enormous body at Manhattan Beach. Finally there are pictures of him at the end, after he left Rae and me for good and reunited with his brothers in New Jersey. He's thinner in these photos than I have ever been but he still has all his hair and his skin is stretched taut over his face without a bit of turkey neck. Encouraging signs.

The photos dissolve and out of the haze comes a single memory so clear that it's exactly like I'm watching a movie—again as Rae described it. My father and I are at a miniature golf course. I'm ten or so and about to putt a golf ball into the jaws of a giant concrete shark and he starts in on a confession about "the sickness in [his] mind." I slam the ball down the shark's throat and walk away from him in mid-sentence. He never brings it up again. The next time he comes to visit, I hide at the top of a cedar tree as he searches the back yard and calls my name. I stay up there until his car is long gone. Fear rises in me now like a black tide, the fear of an overly-cautious boy who was just beginning to grow his claws out. Why the hell would anyone want to wade into this?

I take another Oxy and sit on the bed next to Rae and touch her forehead. Skin temp normal. The fear gradually burns off in opiate-induced euphoria and I spoon with my sister and make my breaths match hers.

Christmas season is the hardest time of year for my half-sister Patti and me, but Christmas of 2010 was especially dismal. We tried to help each other but fell short. At the time I was reading Carl Jung's "The Transcendent Function," an essay about how tolerance for internal paradox allows the opposites within us to grind together and set fire to a divine state of being he called "The Third Thing." Blake called this phenomenon "the marriage of heaven and hell." Nietzsche contemplated a state "beyond good and evil." Jim Morrison urged us to "Break on Through to the Other Side." With Jung's essay in mind, I built "Twinning" from three disparate images: a scorpion, a sea bed, and money on a table.

Creative people are walking paradoxes: both shrewd and naïve, libidinous yet prudish, and so on. I believe that this paradox forms the basis of the creative tension so essential to artistic triumph—the friction of opposites setting fire to that "third thing," which goes by yet another name: the Sublime. People with bipolar live more closely with the friction of internal paradox than most, and I've come to believe that this most definitely links bipolar with artistic temperament.

Megan Granata

THE SITTING

No one at this summer's festival would call me a caricaturist, although that's exactly what I am. Caricaturists belong at a carnival. Their portraits share the same sticky grip as a corndog or a cone of cotton candy, and are destined for the same trash bin. At least, that's the opinion of the Sawdust Festival's summer committee, whose rejection letter last year ended with a hand-scrawled note: "Try the OC Fair." Laguna Beach itself seems to agree. Compared to Venice up the coast, Laguna is straight-backed and tight-laced, its flair carefully measured in the ordered blocks of its Civic Art District. Its crowd of twenty-something beachgoers spared no more than a passing glance at my boardwalk caricature stand. As they strolled by, their eyes smirked above their sunshades as if to say, *Our faces don't look like that here.*

This year, I traded my Quikdraw markers for graphite pencils, switched from airbrush to pastel, and called myself a portraitist. I rented out a corner of a friend's gallery on the lip of the Pacific Coast Highway and built up my new portfolio. I tossed my paint-stained overalls and wore hemp belts, turquoise rings, and corded lace dresses in coral and teal. And this was the year Sawdust let me in.

"Rae, can you spray and sleeve this?" I ask, peeling off my gloves and giving the portrait a final once-over. As I proclaim it finished, my assistant sidles out from behind the wooden purchasing counter with a can of fixative. "I haven't had a break since lunch," I say. "I swear I'll go cross-eyed if I sit here any longer."

"The Kleins should be back soon. Want me to ring them up?" says Rae, shaking the spray can.

I glance at my easel, where Ken and Cassie Klein stare back at me. Like many of my sitters, they're newlyweds. Their heads tilt together as though they share a secret. They brandish clean white smiles, their cheeks gently kissing and flushed with Geranium Lake—a color I normally reserve for children. I would've drawn them much differently on Laguna's boardwalk. Cassie was six months pregnant and had grown puffy with baby weight, her face moonlike above the swell of her maternity dress. "You can leave that out, right?" she asked me in private, her voice a whisper. "I mean, I'll only look like this for three more months." I told Cassie yes, of course, a family portrait is meant to be flattering, all the while sketching her caricature in my head with a face full and glowing.

"If they're back before I am, then sure, that'd be awesome," I say, a bit too gratefully. Portrait hand-offs—even as a caricaturist—have always made me nervous. "Give Cassie my business card and let her know I do children's portraits, too, all right?"

Rae gives me a swift nod as I slip out of the booth.

The aisles winding through Sawdust's grounds are mainly empty. Most of the festival's guests are dining at the food court or listening to live music on the terrace. I can hear the guitar pluck and accordion flourish of the local Cajun band, which plays the pre-dinner crowd on weekends, serenading the food stands with its breathless Louisianan tempo. Craving Greek, I line up at Thasos. Saturday's packed, as usual—especially in the food court, with children charging underfoot and much bumping of hips. In the surge of hungry guests, there's also the occasional brush of bare skin, moist with sweat and sunscreen, or chapped with sand and sea salt, and always pulled briskly away before I can figure out who it belongs to.

A group of women my age stands in line behind me. Wrapped in sarongs and summer scarves, they teeter on heels that sink into the wood mulch covering the festival's grounds. Their half-drunken laughs bob above the Cajun music. While waiting to order, I sketch them in my mind as I did Cassie Klein: with sharp-raked brows, carnival eyeshadow, and wide, painted mouths in the shape of lime slices.

"Hey, you're an artist," one woman says, jabbing a bottle of hard lemonade at my nametag.

"Yeah, I do portraits over by the glassblower," I answer. "But I'm actually more into caricature. I used to run a stand on the boardwalk—Speedsketch?"

"Oh God," she groans. "I got one of those done at the fair last year. The guy drew me with this huge, gross birthmark on my face." The woman, a dishwater blonde whose hair is pinned in a sloppy chignon, has a mole on her cheek that she's hidden with makeup. My Quikdraw pen would've marked it as well, without apology, without hesitation, the same way I'd draw a pupil or a nostril or the dark hollow of an ear. "It was the most god-awful thing I've ever seen," she says, drawling into the mouth of her lemonade bottle.

"Some caricaturists definitely go for the jugular," I reply, feeling suddenly defensive, as though it's my responsibility to justify this anonymous caricaturist's motives. "We're just trying to make people laugh."

The woman takes a slug of her lemonade. "Made my date fuckin' laugh," she says.

At that moment, my turn comes at the order counter. I excuse myself, eager to escape the tailspinning conversation, and buy my usual vegetarian pita. I've drawn plenty of sitters like that dishwater blonde before. During the portrait hand-off, their smiles pucker, their noses crinkle, and they say, airily, "Thank you," with the same gratitude they'd show a family pet that left a dead animal on their doorstep. I've never figured out how to handle those situations tactfully. In them, I always find myself caught between a politely gritted smile, an awkward apology, and the urge to snatch away my caricatures before they wind up in the trash.

Grabbing my pita plate, I begin wandering back through the grounds. Crowds have gathered near the glassblowing display. Behind a metal safety grate, the blower and his assistant weave ruby strands of molten glass around the end of a blowpipe. In another booth, children spin pottery while their parents browse the nearby aisles, turning ceramic mushrooms in their fingers or patting the heads of hand-carved drums. With its wooden booths that remind me of small, rickety cottages, and the watermill tumbling at the edge of its grounds, the festival seems like something out of my old Children's Book Illustration class—less Laguna Beach, more Pixie Hollow. The eucalyptus trees above have dropped their leaves into some of the sculptors' bowls. The falling evening smells of their bitter mint, and wood mulch, and the scent of wild brush rolling in from the Laguna Hills that overlook the sea.

Just as I round a bend into my own aisle, I glimpse something out of the corner of my eye that doesn't quite belong.

It's somebody's hand. But at the same time, I can hardly call it a hand at all. I spot it at eye-level, only a few feet away, as its owner descends a set of stairs rising to the terrace on my left. Two fingers—and only two—unravel from a leathery knot of flesh lumped with huge knuckles. A child's hand wraps around these fingers. It's smooth and milky white, and it seems to tug the other hand along with it, pulling the wrinkled skin straight like a sheet.

I swivel my gaze forward. I'm a professional now and shouldn't be caught ogling anyone who isn't sitting for me. But whatever I witnessed in the briefest fraction of a glance, when I'd been startled into dropping my guard, jolts me momentarily out of the crowds, the Cajun music, and the picturesque sprawl of beach scenery.

Two figures, a man and a young girl, pass me on their way down the staircase.

"—get our faces done," I hear the girl say, and they sweep down the aisle before I can catch the man's reply.

Leaning against the stairwell, I pick at my pita with furrowed brows. I've found over the years that my mind's eye recalls images in a series of details—a blessing to my festival work, which is based largely on memory, as few guests are willing to sit the entire hour necessary to complete a portrait. In this case, I remember that the man's fingernails were oddly colored: maroonish, Sennelier's Red Gold, and also somehow puckered, as though he'd just gotten out of the bath. It strikes me then with a shivering weight that this man might've not had fingernails at all.

Burns, I figure, biting into a slice of red onion. He must've been burned.

But whatever caused this man's disfigurement is none of my concern. Time is my priority now. The Sawdust Festival closes for the day in a little under two hours. As daylight fades, the other artists will switch on the sodium bulbs lining the ceilings of their booths, bathing their wares in a golden glow reminiscent of candlelight. I'll plug in my fluorescents—ideal for portraiture, but blinding as a beacon among the dimly lit aisles. Then, after the guests have gone, we'll all tarp our walls and counters, unplug our bulbs, file out in exhausted silence, and return home ourselves.

I can finish one last portrait in that time. Tossing the remains of my pita in a nearby trash bin, I center my belt buckle, straighten my nametag, and head back for the next round of sitters.

The man's standing at my booth when I return.

"—oil pastel, more of a blended effect," says Rae, struggling to engage him in conversation as the young girl browses my sample portraits. Though my assistant seems composed enough, her smile broad and her glasses perched firmly on her nose, I notice that the tips of her ears are smoldering red.

He's just another guest, I reassure myself, attempting to ease the tightening knot in my stomach. As I approach the booth, though, I can't help but gape at the man's stature. So do a few children, hovering in the aisle with half-dropped jaws before their parents tug them away in anticipation of tactless remarks. The man is barrel-chested and built like the head of a battering ram. With his back to the aisle, he towers over the other guests, his head almost grazing the fluorescent bulbs in my ceiling. A long-sleeved T-shirt bearing the Colts' blue horseshoe stretches over the plane of his shoulders. *A football player?* I wonder, attempting to place his physique. But his left sleeve is safety-pinned at the elbow where what would've been his playing arm apparently ends. A strip of bare skin peeks between the T-shirt's collar and a low-pulled baseball cap. I can see nothing yet of his face.

Shaking off my nerves, I stride forward, planting each step squarely in the wood mulch. There's no reason to dread his appearance. However bizarre it might be, I'm sure Picasso painted worse.

"Sorry to keep you waiting. I'm Mona Eristavi," I say, and as I instinctively thrust out my hand, it occurs to me too late that the man will have nothing to shake it with.

When he turns toward me at last, a sensation like ice water trickles over my ribs.

This man is made of human patchwork. His appears not to be a single face, but several: one person's borrowed ear, another's borrowed cheek, each parcel of skin varied slightly in color and crumpled at the seams into a roadmap of half-healed scars. Whatever fire had ambushed him razed the topography of his features, flattening them into a glazed mask the color and texture of chewing gum. He has no nose. No lips. No eyelids. A jolt of déjà vu seizes me as I realize that I've drawn this face before. It's my pre-sketch face, the preliminary stage of every portrait, which I outline in pencil before adding cheekbones, the contours of the lips, the curvature of the nose—any distinguishing traits that would identify this particular face as my sitter's.

The man slips his two fingers into my outstretched hand. The remains of his lips roll up over his teeth, and he meets my gaze unflinchingly from beneath his baseball cap. Although his brows are naked as thumbs, framing both eyes, I notice, is a fringe of blonde lashes so delicate that it seems one of Laguna's onshore breezes might sweep them from his lids.

With no way to sidestep the social ritual I initiated, I grasp the man's fingers and shake. His skin is unexpectedly warm, and unfixed above the bone so that his joints slide beneath it in my hand.

"Joey," he says, his lips still curled above his teeth. "My daughter and I would like to get our portraits done."

I drop his fingers.

Our portraits.

"I—sure, I can do that for you," I stammer. "You want two singles or a double?"

"A double," he says.

Our portraits. A double. This man wants his face on a canvas.

"That's not a problem, is it?" he asks.

"No," I say, recovering myself. "No, not at all. Here—take a seat while I set up."

As I clip a fresh nine-by-twelve to my easel, the man levers himself onto the sitters' bench. This booth wasn't built to accommodate such an imposing figure. The framed sample portraits rattle on the wall behind him, and the bench creaks beneath his weight. Once seated, Joey calls to his daughter, Jacqueline, who looks up from a leaning stack of poster prints.

Stomach knotting further, I glance twice at her face as well.

Where I expected fair skin, a milky white to match the fist I spotted on the stairwell, hers is a deep and vivid cerulean. Her forehead ripples with layers of what appear to be clouds. A pale crescent moon encircles her right eye. An intricate black lattice, snagged with four-pronged stars and smattered galaxies, climbs up to her left. The illustration covers even her lips and eyelids, so that when she blinks, her face dissolves into a portal opening directly into the darkening sky above.

"Take your hat off," she whispers. "We're s'posed to look nice in portraits."

I can respect another artist's work—Star Shields is Sawdust's resident face painter, the hiss of his spray pen familiar to all—but not when it interferes with my own. Beneath the paint, it's impossible to tell her age. Shooting stars trail highlights where there should be shadows. The black lattice muddles all dimension on her left cheek. Oblivious to my panicked appraisals, Joey and Jacqueline huddle together on the sitters' bench, their faces matched pink to blue, each alone a portraitist's nightmare.

Before I've even readied my pre-sketch pencils, I sense the slowing of foot traffic behind me. It's not much—just a few stalled footfalls here and there. I've arranged the booth so that both sitters and easel face the aisle, attracting a crowd of guests as the portrait nears completion. Rarely, though, does anyone stop by before a single line's been drawn.

"How long do these take?" Joey asks.

"Depends," I say. "Once I get the first few lines down, I can handle the rest on my own. Stay for fifteen minutes, then come back in an hour."

Joey nods. His eyes flicker back and forth, appearing to track the movement of people behind me. Then, when the timing is right, he pinches the brim of his baseball cap and lowers it onto his lap. In one swift, almost gentlemanly gesture, his head is fully bared to me. His scalp is crisscrossed with that same roadmap of scars, that same human patchwork, and appears much more tender than a skull should be, seemingly built of something softer than bone. It's also the same chewed-bubblegum pink as his face—the color of skin beneath skin. Flushing, I pin my gaze to the empty canvas as though he'd removed his shorts instead of his hat.

"We'll stay for the hour," he says.

I peer back around the canvas. "What, the whole thing? There's no need—"

"We want to make sure it's done right."

At that, he flicks his wrist as if to say get on with it. I shake open my box of graphite pencils with trembling fingers. How can I possibly draw this man when merely looking at him seems an invasion of privacy?

Breathing deeply, I trace two circles with my 6H graphite pencil—the lightest of lights, the most tentative of artistic introductions. Joey and Jacqueline talk amongst themselves. Their chatter is a relief to me. I usually make conversation with my sitters, but now I've abandoned my faculties of speech, visualizing the final portrait with a desperate urgency. Should I mold features into this man's face? Puff his lips, carve his jaw, crease his eyelids? And the girl—should I strip the stars from her cheeks? Paint her with a normal child's skin?

More guests linger behind me. A couple murmurs just over my shoulder. The pressure of an audience, no matter how small, compels the hand gripping my 6H pencil to move.

Draw something. Draw anything.

I shade the girl's hairline, stalling as I consider the different possible compositions. If I take the realist's approach and censor nothing, I may overstep my bounds as a commissioned artist. I think of the dishwater blonde in line at Thasos, sipping her lemonade humorlessly. *Made my date fuckin' laugh.* But this isn't a five-dollar caricature—it's a hundred-dollar portrait, which could easily become a very expensive insult. At the same time, though, I've heard stories of a fellow artist whose client flew into a frenzy during the portrait hand-off, when she saw that he'd painted over her cleft palate. *You think I'm blind?* she said, hooking a fingernail into the gap in her upper lip. *You think I don't know how I look?*

Down the aisle, two booths switch on their sodium bulbs. Their candlelight glow glints off of the Japanese wind bells hanging next door.

Still deliberating, I sketch the lightest possible outline of a pair of lips. I regret them as soon as my pencil leaves the canvas. They aren't even an embellishment—they're a boldfaced lie. This man has no lips. The skin beneath his nostrils tucks directly into his gums. My adjustment is embarrassing, a blatant acknowledgement of the man's defect, and I wonder now if the guests gathering in the aisle are watching me struggle, attempting to fashion his face into some semblance of normalcy.

Another booth switches on its sodium bulbs. Shadows deepen on both sitters' faces. Pinching my gum eraser, I blot out the man's lips and start again from scratch.

On the bench, Joey and Jacqueline have fallen silent. Both gaze into the crowd behind me, which—from the volume of chatter and footsteps—I'm guessing has swelled to over a dozen. I've never pulled such a large audience before. These guests clearly aren't here to ogle my portrait, though, which has barely enough lines to make a stick figure. They're here to stare at the girl, with her face like the cosmos, and the man, with his face flipped inside out.

Jacqueline blossoms under the attention, baring a half-moon of teeth at the gathering crowd. But Joey—massive Joey, with his bowling-ball shoulders and fire-hydrant neck—Joey withered at first. His back hunched. His head bowed. He removed his baseball cap with the hurried self-consciousness of a fly zipped, or a shirttail tucked. However, Joey is not hunched anymore. Over the course of the sitting, his back slowly straightened. His head rose. His baseball cap tumbled from his lap onto the bench, forgotten. Now, he sits upright, eclipsing the back wall of sample portraits, drawing guests into orbit around my booth as if exerting his own gravitational pull. His chin tilts upward as he peers down at the crowd, stretching tight the gnarled skin beneath his jaw. He grins as though the sitting itself is alone an accomplishment.

While observing him, I suddenly recall the first time I ever drew a naked model.

Figure Drawing 101. Thirty-five easels arranged around a single sitter. I remember wishing the woman would cover her more delicate parts with her hands or at least sit with her legs crossed. Instead, she splayed open her body on the sitter's stool. Her hair tumbled over her shoulders, one strand of it stuck to her lower lip, and grew on her body in shameless patches that would soon become conté scribbles in dozens of sketchbooks. The great pads of her breasts hung cockeyed from her chest. Eyes closed, she tossed her head back as if in ecstasy.

Staring at this woman was a conscious and deliberate choice for every moment of those first few sketches. But after I'd given up masking the overflow of her flesh with flattering angles and softened lines, the woman began to take her true shape before me. The blush retreated down my neck. My eyes were no longer repelled by her, but drawn to her.

This body. Her body. Blooming unabashedly on the white of my canvas.

My sitters' faces, now, are too dark to see. Around me, the other booths' bulbs douse the aisle in a dim wash of gold.

"Rae," I say.

At the purchasing counter, my assistant snaps to attention.

"Lights, please."

Reaching into the rafters, Rae fumbles with a plug, and the booth blazes with light.

Fluorescence is not gentle. It does not flatter. Instead, it invades every bodily nook—the cup of every ear, the hollow of every pore, every crease, buckle, and bend over which sodium light politely glosses. My fluorescent bulbs buzz hot overhead. Joey sits at the spotlight's center, illuminated. Exploded veins branch beneath his scalp. His scars glisten like a running liquid where they catch the light. The pores were melted clear from his nose and cheeks, and in their place, the skin is impossibly smooth, less chewing-gum pink and more the delicate, hidden pink of a tear duct. Beside this man's face, with its exquisite and inscrutable complexity, the young girl's painted galaxies fall flat.

With my 6H pencil, I etch in guidelines—three horizontal for the eyes, nose, and mouth, one vertical to divide each face in half. The lightest crescents for eyelids. Flicks for nostrils. Dashes for lips. This is my pre-sketch: the lowest common denominator of the human face. My wrists tremble. I can see it now: the finished portrait, surfacing slowly in the empty canvas. Ripping a pair of gloves from the dispenser and unlidding my tin of Sennelier oils, I lift two pastel sticks from the tray.

For Jacqueline, Azure Blue. For Joey, Geranium Lake.

As a caricaturist, I'd play up quirks—exaggerate the slant of an eyebrow, the slope of a forehead, the grade of an overbite. As a portraitist, I'd tone them down, smother asymmetries so that only the smooth, firm, and pleasant remained. But this process is new to me. I don't search beneath either face, the painted or the scarred, for the one I'm commissioned to draw. I layer onto my pre-sketch the precise, unearthly colors of their skin. Jacqueline's hairline crumbles with blue paint. I shade it with Cobalt. Amber scabs dot what's left of Joey's lips. I add these in Cinnabar. For the first time in years, I draw my sitters precisely as they are, mapping the uncharted territory of their faces with my Sennelier oils.

The crowd's murmuring fades. As I work, I can hear nothing except for the fluorescent bulbs' buzzing and the stroke of pastel on canvas, feel nothing besides the stiffening of joints in my right forefinger and thumb.

The hour's gone. I'm almost there.

I tuck a strand of hair behind my ear, smearing my temple with Jacqueline's Azure Blue. Joey's Geranium Lake has crept beyond the rolled wrists of my gloves as well. Try as I might to contain the spread of oil, my sitters' hues always inevitably invade my own, though never as vibrantly. All over, my skin is a palette of blue and pink. After I've tarped my walls and counters, unplugged my bulbs, and joined the exodus of Sawdust's artists down the night-cooled Pacific Coast Highway, I will carry their colors home with me in swaths on my arms and cheeks.

I sit back, angling my head this way and that, measuring the completed portrait against the models before me. And then, there's that sudden rush of calm—the extinguishment of some creative spark into smoke. My nail beds tingle with sweat pooled in my gloves' fingertips. From the terrace, I can hear the distant zip of the Cajun band's violins, the tumble of Sawdust's watermill.

It's finished.

"Done?" the man asks.

My stomach knots once more. There's still the hand-off. As satisfied as I am with the portrait, there's no guarantee my patron will feel the same.

Peeling off my gloves, I flip the canvas toward my sitters. It's my turn to gaze unflinchingly forward, to meet the appraising eyes of my audience. This time, though, there will be no politely gritted smiles or awkward apologies, no defensive grabs at my work. There will be only the portrait's exchange—nothing more.

The man leans forward. With one finger, he traces the canvas's frame, poring over the cavernous nostrils, the naked brows, the vast planes of puckered skin, an exact mirror in oil of his own.

Then, he turns to his daughter with the remains of his lips rolled up in a grin.

"Your dad's a handsome bastard," he says.

With my 6B pencil, I scrawl my name in the corner, smudging one end of the signature as my wrist—still shaking—bumps the canvas. *M. Er—*.

I leave it be. Rae sprays and sleeves the portrait, runs the man's credit card, and hands his daughter the bagged canvas. The plastic rubs the paint from her chin to reveal a spot of freckled white. It's hardly noticeable, so small that it could be yet another star. But it's her skin—its true color, thrilling and pure. I'm sure of it.

From a young age, we're trained to look away from disability. Of course, there's an element of politeness and consideration in this—*don't stare,* gawking children are told, *you'll make her feel uncomfortable*—but just as often, this seems to be about the viewer's discomfort as well. Disability can be difficult to look at. Disfigurements like Joey's can be unsettling in their strangeness, their out-in-the-open vulnerability. But rather than ignore it wilfully, the protagonist in "The Sitting" is forced—with her meticulous artist's gaze—to stare directly at what she's been conditioned not to, and to treat the disabled body as aesthetically valuable. And what she finds is that bodily difference is worth viewing—and worth viewing closely. It is sublime, and intimate, and deeply human. In a way, it is art.

Kara Dorris

IN THE WAITING ROOM

"...I'd take a look at my own self in the mirror and wonder how
it was possible that anybody could manage such an enormous thing
as being what he was."

—Chief Bromden in *One Flew Over the Cuckoo's Nest*

Rose loved waiting rooms: the drama and the intimacy, as enthralling
as any daytime soap opera, any AA meeting. Support groups existed for
everything and anything could become an addiction. She sat in the light
beige waiting room of Dr. Tucker, plastic surgeon: the upper walls, an
oatmeal cookie tan and, under a surprisingly crisp white chair rail, a darker
paisley wallpaper. Elvis played over the speakers. Rose was over an hour
early an hour ago. After giving her name at the front desk, she had settled
in the far left corner to observe. Medical waiting rooms were migratory.
The inhabitants searched for warmth and survival, sometimes finding one
or the other, but rarely both. The doctors and their diagnoses were like the
sun: hot, bright and unquestionable, bits of burn and ash that couldn't be
looked at or faced directly, but covertly studied from the corners of eyes and
beneath eyelids.

In the last hour, Rose had watched a woman in her late 40s repeatedly
pull and smooth the sides her face, as if in a wind tunnel, achieving an
effect not unlike a dog's head out the window. *Face lift*, Rose thought.
Another woman kept puckering and smacking her lips. *Collagen*. A man
with extremely muscular arms kept pinching and massaging his skinny
calves. *Calf implants*. Currently, one mother and daughter duo flipped
through a catalogue of noses; each looked for the perfect nose, each chose
differently. More than perfection, Rose knew, the teenage girl looked for
the nose that would make her life bearable, as if her nose made the girls at
school tease her, the boys look through her.

Rose fiddled with the tiny, silver stethoscope necklace hidden under her
shirt. Dr. Tucker would want x-rays and lab work. In x-rays, her body was
just a container where fat and skin didn't exist, just space and what is left
empty; yet, she felt heavy, wrapped in a lead jacket, protected from drifting

away. At the end of the day, her body was hers. And you could do so much, and so little, to the body: ear plugs, nose bars, tattoos, breast implants, nose jobs, broken then stretched femurs.

Last month, Rose had volunteered in at Memphis General, in a wing that specialized in bone disorders. In each patient, tumors jutted from beneath skin and were framed by bruises in various stages of decomposition. She witnessed baseball-sized tumors attached to trim ankles, sharp edges protruding from rounded kneecaps. Surgery was the only treatment, but taking away the tumors weakened the bone's integrity. Sometimes, doctors inserted metal plates and screws.

Rose realized the bones grew to need the tumors; the body learned to deal, to adjust to so much. And if the body didn't adapt, the individual would. In several patients a leg grew shorter than the other, sometimes a leg and an arm, but shoe lifts and long sleeve shirts counterbalanced DNA and gravity.

Somewhere between emptying bedpans and sweeping the floor, Rose had decided she wanted this excess. That night she went home and began fasting. Over the weeks, she lost enough weight that her bones seemed more prominent, her skeleton stuck out. As she fasted, Rose imagined her Aunt Earlene canning jam, imagined the moist, fresh fruit leftovers squishing between her fingers and she wasn't hungry anymore. Rose had been born and raised in Tupelo, Mississippi, as had her mother and her grandmother, even Elvis. Tupelo had always seemed magical with skyscraping trees; the twisting and winding hills and back country possessed an extra special voodoo.

Rose thought of stories she had overheard at Memphis General, how tumors built up directly under nerves, so that every touch caused pleasure and pain. Each new tumor, a potential foreplay delight. If hit too hard, the entire area surrounding the tumor would vibrate like a bell becoming numb. As she stocked shelves and gave out directions, Rose had watched knotted knees knocking together, so that even walking became a carefully thought-out event. Running became dangerous.

Rose wanted to feel the bumps and ridges beneath her flesh like stones in a shallow stream. If she had this bone disorder and she died, if she was violently murdered or disfigured in an accident, the medical examiner would easily identify her body based on her bones, no dental records or DNA needed. He would say, *Oh, look, this girl has tumors, no one else will have a skeleton like hers.*

In the waiting room, the nurse called the name of the teenage girl. Her mother stood up in tandem with her daughter, but the girl just stared.

"I'm eighteen," the daughter said. "You don't need to come in with me."

"Are you sure?" her mother asked.

"Just wait here."

"Alright, but don't come back with plans for breast implants, because that's not what your father and I are paying for."

The daughter rolled her eyes and walked through the door with the nurse.

"I swear," the mother said to Rose. "I know her nose is too big. She gets that from her father. But breast implants at 18? I don't think so."

"Everyone draws their line somewhere," Rose said.

"Teenagers don't have lines," the mother said. "I swear, when she was nine she colored anatomy charts and drew red-dotted lines in potential liposuction areas. Then she started drawing on herself: an egg-like mark on each thigh. A tummy-tuck incision around her bellybutton. Kids."

"At night I used to name each organ and bone in my body," Rose said, "then list potential diseases and symptoms." She didn't need anatomy charts to know where to cut; she felt an internal radar, her body a homing beacon.

"Well, that's a little bit morbid," the mother said.

"Self-mutilation is self-mutilation," Rose said. Last night, to practice, she had created paper-mâché knots to strap on her ankles and knees.

"A nose job is just a nose job," the mother said. "Everyone does it."

"It's like canning jam," Rose said. "Either you seal your goods in an unreachable, airtight container and move on, or you don't tighten the seal enough and deal with mold. It's either preservation or survival. Stasis or struggle. A choice."

"Survival is an instinct, like breathing," the mother said.

"Not always. Breathing is a choice."

"Yeah, who wants to breathe anyway?" the mother asked sarcastically.

"Your daughter. That's why she's here," Rose said. The mother flinched.

"So why are you here, anyway?" the mother asked.

"I'm going to have this bone disorder," Rose said. "I feel the tumors rising up underneath my skin."

"Why would you want something like that?" The mother asked.

"Why wouldn't I?" Rose answered.

For a moment, the waiting room was quiet. Rose flipped through a *National Geographic* magazine, studied the insides of volcanoes; all that black ash and molten, overflowing lava reminded her of the human body. Why did we worship the body? After his first burial, grave robbers tried to steal Elvis' body. But the body always undoes itself until nothing is left behind.

How was implanting prosthetic bone tumors any different from getting breast implants? Rose knew some girls wanted desperately to be normal, which, to Rose, was like death or a blank wall, a clear canvas to fuck up with paint and collage, tattoo and pierce. To be beautiful. What was beauty? Rose's mother started entering Rose in beauty pageants as a baby. At eight, Rose competed in the Little Miss Tupelo Pageant, her dark curls bouncing, wearing a red polka dot, ruffled dress. In the talent competition she sang "Devil in Disguise." The first time she watched an Elvis concert on TV, she studied the way he smiled, rolled his hips, and made the girls scream. Although she entered dozens of pageants, she never won.

Rose felt the mother staring her from across the waiting room.

"I knew this girl once," Rose said without looking up, "pretty but weak and scared of everything. She was in a hospital and she met another girl, Miranda, who had strange knots on her knees. One was the size of her fist, the other smaller, sharp, like a kitchen knife. Miranda said as she walked, she could feel the bruises forming as the knots knocked together. She was in that office to have those knots removed. She wanted to walk without thought, to be just another girl on the street."

"That's understandable," the mother said.

"Is it? Her mother thought so too," Rose said. "The other girl in the waiting room, the one waiting, asked, 'Aren't you scared, what about the pain?' Miranda just smiled and said, 'When you're told your body has failed you from birth, you grow up tough.' The waiting girl didn't understand."

"What happened to Miranda?" the mother asked.

"She had the surgery," Rose said.

"Was she okay?"

"That's not the point," Rose said. "Her surgeries didn't stop. She just kept taking from her body. Until she wasn't herself anymore."

"That's so sad," the mother said.

"I thought you said it was understandable," Rose said. "We try to name our pain and fix it. But we never fix it, because something else always hurts. When someone asks you what's wrong, it's easier to say I hurt and to physically show it."

"But does it hurt any less if it's made visible?" the mother asked.

"Once you name it, see it, maybe you can understand it," Rose said.

"Then what comes next?" the mother asked. "Sympathy?"

"Empathy, maybe. I don't know."

"So you're going to have prosthetic knots inserted into your body, like the knotted girl in the other waiting room," the mother said.

"Yes."

"But that doesn't make any sense. Why would you do such a thing?"

"I want to be the person I dream of being."

"But why go to such extremes?"

"We'll do anything."

Neither spoke.

Rose's mother taught her to arrange flowers and fill in the gaps with baby's breath, to arrange displays in 3s and 5s, how to apply makeup, to use light colors for day eyes and heavy, darks for night eyes, to walk and turn and smile, how to hang paintings in big, empty spaces, to arrange furniture to maximize floor space, fung shui, how to stage. But staging the body, out of balance or not, was so much harder.

Rose remembered her mother playing the piano and singing Elvis songs. Rose used to turn the sheet music and stand so close she breathed in White Linen by Estée Lauder and gin. Together, they had formed a duo, spoke to each other through Elvis. On her ninth birthday, Rose learned about Elvis' death. How people loved how far he fell, how slow and fast, how low he laid on the bathroom floor.

—KARA DORRIS—

This story stems largely from my past, especially my teenage years when the focus on the body is so absolute and unforgiving that everyone is found wanting. I have deposits of excess calcium throughout the bones of my body, mainly at the joints, which is caused by a genetic disorder called osteochondroma. Through surgery, I cut away two knots protruding from my left knee, thinking that would make me "normal." Two more surgeries and three years later, I was obsessed about the baseball size tumor on my ankle. Doctors didn't know how to remove it, or even if they could, since the tumor itself was holding my ankle in place. I turned to clothing, and, even in the Texas heat, I wore jeans. Many years later, through writing, I was forced to ask myself: Who would I be without this genetic disorder? Why would someone be thankful to have it? So I started writing this story, and I discovered it takes constant strength to walk through the world without hiding.

Ellen McGrath Smith

TWO REALLY DIFFERENT THINGS

Sharon sat straight up in bed and was suddenly cold.

Where she'd just been at work in deep musky efforts to make Abby, her girlfriend, feel good.

Which reminded her of torrid but slow summer afternoons in childhood when she'd crawl inside the blackberry bush in a neighbor's backyard and sit there, eating the berries, tatooing her arms and legs with runes from their juices, the whole time aware that no one could see her, no one could ever find her. And if the lady whose yard she was in—Mrs. Welty—did find her, she wouldn't mind her being there. She was a kind old woman in a housedress who spoke in a globby and plaintive way, her completely unmanageable tongue lolling out every two syllables or so. At first, Sharon thought it odd that a lady so old would, like her, be the victim of a ridiculously oversized wad of Bubble Yum. Given the chance to buy a pack at the Corner Store, Sharon often went too far, inserting piece upon piece into her mouth until her jaw ached and words were, like the bubbles themselves, stretched beyond the shape of anything containing meaning.

Sharon's mother soon explained it all to Sharon:

One. Mrs. Welty had suffered a stroke, which meant that certain nerves controlling her jaw and tongue no longer connected right.

Two. If you get 5 cents to buy a pack of bubble gum and chew it all up in one blob in one day, you should not be given 5 more cents the next day to buy another pack at the Corner Store.

Where she'd just been at work inside the legs of her girlfriend, the powerful half of the power-couple Grace Howers said they would be when she fixed them up, Sharon now sat up, spine straight; still and cold. She was trying, as usual, to hear what she thought she'd just heard. She'd been hearing impaired all her life, so this delayed processing of things others said to her was normal, though now more emotionally charged. She just had to figure out:

One. If Abby, from her place up on top of her body-being-pleasured, head on the pillow, muttering directions like *over a little. To the right. There yes,* had really just raised her voice, exasperated, and barked out, "I don't know why the fuck you took out your hearing aids!"

Two. If it was reasonable to request that one's lover wear hearing appliances when doing it.

Since Sharon couldn't figure out *Two* even after she got Abby to repeat and confirm *One* (without saying "fuck" the second time), she got up, threw on a T-shirt, and walked out of the room with a pillow, her plan to go sleep on the couch.

"Thanks a lot," Abby said.

Abby was a soft butch superstar real estate lawyer with straight black hair that hung down just below her jaw. She served on the board of every other charity in Pittsburgh, had been open and out about her civil union with a local radio disc jockey. At 35, she'd made the local paper's "Most Powerful Pittsburgher Under 40" spread. Sharon had seen her at arts events before and (take a number) thought she was hot. She gave off a kind of energy that made you think she had an engine implanted that only a few other humans get. Abby never considered not getting what she wanted, a trait that, when they started dating, drew Sharon to her. Sharon was a painter with an expensive arts degree (and huge loan debt to go with) and one show in New York (Buffalo) under her belt. Most fellow artists made it clear that her work was outstanding and deserved a wider reach, but she just wasn't good at the self-promotion thing. Her stature as an artist in Pittsburgh had still managed to improve despite that deficiency. She'd received, some years ago, a $40,000 award for her work. She hadn't even applied for the award, but she used half of it to begin a cooperative art gallery on the west side of Pittsburgh, where there was a need for more arts-based programs and facilities. Abby was not on their board.

Grace Howers had fixed them up because she knew both of them. Abby's much-publicized partner of 10 years had quietly dumped her for a man, her high school sweetheart. And Sharon was generally on hiatus from dating after a series of two- to three-year relationships that began while she was at the expensive arts college. She was 31, she'd begun thinking hard about that two- to three-year span, what it meant about her and what it could mean for her in the future. Most of those years involved drinking, though she'd stopped drinking altogether when she was 28. It was easy for Sharon to meet people, easy even to get very familiar very fast, but she was using the hiatus to read self-help books, teach advanced painting classes at the community college, work on a series of self-portrait-as-bird paintings (some with actual feathers), attend meetings (AA), run the co-op gallery, and train for a marathon. Men and women had asked her out, but she just didn't want to be dating, she told them nicely. Only in retrospect would she realize that the day Grace called about introducing them was about a year after she'd first started her hiatus, or what she sometimes referred to, with friends, as her "ceasefire." She'd just completed her first marathon, in Pittsburgh, the day before Grace's call. Maybe that sense of full-circularity was what led Sharon to agree to be fixed up.

They hit it off right away. Abby had a lot of questions about the co-op gallery and how it worked. "You could open me up to my artistic side," she'd said, in that early part of a relationship when, no matter what you're talking about, it seems inordinately sexy. "And I could open you up to the competitive business world and help you grow your gallery."

Sharon distrusted the use of the word "grow" as a transitive verb except within the context of gardening, which she loved more and more each year she did it.

Abby loved that Sharon gardened as well. She was always travelling for business and for speaking engagements, always eating lunch and dinner away from home. She loved when Sharon made some organic meal. As the relationship advanced to a half a year, Sharon realized that she and home were to be one and the same for Abby. Not necessarily that she would be Abby's housewife, but, rather, that she was to be the constant to Abby's variable. Around that time, Sharon picked Abby up at the airport. The flight from Chicago had landed at midnight, and Sharon was there. Upon seeing Sharon, Abby was upset by two things:

One. That Sharon had, as a surprise, done something she'd long been wanting to do, which was have a good colorist strip her bleached blond hair back to its original auburn color, which it hadn't been since right before she'd stopped drinking.

Two. When Abby said, "Oh, I'm starved. Do we have anything to eat at home?" and Sharon started listing what was there and Abby interrupted her and said, "No. I mean *made*?" and Sharon said no.

Abby went into a funk about how Sharon probably hadn't even missed her, and Sharon threw in a comment about how, if Abby hated her hair now, then she must hate who Sharon really was.

"Well, no," Abby said. "I think you look gorgeous, I always do."

"I know what it is," Sharon said, herself still able to be surprised by the lack of blondness in the rearview mirror. "When we first hooked up, you told me that one of the things your ex always accused you of was looking at blondes. You told me, remember—you were wearing your big Michigan shirt—'Yeah, she always said I really wanted a blonde on my arm and now, ha! wait until she sees me with you.' And then you went out of your way to get tickets to that one fundraiser where we had to sit with that couple that looked like twin turtles?" Sharon rehearsed this all in a joking way, and Abby didn't interrupt her. In fact, she left a pause after Sharon finished, then sighed and said, "No, really, of course that was unrealistic of me to expect you to have dinner for me at midnight. It's just that I missed you so much and I've been eating such fatty food."

When they finally settled in to sleep for the night, Sharon said to the dark ceiling, "The opening went really well tonight. We sold two pieces. One to your ex and, you know, the guy she's with. Who's really nice, by the way."

"Thanks for ruining my chances for a good night's sleep, Sharon."

Sharon had been really anxious about the opening the gallery had held that night. It was a group show of really amazing work from all over the country on the general theme of STRUCTURE. After all the pushing Abby had been exerting on her to change it from a co-op to a nonprofit corporation so that Abby could work on the leasing of a new multi-use warehouse space in that area, Sharon assumed that she'd be pleased that they'd sold two pieces in a non-buying city like Pittsburgh, or that she'd at least have asked how much the pieces sold for. As she turned to her own mound of pillows, she simply pretended that she hadn't heard the only thing Abby had had to say about it. This was one of the uses to which she put her hearing impairment. Everyone she'd ever been close to—parents, siblings, roommates, lovers, friends—had been happy to enable her in this.

The first and only time she had sex with Abby with both of her hearing aids in, Sharon flashed on the image of tiny transistor radios tossing in an endless sea of 500-thread-count Egyptian sheets and goose down.

Abby's solar plexus sounded like a boiler in the basement of a large institutional structure, say a casino complex or hospital. Intimacy's noises were not meant to be this loud. On top of this, Sharon had to be vigilant about how she moved or positioned her head because those suckers cost a lot of money—and time, when you count all the programming. When Abby put two fingers inside her and she moaned, she heard not only the sound of her brain wiring but also her moans magnified to whalesongs underwater over great distances.

These were the whole clauses Abby said during:

—Baby, you're so wet for me.

—Point your tongue like it's a bullet.

—What did I ever do before you?

But many fail to understand—and though Sharon often tried to explain, Abby didn't get it—that volume and frequency are two really different things. So, for at least three weeks after she broke up with Abby, sure she was doing the right thing but often tempted to pick up the phone, Sharon kept her resolve strong by reminding herself of what it was she'd heard:

—You'll never get real love from me.

—What you do is bullshit.

—You are what I make you.

"Two Really Different Things" came from a writing day with my friend, the fiction writer Keely Bowers. I was finally building a story around something that had happened to me: the experience of having a lover suggest I wear my hearing devices in bed after I didn't hear something she'd said. I turned it into a fictional exploration of dualities—of perspective, of experiences, of the identities of words—because I wasn't interested in lingering on the outrageousness of this expectation but, rather, I was interested in the other ways in which the balance of power in this relationship was coming to seem, to Sharon, unacceptable. These other ways can be traced, though, to Sharon's hearing, which is right enough most of the time for Sharon to keep hoping it won't fail her but wrong enough to make her doubt herself and her feelings. I liked that it's about two women in a sexual relationship, but that it doesn't have to be about that—it could just as easily have happened in a hetero or gay relationship.

Anne Finger

COMRADE LUXEMBURG AND COMRADE GRAMSCI PASS EACH OTHER IN THE CONGRESS OF THE SECOND INTERNATIONAL ON THE 10TH OF MARCH, 1912

Italicized sections of the text are quotations from Johann Goethe, Rosa Luxemburg, Johnny Cash, Alfred Döblin, Antonio Gramsci, Vladimir Lenin, Benito Mussolini, Adolph Hitler, Karl Koch, and the Bible.

It never happened.

It could not have happened.

It could not have happened that at a crowded congress of the Second International held in a resort hotel on the shores of Lake Catano in the foothills of the Swiss Alps, alongside a snow-fed lake with waters of such pure, crystalline blue that even in the very center one could peer straight down and clearly see the fluid shadows of the waters' ripples speckling the rocks at the bottom, the delegates from the socialist parties of the world gathering in clots in the hallways, doing the real business of the congress there, with urgent imprecations, hands grasping forearms, voices dropped almost to whispers and glances over their shoulders, while upstairs an overworked chambermaid with varicose veins, Madame Robert, flicked a sheet in the air, sending motes of dust dancing in the afternoon sunshine, Comrade Rosa Luxemburg and Comrade Antonio Gramsci limped past each other.

It never happened that Luxemburg, who had been detained after her speech by those anxious to get her advice, to give her theirs, to merely say that they had spoken with her, yes, *individually, personally,* at last signaled to her companion with her eyes, who worked his way through the knot of people surrounding her, laid a paternal hand on her arm, said, "Rosa, you must..." and Rosa allowed herself to be led away, departing the Geneva Room at 2:52 in the afternoon, while at 2:51 Comrade Gramsci had sneezed, futilely searched his pockets for a handkerchief, and, having wiped his nose surreptitiously with the back of his hand, bowed his head and hurried through the crowded corridor to ascend to his room on the fifth floor to fetch one, so that, two-thirds of the way along, the two of you would pass each other.

No, it could not have happened.

On March 10, 1912, at eight minutes to three in the afternoon, Rosa Luxemburg was in her apartment on Lindenstrasse in Berlin, preparing a lecture for the Party School, thumbing through Goethe's *Faust*, looking for the quotation *No one yields empire / To another; no one will yield it who has gained it by force…*, the same volume that she will drop into her purse when she hears the footsteps coming up the stairs of the house in Neukölln to take her to her death six years later; and Gramsci was a twenty-one-year-old, a poverty-stricken Sardinian student, eating his first meal in three days, a plate of *spaghetti con olio*, at a trattoria on the Via Pereigia in Turin, reading a linguistics text as he ate, at a table just a little bit too high for him, so that his arms ached slightly from the odd angle at which they had to be maneuvered. At the next table a father moaned and patted his belly, pushed his chair back from the table, then urged his plump daughters to eat dessert, accompanying his coaxings with tugs at their flesh: they were too thin, altogether too thin, his dumplings, his darlings. The coy daughters protested; the *padre* signaled the waiter to clear away the platters of calamari and pasta, the remains of the spring lamb, the half flask of wine. Later, limping home alone in a sharp wind with his half-empty belly (why does one feel the cold so much more when one is hungry?), Gramsci tried to name the force that allowed him to watch the remains of the rich man's dinner being taken away while he still hungered: a dog, a dumb brute, would have leapt for it, seized the lamb in his teeth. The dog would have been a better socialist than I am, he thought.

No, Comrade Luxemburg does not pass Comrade Gramsci as she heads down the corridor on her way to sit next to Karl Liebknecht at dinner, on her way to dine with him and twelve Judases, on her way to *the unprecedented, the incredible 4th of August 1914*, when the men she thought of as her comrades will vote for war appropriations so that the workers of Germany can kill and in turn be killed by the workers of Italy and France and England; on her way to the gloomy evening a few weeks later when she and Clara Zetkin will sit in her parlor, four feet in scuffed slippers resting on the fender before the fire, debating not the woman question, not organizational questions of the party, but whether laudanum or prussic acid would be a better way to go: because *mass murder has become a boring, monotonous daily business*; on her way to listening to the whistle of the 3:19 train carrying Mathilde away from her in the prison where Rosa was locked up for her opposition to the war (*If they free me from this prison / if that railroad train was mine / you bet I'd move it on' a little further down the line / far from Folsom prison...*); she will promise Sonja Liebknecht that she will go to Corsica with her after the war (*On high, nothing except barren rock formations which are noble grey; below, luxuriant trees, cherry trees, and age-old chestnut trees. And above everything, a prehistoric quiet—no human voices, no bird calls, only a stream rippling somewhere between rocks, or the wind on high whispering between the cliffs—still the same wind that swelled Ulysses' sails...*), but she will never see Corsica again; instead she will spend her first night of freedom, a sleepless night, at the railway workers' union hall, preparing for a demonstration the next day; on her way to Berlin, where red flags will be flying everywhere (*...precisely when on the surface everything seems hopeless and miserable, a complete change is getting ready...*); on her way to her dazed, lurching walk through the corridors of Hotel Eden (*You know I really hope to die at my post, in a street fight or in prison*), past the chambermaids and valets who, a few weeks previously, might have joined the throngs in the streets of Berlin, might even have a sister or brother who took part in the occupation of the *Vorwärts* building demanding of a newcomer, "*Why have you come so late? And why have you not brought others with you?*", who will now join in the jeering: Jew, sow, red whore, cripple, Jew; on her way to the black car, on her way to the bullet to her brain that pierces her left temporal lobe and wipes out the throne within her brain where reason sat; on her way to becoming, for a few brief minutes, no longer Dr. Luxemburg, no longer the visionary, the prophet, just a body, an unconscious (*...sometimes it seems to me that I am not really a human being at all, but rather a bird or a beast in human form...*); a body whose dead weight will plummet into the waters of the Landwehr Canal.

She does not pass Comrade Gramsci on his way to his room on the fifth floor to fetch a handkerchief; on his way to the Petrograd train station where he will be met by a delegation of four men and one woman who will stand on the platform scanning the air above him, and he will pretend not to notice the few seconds lag after he announces himself in a voice he has made as deep as possible (this shrunken hunchback the famous leader?—sometimes they will have been warned ahead of time that he is *handicapped, deformed*, but then they will expect some Cyclops, a Minotaur, not this limping dwarf); on his way to being led into the courtroom, where everyone save the prisoners will appear in tragicomic fascist splendor, a double cordon of militiamen in plumed black helmets, heels of well-polished shoes clicked together, backs straight, an emblematic dagger poised in an identical position in the belt of each one, the marshals bearing standards that read SPQR, Senatus Populusque Romanus—this will, of course, recall to him Marx's comment about history repeating itself, the first time as tragedy and the second as a farce; he will limp in dirty, unshaven, feeling like a wounded, crawling animal: a ferret, perhaps, slithering and predatory; he will feel a sense of physical shame and understand again a sentence he will have written years before when the Turin workers councils failed: *the bourgeoisie lies in ambush in the hearts of the proletariat*; on his way to becoming the great mind, the Gramsci who floats, a head without a body, on fading posters once thumbtacked to apartment walls in Madison, Wisconsin and Berkeley, California, now matted and framed.

Rosa, you warned us, *we can no more skip a period in our historical development than a man can jump over his shadow.* But still I spray-paint walls on the Hotel Leveque a slogan that wouldn't be heard for fifty-odd years hence: "All power to the imagination!" I imagine that in those days when we didn't yet have a name for ourselves, when the only words were *handicapped, lame, deformed, hunchback, dwarf, cripple,* when the only words were silence, that we could speak.

I imagine that Comrade Luxemburg stares, looks away, but then laughs at herself for doing so: not so loud, not a full-throated, rich deep laugh, but only a laugh of mild amusement at her "instinctive" reaction. And then she turns, smiles, as you or I might do passing each other in the corridor at a meeting filled with ABs.

She stops, stretches out her hand, says, "We haven't met. I'm Rosa Luxemburg."

"Of course," he mutters. "Yes, of course," stretching out his hand in return, conscious of the fact that it's the one he used in the absence of his handkerchief.

"And you?" she says, helping out the flustered young man. He gives his name. "Let's talk," she says.

After dinner when the coffee's served, they meet out on the veranda. Of course the stone benches out there are backless, and so they'll schlep three chairs out—one to prop their feet on, which otherwise would dangle above the ground.

"So," Rosa asks right out, "has your disability made difficulties for you, in the party?"

Antonio shrugs, "They—the workers—trust me."

She nods, she knows. The wound on the outside so that strangers on a train pick you to tell their tale to.

"But they fear it, too," she supplies.

"Yes, they fear it, too."

"And yet," she says, "I often wonder if I would have got as far in the party as I have if it weren't for—"

"The de-sexualization—"

"De-gendering was more what I was going to say," she says. Because of all those years of her growing up when it seemed that she was destined to be permanently outside the realm of desire, his words make her a bit prickly. If she were honest with herself about this—although she couldn't be— she'd admit that it was one of the things that led her to socialism: that it was the place where her strength of mind, of character could overcome her physical flaw, allow her to be desired. She only lets herself know that she felt freedom here, a freedom she couldn't feel anywhere else.

Comrades, I want you to go on but his conversation has grown awkward, studded with anachronisms, impossible to write. All power to the imagination? As difficult a slogan to put into practice as *All power to the soviets.*

And although I want to holler back through time: "Please, speak to each other," I cannot let you know what's to come. Mussolini is not yet a fascist, he has not yet become a man of steel, a man who will slap cold water on raw morning flesh, his chest puffed out like an enormous steam engine: *the masses are a woman*, he will say, and, at a certain moment when, haranguing them from a balcony, he feels their submissive spirit reach up towards him, he will strip off his shirt to show those muscles like iron bands, jut forward the great leonine head, the lumpishness of his bald skull giving the effect of a Roman head chiseled in marble. Hitler is still nothing more than a gleam in the evil eye of history. He has not yet spun that web of propaganda where disease, prostitution, the caftaned Jew lurking in the alley waiting to defile the Aryan woman, *the suffocating perfume of our modern eroticism*, the degenerates contaminating the healthy and passing their defective genes on to their offspring, blur together and become one. He has not yet declared that Germany must become a healthy state. Kommandant Koch of Buchenwald has not yet said, *There are no sick men in my camp. They are all either well or dead.* Mussolini, Hitler, Koch will understand: the worship of the healthy body, the fear of us, is the taproot of fascism.

But Rosa, sober Rosa, leans forward through time to reprimand me: *In the beginning was the act.* No, they can't yet speak to each other. We don't yet exist. We are the sons and daughters of fascism as well as the daughters and sons of ourselves.

So I try again. I fast-forward through the next four bloody years of history: the soldiers like Keystone Kops as they rush out of their trenches, grimace, fall to the ground, and the next wave of soldiers rises and does the same, and the next does the same, and the next does the same, and the next does the same, and the next does the same, until twenty-two million have died and I hit the "play" button and return to normal speed.

Rosa walks out the doors of Breslau Prison, she speaks at the rally in Berlin, she writes, *There is order in Berlin...your order is built on sand.* But she never takes that last dazed, lurching walk through the corridors of the Hotel Eden; she is never found, a bloated marshmallow of a corpse, eyeless, bobbing against the locks of the Landwehr Canal. Instead she escapes to the Soviet Union, from there she hopscotches to New York. Antonio, at first I imagine that you were persuaded to leave Italy before your arrest, but even in the world of imagination I can't wish *The Prison Notebooks*, the *Letters*, out of existence. Forgive me, Nino, but I am sending you into that filthy cell in Regina Coeli Prison, where the single bare bulb burns all night long and the lice scuttle through the mattress; and into all the prison cells that follow that one. Let's suppose that Romain Rolland, who has worked so diligently for your release all these years—circulating petitions, writing endless letters, lobbying in the court of world opinion—despairs of those tactics: instead, knowing how close you are to death, he organizes a commando raid against the Quisisana Clinic. Chuck Norris is the advance man, he disguises himself as a taciturn (male) nurse—we'll explain away his fair complexion by having him pretend to be German; at the appointed hour, while a helicopter lowers itself toward the roof, he'll pick you up in his arms like a baby (you weighed only forty-two kilograms then), toss you over his shoulder and, a machine gun in his free hand, take out a few fascists as he rushes the roof. Chuck will cradle you in his arms, stroke your black hair away from your hot forehead, say, "Hey, guy, it's okay. You're all right, Comrade." There will be no flyer headlined "Italian Fascism Has Murdered Gramsci." No, Comrade, you will live.

Neither of them will become famous. Sorry, there's truth to the old saw about death being good for your career. Rosa ends up giving lectures at the New School, writing for magazines with ever-dwindling circulations. She began her article "Either/Or" with a quote from Revelations: *I would thou wert cold or hot. So then because thou art lukewarm, and neither cold nor hot, I will spew thee out of my mouth.*" But now the masses have moved to White Plains, they drive DeSotos, she has become an apocalyptic crank. Antonio sits out the war years in the warm dry air of southern California, regaining some measure of health, joining up with that colony of squabbling, quibbling, squalling leftist exiles.

What will I do with them now that I've saved them? Have them meet again, on a subway platform in Brooklyn? Rosa, 103 with that papery, almost smooth-as-a-baby patch of skin on her cheeks that old, old women get; and Antonio, in his eighties, lumbering and wheezing up the steps. But then, it could only be the early 1970's: too early still. No, I'll have time pass but the two of them stay in their forties, the ages they were when they died; it's 1990: Rosa is sitting on the bench at Ditmas station in Brooklyn, waiting for the F train, the Americans with Disabilities Act has just passed; she's reading the article about it in *The New York Times*. Antonio comes and sits down next to her. He knows enough to leave a couple of New York inches between the two of them, but still she sidles a bit away. He can't help looking over her shoulder, reading the same article she is. She shakes the newspaper a bit, casts him a quick cold glance. He looks away; but then she says, "Excuse me. We've met, haven't we?"

What shall I have the two of them say? Shall I have Antonio say that our movement must concern itself with more than legislation, *must reach for the solution to more complex tasks than those proposed by the present development of the struggle; namely, for the creation of a new, integral culture…;* shall I have Rosa come back with the necessity of our movement being democratic, that we must make our own errors, *errors…infinitely more fruitful and more valuable than the infallibility* of any CIL board and all its high-powered consultants?

But no, it's another conversation I can't imagine.

No, I have to go back to that hotel corridor.

Although it could not have happened on the 10th of March, 1912, at a congress of the Second International, in a corridor of the Hotel Leveque at precisely 2:53, that Comrade Luxemburg, heading in a southerly direction down the corridor towards the dining hall while Comrade Gramsci headed towards the north staircase, passed each other, still, had it happened, Rosa would have startled slightly as she glimpsed him, the misshapen dwarf limping toward her in a secondhand black suit so worn the fabric was turning green with age, her eye immediately drawn to his disruption in the visual field.

Realizing she was staring, she would have glanced quickly away. And then, the moment after, realizing that the quick aversion of her gaze was as much of an insult as the stare, she would have turned her head back but tried to make her gaze general. Comrade Rosa would have felt a slight flicker of embarrassment? shame? dread? of a feeling that had no name?

Would Gramsci at first have bowed his head in shame, then raised his head, stared back deciding that her right to look at him equaled his right to look at her? Did a slight smile pass across his face because he was glad to know that such a prominent comrade shared his condition?

It is all over in a matter of seconds.

But this never happened. And even if it had, it would have not have mattered. What passed between the two of you belongs to the realm of thought before speech, of the shape of the future before it can be seen: a nameless discomfort, not even a premonition.

No, there is no such place on earth. You will not find this Lake Catano on any map: I have created it out of words. This congress never happened; the two of you were not there.

Look down through those clear blue waters of Lake Catano to shifting shadow of the lake's ripples that speckle the rocks at the bottom; see the shadows grow larger and larger until they dissolve into nothingness. Now the lake itself, which never existed, disappears. The scullery girl scraping onions in the kitchen automatically wipes her cheeks with the backs of her hands and discovers that her cheeks are not wet with onion tears; surprised, she sniffs the air; it does not smell of onions, it does not smell of anything. Upstairs, the chambermaid, old Madame Robert, stands on her aching legs and snaps a freshly laundered sheet through the air. Madame Robert, your legs will ache no more: I am writing away your pain, I am writing away your very existence. For a moment the motes of dust you have disturbed dance glistening in the air, but then they cease, and first the sheet itself and then you yourself turn to shadows and vanish.

—ANNE FINGER—

I have long been fascinated with how histories of disability are still hidden, ignored, treated as shameful, even by those who should be our allies. I learned about the great Italian intellectual Antonio Gramsci's disability when reading the introduction to an edition of his *Prison Letters* which described him as "having the appearance of being a hunchbacked dwarf," as if assuring the readers that he wasn't *really* a hunchbacked dwarf, he just looked like one. And I only learned about Rosa Luxemburg's being a "semi-cripple" when I read that description of her in Nazi propaganda. In this story, I imagine the impossible—that these two people could have passed one another, could have, to use Simi Linton's term, "claimed disability" in a time before it could have been claimed. I should also add that I had fun writing this story—making the impossible happen and dissolving these two characters into air.

DEEP END

The pool was supposed to be like freespace. Enough like it, anyway, to help Wayna acclimate to her download. She went in first thing every "morning" as soon as Dr. Ops, the ship's mind, awakened her. Too bad it wasn't scheduled for later; all the slow, meat-based activities afterwards were a literal drag.

The voices of the pool's other occupants boomed back and forth in an odd, uncontrolled manner, steel-born echoes muffling and exposing what was said. The temperature varied irregularly, warm intake jets competing with cold currents and, Wayna suspected, illicitly released urine. Overhead lights speckled the wall, the ceiling, the water, with a shifting, uneven glare.

Psyche Moth was a prison ship. Like all those on board, Wayna was an upload of a criminal's mind. The process of uploading her mind had destroyed her physical body. Punishment. Then the ship, with Wayna and 248,961 other prisoners, set off on a long voyage to another star. During that voyage, the prisoners' minds had been cycled through consciousness: one year on, four years off. Of the eighty-seven years en route, Wayna had only lived through seventeen. Now she spent most of her time as meat.

Wayna's jaw ached. She'd been clenching it, trying to amp up her sensory inputs. She paddled toward the deep end, consciously relaxing her facial muscles. When *Psyche Moth* had reached its goal and verified that the world it called Amends was colonizable, her group was the second downloaded into empty clones, right after the trustees. One of those had told her it was typical to translocate missing freespace controls to their meat analogs.

She swirled her arms back and forth, creating waves, making them run into one another:

Then the pain hit.

White! Heat! There then gone—the lash of a whip.

Wayna stopped moving. Her suit held her up. She floated, waiting. Nothing else happened. Tentatively, she kicked and stroked her way to the steps rising from the pool's shallows. It hit her again: a shock of electricity slicing from the right shoulder to left hip. She caught her breath and continued in.

The showers were empty. Wayna was the first one from her hour out of the pool. It was too soon for the next hour to wake up. She turned on the water and stood in its welcome warmth. What was going on? She'd never felt anything like this, not that she could remember—and surely she wouldn't have forgotten something so intense… She stripped off her suit and hung it to dry. Instead of dressing in her overall and reporting to the laundry, her next assignment, she retreated into her locker and linked with Dr. Ops.

In the sphere of freespace, his office always hovered in the northwest quadrant, about halfway up from the horizon. Doe, Wayna's honeywoman, disliked this placement. Why pretend he was anything other than central to the whole setup, she asked. Why not put himself smack dab in the middle where he belonged? Doe distrusted Dr. Ops and everything about *Psyche Moth*. Wayna understood why. But there was nothing else. Not for eight light years in any direction. According to Dr. Ops.

She swam into his pink-walled waiting room and eased her icon into a chair. That registered as a request for the AI's attention. A couple of other prisoners were there ahead of her. One disappeared soon after she sat. A few more minutes by objective measure, and the other was gone as well. Then it was Wayna's turn.

Dr. Ops presented as a lean-faced Caucasian man with a shock of mixed brown and blond hair. He wore an anachronistic headlamp and stethoscope and a gentle, kindly persona. "I have your readouts, of course, but why don't you tell me what's going on in your own words?"

He looked like he was listening. When she finished, he sat silent for a few seconds—much more time than he needed to consider what she'd said. Making an ostentatious display of his concern.

"There's no sign of nerve damage," he told her. "Nothing wrong with your spine or any of your articulation or musculature."

"So then how come—"

"It's probably nothing," the AI said, interrupting her. "But just in case, let's give you the rest of the day off. Take it easy—outside your locker, of course. I'll clear the bunkroom for the next twenty-five hours. Lie down. Put in some face time with your friends."

"Probably?"

"I'll let you know for sure tomorrow morning. Right now, relax. Doctor's orders." He smiled and logged her out. He could do that. It was his system.

Wayna tongued open her locker. No use staying in there without access to freespace. She put on her overall and walked up the corridor to her bunkroom. Fellow prisoners passed her heading the other way to the pool: no one she'd known back on Earth, no one she had gotten to know that well in freespace or since the download. Plenty of time for that on planet. The woman with the curly red hair was called Robeson, she was pretty sure. They smiled at each other. Robeson walked hand in hand with a slender man whose mischievous smile reminded Wayna of Thad. It wasn't him. Thad was scheduled for later download. Wayna was lucky to have Doe with her.

Another pain. Not so strong, this time. Strong enough, though. Sweat dampened her skin. She kept going, almost there.

There. Through the doorless opening she saw the mirror she hated, ordered up by one of the two women she timeshared with. It was only partly obscured by the genetics charts the other woman taped everywhere. Immersion learning. Even Wayna was absorbing something from it.

But not now. She lay on the bunk without looking at anything, eyes open. What was wrong with her?

Probably nothing?

Relax.

She did her body awareness exercises, tensing and loosening different muscle groups. She'd gotten as far as her knees when Doe walked in. Stood over her till Wayna focused on her honeywoman's new face. "Sweetheart," Doe said. Her pale fingers stroked Wayna's face. "Dr. Ops told a trustee you wanted me."

"No—I mean yes, but I didn't ask—" Doe's expression froze, flickered, froze again. "Don't be—it's so hard, can't you just—" Wayna reached for and found both of Doe's hands and held them against her overall's open V-neck and slid them beneath the fabric, forcing them to stroke her shoulders.

Making love to Doe in her download seemed like cheating. Wayna wondered what Thad's clone would look like, and if they'd be able to travel to his group's settlement to see him.

Anticipating agony, Wayna found herself hung up, nowhere near ecstasy. Doe pulled back and looked down at her, expecting an explanation. So Wayna had to tell her what little she knew.

"You! You weren't going to say anything! Just let me hurt you—" Doe had zero tolerance for accidentally inflicting pain, the legacy of her marriage to a closeted masochist.

"It wouldn't be anything you *did*! And I don't know if—"

Doe tore aside the paper they had taped across the doorway for privacy. From her bunk, Wayna heard her raging along the corridor, slapping the walls.

Face time was over.

Taken off of her normal schedule, Wayna had no idea how to spend the rest of her day. Not lying down alone. Not after that. She tried, but she couldn't.

Relax.

Ordinarily when her laundry shift was over, she was supposed to show up in the cafeteria and eat. Never one of her favorite activities, even back on Earth. She went there early, though, surveying the occupied tables. The same glaring lights hung from the ceiling here as in the pool, glinting off plastic plates and water glasses. The same confused noises, the sound of overlapping conversations. No sign of Doe.

She stood in line. The trustee in charge started to give her a hard time about not waiting for her usual lunch hour. He shut up suddenly. Dr. Ops must have tipped him a clue. Trustees were in constant contact with the ship's mind—part of why Wayna hadn't volunteered to be one.

Mashed potatoes. Honey mustard nuggets. Slaw. All freshly factured, filled with nutrients and the proper amount of fiber for this stage of her digestive tract's maturation.

She sat at a table near the disposal dump. The redhead, Robeson, was there too, and a man—a different one than Wayna had seen her with before. Wayna introduced herself. She didn't feel like talking, but listening was fine. The topic was the latest virch from the settlement site. She hadn't done it yet.

This installment had been recorded by a botanist—lots of information on grass analogs and pollinating insects. "We know more about Jubilee than *Psyche Moth*," Robeson said.

"Well, sure," said the man. His name was Jawann. "Jubilee is where we're going to live."

"*Psyche Moth* is where we live now, where we've lived for the last 87 years. We don't know jack about this ship. Because Dr. Ops doesn't want us to."

"We know enough to realize we'd look stupid trying to attack him," Wayna said. Even Doe admitted that. Dr. Ops' hardware lay in *Psyche Moth's* central section, along with the drive engine. A tether almost two kilometers long separated their living quarters from the AI's physical component and any other mission-critical equipment they might damage. At the end of the tether, Wayna and the rest of the downloads swung faster and faster. They were like sand in a bucket, centrifugal force mimicking gravity and gradually building up to the level they'd experience on Amend's surface, in Jubilee.

That was all they knew. All Dr. Ops thought they needed to know.

"Who said anything about an attack?" Robeson frowned.

"No one." Wayna was suddenly sorry she'd spoken. "All I mean is, his only motive in telling us anything was to prevent that from happening." She spooned some nuggets onto her mashed potatoes and shoved them into her mouth so she wouldn't say any more.

"You think he's lying?" Jawann asked. Wayna shook her head no.

"He could if he wanted. How would we find out?"

The slaw was too sweet, not enough contrast with the nuggets. Not peppery, like what Aunt Nono used to make.

"Why would we want to find out? We'll be on our own ground in Jubilee, soon enough." Four weeks—twenty days by *Psyche Moth's* rationalized calendar.

"With trustees to watch us all the time, everywhere we go, and this ship hanging in orbit right over our heads." Robeson sounded as suspicious as Doe, Jawann as placatory as Wayna tried to be in their identical arguments. Thad usually came across as neutral, controlled, the way you could be out of your meat.

"So? They're not going to hurt us after they brought us all this way. At least, they won't want to hurt our bodies."

Because their bodies came from, were copies of, the people they'd rebelled against. The rich. The politically powerful.

But Wayna's body was *hers*. No one else owned it, no matter who her clone's cells started off with. Hers, no matter how different it looked form the one she was born with. How white.

Hers to take care of. Early on in her training, she'd decided that. How else could she be serious about her exercises? Why else would she bother?

This was her body. She'd earned it.

Jawann and Robeson were done. They'd started eating before her and now they were leaving. She swallowed quickly. "Wait—I wanted to ask—" They stopped and she stood up to follow them, taking her half-full plate. "Either of you have any medical training?"

They knew someone, a man called Unique, a nurse when he'd lived down on Earth. Here he worked in the factury, quality control. Wayna would have to go back to her bunkroom until he got off and could come and see her. She left Doe a message on the board by the cafeteria's entrance. An apology. Face-up on her bed, Wayna concentrated fiercely on the muscle groups she'd skipped earlier. A trustee came by to check on her and seemed satisfied to find her lying down, everything in line with her remote readings. He acted as if she should be flattered by the extra attention. "Dr. Ops will be in touch first thing tomorrow," he promised as he left.

"Ooo baby," she said softly to herself, and went on with what she'd been doing.

A little later, for no reason she knew of, she looked up at her doorway. The man that had held Robeson's hand that morning stood there as if this was where he'd always been. "Hi. Do I have the right place? You're Wayna?"

"Unique?"

"Yeah."

"Come on in." she swung her feet to the floor and patted a place beside her on the bed. He sat closer than she'd expected, closer than she was used to. Maybe that meant he'd been born Hispanic or Middle Eastern. Or maybe not.

"Robeson said you had some sort of problem to ask me about. So—of course I don't have any equipment, but if I can help in any way, I will."

She told him what had happened, feeling foolish all of a sudden. There'd only been those three times, nothing more since seeing Dr. Ops.

"Lie on your stomach," he said. Through the fabric, firm fingers pressed on either side of her spine, from mid-back to her skull, then down again to her tailbone. "Turn over, please. Bend your knees. All right if I take off your shoes?" He stroked the soles of her feet, had her push them against his hands in different directions. His touch, his resistance to her pressure, reassured her. What she was going through was real. It mattered.

He asked her how she slept, what she massed, if she was always thirsty, other things. He finished his questions and walked back and forth in her room, glancing often in her direction. She sat again, hugging herself. If Doe came in now, she'd know Wayna wanted him.

Unique quit his pacing and faced her, his eyes steady. "I don't know what's wrong with you," he said. "You're not the only one, though. There's a hundred and fifty others that I've seen or hear of experiencing major problems—circulatory, muscular, digestive. Some even have the same symptoms you do."

"What is it?" Wayna asked stupidly.

"Honestly, I don't know," he repeated. "If I had a lab—I'll set one up in Jubilee—call it neuropathy, but I don't know for sure what's causing it."

"Neuropathy?"

"Means nerve problems."

"But Dr. Ops told me my nerves were fine..." No response.

"If we were on Earth, what would you think?"

He compressed his already thin lips. "Most likely possibility, some kind of thyroid problem. Or—but that would be elsewhere, that's irrelevant. You're here, and it's the numbers involved that concern me, though superficially the cases seem unrelated.

"One hundred and fifty of you out of the Jubilee group with what might be germplasm disorders—one hundred fifty out of 20,000. At least one hundred fifty. Take under-reporting into account and there's probably more. Too many. They would have screened fetuses for irregularities before shipping them out."

"Well, what should I do then?"

"Get Dr. Ops to give you a new clone."

"But—"

"This one's damaged. If you train intensely, you'll make up for lost time and go down to Jubilee with the rest of us."

Or she might be able to delay and wind up part of Thad's settlement instead.

As if he'd heard her thought, Unique added "I wouldn't wait, if I were you. I'd ask for—no, demand another body—now. Soon as you can."

"Because?"

"Because your chances of a decent one will just get worse, if this is a radiation-induced mutation. Which I have absolutely no proof of. But if it is."

"By the rivers of Babylon, there we sat down, and there we wept..." The pool reflected music, voices vaulting upward off the water, outward to the walls of white-painted steel. Unlike yesterday, the words were clear, because everyone was saying the same thing. Singing the same thing. "For the wicked carried us away..." Wayna wondered why the trustee in charge had chosen this song. Of course he was a prisoner, too.

The impromptu choir sounded more soulful than it looked. If the personalities of these clones' originals had been in charge, what would they be singing now? The "Doxology?" "Bringing in the Sheaves?" Did Episcopalians even have hymns?

Focusing on the physical, Wayna scanned her body for symptoms. So far this morning, she'd felt nothing unusual. Carefully, slowly, she swept the satiny surface with her arms, raising a tapering wave. She worked her legs, shooting backwards like a squid away from the shallows and most of the other swimmers. Would sex underwater be as good as it was in freeespace? No—you'd be constantly coming up for breath. Instead of constantly coming... Last night, Doe had forgiven her, and they'd gone to Thad together. And everything was fine until they started fighting again. It hadn't been her fault. Or Doe's either.

They told Thad about Wayna's pains, and how Unique thought she should ask for another clone. "Why do you want to download at all?" he asked. "Stay in here with me."

"Until you do? But if —"

"Until I don't. I wasn't sure I wanted to anyway. Now it sounds so much more inviting. 'Defective body?' 'Don't mind if I do.'" Thad's icon got up from their bed to mimic unctuous host and vivacious guest. "And, oh, you're serving that on a totally unexplored and no doubt dangerous new planet? I just totally adore—"

"Stop it!" Wayna hated it when he acted that way, faking that he was a flamer. She hooked him by one knee and pulled him down, putting her hand over his mouth. She meant it as a joke. They ought to have ended up wrestling, rolling around, having fun, having more sex. Thad didn't respond, though. Not even when Wayna tickled him under his arms. He had amped down his input."

"Look," he said. "I went through our 'voluntary agreement.' We did our part by letting them bring us here."

Doe propped herself up on both elbows. She had huge nipples, not like the ones on her clone's breasts. "You're really serious."

"Yes, I really am."

"Why?" asked Wayna. She answered herself: "Dr. Ops won't let you download into a woman. Will he?"

"Probably not. I haven't even asked."

Doe said, "Then what is it? We were going to be together, at least on the same world. All we went through and you're just throwing it away—"

"Together to do what? To bear our enemies' children, that's what, we nothing bunch of glorified mammies, girl, don't you get it? Remote-control units for their immortality investments, protection for their precious genetic material. Cheaper than your average AI, no benefits, no union, no personnel manager. *Mammies.*"

"Not mammies," Doe said slowly. "I see what you're saying, but we're more like incubators, if you think about it. Or petri dishes—inoculated with their DNA. Except they're back on Earth. They won't be around to see the results of their experiment."

"Don't need to be. They got Dr. Ops to report back."

"Once we're on Amends," Wayna said, "no one can make us have kids or do anything we don't want."

"You think. Besides, they won't *have* to make people reproduce. It's a basic drive."

"Of the meat." Doe nodded. "Okay. Point granted, Wayna?" She sat down again, resting her head on her crossed arms.

No one said anything for a while. The jazz Thad liked to listen to filled the silence: smooth horns, rough drums, discreet bass.

"Well, what'll you do if you stay in here?" Doe asked. "What'll Dr. Ops do? Turn you off? Log you out permanently? Put your processors on half power?"

"Don't think so. He's an AI. They stick to the rules."

"Whatever those are," said Wayna.

"I'll find out."

She had logged off then, withdrawn to sleep in her bunkroom, expecting Doe to join her. She'd wakened alone, a note from Dr. Op on the mirror, which normally she would have missed. Normally she avoided the mirror, but not this morning. She studied her face, noting the narrow nose, the light, stubby lashes around eyes an indeterminate color she guessed could be called grey. Whose face had this been? A senator's? A favorite secretary's?"

Hers, now. For how long?

Floating upright in the deep end, she glanced at her arms. They were covered with blond hairs that the water washed into rippled patterns. Her small breasts mounded high here in the pool, buoyant with fat.

Would the replacement be better-looking or worse?

Wayna turned to see the clock on the wall behind her. Ten. Time to get out and get ready for her appointment.

"I'm afraid I can't do that, Wayna." Dr. Ops looked harassed and faintly ashamed. He hadn't been able to tell her anything about the pains. He acted like they weren't important. He even hinted she might be making them up just to get a different body. "You're not the first to ask, you know. One per person, that's all. That's it."

Thad's right. Wayna thought to herself. *AIs stick to the rules. He could improvise, but he won't.*

"Why?" Always a good question.

"We didn't bring a bunch of extra bodies, Wayna," Dr. Ops said.

"Well, why not?" Another excellent question. "You should have," she went on. "What if there was an emergency, an epidemic?"

"There's enough for that—"

"I know someone who's not going to use theirs. Give it to me."

"You must mean Thad." Dr. Ops frowned. "That would be a man's body. Our charter doesn't allow for transgender downloads."

Wayna counted in twelves under her breath, closing her eyes so long she almost logged off.

"Who's to know?" Her voice was too loud, and her jaw hurt. She'd been clenching it tight, forgetting it would amp up her inputs. Download settings had apparently become her default overnight.

"Never mind. You're not going to give me a second body. I can't make you."

"I thought you'd understand." He smiled and hunched his shoulders. "I *am* sorry."

Swimming though freespace to her locker, she was sure Dr. Ops didn't know what sorry was. She wondered if he ever would.

Meanwhile.

She never saw Doe again outside freespace. There'd still be two of them together—just not the two they'd assumed.

She had other attacks, some mild, some much stronger than the first. Massage helped, and keeping still, and moving. She met prisoners who had similar symptoms, and they traded tips and theories about what was wrong with them.

Doe kept telling her that if she wanted to be without pain she should simply stay in freespace. After a while, Wayna did more and more virches and spent less and less time with her lovers.

Jubilee lay in Amends' Northern latitudes, high on a curving peninsula, in the rain shadow of old, gentle mountains. Bright-skinned tree-dwelling amphibians inhabited the mountain passes, their trilling cries rising and falling like loud orgasms whenever Wayna took her favorite tour.

And then there were the instructional virches, building on what they'd learned in their freespace classes. Her specialty, fiber tech, became suddenly fascinating; baskets, nets, ropes, cloth, paper—so much to learn, so little time.

The day before planetfall she went for one last swim in the pool. It was deserted, awaiting the next settlement group. It would never be as full of prisoners again. Thad and Doe weren't the only ones opting out of their downloads.

There was plenty of open freshwater on Amends: a large lake not far from Jubilee, and rivers even closer. She peered down past her dangling feet at the pool's white bottom. Nothing to see there. Never had been, never would be.

She had lunch with Robeson, Unique, and Jawann. As Dr. Ops recommended, they skipped dinner.

She didn't try to say goodbye. She didn't sleep alone.

And then it was morning and they were walking into one of *Psyche Moth's* landing units, underbuckets held to the pool's bottom, to its outside, by retractable bolts, and Dr. Ops unlocked them and they were free, flying, falling down, down, down, out of the black and into the blue, the green, the thousand colors of their new home.

I wrote "Deep End" in response to an invitation from another black woman science fiction author, Nalo Hopkinson. For the groundbreaking anthology *So Long Been Dreaming*, Nalo wanted a post-colonial story about interstellar colonization. What I came up with seemed to me a logical extension of Britain's use of penal servitude as a tool for the settlement of Australia. I've since written three further stories based on this premise: "In Colors Everywhere," "Like the Deadly Hands," and "The Mighty Phin." I hope to eventually complete a total of eight, to be published as a collection titled *Making Amends*.

Both Nalo and I have been diagnosed with fibromyalgia, an invisible disability consisting primarily of chronic pain and fatigue. It's a highly problematic condition with no known cause or cure. Nalo helped me learn how to treat and come to terms with it, and Wayna's experience of a similar though unnamed syndrome is in a way a love-note to Nalo, an ode to our shared hope and obstinacy in the face of this shared difficulty.

Dagoberto Gilb

please, thank you

at first, their people came and went. my children or the few close friends who worried about me dying, they came and stayed some too. im talking about staff people. nurses? not all of them. or they all werent schooled as nurses, years of classes, even if they acted like they are or even do what nurses do. they do something every hour. if i tried to say something, they started asking the same questions. what is your name? what is the date? where were you born? like that. or sometimes, como te llamas? que es la fecha de hoy? like im from mexico and just crossed, not american like them. im from here! ill bet my familys been here longer than yours! i was semper fi, cabron, and then i was an ironworker for ten years, were you? always, always has made me so mad, even if i dont say it out loud to these people here. i was cooperative the first few times, but then i just wanted to be given answers to what i was asking. like, am i going to get better? or worse? i didnt like them ignoring me, or acting as if what i said was not important. even if it wasnt. i knew what they were thinking. i was someone who didnt matter, who didnt count much. in the large, i know its true. I am a name, just another, one they think is foreign even, when there are so many hurting. but then, so what? I accepted it always, in my life, but now too? it makes me mad.

so i started not answering, ignoring them back, or yelling at them. maybe yelling is what i was doing in my mind. maybe muttering under my breath is what i did. like, oh fuck off. what would yelling at them do for me? i practically couldn't move. so sometimes i did answer but lied, made up names and places. Just say anything to shut down the questions.

every hour or few they would wake me up. i was dazed because i was messed up, but as much, i finally realized, because i didnt sleep enough. I wanted them to stop, and they kept coming at me in my haze. Strangers with no names who just ignored what i would try to say who would say my name off a sheet. at night i became scared even, like my thoughts were exposed, like these people would be mad if anything wasnt exactly what they wanted. night, that is, early, early morning. Nobody can really be feeling good to be awake, to be alive, then. not one of these workers. and i cant see their faces. I dont believe they look at mine. they dont care. i am weak, and everyone is bigger, stronger, tougher than me. they take blood or pull my body around. they turn on a light when it is supposed to be sleep-time dark. what does it matter what i think or feel? Nobody sees this work they do, and i am justmeat, a carcass. if i kick them with the one leg that can, will i at least be more wild-tasting meat?

a few days like this i am so tired I can barely function. hard to think where i am and what happened to me. i dream but nothing familiar to my own history. one of them comes in and is telling me something. Words as blurry as sight. i cant tell if it is kind or hostile but i am being shoved around, like i am doing something wrong, something bad. my body seems to be on something that i don't feel and i dont care but they care and act like i should too and they throw it on me. an arm with a hand, a third arm and hand, not from my body. no, it is mine. or was. i recognize it but it is inanimate, lifeless. i touch it with my other hand, pick it up. i was lying on my own arm. this hand. My hand and fingers. i know them. I knew them. im shocked.

my own arm?

i am glad to be moving from intensive care. id say i counted the days but i dont know how many. my children are here to help me. i trust them. i wish they could stay, back me, protect me. its how it is now. I feel so small, and they are big, lifesize, as big as them, unlike me. They are not weak. i dont trust these hospital people but i know i cant say too much. its hard to say much anyway. I dont want to say anything to my children either because they are doing so much already, and i dont want to worry them, or, worse, i am afraid they will think its me.

you werent making sense, my daughter says. they couldnt understand you.

i lied to them. they werent listening to me.

daddy, im telling you, you weren't making sense. you couldnt talk.

it wasnt that, i say. besides, i know i made sense, i have a brain still.

but your speech was bad, she says. its better now. sometimes you said things that nobody could follow. or said things that were wrong.

wrong?

once you said you were born in new mexico. another time you said argentina.

i lived in new mexico for a while.

133

you said you were born there.

ive never been to argentina. I would never go there. a bunch of gringos. i said argentina?

one time they asked and you said you were born there. you said the year was 1994.

when did i say that?

when they asked.

maybe i got confused.

thats what i mean.

i hate argentina.

you said it.

i didnt want to answer their stupid questions. i started saying anything because i didnt care. thats why i gave a wrong name too.

it was that strange name, daddy.

harry?…i dont even know what last name you said now, but it was odd. we all wanted to laugh.

truth is, harry was a name i didn't know. ive never known a person with a name harry. harry anything. ive never met a harry, dont even know what kind of name it is, where a harry would come from. and i dont remember giving the dates or saying new mexico either. definitely not argentina, but it doesnt change anything. this is how they beat you down, and they make money. im meat to them, i know it. im nothing, im nobody. just nothing else is possible for me to do and im not going to do nothing. im not not saying something.

it isnt that i dont want to jump and hop around and be wide-eyed sparkly. if i could, i would dance for everyone. though i really didnt feel like any of it, even if i dont say so. I cant, much as i wont admit it out loud. any moving much is hard for me. i used to be strong. just the other day! just the other day, a couple of weeks ago. now, now these people come in my room. my room is more my bed. a modern bed that moves up and down with a control.

i cant find it, i say. i couldnt even buzz you.

she looked around the edges of the bed, under and in the sheet knotted around me. she found it under me, behind my right shoulder. had to leave a big impression in my skin, deep enough to cast a souvenir pewter model.

i couldnt even feel it? i say. how is that possible?

its okay, mr sanchez. you have it now.

✳

her name is stephanie. shes mexican, mexican-american. has that happy
pocha kind of name. i remember the era, just the other day, when those
educated lefties of ours named their children after aztec deities. My
daughter we named gloria, my wifes choice. my son was joe, like my own
dad and my suegro both.

but youre all good now, she says cheerfully. do you need anything? maybe
youd like to take a shower?

i dont think i can stand up, i say. and with all this added weight,
probably cant.

you probably havent gained weight, mr sanchez. and youre not fat.

i meant all the dirt on me, the layers of it with several coats of laying
around sweat.

i could help you in the shower. shes like sixty pounds and four foot tall.
the other day i wouldve had to use binoculars to see her if i were on my two
legs. from the bed, she almost seems full-size.

i dont know.

i wouldnt look at you. id just stand there outside the curtain.

i meant i dont think you can handle me. your size, my size.

of course i can. i thought you were embarrased.

embarrassed? hell, im proud when im naked.

mr sanchez, youre such a joker. I thought it was because im a girl.

normally id like it better because youre a girl. i dont feel too normal is all.

if you change your mind, she says, stephanie-like, sleepy and positive
both.

its a good idea, this shower. and after i think about it, decide i will.
but Stephanie doesnt come back. now its scott, the other one who comes
sometimes. there are quite a few of these employees. scott is the one who is
confused like its three in the morning, not afternoon. he repeats things. for
example, he says thank you even when it should be a tense there you go! or
a relieved finally its done, or maybe he has to change the sheets, or dump
the urine in the piss bottle, and always when hes leaving and cant believe he
has this job and isnt still in the army.

he brings over the wheelchair. i roll and squirm and push myself to sit
in it like its any chair to take a seat in. i land hard, as though the side that
barely moves has petrified into heavy rock on the bottom and drags me
down faster than i want.

thank you, says scott.

no problem, i say. the problem is standing up. the problem is not standing up. the problem is slipping off my clothes, even when its a tshirt and gym shorts. the problem is holding soap and washing when I bobble like im in a torrent of winds all blowing into me from all cardinal directions. and im even sitting in a yellow plastic chair, a toilet-seat throne. it is pounding to feel the water against me. it feels so good to get clean.

i cant reach the button that means enough. i talk. i cannot talk loud enough without screaming, which i wont.

i hear, is everything okay, mr sanchez?

i say, i am done. i cant yell.

i hear, when youre ready, ill be there.

im ready, i say. hes not hearing me.

finally i can turn off the water with my left hand. i just wait there, trying to figure a way to reach the help button. i try to lean and get it with my left hand, but it is a little behind me too. stand? try to stand? i lift off with my left leg and groan and there i am, standing! but i feel like a golf ball balanced on a plate. the tile wall isn't that close. not sure what to do, i begin careful movements. turn a little, turn a little, a little more, like a firsttime rock climber. i reach for the button and miss. the second shot is a hit though, i think, but theres no apparent buzz ring anything from the button. i push it again and again. Im expert at punching it, could do it for many, many minutes if i can stand much longer. i am there naked and wet, and i feel lost and pathetic because i cant do much besides this.

good shower, mr sanchez?

great shower, i say.

thank you.

he is drying me. it feels good. i am grateful.

i sit back into the safe wheelchair and he gets me a t-shirt and a clean pair of gym shorts. i dont want underwear, so i can pee quickly. He pushes me to my bed home. he pulls the sheet over me and it is comforting. i am clean. i am back to what i know.

thank you, i say to scott.

least i know can stand, i tell my son. next stop, up and down from the toilet. and then flushing by myself.

itll take some time, dad. you know that.

no rush. its all good exercise too.

we were watching basketball playoffs. he likes them. i really like it that my son and daughter visit me and sit here.

whos winning? asks jannette. She doesnt even look up at the tv when she says that bursting in. shes come in to take my blood pressure and give me my evening cup of pills.

the girl across the hall, i say. shes got a no-salary-cap team. the girl across the hall, who cant be more than thirty, has so many visitors all the time i think they had to rent chairs. she had a stroke too, same every symptom as me.

shes popular, says jannette. she got lots of family.

my bp is still high.

whatre you doing in here, mr sanchez?

i think its the pills you people give me to keep my people down.

jannette laughs. we trying to keep you here cause you so pretty.

 aside from the young one across the hall, how many victims arent Mexican or black?

mr sanchez, you a nutcase.

see? im right, arent i? its an experiment being conducted.

you know you are a wrong man, mr sanchez, you always messing. but i am here for you, so you need something, you just buzz.

what i notice, i tell my son, is that all the help is black or brown until its like from two in the morning to six. those are the crazy-people hours.

whatre you talking about? Asks my son.

when they come in at three or four, and you can barely see them, its these deranged, sleep-deprived white people out to get even. actually, those visits at those hours are harsh and blurry and 100 percent unfriendly. i don't know for sure what theyre for.

well, first of all, those sound like the worst jobs, so there goes your conspiracy. second, they must have something to do with your health...

they wake me up so ill be tired all day like they are. either become like them or die from fear. this one guy just turns on a light when he comes in and starts talking like im the weird sleeping man in the dark. one night, reacting like a human, i cry out whyd you turn on the light? he gets mad, you know, says its so he can see. now I know he turns on the brightest one to torment me and teach me whos boss. if i werent a cripple in bed helpless, id bust the fucker in his face.

i can ask about that, about you not getting to sleep.

youll probably piss them off more and theyll do more cruel shit to me. get to me when im finally having a sweet dream.

and third, says my son, i think over half to three fourths of the staff i myself see here is anglo. and the patients too.

and almost all the therapists too, I say. my point therefore proven, that they rule the world, even if they don't have any players of importance on any playoff team.

pau gasol is on the lakers.

spaniards and argentineans don't count. and you notice how they don't even bother to learn to pronounce his name right? like its ga-salt, which they insist is not healthy, even though theyre the ones who soak everything in it, not ga-sun, which is the one and only source of all our light and energy! hes a star on the team too, not just kobe, whose name they did learn, as strange, and two syllables, as it is. always treating our heritage like its common and unimportant even when it's a pinche spaniard, even.

youd think speech therapyd be about speech. half my body went dead. that means half my face too. kristen, my therapist, even taught me that half my tongue went too. It is what i learned from her, that its the most complex muscle in the body. thats why i sound drunk when i talk. however, we dont seem to ever deal enough with speech or my numb face.

kirsten, she corrects me again.

maybe its because of the stroke I cant get that right, i say.

nice try.

at least i got cover for my drinking.

i do think your focus might be affected.

i cant tell if shes teasing or not. she really takes her tests seriously. like there are answers in them. she has a library of three-ring binders she looks through until she finds tests for my homework, though sometimes i have to take one or two right there in her office. she times things i do. i hate this. i hate this speech therapy. i think shes making it up, doing some project on her own. wheres the speech part? i feel like its sunday school with mormons.

i do not believe. im not a mormon.

excuse me? she says.

i didnt say anything. or mean to.

howd you know i was a mormon?

i didnt. maybe you told me.

no.

in truth, i had no idea. i was just thinking to myself and that sentence came out in public.

anyway, you need to put all the pills from the jars into the organizers. all these? there must be a dozen jars of pills.

theyre all yours.

no wonder i cant talk right.

you have to be able to do this without getting confused.

what?

into each day. into the morning slot or afternoon, or…

i know what you meant.

and you have to look at what each pill requires. if its twice a day, or morning only…

yeah yeah okay.

you have to do it with your right hand.

but i can barely use it. i cant feel anything with it.

youll get used to it. we want you to do this when you get home.

they arent pills. theyre colored beads and nuts and washers. i drop every one. i dont drop every fifth one. i make it first try into the organizers slot only one in the five of the beads i do manage to get between my numbed fingers. not very good success odds.

i miss a lot, i say.

youll get better with practice. You have to be able to do this right.

so important that i am using my almost worthless right hand. i would never try to pick up real pills…but its good. it takes up time. i hate speech therapy and this will take me days of practice.

nancy insists on my being buckled up in my wheelchair to go to physical therapy. and she wont push me, unless were in a hurry. that is, she is. today shes in a hurry, and we have to go through an uphill hallway to the therapy room. I dont think shes a lesbian, though she has that short hair, ironed, tucked-in t-shirt, fitted jeans, and never-married-to-a-man bark and fire-hydrant frame of…maybe its just her, who knows. shes nice to me, or means to be, when shes snapping. i like her like you do your hardass coach. even if i dont know her win-loss record.

move your arm in. you want to lose those fingers?

my right arm often hangs too limp and casual near the spoke wheels of the rolling chair.

i tell you all the time. you want to learn when its too late?

shes right. i pull my arm to my lap.

now youve got it like you had a stroke and cant use it. put it on the armrest. it has to do what the other arm does.

i obey and put it on the armrest. I understand her, shes right. when we get to the room, she makes me stand up with no hands. shes taught me and i try very soldierly to please her. i have to lean my body forward. apparently, this is how i used to and everyone not in a wheechair does it all the time.

almost have it, she says.

almost?

youre still favoring that other side. like its too weak.

i want to suggest that it is, really, kind of weak, but i dont want to sound weak or make her mad.

do it again, nancy says.

what?

stand up, then sit down.

seated on the edge of a padded table, i muscle my way up, i sit down. like its an exercise, which it is for me now, not just standing and sitting. i do this until she tells me to rest. up, back down. i feel sweat everywhere, im hot, im out of breath.

you have to get more control, especially when you sit down. Not just drop.

i meant to get them all.

the last ones were sloppy.

oh. sorry.

you got tired, she says.

im afraid of agreeing or disagreeing. i do exercises on the padded table. stretches of the calves. then the quads. then i get on my stomach. I am supposed to lift the foot and calf ninety degrees, starting with my left. nothing, easy. when i try my right, its like nothing connects the two leg bones but kneecap. my calf flops on either side of my body. it doesnt hurt, theres no physical pain, but inside me, silently, it might be the worst indignity yet, so harsh i cant cry or rage. its as though i have been slugged very hard and the pain hasn't checked in.

this is nothing ever. i cant do it?

you have to work on it.

work on it? you dont work on moving your leg.

your hamstring. you have to.

i am on my stomach. i have no strength where i never even thought of strength. the plastic of the mat against my face, the pressing on it is how far ive fallen. how messed up this body is. my body. my life. My past is past, is back then when I didnt know, when i never gave a thought to…this. how is it possible i am this way?

you had a stroke.

i know, but i cant believe i cant pull my stupid leg up.

you had a stroke.

its not time to quit yet. Nancy wants me to walk. i stand to the aluminum walker and take one step, then another. i have to move my right leg right. bend it, pick up my toe. pick up my toe. dont hyperextend. she grabs my knee. now go on. go. pick up my toe and put it out in front and dont do this. thats good. thats good. dont go so far back. don't try to go so fast. step. step. step. Not like that. stop that. dont hyperextend. better. better.

nancy buckles the seatbelt in my wheelchair because she thinks its unsafe to be unbuckled, even though I do it all the time. im too wiped out and whatever to talk. i am going to wheel myself in the chair because I dont want her to even if she were willing, which of course i am sure she isnt. i pretend to use my right hand to help push the wheel, like two sides of me are equally doing the job. i push as hard as i can but act like im not. I want to get to my room and when i do she says see you tomorrow and i say the same like i am looking forward to it and her.

1, patty speaks chinese. 2, the elevator operator plays tennis. 3, teresa does not speak french. and so on. this one, i tell my son and daughter, is easy too. but you see how it is. heres another, which is worse, watch. i have to record the following in a checkbook ledger. 1, ace insurance company, $90, march 17, 1981, no. 19. 2, deposit, $200.53 on april 20, 1981. and so on, each a puzzle or test that is part of my speech therapy. Least this one you could say gets me practicing my writing with my left hand. otherwise, i pretend i forget. if i say i forget, then i guess it seems like i have more speech problems with addition.

just dont do them, my son says. Im sure it cant matter.

i have to see her almost every day. i did those pills so long she thought something was wrong with that speech too. but if you do these for for me, i wont look so bad, and my speech will be much better too.

hello, says scott. hola. Buenos noches? is that right?

its perfect.

just checking to see if everythings good.

too good.

good, thank you! just making sure.

alls good.

im finally leaving for the day.

you work some long hours, scott.

they never let me go. techs don't show, i get a double shift.

get some rest.

i wanted to tell you.

appreciate it.

thank you.

thank you, scott.

he is strange, my daughter says quietly as he leaves. very odd character.

but you know, i say, i think hes harmless. hes here, doing this.

are you okay, dad? asks my son. you almost sound soft.

i do need that other test done. you guys can do that for me? i really dont want to. my brain fries. Not how she thinks, or why she thinks, but in the me that evolved long before the incident. apparently thats a speech problem.

i got it, daddy, says my daughter. its like that sudoku thats gotten so popular. only easier.

i could do it if i didn't hate to. I did them at first, a couple. just put it on some paper and ill write in the boxes.

she really checks on this like its homework?

you kidding? i swear shes going to detain me for an all-day speech camp for those of us with special speech trouble.

im not getting soft on the place or any of them. its like this typing though. which i hate. i hate the mistakes i have to fix, the waste of time, the enthusiasm they drain. you dont see them because of me. I make them right. im better at it too because im doing it, as you see. i type with my one hand. really its more one finger on the wrong hand. im right-handed, and now I can only use the left. im not bothering with the shift key or the apostrophe. i fix the other mistakes, slow as that is. even by staring right down at the keys, i type y for t often, for instance, or o for p. i make extra letters where they dont belong, or i forget letters or spaces. i could make caps. not easy, but I could. and apostropkes. see those mistakes? im noy

142

fixing them to show my point. that last little sentence only has one usual letter y instead of t typo in it. when i started typing it, there was one in every word. sometimes now i put my right hand on this keyboard too, even though it really isnt close to helping much. the index fi nger cant feel the keys. the right hand, and its fingers, has like a thick glove on it. the glove fits my hand so organically it looks exactly like my hand used to. you cant tell them apart. im not getting soft. i am not wanting to scream and fight as much though, punish the keyboard like I used to. i fi x the mistakes like i did it, like im responsible for them. there are less of them to fix. i learn patience. i come back to the keyboard when im not so tired or just not so mad at all, any, every. i hate it, i know i do, that is the truth, but i get better at this.

im wiping the window clean with my right hand. its not really a window. its the wall in the therapy room. im using a washcloth. its an exercise. i am upright for this. sometimes i sit and do something similar to this on an ironing board, where i also reach as high as i can.

    you think im going to get better?

    you already are, says deena.

    she, mostly, has been my occupational therapist for weeks. Deena is korean. or her parents were. That is, her grandparents were from there. she is always calm and slowmoving.

    i think it explains why she gains weight so easy. no metabolism. its what makes her seem like she knows more, has deeper insight, something like that. a buddha. I know its stupid. youd have to be here, youd have to meet her. Even if she told me that her family has always been christian. presbyterian, she frowns, which, she says, is so lame. but she says the word lame so profoundly and frowns with great, calm buddha wisdom.

    i guess i am. id definitely outrun a slug, crush him if i had to. i think. but i mean my hand. you think itll get better?

    i dont know. we never know. Its hard to predict. brain injuries...

    yeah, im always hearing that. i just want stats, not legal promises.

    i dont know any.

    seems like nobody does.

    ive only been doing this for a few months.

    youre joking.

    no.

    but dont you

im interrupted typing by erlinda, the custodian. she washes the floor in my room, dumps the wastebaskets, and cleans the shared bathroom. For six years. shes from morelia and the outskirts of mexico city last. she likes to talk to me because the only other person she gets to talk spanish to all day is the other janitor, beatriz, and thats only at lunch break. she wants to know what i think. she was in walmart yesterday, with her husband and two girls who were excited because it was the youngests birthday. they were in line to pay. they were buying lots of things when she heard this woman in the line behind them complain. about them speaking spanish. so, she says, she told that woman in english that it was none of her business. that, see, she could talk in english. the lady started yelling at her, threatening her, and so she started yelling back at the woman. They just yelled because erlindas husband held her back. then the guards came and stood between.

what was she yelling? i ask.

i dont know. i was so mad. im not like that.

of course.

even now she is upset. was she wrong? it was her youngest daughters birthday too, that was a lot of it.

i really dont know what to say. Im okay with erlinda, but do i know what this other rude lady was talking about really? erlinda is slow. thats not because she speaks spanish and is mexican. its because she is slow. Not lazy. she is here at six every day, and the rooms are mopped and picked up. still, i wouldnt want to be behind her in a line, and not at walmart. but erlinda is nice. but i dont know why she asks me. only because theres no one else, besides beatriz, to tell?

low-class people, i say. theyre everywhere, but especially at walmart. even though you save so much money there.

what could she do? she asks me. she has stopped swabbing the floor. shes not even resting with the mop as a prop to lean against. she holds it steady. what should she have done?

are you really asking me? do you really want me to answer?

yes, she says. please.

she says please? that makes it even harder. not because she is incapable of being so polite, but because she means it, wants my answer. if it were me, and i were her, with her family, which i dont even know about. please. sure, i sit in the wheelchair much of the time now. i go to the toilet with no help. i can sit and stand, hold myself to pee, clean myself. an hour ago i showered and didnt tell them. i felt like that was accomplishment. like i was a big boy. i was proud and pleased with myself. she wants my opinion?

im not sure what else anyone would have done, i say.

she doesnt speak. she is listening, waiting for what i offer.

well, you know, i dont think...no. okay. youre a good person. i know youre an honest worker, just like you say. I know it. its not your fault where you were born, what language you speak. people like that woman, ignorance like that...you have to ignore those stupids. do your best, what you can, the best you can. what you do. what more is there? you cant help it if someone like that is in your line at walmart. wherever. stupid, mean people, theyre just that. theyre not most people. Just like people who dont bathe. its not everybody, its not all the time.

thank you, mr sanchez.

you dont have to thank me. it shoudnt have happened.

my family was upset. i was. My husband is still. mad,

for you. of course.

we are so happy. we had such a nice day shopping.

beautiful.

i dont want my husband to think more about it. i am so sorry. i am never like that.

he cant help it.

but i didnt tell him what she said. i was crying.

well, okay.

he doesnt speak any english.

lots who do dont make any sense.

i shouldnt tell him?

you dont have to. tell him you just want to forget it.

thank you, mr sanchez.

please, no reason to say that.

its not the worst that has happened. im not sure why that made me so angry.

you were having a nice day.

exactly.

at walmart.

and my girls were so happy.

theyre still happy, im sure. They'll be proud of you. look what you do for them.

thank you, mr sanchez.

no, no. how old is your daughter now?

she turned three. the other is five.

so lucky.

see you tomorrow.

yes.

maybe make a special meal. Tell your daughters you guys are having an extra birthday dinner.

she nods and smiles.

you just…move forward. why dwell on that ugliness? youre fine now.

ill see you tomorrow, mr sanchez.

i clear out in an hour. my daughter and my son are coming for me and I cant wait to see them and leave. Im not good at goodbye, and not here either. im in the wheelchair i take home with me. it moves on its own. i didn't know how rickety my old one was. Nobodys here to say goodbye to anyway, to thank, except stephanie. she works all the strangest, longest shifts.

i bet you cant wait to leave, she says.

i bet you cant wait to go home either.

i am so sleepy.

you do it all the time.

i only work these three days, but I have to sleep four days to recover.

shes still so little i feel like i have to hold the fired-up wheelchair so it doesnt accidentally take off and roll her down.

you need anything? she asks.

alls good.

see you tomorrow, she says.

yeah.

i like sleepy stephanie. ill miss her too.

i want to say thank you to all of them, even though theyd forget in sixty seconds. were all moving onward. tomorrow someone else here.

Though the details of what Mr. Sanchez went through parallel what happened to me (I too was hospitalized for what has become a permanent brain injury), and I hope are good for those to read who've had a stroke, they are incidental to this story. It's fiction and not nonfiction because it's not about my small experience. What I wanted seen is how Mr. Sanchez' recovery exaggerated his awareness of his place in society. And what he learns as he comes back peaks in the interaction he has with the custodian Erlinda. I'd say she reminds him that those doing seemingly the least valued can offer him what's most important.

Thom Jones

BOMBSHELL NOEL

Mickey bought me a goldfish he named Seven Cent. He's got an orange streak along his lateral line running from forehead to tail. His dorsal fin is as black as night and appears to have been chewed. Otherwise he is albino in coloration except for his tail, which is translucent. You can see clear through to the bone. Me personally, I would have named him X-Ray, but you can't judge a book by its color. Seven Cent is a showman, a gifted performer, and he's got some pretty smooth moves.

He swims the perimeter of his little fish tank hugging the side of the glass with one eye, in full presentation for effect, as he swims around in concentric circles with his mouth going open-close, open-close like a normal fish until he begins to pump his gills and then shoots himself skyward, partially breaking the surface, where he executes a well-timed flip, wagging his tail for propulsion, right down to the bottom, where he shakes things loose.

When you are on the Highway to Death, like me, everything is interesting. Everything is important. You see different, taste and smell different; everything has wonder written in it. Things you have done 6 million times seem new, and likewise you run into a seven-cent celebration of life in its otherwise impenetrable glory.

As Doomgirl, I host a show called *Bomb Shelter Radio* broadcast at 147.859 kHz. The program is directed to survivalists. Mickey roped me into doing it because I have a pleasantly low voice. It's his radio, and he rigged up an antenna, which bounces radio waves at a communications satellite so the show can be heard worldwide. I play classical music, do some astrology, but the show is mostly about survival.

Mickey taught me a lot of survival stuff and this is what the listeners tune in to hear. I can build an igloo in frozen Antarctic wastes or a cozy tropical shelter poised to withstand apocalyptic tornadoes and hurricanes. I can read a compass, hunt, fish, forage edible roots high in vitamin C, and I have helped Mickey construct our bomb shelter, which is A1 deluxe.

*

Watching Seven Cent, I sometimes feel like I'm drifting through the icy rings of Saturn, sight unseen, far far away, safe and secure amid grains, flakes and pieces of smashed comets. Chunks of rock the size of trucks are there, to be sure, but mostly it's snow and ice. Who knows? I feel like those odd people reading your fortune at the carnival when I begin to speculate on things unknown. When I told this to Madame Rosa, she threw back her Roma head and laughed like a hyena. Madame Rosa is a tarot reader with advanced paranormal skills. She asked me, "What's your blood sugar? Ten?"

I am a type 1 diabetic with hypoglycemic unawareness. Because of this, I'm on a first name basis with every paramedic in town. "Laura! Laura! Can you hear me?"

You wake up with an IV in your arm, totally spaced. Every coma I have is different. When I have a rock-bottom seizure, I come out of it feeling pretty good. It's the light stuff that contains the most terror. They are the realm of the Bone Crusher and his dancing Salvador Dalí demons. You come out of those ice-cold and soaking wet. I follow my diet religiously, eat in a timely fashion and test my blood sugar on the hour. People think you just go around like a reckless fool. "Here comes that stupid with her big bag of Halloween candy."

Last night in the 60-watt glow of my Aladdin kerosene lantern down in the bomb shelter, I was reading about a family in Ulaanbaatar, Mongolia. Ulaanbaatar is the coldest capital city on the planet but only three percent of the population over the age of 20 is diabetic.

Three percent in a world where eight percent is average! Many of the rural population of Mongolia, the prosperous ones anyhow, live in snazzy yurts. The people of Ulaanbaatar eat mutton dumplings, tinned herring and cabbages. They smoke L&M cigarettes. Ulaanbaatar is like any other city except for the extreme cold.

At the Dialysis Center some of the day patients brought in a Christmas tree. Someone wrote, "Christmas is just around the corner," on the green chalkboard at the well-lit entryway. Dixie Platte picked up a piece of chalk before a treatment and added, "Have a Holly Jolly Christmas!"

Dixie is one year and seven months older than me, like that makes her the final word on subjective topics. Dixie is a lap dancer at the Zebra

Club. She says the dialysis fistula planted under her wrist looks like a 1965 portable phone from Botswana. Dixie gets by on a cadre of older customers who don't look at her wrists.

A dialysis fistula is a special tract placed under the skin of the forearm connecting an artery and vein to provide access to a dialysis machine. Without the surgically implanted fistula, a patient's veins and arteries would quickly break down altogether.

A few people on the midnight-to-four a.m. shift still have jobs. They will sleep, read, maybe engage in a little lighthearted banter while the techs hook us up. Occasionally someone will have a mini nervous breakdown. Some of the dementia patients are screamers. There is an adjunct room in the back, but you can hear them anyhow. You wonder why they never get hoarse.

Mickey and I used to drive to the hospital emergency room on Friday and Saturday nights as well as nights of the full moon since there are so many drunken automobile and motorcycle accidents, and drive-by shootings, random shootings, knifings, etc.

This is how Mickey got his new pancreas and kidney, from a 25-year-old man, blood type O, cause of death unknown. Mickey wanted me to get them, but the man's organs were too big, or I'm just a little shrimp. I didn't know it at the time, but a donated organ has to fit or it won't work right. Mickey takes prednisone so his immune system doesn't destroy the new kidney and pancreas. He's got a swollen face, but apart from the pills, he's cured. He tells me over and over that he wishes I got the cure, not him. He said he would die to save me. He said he will protect me from any harm that might befall me and that I'm the only person he can trust.

When I turn 17, we are driving to South Carolina and getting married. Dixie helped me pick out lingerie to wear on my wedding night. When we were at the Laundromat, she told me that my underwear was too "utilitarian." Personally I think her thongs, bustiers and other sexy garments are uncomfortable looking. She badgered me into buying a black ruffled petticoat. It's not the kind of thing any girl in Ulaanbaatar would ever put on.

I can fell an edible crow with a blowgun or drop a hefty vulture with a boomerang. I can practically start a fire under water. Ha-ha. Additionally I can handle .50 caliber machine guns, crush a villain's trachea or knife him through the heart even though I don't like seeing people get hurt.

*

Hen Pierson sits in the geri chair across from my own. He has been on dialysis 19 years interspersed with two short-lived transplants. He was diabetic at 12, BP 150/95 mm Hg. His albumin-creatinine ratio (ACR) at 3.4 is better than my own.

Hen is 64. His brother was thrown in prison for murder, and while he sat many a long year in his death row cell, the weight of his crimes weighed heavily upon him. Hen asked his brother for a kidney, but his brother wrote back, "Why should I give you a kidney? Nobody ever gave me anything worth having."

A week later Convict Pierson, age 57, was stabbed to death in the prison infirmary. Madame Rosa said she knew this was going to happen. "It was plain as day."

She said she was glad it happened. I think her lumbago puts her in a bad mood sometimes. She is not a mean person. I have seen her read the Bible from time to time.

Hen came to treatment looking pretty down after the incident at the prison. He wanted the kidney, sure, but he loved his brother and he was always loaning him money or paying off lawyers, money he could have spent on himself.

He was wearing a suit that looked three sizes too big on him. He removed his jacket and rolled up the sleeve of his left arm, exposing his arterial fistula.

The dialysis technicians were coming down the line, hooking everyone up, but when they got to Hen's chair, I heard a terrible scuffling of shoes against the tile as Hen stumbled out of his chair and started to fall. The clinic nurse hurried down the aisle and helped him gain his balance. "Are you okay, Mr. Pierson?"

Hen's face was white with fear. "I'm done," he said. "I'm just going to go home."

The long room fell dead with silence.When Hen realized he was the center of attention, he tried to put a good face on things and said, "I want to thank everyone for being a pal for so many years. I sincerely wish you all the best."

Hen approached my geri chair, where I lay with my lower lip trembling. I was crying big tears, snot coming out of my nose, choking. I just couldn't control my feelings. I was so ashamed. I didn't want him to feel still worse.

It felt like someone stuck a spoon in my heart and twisted it. Hen always looked after me. He knew me since I was little. We were solid. He gave me a hug and said, "Don't you worry about a thing, sugar britches. Everything is going to be all right."

I said the same stupid thing to him I always said after dialysis. "See you later, alligator."

The ultrafilters on my machine took three liters of water out of me after that. I can't urinate. The machine does it for me. Losing all that water at one go is a shock to your body. I had cramps, my knees hurt and I itched everywhere, but I put on my winter coat and staggered to the bus stop. Dixie and Vera T. Bailey, who is slightly retarded but nice, offered me a ride home. I should have taken it. I should have gone back to the clinic. People actually get angry with you if you don't ask for a stupid ride. They all seemed like mechanical people to me. Machines and robots like the damn Tin Man in *The Wizard of Oz*, who was so fake he wrecked everything in that movie. What a bozo.

The next day Mickey and I bought a four-gallon BiOrb aquarium at the Goodwill. It looks just like a crystal ball. It came with a filter, bubblers, air stone and magnetic algae cleaner. It was just too cool for words. I was so happy, I couldn't wait to get home and fill it.

Mickey said, "Looks like Seven Cent got him a $55 crib."

I hugged Mickey and kissed him until some Goodwill shoppers told us to "Go get a room."

"We don't need a room, what we need is a mortgage," Mickey said.

Ha-ha.

The BiOrb was the talk of treatment at the clinic, 12 midnight to four a.m. I went on and on about it. Finally Dixie said, "Most of the stuff you get for Christmas is crap you don't want, just stuff you have to get rid of, a used piano or something. An anvil."

Ha-ha.

A young man named Jerome now sits in Hen's geri chair. He's tall, thin and good-looking, from New York City. He's got a crush on Dixie and won't lay off. Dixie told him to zip his lip, but it only heightened his ardor. Pretty soon Dixie has a big crush on Jerome, and listening to their crazy infatuation talk was almost scary. They begin to sound like mental patients in their heated excitement. By that I mean they can be talking about normal everyday stuff and something insane will pop out like a jack-in-the-box. *Pow*!

Dixie started in with a story she read in the *National Examiner* about an ostrich that swam from Nelson Mandela's prison island to Cape Town, South Africa.

"Why would an ostrich go to the trouble?" I said.

Dixie said, "I don't know. To pull rickshaws or have chariot races. They got the legs for it."

Jerome said, "An ostrich is no more than a giant chicken, too heavy to swim or fly. All they can do is the 50-yard dash."

Normal non-in-love people don't talk at length about things no one else cares about, fighting over nothing. Mickey is the love of my life, but I have never broken into this sort of gibberish pining over him.

"Jerome, you are just an ignorant fool," Dixie said. "All you do is lay over there acting gangster. You should go back to New York City and live in the hood again."

"I was starting to like you, but now I have changed my mind," Jerome said.

Dixie lay back in her chair. She said, "I'm right and you know it."

I used a commonsense voice with levelheaded humor and said, "Let me get this straight, jobless ostrich braves howling winds, tenebrous currents in search of work, ha-ha—"

Jerome wheeled on me in a fury. "Why don't you just shut the fuck up? You aren't funny. You think you are, but you aren't. I am not gonna lay here for four hours three times a week, 12 hours total not including the fucking goddamn Mickey Mouse of coming and going only to get ha-ha'ed to death by you."

Super Huge Hudson, a dialysis technician and martial artist, came thumping down the aisle on his size-14 feet. He pinched a muscle on Jerome's neck, paralyzing him. "I don't want to hear another word out of you, Jerome, ever again, so long as you live. Do you follow? I am back there at my desk trying to read *The Girl With the Dragon Tattoo*, and I don't want to hear another word come out of your filthy mouth."

Jerome didn't so much as say "Ouch," but later I could hear him sniffling. What was he thinking about? This fresh humiliation? The rigors of dialysis?

I felt bad for him, I who cried bitter tears across the aisle from him over

Hen Pierson, who was never coming back. Hen walked out with a clear mind. He knew without dialysis he had a week, maybe 10 days.

One night when Super Huge Hudson was out sick, I was lying in my geri chair, half flaked, and I could hear Jerome crying again. I said, "Jerome, I know that normally you are a nice person—"

"No I'm not!" he shouted back. He leaped forward at me with such blinding speed, I thought he would rip the tubes to the fistula loose. Instead he half toppled his machine, screaming, "If I could get away with it, I would kill you right now, today!"

Dixie looked over and said, "Put a lid on it, dorkhead. You aren't supposed to talk. Jesus H."

I spoke to Jerome in low confidential tones, "Down deep inside you are a nice person, Jerome. Down deep you are wonderful and I love you."

None of what I said was true, but why hit someone when they are down? I was freezing cold. It felt like a Jack Frost crew of half-inch Eskimos had infiltrated my machine with sacks of dry ice over their shoulders. My blood sugar was so low that I fainted amid a room of fellow sufferers. Dixie said, "That's the third time this month."

The skies cleared and it got colder. I went back to the Goodwill store, where I saw a coat that wasn't too bad. More importantly it was lined with sheepskin. Like some hand-me-down from Cinderella. I like a coat with loose sleeves. I wear long sleeves even in the summer to hide my fistula. For knock-around activities, I wrap an Ace bandage around it.

Damn! Look at the lovely bride wearing a black ruffle petticoat with a large conspicuous fistula bulging out of her arm. Isn't she lovely?

Ha-ha.

I was at the bus stop and along comes Hannes Smit, another type 1 diabetic, and he's back to drinking again. He's on the list for his third kidney. He won't get one; he's 62 years old. He was some kind of part time janitor.

"You live in a dangerous neighborhood," he said. "Let me walk you home."

"Naw, the bus is good."

Hannes said the whole world would end before dawn, and being gay, could he fuck me since he never had sex with a woman before? Tell me what chick hasn't heard that come-on a thousand times?

We were on a long desolate street inhabited by empty shops and failed restaurants. Down the road I watched the approach of the yellow Union Street bus, bumping and squeaking along on a leaf-spring suspension and razor-thin drum brakes, its headlights imperceptible.

I hopped on and moved to a seat with an open window. Outside Hannes was having an argument with the parking meter I had been hanging on to moments before. At least I knew that it was a parking meter. I wanted the bus to get going but the driver sat behind the wheel trying to light a wet stub of a cigar, and outside Hannes had now turned his vitriol on a fire hydrant. Hannes wasn't right in his mind from a stroke he had. Once he split his pants and I saw he was wearing aluminum foil underwear.

Mickey and me live kind of far out, and when I got off the bus the sidewalks were extra slick. I unlocked the iron gate surrounding the house and struggled up the incline to the front door. I could hear the low rumble of the diesel generator.

There were three access portals to the shelter, all sealed with blast-proof doors. There was one in the basement, another in Mickey's shed and the third out in the field covered with thorny blackberry bushes. Mickey called it "hiding in plain sight."

He was down in the basement shoring up a section of a narrow tunnel. He crawled out and wiped the grime off his face and hands with a clean rag. He was sweating in spite of the cold.

I asked him why he had the generator going.

"Air movement," he said. "I just put in a backup filter. Now we got two."

A strong current of air came out from the tunnel, which was constructed with a lot of 90-degree turns designed to block the forward path of nuclear radiation.

"As long as the generator is going," I said, "I'll go do 20 minutes of my show. I don't feel like it, but I'll do it anyway."

"Have you sketched out a script?"

I shook my head no. "I know what I'm going to do." He shrugged his shoulders. I knew he wanted to get back to his project. I went to the radio shack, where I had a hidden six-pack of lime Diet Coke. I had been sneaking one too many only to pay the piper on the ultra filters. Back at the bus stop, I swore up and down I would never do such a thing again. But I was so thirsty I guzzled an entire can and opened another.

I put on the radio headset and adjusted the microphone.

"Good evening all and sundry. Welcome to another fabulous hour of *Bomb Shelter Radio*. This is Doomgirl and you are dialed in at 147.859 kHz. Hang on to your hats; this is going to be a truly fantastic show."

The words coming out of my mouth were hollow, but I pressed on. "I'm sort of rattling things off the top of my head, but there is this young man, Jerome. I wish to dedicate tonight's show to Jerome. I hope you are okay, buddy. I just want to tell you that you are not alone in thinking your stalwart plans will only vaporize and disappear in the weak rays of light. I have Mickey and Seven Cent and all you out there listening, but can someone tell me why life is so hard?

"I want to ask about loneliness and tears, about frustration, lots of frustration, about my head exploding, about how I ache for love, unconditional love that will last and last, about how hopeless I feel no matter how much I know, of how I will die soon, about how I have so few friends, about all the bad things I've done, about how afraid I am of dying in pain, about how I am such a disappointment to those who love me, about how slow I am, about blood coming out of me, about the places I go and don't come back from, and really, Jerome, for all this the only thing I have to offer is the first tune of the evening, from Waltz in C-sharp Minor, op. 64, by Frédéric Chopin, the man who wrote poems with the piano, who wrote for Saturn's icy rings and Ulaanbaatar, for Madame Rosa and beautiful Hen and Dixie in her thongs, here we go. I love you all out there in Radioland. Stay warm. Merry Christmas."

—THOM JONES—

Type One diabetes was a death sentence until the manufacture of insulin in 1922. Today many diabetics live near normal lives using it, but there is the ultimate downside of heart attack, stroke, amputations, blindness, frozen shoulders, burning neuropathies as well as kidney failure and dialysis suffered by my heroine, Laura. Diabetes is a balancing act, carb counting, exercise and insulin. A little too much of the latter can lead to coma and death. Long-time diabetics develop hyperglycemic unawareness and can run perilously high or low without knowing it. Fortunately there are test strips and glucometers to monitor sugars.

In 1922, insulin came from the beta cells of cows, horses and pigs. It could be putrid brown in color, but it worked. Today synthetic insulins are pristine but end stage mortality remains common. Laura, in my story, like nearly everyone on dialysis, is waiting for a kidney transplant. The best of these come from living relatives and the worst from cadavers. Laura is one of my favorite characters. I love her radio broadcasts, her humor, thoughtfulness and ingenuity. In a world where something has gone terribly wrong, I hate to think of her chances, kidney or no.

I had a Nighthawk friend who received dialysis treatments on the graveyard shift. I sometimes drove him to his treatments and sat near him reading. One evening I wrote the first draft of this story in a notepad using a golf pencil. He kept asking me what I was doing and I said, "I'll show it to you when I'm finished."

Paul de Anguera

RIDING THE BUS

That nurse with the glasses is fooling around with something that looks like a television and not paying attention to my good news. So I tell her again, "The bus is coming!"

She swivels her chair a little and pats my poor knobby hand that's resting on a handle of my walker. *Young people's hands are so warm!* Then she starts typing again. "The bus is coming!" I insist. "What time is the bus coming? I don't want to miss it!"

The nurse stops typing. She pulls a big card out of a shelf and swivels her chair to face me. "The bus isn't here now, Amanda. It comes at five p.m." She holds up the card and adds, "See?" It shows a big picture of a bus and, underneath it, the words "THE BUS LEAVES AT 5 PM."

Amanda is me. I think I'm ninety-something. I don't know much else about me, and I'm not sure how I came to live here. I wonder why she is holding up this card when she could be taking me downstairs to get on the bus. A bearded fellow with a nametag that says, "Steve, Volunteer" bends down to talk to me. "Where does this bus go?"

"Portland!" I tell him.

"But, we're already in Portland."

"Oregon!" But it's really the bus to home. At home, I'll be young again. I'll be surrounded by people who love me, especially Ma and Pa. And I'll get back all the wonderful things I've lost, like my dog Jippy that I got for my sixth birthday.

But it takes too long to say all that. And besides, if we stand around yapping, I'm going to miss the bus. "Help! Help!" I shout, scooting into the common room. I scoot by pushing my walker and my feet ahead of the chair I'm sitting on, then pulling my chair up to them with my bottom, and then doing it again.

Steve is following me. "Look, Amanda!" he says. "There's a jigsaw puzzle on that table. We could go over and finish it." Now I see that we've reached the puzzle table, and I am huffing and puffing from the trip. So I stop and look it over. The puzzle is half done. In it, I see tractors and smiling construction workers. Each puzzle piece is bigger than my hand.

Some of them have flat sides. I don't like those pieces because it's harder to stick them onto the other ones, so I reach for some others.

"Look at the colors on the pieces," Steve says. "They're parts of a picture. If two pieces have the same color on them, there's a good chance..." *Blah blah blah*—so much talk! The pieces won't fit together, so I pound on them. "If you pound them, you'll spoil the puzzle," Steve points out. Well, it's a rotten puzzle anyway. I'd rather catch the bus home! I pull my walker close, stand up first and then put my weight on it, like the occupational therapist taught me.

It hurts my back to stand, but now I'm tall, like somebody who still matters. "Help! Help!" I call as I push it down the hall. All the bedroom doors are shut. So I go on to the next common room. "Help! Help! Who wants to ride the bus?"

But this is not a good room. There are only two people like me here, and they're sleeping in their chairs. I see some staff people having a meeting at the next nursing station. One lady looks up at me and says, "That bus doesn't run on Sunday." She's no help at all, so I go on down the hall.

Steve is still following me. "I found a schedule," he says. For a minute I think it's a bus schedule, and my heart leaps. But it's just a list of the activities they put on in this building where I live. "There's going to be an art class," he goes on. "Maybe you could go to it and make pictures."

"Help!" I say. Then I see an open door. In this room, a man is lying on a bed. I start in to tell him the good news, but Steve is still there. "You shouldn't go into people's rooms," he says. "You wouldn't like it if other people went into your room, would you? Other people feel the same way."

I stop. He's right; I don't like other people to come into my room, because it's mine. Well, these people had their chance. I go to the elevator and push the button.

The first time the door opens, the elevator is full of people. But the next time, it's empty. I get in, and Steve comes in too. I remember seeing an outside entrance on Floor 1, so I push that button. When the elevator doors open again, the air feels chilly. I'm cold already, and my coat is a million miles away, back in my room. My back is starting to hurt, too. I go quickly toward the entrance. It will be worth all this trouble to get home.

But before I can get to the entrance, a pair of inner doors slides shut. A beeper goes off, and a recording repeats, "Code purple at exit 7."

"I heard that the bus doesn't come on Sunday," Steve says. "We'll have to wait a long time. It's a good thing we're inside. It looks cold out there." A gentleman would open the door for me, but clearly I'll have to do it myself. I push my walker against the door and give it a shove.

Some staff people come into the lobby, and they are very nice. "You look so tired, Amanda. Would you like to sit on the bench?" says a woman. And I am tired, so I sit.

A young man with a moustache gets a little television out of his pocket. "Look, I have some pictures of my kids!"

"That bus won't come today, because it's so cold outside," another woman says.

The first woman sits next to me and puts her arm around me. She is so warm! But the other people are blocking my view of the door. "Move out of the way!" I tell them. The bus might come, and I want to see it. And they do move.

Then the elevator door opens. A pretty girl rolls a wheelchair out of it toward me. A wheelchair is better than a bench, so I get up with my walker, the way the occupational therapist showed me, and sit in it. She says, "Shall we go home now?"

What a relief. "Yes," I agree. But then she rolls me into the elevator. "No! No! I want to catch the bus!"

The girl pushes me back out of the elevator. She lifts the necklace from around my neck and hands it to someone. I always seem to be wearing it, although I don't know where it came from. "Shall we wait for the bus outside?" she asks me.

"Yes!" I shout, smiling. At last, after all this trouble and pain, someone is going to help me. She rolls me toward the doors. The first door slides open, and I don't hear any buzzers or recordings. It's colder in this little porch-like room. Then the second door opens, and a very cold wind blows around me. It makes ripples in puddles that reflect clouds full of rain. I see no bus anywhere.

"It's so cold out here," the girl says. "That's probably why the bus didn't come today. Maybe another day. Let's go up and get something warm to drink." She is the sweetest girl, and her poor arms are bare.

"Yes," I tell her. "And I want to go to bed. I'm so tired." Then we're back in the good warm building, and my loving friends are taking me to my own area and my own room. What a wonderful day it has been! But, that bus. I just can't count on it. Maybe tomorrow?

Tomorrow won't be Sunday any more, that's for sure.

—PAUL DE ANGUERA—

I was inspired to write this story by Aleksander Solzhenitsyn's novel—*One Day In the Life of Ivan Denisovich*—an oddly upbeat tale of adventure and fulfillment in a place of suffering and oppression. "Riding The Bus" presents a composite of people I've known and events I've witnessed over the past twelve years as a volunteer at a nursing home. Here, the people who are using canes and walkers are the athletic ones. Those in wheelchairs are more the norm. Some laugh about their lost youth, while others mourn it. And a few, childlike, seem unaware that they've lost anything. They're our mothers and fathers and, ultimately, ourselves. And every one of them longs to go back home

Christopher Jon Heuer

TRAUMA

There are two police officers in our dining room. They've come to take my father away. He's standing by the table in his underwear, hands cuffed behind his back. My mother is trying to place her burgundy housecoat over his shoulders so he won't be naked when they take him outside. The housecoat has feminine floral patterns and looks ridiculous on him. She looks ridiculous too, being all concerned for his appearance when she's the one who called the police in the first place.

Dad is completely out of it—if he knew what was going on he would be shouting and bitching. Instead he's in a stupor. I can't hear what he's mumbling.

The police officers take him by the elbows and lead him out the door. Mom's burgundy housecoat falls from his shoulders when he stumbles on the porch. Nobody stops to pick it up.

The clock reads eleven-thirty p.m. Mom closes the front door behind them and sees me standing in the stairwell.

"Go up to your bedroom," she says, pointing up behind me.

Her eyes are puffy and dark with exhaustion. Behind her I can see red flashing lights on the wall. She shuts the door, leaving me standing in nearly complete darkness. I run up the stairs to the hallway window so that I'll be able to see where the cops are going.

There's an ambulance and two police cruisers in the driveway. The ambulance pulls out first—after a few minutes my mother gets in her car and follows it up the road. Then the cruisers leave. I watch them until the line of taillights disappears over the hill.

Mom still isn't home in the morning. She used to have to wake me up when I stopped being able to hear the alarm clock. But now waking is internal, and I usually leave for school without seeing her.

Everyone is watching me closely when I get on the bus. After a few minutes this senior girl I know, Jill, sits down beside me. She already has something written on a notepad.

"What happened at your house last night?"

Note-writing is a delicate system of avoidance that I've worked out with the hearing population of Juneau, Wisconsin. We've been using it ever since I transferred back here from the Wisconsin School for the Deaf. On the very first day of school, I made the mistake of asking one of the senior guys to repeat something. We just happened to be right in front of some girls, so the location was very strategic for him. He put his hands on my shoulders and very slowly said:

"Suck…my…dick."

After that I've always tried my best to make lip-reading as much of a pain in the ass for them as they make it for me. Hearing people will do just about anything to avoid writing things out—they'll puff in and out like suffocating goldfish for fifteen minutes, they'll repeat something fifty times. Anything but write. If you refuse to lip-read them, they'd rather pretend you don't exist. Thus you're spared any further *suck my dick* adventures. The only downside is that if they actually hand you a note, it means that they have something important to say, and you're stuck.

I read Jill's note, and all I can think to do in reply is shrug.

"Didn't your mom leave you a note or something?" she writes.

I say no and Jill does a little double take, shocked that my mother didn't tell me anything.

She doesn't understand—that's the beauty of the system. No note, no hassle.

"I didn't really look for one," I tell her.

People are still looking at me strangely all through Homeroom and at the start of gym, but by fourth period World History things have died down a little. I keep to myself so it stays that way. In Juneau more people own police scanners than televisions. The local paper even publishes a weekly list of everyone who gets a speeding ticket. People eat it up out here. It's either that or *Dukes of Hazard* re-runs.

Instead of eating in the cafeteria, at fifth period I go get a sandwich at the gas station/deli on the corner. Brad is down there smoking a cigarette by the dumpster.

"Heard about your dad," he says, making a little drinking motion with his hand.

The only kind of thing Brad ever bothers to sign is the one word that will sum up the last fifteen minutes of conversation. The rest I have to fill in on my own. But with him it's not hard. Lip-reading is a question of making educated guesses from a limited selection of things the other person is allowed to say.

The McDonald's guy isn't supposed to ask you if you like Sumo wrestling when you're waiting for your Happy Meal. He's got to say, "Would you like Coke with that?" or "Thank you! Have a nice day!" So long as they stay in character, you're set.

"Hello?" Brad says, waving in my face.

"I don't know what to tell you."

"Well, how many cops were there?" He knows the sign for "cops" and uses it.

"Two. And an ambulance."

He hands me a cigarette. We stand there smoking in silence while he rubs his collarbone. His real dad threw him down the stairs when he was four and broke it. Twelve years later there's a big knot in the bone. He says it never hurts. But he never stops rubbing it.

Finally he finishes his cigarette and tosses it down, crushing it out under his shoe. He says something I don't catch, and then repeats it.

"What you doing tonight?" he asks, signing "do."

"I don't know. Nothing."

"Come out with me later. We'll go to Hartford."

Juneau hasn't got shit. Hartford is where everyone goes—to cruise Main Street, to park in the lots by McDonald's and Burger King and hang out, to drive out to the parks and get drunk.

"I don't know." I glance at my watch. Sixth period starts in ten minutes.

"C'mon."

"My mom's going to be home."

"This is a problem?"

My mother basically lives her life from one holiday to the next. One day after Labor Day, she's getting ready for Halloween. She's taking down the black cats while putting up the Thanksgiving turkeys—all of this done, year after year, around and sometimes over my father. His body passed out on the couch is practically the only permanent showpiece in the room. For her to go calling the cops on the guy after all this time is not in character. It's the McDonald's guy asking you if you like Sumo wrestling. There's no limited selection of responses to choose from.

"Listen," Brad sighs. "Go home, get a sleeping bag, and just...come over tonight. Okay?"

"Just come over." He signs "home" and "sleeping bag."

He said the same thing three years ago, the summer before I left for WSD. He was outside the bowling alley trying to pick the lock on the soda machine. I had just biked into town and couldn't remember why, couldn't remember leaving my house.

He pointed at my forehead and said: "You got something up there, man."

Sweat trickled down my nose. I wiped it off and my fingers came away sticky with blood.

"Did you wipe out or something?"

Weird how I understood him perfectly: weird to be so hyper-aware of everything. I began to shake as if it were winter instead of mid-July.

"Hey."

I couldn't respond. Brad slowly reached out and pulled a jagged piece of glass the size of a dime out of my forehead.

I couldn't move.

Brad said, "Come over to my place. Come on."

In the end he had to park my bike by the soda machine and guide me by the elbow.

Sure enough, Mom is sitting at the kitchen table, wearing a gray sweatshirt and black polyester pants—not the regular white of her nursing home uniform—which means she hasn't been to work today. She has a note ready, too, and holds it out. It reads: Your father is in the detoxification clinic in Hartford.

Well, no shit, hey? Let's do the difficult math of adding two and two and subtracting one from five.

When she's sure I've had enough time to read it, she takes the notepad back and writes: "He's staying for four weeks."

"Good for him."

"I needed to do it," she says.

This is exactly what I mean—the limited selection of things people can say.

"Good for you."

She slams her fist on the table in real frustration, startling me. She almost never acts out. She puts a hand to her temple, fights to control her breathing, and then picks up the pen again.

I read over her shoulder: "Don't you blame me!" "Me" is underlined.

"I don't blame you."

But I've answered too quickly. Sometimes you know a person is lying based on how fast they answer. Too fast, its' a lie—too slow, it's a lie. You've got to nail it right in the middle.

"Then why are you so angry with me?"

Again I miss my window. Nothing I can say at this point will be the truth. I tell her that I'm going to Brad's for a while and head upstairs to get my stuff.

Brad and I wind up at some house party in Hartford. It's nothing big, just a couple of people sitting around finishing off a few cases of beer. I don't know anybody and focus on getting as drunk as I can as fast as I can. It's too hard to lip-read groups and nobody is talking to me anyway.

Here's something about hearing people's parties—they all stop being real and instead become animated mannequins running on battery power. Their mouths open and shut and their arms go flapping around, but that's it. Nothing comes out. I told this to Brad once. He looked at me like I was nuts.

I get a buzz going and lean back to rest my head on the couch. Sometime later Brad slaps my knee and I jerk awake. He hands me a can of beer. In the background the mannequins are reeling back and forth in a mocking parody of laughter.

Brad goes away and I drain the can in a few swallows. A mannequin notices me and shambles forward with a fresh can. I take it and drain that one too. The mannequin reels back laughing. During the five-second pause it takes for his battery to stand him upright again, I ask the mannequin where the detox clinic is in Hartford.

Now I am wavering against the side of Brad's car. He's talking to one of the guys from the party. Everyone seems angry. Brad comes up and gives me a look: "You puke, you die." Then he motions for me to get in the car. I lean my head back against the seat and close my eyes.

Five minutes later Brad slaps my shoulder and wakes me up again. We're parked in a hospital parking lot.

"It's up there," Brad says, pointing.

"What?"

"The detox clinic."

He's pointing over at a lit blue and white sign that says "Mental Health" in bold print. The sign below it says "Emergency Room." I stare at the letters until they blur out. Brad asks if I want to go up.

166

I shake my head no.

He says something about my shirt that I don't catch. "What?"

He flips on the dome light and points at my hand. Something about keeping it wrapped.

My hand is wrapped in a tee-shirt. There's blood soaking through at the knuckles.

"If it's broken," Brad says, "tell me now while we're here."

I'm not wearing a shirt. I'm wearing my jacket but no shirt. "Where's my shirt?"

"Is it broken?" Brad asks again.

I don't understand. "How'd it get broken?"

Brad grips the steering wheel and breathes deeply—a flashback comes of my mother massaging her temples. He snarls something about how I'd "better not get blood all over the fucking car" and angrily reaches up to flip off the dome light. The tires squeal as we tear out of the parking lot. I know because nurses in white pants and multi-colored tops come running to the big hospital windows to see what's causing all the commotion.

Brad is already gone when I awaken on his bedroom floor, feeling sick. It's nearly ten in the morning. Third period is half over. I'll make it in by lunch if I get a move on. I can forge a note from my mom—I've done it before. When I think about writing my right hand starts itching. It's still wrapped in my shirt.

Brad's room is in the basement—he's completely self-contained down there with his own bathroom and even a refrigerator. He's probably not sophisticated enough to have Peroxide, but I'm hoping for at least soap and a better bandage. Wonder of wonders, though, he has both Peroxide and an old roll of football tape.

The first three knuckles of my hand are caked with blood and bruised purple-black. The swelling is bad. Miniature geyser spouts of acid are shooting through my stomach. It doesn't help to watch the Peroxide bubble in the cuts as I dump it on. All I can clearly remember is getting into Brad's car. Did I slam the door on my hand? The face staring back at me in the mirror is strung-out, pasty skin and long, greasy-wet strands of hair clumped together.

Standing behind me in the mirror is my mother.

She's younger and thinner, kneeling next to me as I stand in front of the toilet. I'm five years old and sick with the flu. I'm wearing my dark red pajamas with the blue collar and cuffs. One of my mother's hands is on my stomach, the other is massaging my neck, gently pushing downward so I'll bend over and throw up.

"Let it come," she says. "Don't be afraid. Just let it come."

But I am afraid. I won't let it come.

My hand is almost too swollen to write the note, but it passes muster. Then again the secretary gives me a wary look, so who knows? As I walk through the hallways, guys laugh and clap me on the back. Apparently I'm cool now and have some sort of party-animal reputation from being drunk last night. I wonder how they all found out so fast.

I don't even know if Brad will be in the cafeteria, but I don't feel like walking the extra block to the deli. My stomach isn't doing too hot. Hopefully some milk will take the edge off, along with a bottle of aspirin I found in Brad's medicine cabinet. As it turns out I can barely force down even that, and when Brad claps me suddenly and sadistically on the shoulder as he sits down across from me—"How ya doing!"—I nearly choke.

"Fucking hand hurts, man," I tell him.

Brad says something with the gesture "fight" in it, but I don't catch the whole thing.

"What?"

"You," Brad signs. "Fight." Then something more I still don't catch. Then he points at my backpack.

"What?"

He points again with a "Wait a minute and I'll tell you" expression. When I still don't understand, he impatiently leans over and grabs my backpack, rummaging around. He pulls out a notebook and a pen just as I finally realize what it is he wants.

At the party, he writes.

"What about it?"

Brad signs "drunk" and points at me.

"Well no shit, Sherlock!"

He writes again: "You hit that guy."

"What?"

He holds up his hands defensively, mistaking my irritation for denial. "You did!"

I can't focus. "I have no fucking idea what you're talking about."

He busily scribbles on the notepad: "You asked where the detox clinic was in Hartford. You were completely fucked up. Some guy laughed and you hit him."

I close my eyes and see blood spurt from my knuckles. The other mannequins in the room scramble away from me, shouting. The guy I just hit is huddled up on the floor holding his nose. Blood is spraying out between his fingers.

Brad is watching me. "Do you remember now?"

"No." *No, no, no.*

He shakes his head and writes: "You dragged him outside and kicked the shit out of him."

Now that I don't remember at all. So he's bullshitting me. Fucking playing me. "Please stop, man," I whisper. I'm going to puke if he doesn't leave.

He points down. "Look at your shoe."

There's blood smears all along the toe of my right sneaker. And something else. At first I think it's grass, but it's hair.

How does anybody really get around? I wonder about this all the time. How does your brain get you from one place to the next on autopilot, remembering some things and blocking out the rest? The stop signs…every turn and shortcut? Suddenly you're home with no idea how you got there, no sense of passing time. People say this happens all the time when they drive. But I think it can be a whole way of life. Nobody says anything about it because it doesn't occur to them until they do remember something, and then they're too freaked out.

Like now. I'm home. In front of me is our kitchen table. I'm fourteen years old. We moved in a little over a year ago, leaving behind our farm in Hustisford. I'm drawing pictures of X-Wings and TIE Fighters. My father comes in drunk and asks what I'm drawing.

Maybe it's because I don't look up at him immediately, or because my family no longer has the farm—if we did I would be out picking off stones or bailing hay instead of sitting at the table drawing. I would be working toward something meaningful and worthwhile. I'm pretty sure this is what my father wants me to understand.

He overturns the table with one hand and grabs me by the throat with the other, shoving me into the wall. I can't get free and I can't breathe. He moves in close, breath reeking of beer, and pins my legs with his knee. Then he rips a framed sketch of an old barn from the wall above my head—a drawing of one of those rotting wooden sheds and half collapsed silos that you see all over Wisconsin. People sketch and frame them and sell the drawings at craft shows. They bring in good money.

"Why can't you draw something people want!" my father screams, and pushes the picture into my face until the glass shatters.

Sometime later the light flashes. It's nighttime outside. My mother has come home from work.

She says, "Daniel, when did you come home?" I'm seated at the dining room table. The last thing I immediately remember is sitting in the cafeteria. I reach up to pull the glass from my forehead but there's nothing stuck in my forehead and there's no broken picture on the floor. I feel stupid.

"Daniel, what's wrong with you?"

My mother is talking in slow-motion, her hand frozen on the doorknob. She'll cry soon.

"Please tell me what you're so frightened of," she says.

I look away slightly. Brad is picking bloody glass out of my forehead.

"Daniel, please!" I'm in the dining room again. My mother is shaking my shoulder.

Brad wrote: "You dragged him outside and kicked the shit out of him."

"What did I do?" I ask.

"Look at your shoe," Brad said.

The barest pause.

Then my mother says, "You didn't do anything, baby."

I can feel my heart beating, so very badly do I want that to be true.

"I was the one who sent him away," she says. "I called the police. Me."

For a second I'm confused. She called the police on me? What did she call the police about?

"Your father did it to himself, Daniel. It's not your fault."

She doesn't know what I'm talking about. Even I barely know what we're talking about. I'm going to be sick. How long is it going to take to not be sick anymore?

"We can fix this, honey," Mother is saying. "We can pull ourselves together..."

How can we do that when we're not even talking about the same thing?

She says something more that I don't follow. I've stopped trying to lip-read, to predict, make educated guesses. There's no more limited selection of things she's allowed to say. Then is here and now is nowhere. The character of everyone and everything—completely shot to hell.

Brad and I skip school on Friday and spend the day in his room, drinking beer and watching *First Blood* on his VCR. During the part where Rambo stitches his side back together with fishing-string, Brad says that the guy I hit is going to be looking for me. We watch television in silence for a while.

"I was talking about my dad," I say, suddenly.

"What?"

"That night, at the party."

Brad makes a gesture—"I don't understand."

"When I asked where the detox clinic was. They all laughed. That guy especially. They thought I wanted to go get my own stomach pumped or something."

Brad watches, silent.

"But I was talking about my dad," I say.

"Well, how the fuck could they know?" he asks.

"Yeah."

Brad starts rubbing his collarbone.

"Do you ever think about him?" I ask after a while.

"About who?"

"Your dad."

It was a mistake to ask. Brad stands up suddenly, and tosses me the roll of football tape.

"No," he says, and walks past me toward the bathroom.

I feel sick all the way to Hartford. If Brad notices he's not saying anything. But halfway though *Hotel California* he gives my shoulder a good-natured thump and starts slapping the wheel in time with the beat, trying to lighten the mood. It kind of works. The stereo is cranked up all the way and the enclosure of his car is the best hearing aid in existence.

We go to Burger King for some food. Brad goes in to get us a couple of cheeseburgers. I stay in the car, draining one can of beer after another from the case in the back seat. Part of me wonders if this is how my dad got started, drinking for the nerves.

Eventually Brad comes back with cheeseburgers, fries, and Cokes. He sets the food on the hood and makes a "come out" gesture.

"I want to sit in here."

He shakes his head "no." He wants me to come and sit on the hood. That's how we wait guys out around here—you don't go driving all over town looking for a fight. You sit out in the open and sooner or later one will come to you.

Once I'm sitting on the hood he pours Southern Comfort into the Cokes from a flask in his jacket pocket. He gives me one and we sit in silence for a while, watching the sun go down and the cars go by.

"I don't want to do this." I have no idea I'm going to say it until I say it.

Brad looks away, because what is he supposed to do about it? It's not like I can call the guy up and apologize. Nobody's going to say, "Hello, this is Dan's mommy. Can I please speak to your mommy?" No: "Look my father is in a detox clinic and these are my feelings and what should I do about my feelings?" What would the guy say to something like that? And even if he said something, how would I ever follow it? Lip-reading is a question of prediction.

Eventually some Hartford guys pull in and talk to Brad. He comes walking back and tells me "It's on. We're going to the park. Get in the car."

It's violently cold on the way there. I can't stop my hands from shaking—my arms and shoulders.

"Turn off the air conditioner," I try to say, but my teeth are chattering and my cheeks are numb.

Brad shrugs and makes a dismissive gesture with his free hand—"It is off."

We reach the long gravel road that leads to the park and I tell him I have to puke. He slams on the brakes and I barely make it, already vomiting up beer and Southern Comfort as I push open the door and stumble away from the car. Finally it turns to dry heaving and I steady myself against the trunk. I stare at my bad hand then look up. My mother is sitting on one of the front wheels of a John Deere tractor like the one we used to have back at the farm. But this one isn't ours. We lost our farm and had just moved. My father now worked as a farm hand for another farmer. My mother took the stitches out of my forehead that morning. I tell her I want to go swimming with our neighbor's kids up the road.

She says "No."

"Why not?"

"Just…no!"

No, because the pool hasn't been cleaned and she doesn't want me to get an infection, or because we'll be having lunch in fifteen minutes. There are a dozen potential explanations, but it's not them I react to—it's the fact that she doesn't explain at all. She treats me like I'm six, crying when she takes stitches out and it's not even her with her head that was cut open. It's the expression on her face now, the impatience, the exasperation, like it's my fault.

"I hate you!" I scream at her suddenly. She's steps back, blinking from the fury in it, but the swimming pool is right there! Everything I want is right there, and I can't have it. I can't have pictures of TIE Fighters. A father. A family that can talk to me. Friends that can talk to me. Everything right in front of my face, and for some reason that nobody will explain, that everyone is too exhausted and irritated to explain, I can't have any of it.

I kick her knee. She lies about it later to her friends, but that's really how it got broken.

Brad's hand slaps my shoulder. "Fucking get it together, man!" he shouts. I look at him and try but can't.

It's dark. The headlights are on. I'm sitting in Brad's car dry heaving into my hand, and he's out by the picnic tables fighting two guys at once. One guy's nose is in a splint. The other guy gets a good hard kick in the nuts, and then it's one-on-one. But the guy with the nose splint turns and runs up the road. Brad walks up and gets in the car.

"Just shut up," he says, and signs "shut up." He rips the gearshift backward into drive and sprays gravel all the way out of the park. We take back roads on the way out of town and head for Juneau in a completely roundabout way. At first I think Brad is trying to avoid the cops—and he probably is—but eventually I realize that we're heading towards the highway that leads to my house. Right before we get to my driveway, Brad shuts off his headlights and we cruise slowly past it. He stops behind one of the trees that border my front lawn. When I fumble drunkenly with the door handle, he reaches past me and opens it. His expression is stony. I can't read him at all. Once I'm out, he pulls the door shut and drives away, heading toward Highway 60. Either he's going back to Juneau the long way or he's just going out cruising. I get the feeling I'm not welcome to know which.

I go into my house through the back door because it's quieter, but my mom still wakes up. When I look up from the refrigerator she's standing next to the living room table—the exact same place my father had been standing when the cops cuffed him only a week earlier. Then is now, there is here.

"Are you drunk?" she asks. She looks tired.

I set my glass of milk down on the counter.

"What would your fath—," she begins to say, but stops herself.

No matter. "What would your father say if he were here?" is what she would have said. The day after Dad broke the picture over my forehead, I biked home from Brad's house and walked through the front door. My father was standing in the dining room with the phone in his hand. I found out later he had been about to dial the cops. When he saw me, he hung up and put his fingers over his eyes, then walked quickly into the bedroom.

My mother came out of the kitchen, her mixing bowl tucked in one arm. She said, "Daniel, if you're going to stay out at a friend's house, make sure you tell us first." No question on why I left, about the bandage on my forehead, nothing. "You're father doesn't like it when he doesn't know where you are," she added. She didn't even put the bowl down.

"I don't know what Dad would say," I tell her. It's now again. I know because my hand is still taped up. If not for that, I wouldn't.

My mother says, "I'm trying," as if apologizing. How to respond to that? I don't know. She doesn't know. Even Brad probably wouldn't know.

All of us trying, yet nobody knows.

—CHRISTOPHER JON HEUER—

"Trauma" is based on a mixture of events from my own life and the lives of friends I hung out with in high school. My father is dead now. He died of heart failure brought on by old age. My friend Brad (his actual name) is dead too. He was in a car accident during my second year of college, remained in a coma for approximately a year after that, and never woke up. I wrote several short stories about Dan. I remember reading a review of one of these. Someone called him the perfect example of an anti-hero. I don't see him as any kind of hero. Or as deaf. I don't see "Trauma" as "disability fiction" (or non-fiction). It's just a story about a horribly screwed up, frightened kid and his situation. I'm amazed he's still alive. *He* is, too.

Ana Garza G'z

ROCKS AND PROCESSES

A partition divided the room where the university's geology department buried its teaching associates, giving the slit of a space the general proportions of two boxcars. An unbroken line of office desks pressed into one another along three walls, and a row of floor-to-ceiling cupboards leaned against the fourth. The door was cut into the wall with the cupboards giving short-lived haven to anyone—okay, me—standing in its shelter with a guide dog and the third internal pep-talk of the week. I didn't want to think about the previous two, especially since I had another couple of seconds to make up my mind about whether to stay in the class.

I could still leave. My TA, sitting beyond the divider with his back to me, hadn't seen me yet and hadn't heard me over the bustle of class changes in the hall outside. He was still at his desk, discussing fault lines with another graduate student. So I could go away and maybe drop the class—or at least change sections, but with my luck, he would turn out to be a supervisor, in which case the soul blighted enough to get stuck with me would appeal to him for advice. Or I could just leave for now and innocently return next week with my gift of metamorphic transformation, when I had screwed my nerve up to the point of dealing with him, pretending to have forgotten all about our arrangement, made yesterday— when I showed up late to lab.

That had been a Big mistake. And to think, yesterday I'd even tried to get there on time. I got out of bed early. I rushed to the university, the dog and I jogging across campus down a breezeway, through a glass door, and into the building. But then a friend stopped me in the stairwell to catch me up on the latest chapter in the saga of her recent divorce, and since even I thought it tactless to say, "That's horrible! Gotta run," I was late, ten long talk-show-tragedy-ridden minutes late.

When I walked in, the lab had already started. Students were sitting in the rows of work tables, and the TA was lecturing at the chalkboard in front of the room. So much for the plan to sneak in early and take a seat in one of the rear corners to keep him from noticing me or rather my sixty-eight-pound golden retriever. I would just have to get the inevitable "What do I do with you?" discussion out of the way early. And in the florescent light hum that hovered over us all while I hesitated in the doorway, I braced myself for getting to that discussion as soon as possible.

"Over here," the TA said, almost convulsing forward to grab my arm, awkwardly seizing my right elbow and pulling, never losing sight of the other students.

I couldn't place the accent right away, but I noticed that he directed me with his right hand when the unclean left would have been easier for us both, and he actually bunny hopped to avoid contact with the dog. "Middle Eastern," I thought sinkingly, "and devout Muslim. He'll hate the dog." That would complicate things further.

"Sit right there," he barked, ending in the classic level-fall inflection of the Arabic speaker.

"Absolutely wonderful," I thought sourly, settling the dog and clipping paper into my slate as quietly as possible.

"Alright," he resumed when I had the stylus in my hand, "in addition to the weekly lab reports, you have one midterm, one final…" and proceeded with the class as if I'd never disrupted it, moving, after further preliminaries, to the thirty-to forty-minute lab explanation, which he promised would not only supplement the four-hours Ph.D. lecture but also prepare us for the lab activity, the greater part of our two-hour time with him.

Sixty minutes later, when people were wandering around looking at minerals (rocks have histories and personalities. Who knew?), and I was sitting at my seat examining a palm-sized slab of talc, he approached me.

"What's your name?" he asked.

Not snapping: Just "overlaying L1 suprasegmentals on his L2" or something (linguistics courses were a trove of useless information).

I said my name.

"You're taking Geology 2?"

Duh. I focused on keeping my tone neutral. "Yes."

"Do I need to do something special for you?"

"No."

"Do you think you will be able to participate in the lab?"

"Yes."

"Will you be able to do the work?"

"I'll need permission to turn in in-class assignments late so I can type them up."

"Alright," he said, and strolled off to answer other people's questions.

After another twenty minutes, he was back. I was handling a pencil-shaped laboratory-grown quartz crystal and comparing it to a slightly warped natural spur jutting out of a porphyritic mass.

"I was thinking," he began, three words that always put a chill down my spine, "maybe it would be better for you if you came to my office instead of the labs."

I tried hard to look confused in the hope that he would think again. "Every week?" I feigned uncertainty, drumming my fingertips against the crystal.

"Yes," he softened. I couldn't tell whether doubt or politeness accounted for the shift. "I can explain things to you better that way."

Imagining an introductory level lab activity so complicated that I would need extra assistance only added tone to the scraps of response that fluttered around my head.

I drummed on the quartz some more. So far this morning, two other instructors—the ones for Lesson Planning, whom I'd had earlier in my endless college career, and Statistics—had each asked whether I might reconsider enrollment in their classes, presumably believing the eyes, not the brain, to be the primary processing organs. And of course, beliefs are facts until consensus says different. Lucky me, having this revelation while dealing with a pissy sub-teacher who was joining ranks with the other two.

"Do you think that would be alright?" he was asking.

I put the quartz down.

"Alright," I snapped, careful to confine the tone to his inflection.

"When can you come?" He was all business again.

"When are you available?"

He took stock for a moment, and we agreed on time, day, and place.

"We'll start tomorrow," he decided. "So come by the office. We'll talk about today's lab. If I'm not around, just ask for me."

I nodded crabbily, still taking down the place and time, waiting till I finished before bothering to speak.

"What is your last name?" I asked mechanically.

"Ouassou [uh-/sou]," he said, pronouncing the name carefully. "O-u-a-s-s-o-u."

"Ouassou," I repeated, writing the name phonetically after the spelling and mentally chanting in beautiful anapest, "You're *not* just a *pig*, but a *sow*." The mnemonic amused me. I felt my mouth twitch into a smile.

"Alright then," he was smiling too now. "I'll see you tomorrow."

So here I was, standing in his office doorway, listening to him talk geology, and debating whether to stay and make the best of it or turn around and leave. The dog shook then, flapping his ears and jangling his collar and harness. The conversation beyond the partition stopped. I'd missed my chance.

"Oh, hi," he called out cheerfully, getting up to meet me.

"I've been unfair," I thought, remembering my little mnemonic, and said hello.

"Over here." He guided me awkwardly by the elbow with his right hand as on the day before, again elaborately avoiding the dog.

I dropped into a padded desk chair on coasters, the just quashed irritation flaring when he slid his chair farther away as I settled the dog.

"You'll have to take out a sheet of paper for writing things down," he ordered, flipping through a folder to get out his notes while I obeyed. "Now, the first thing we need to talk about," he began formally, "is minerals," and he barked out the same exact lecture I'd heard the day before, excluding nothing, embellishing nowhere.

I was irritated. Today's notes would be duplicates of yesterdays, so I entertained myself by anticipating his data and writing "prick" and "asshole" when I finished the note before he finished speaking. For the third time this week, I cherished braille for its advantages.

"Now, let's actually observe some of these," he said eventually, handing me the same talc, quarts, and other mineral samples I'd fiddled with the day before, only describing in an awkward kind of lyricism the way the colors layered over each specimen ("this one is pink and gray and brown, like waves on the ocean rolling onto each other and onto the sky"), applying some of the points of his lecture and asking me questions to make sure I understood.

By then, guilt over the bad pun crept through me. I played up a little more interest, asking him questions and bringing up the text.

"Anything else?" he invited finally. We'd finished with the day's activities, and we had ten minutes to spare. He was obviously filling out the time. "Anything from the class you might have questions about?" He was referring to the Ph.D. lecture.

I'd forgotten to be tense. Now I hesitated, suddenly wary again. A stupid question could start him talking at me.

"Well," I paused, "there's this diagram. It shows the minerals..." I trailed off.

"The Bowen reaction series?" he supplied. The tone was helpful. I relaxed.

"Yes. Well…I don't understand what the diagram looks like, so I'm having trouble conceptualizing it. And I don't really get what it means."

He thought for a moment. "Well," he spoke slowly, working out the forthcoming explanation, "it describes the order in which the different minerals form as the elements are cooled or subjected to heat." He brooded. "But I don't think he'll expect you to know what the diagram looks like."

I was irritated again. Not a *pig*, but *A* sow.

"I would like to understand what it looks like for myself," I rejoined, barely disguising the annoyance.

"Alright," he snapped, the level inflection rising slightly in Western finality. "It looks like a 'Y.'"

"Capital or lowercase?"

He gathered his patience in a round exasperated sigh. I'd pushed too hard.

"We can draw this," I backed down, reaching for my backpack and pulling out a sheet of cork.

"We can?" Surprise.

"Yes." Indifference. "Do you have a pencil?"

"Just a regular pencil?" Confusion, wonder.

"Yes," I said again, the fizzing irritation of a second ago petering into weary frustration.

Today's golden opportunity to educate, to enlighten the superior life form on my own inert existence. I'd been educating the sighted since I'd gone blind. I would be educating the sighted the day I died. I wished for one day, just one day, without such opportunities. I laid a sheet of paper on the cork and, reaching for his fingers with my unclean left hand, showed him how to score the page with the pencil by applying the right amount of pressure.

As the weeks dragged on, I attended lab regularly, dropped Statistics—disappeared, really (I'd had enough)—and presented my first teaching demonstration (on the role and function of the preposition) in Lesson Planning, which went better than expected. I started working on the next assignment for that class almost immediately, deciding on the atom and molecular formation during geological processes as a topic. I reread the pertinent sections in my geo book and plied my lab TA with a battery of questions during our ten spare minutes. By then, Lesson Planning had stopped harping on my inadequacies, and the Lab TA actually smiled and sometimes laughed during our sessions, giving every indication of enjoying our meetings.

School interested me again. I read my textbooks just for the thrill of it, wrote my papers ahead of time for a change, and studied for exams to the realization that I'd committed important concepts to memory during the initial reading. I'd dash from class to class, surprised anew that it had all started with geology, out of the hasty chapter readings that I had submitted myself to in both the fear that Ouassou might go into question mode and the guilt I'd felt for doing bad things to his name—"a sow," indeed. Somehow a chore had sparked something I'd forgotten I possessed, kindling first a pleasure, a genuine interest, in rock formation and other geologic processes, then later firing into curiosity about other courses—lesson planning, bilingualism, second language acquisition, Lit of the Spanish Golden Age, and even statistics though I confined this last to reading the textbook and working out problems at my kitchen table. Most amazingly, I thought again in terms of the need to graduate for the first time in eight years, and I was swayed enough by that desire to drop by the Evaluations and Records office for a degree completion eligibility check. I visited the nearby school district offices to apply for ESL teaching positions, dreaming of the day I'd sit down to an interview that would end in handshakes and a two-year contract. Somehow all of that had been ignited by geology lab, which shouldn't have made a difference, but it had.

Sometimes on my dreamy dashes through the campus, I would rush past my TA. "See that blind girl with the dog?" he'd tell whoever was standing with him by the ATM, the library, or the benches near the food court. "She's in one of my classes. She's really smart."

The comment was jarring, annoying, typical, "smart" being the word for pets and children, entities not quite human, who unexpectedly do the ordinary. Others had made it. Others would make it. Again, the tiresome gift of my day-to-day. By the end of the term, he'd be calling me a "person," and a year from now, I'd be a "blind girl" again, as I discovered myself to be when I ran into people I'd gone to high school with or sat beside three semesters before, and for him, as for the rest, I would remain a "blind girl" until the memory of me faded.

I would dash ahead, pretending not to have heard him, letting my mind drift to the material he would probably ask about at the end of our next session, so as to find a reason to return to his lab.

Eight weeks into the semester, my individualized lab session began with an announcement. "I won't be here for the next two weeks. My father is sick. No one will tell me exactly what is going on with him. So I'll be going back to Morocco to see how things are. After today, we'll meet again when we get back from spring break. We'll have to do as much as we can." We'd have a lot to cover both this session and the two or three following his return. There would be no time for his ten-minute reviews. I said I was sorry. He seemed moved, and I sympathized again before I left.

Two evenings later, I waited for my ride in a parking lot at an empty corner of the university.

He called my name, crossing a strip of lawn to come and talk to me.

"Hello," I smiled, surprised to have recognized his gait and scent (warm, light, salty) since I thought I hadn't registered either.

He paced indecisively, mentioned the setting sun, wondered if I'd be alone for long, told me he was on his way to the mosque down the street. His flight would be leaving first thing tomorrow. He fell silent, standing in front of my dog a safe ten feet away, then crossing his feet, evidently deciding to stay a sec.

"So how *are* things?" I asked.

And feeling weak and vulnerable, he told me.

After Easter, I returned to his office. We talked contour maps, water tables, wells, and sewage. Other classes were going splendidly. I'd managed to educate Lesson Planning about my general competence all over again, and the semester overall was good. Four weeks later, my TA read me my final exam questions, jotted my answers down, and reported that my laboratory grade was a ninety-five percent.

"When's your lecture test?"

"Next Friday."

"Good luck." He was beaming like a parent.

"I enjoyed the lab."

That pleased him, and I'd been sincere.

The next afternoon, I walked across campus between classes, mentally running over the list of papers to be completed by the last day of the term. A good thing the lab final had been administered a week early, and getting Lesson Planning out of the way this week would also help. I heard my TA's voice: "See that student," he told whoever was walking into the coffee shop with him, "the one in the white shirt, with the blue skirt and the long dark hair? She's in one of my classes. She's really smart." I'd become a person. I felt a momentary rush of gratitude, replaced by the humiliation of realizing I hadn't been until then.

On the assigned day and time, I showed up to my Lesson Planning professor's office for my exam. I slid the dog under my chair, patting him on the shoulder abstractedly, wondering whether I should ask for a letter of recommendation. It would probably help with the teaching applications and the interviews that never ended in handshakes. I'd decide by the time we finished.

"Good afternoon," he greeted formally, as if I were a roomful of students. "Please sit down. I'll start by reading you the instructions. Then select whichever part of the exam you feel most comfortable with."

It was easier than expected, and we got through it quickly. When we had finished, my professor put the test aside and cleared his throat in prelude to an awkward question. I sat back, laying odds on "Were you born blind?" and planning how I'd transition from that to the letter of recommendation.

"Well," he began, pausing so long I thought he changed his mind. He exhaled thoughtfully. "I don't know how to say this. This may not be any of my business. But I ask because I care and I think it's important."

I waited silently.

"You," he went on after a moment, "were in one of my classes a number of years ago, nine? Or ten? I think?"

That wasn't what I was expecting. I tensed.

"You were a different person then."

He waited.

I waited. He hadn't asked a question.

"I'm not sure where you've gone since."

I sat still, his own beginning-of-the-semester intimations, Statistics', those of so many others who came before rolling over me, slowly, heavily, wearyingly. I blinked rapidly.

"I remember a young, energetic woman," he went on, "eager to learn, to know, to ask, full of life and vigor, ready to conquer the world." He spread his hands out as if to embrace the globe. "But now," he dropped them on his desk, "she's gone."

I squeezed my eyes shut.

"I don't know where she went," he said. "I wonder what has happened to her."

I took a tissue out of my pocket, blew my nose softly, and wiped my face.

He didn't say anything.

I shoved the soiled tissue back into my skirt and sat rigidly, waiting to be dismissed.

"Where has she gone?" He said my name, pressing gently, and I remembered he'd been a seminarian at one time. This was probably the remnant of his confessional technique. "Where?"

I bent, and found more tissue in the backpack, blowing my nose again.

"Where?" he murmured. "Where?"

The room was silent for a long time.

"I've been in school too long to care much about anything," I said at last, my voice much louder than I'd intended. "I'm tired of being questioned and second-guessed and relegated to nothingness because everybody else is too closed-minded to know any better. I'm tired of having job interviewers either tell me that there appears to have been a scheduling error because I'm not on the list or cross-examine me about my blindness rather than my qualifications—" I cut myself off before I said anything about the ones who had the nerve to pray for me, the ones who mention day programs, where I could make dolls and weave baskets, or the ones who went irritably through the motions of interviewing me in a way that made their refusal to take me seriously unmistakable.

"Job interviewers?" he asked tentatively. "Are you having trouble finding work?"

I scrubbed wordlessly at my face with the tissue I'd just used, trying to control myself.

"What kind of jobs are you looking for?"

I didn't answer, working too hard to keep myself together.

"Have you tried finding work in radio, special education, as a telephone operator?"

Damn him. The three most stereotypical 'blind' jobs on the planet. I was suddenly too angry to cry, and zipping up my backpack, I signaled the dog to rise.

"Those jobs don't interest me," I said steadily, swiping at my face one last time and looping the pack on to my shoulders. "I'm not majoring in any of those fields."

Several of my classmates had collected around the door.

I stood and checked my watch reflexively. My professor's last office hour of the semester had just begun. He rose to see me out.

"If there's anything I can do," he urged, "if there's any way I can help you, please let me know and tell me what to do." He meant it, I could tell, but I was angry, and I wouldn't get any help from someone who didn't believe I'd make use of the information I learned in his class.

"Thank you," I recited formally. "I hope you have a wonderful summer."

I pushed through the crowd at the door with automatic hi's, sorry's, and excuse-me's and headed for the spot across campus where my ride would be picking me up. A left and then another left, and then a straight shot to the opposite end of campus, where I'd be met. But I was on the verge of crying again. Pissed and mad and hurt and tired, I wished my professor hadn't decided to play job counselor. I wished he hadn't proved to me that I'd deceived myself in thinking I could win someone over. How dare he do that to me? How dare he be so incredibly closed to the possibility that someone like me could be someone like him? I turned a hundred yards before I needed to and veered into the breezeway of a set of connected buildings. I wanted privacy and space. Late on Friday afternoon, right before finals, the grounds were empty, and both could easily be mine. I stepped into one of the narrow side passages, which spidered off the main one and, noticing no one, walked halfway down the corridor and allowed myself to cry.

This wasn't the same routine I'd dripped through in my professor's office. None of the stony, silent, dribbling tears of a person sealed too far into herself to be touched by anything—this was something different, something frightening, something intense. It was the heaving, gulping, blubbering, bawling, wracking paroxysm of tears, spit, and snot that befits a child's loss. And I didn't understand it. Lesson Planning's question shouldn't have affected me the way it did. Others had asked more destructive questions. One had asked, "What's the point of your being in school?" But none had rattled me like this, depressed me like this. None had gotten me to howl and wheeze like this while standing on a lonely sidewalk. I gasped and whined in incomprehension, my dog motionless beside me.

Then in one of the little silences between sobs, I heard the footsteps, the gait I'd recognized in an empty parking lot, and I caught the warm, light, salty scent I'd filed away somewhere without really knowing. He'd come up behind me. The dog turned around. The steps retreated to beyond leash length. I was embarrassed. I covered my face to hide the redness and the puffiness. I squeezed my eyes to make the tears stop. I held my breath to control the breathing, the sobs, the drip. I felt him hovering.

I understood then.

At some point in the semester, I had begun to have a future again. I had begun to believe that I had a mind and a contribution to make. I had started to read and think and question again, at first in part because I'd feared my TA might ask questions about the course in order to kill time, at first because I'd wanted to quell the guilt for childishly turning his name into a rude private joke, but later because he'd made asking possible for me. He'd answered my questions, excited my intellect, and eventually regarded me as a person—a person. A thinking, seeking, knowing person! He had never questioned my right to enter his classroom, never doubted his responsibility to me. He had rearranged his time for me, a chore for him, to be sure, but his demeanor changed, suggesting pleasure, even genuine interest, in introducing me to the rocks and processes that he knew specifically and profoundly. He had unintentionally reminded me that I had a right to my own specific and profound knowledge and to a dream and that years of lesson planning and statistics profs had worn away at my certainty about that fact. I felt strong suddenly, empowered, despite the interviews that hadn't panned out, despite the interviews that might never pan out. He gave me my mind back. He acknowledged it—always—even that first time: "I thought I could explain things to you better," he'd said. A stream of perfect gratitude flowed through me, gratitude that humbled and enlarged. I uncovered my face and turned to him, still wet and snotty, but easier, relaxed.

"All right?" he asked.

I nodded.

He watched me blow my nose and wipe my face. Then, when I was done, we set off in opposite directions without speaking again.

—ANA GARZA G'Z—

In a graduate writing pedagogy class, one of our weekly prompts was to write a narrative about a teacher who was significant for whatever reason. I knew I would write about my geology lab instructor because he'd helped me rediscover an interest in the life of the mind, but as I wrote, I realized that my Spanish professor was equally important though for a very different reason. He was well intentioned and even broadminded, but he was as entrenched as the rest of the world in misconceptions about what dreams I had the right to as a person with a disability.

I didn't throw the narrative away because I couldn't. The tension produced by the two instructors and the noise in my head were not unique to the semester I wrote about. They were with me always at school and have been with me always in my various encounters with people at work and in daily living, and so have the unexpected moments of betrayal and grief that come from the subtle reminders that, in the minds of others and sometimes in my own, I am other, and my aspirations should be less.

Eventually, I reshaped the piece so it would read more like fiction, thinking no one would be interested in yet another read about a poor blind person feeling oppressed by the sighted world around her. Maybe, as fiction, the experience would be more accessible to able-bodied readers, who could slip into the student's subjective reality, without clinging to the kinds of judgments they would make about her in real life.

Ann Bogle

LETTER TO JOHN BERRYMAN

for Christa Maria Forster

Maybe we'll try elevator music again. That would appeal to the senses. As the book begins to close, Normandberger appears as sister speech, endearing term for summer friend. A friend of a deep friend, a serious secular religious poet living near Chicago, Bill Yarrow. Festschrift my favorite writer. Jane Bowles. Feminine wiles. I'll go Scottish on my oath. An escort from Moscow inspired my friend in writing his novel on bedding. Deep set women laboring deep set men. I thought of Stephen Dunn's poetry about divorce in the bookshop in St. Paul.

Based on a photo: Evie Shockley is protected, a garden herb, better than hosta. I met her mid-flight in a windowed elevator in Atlanta. I met Dunn in the same elevator at ground level going up. Hilda Raz's son's speech on the panel where Dunn described his date with Liza Minnelli left me disconcerted.

Hilda Raz had lost a daughter. Her son gained a persona, backed by biological components. His male-pattern baldness impressed me. In the elevator, Dunn said he'd seen that I had cried at it, the loss to female pride, as I experienced it. Dunn said he had known already about Raz's son.

Leo Kottke and I happened to go to lunch the same day in Excelsior. I ate like a man, soup, as I always do. I tend to be thin yet eat unapologetically. He flickered rue when I said I had bipolar, as if saying so would not go well. It was a publisher who released Janet Frame from her hold in a mental hospital, where she had gone after college, identified schizophrenic by her red, kinky hair. "Fat chance," I said, referring to my own release from a hospital without walls. He said he was in a correspondence with Kay Redfield Jamison. Creativity clears sinus, a middle path, a moral resistance to flight and melancholy as savored by artists. So knock on stove for Sylvia Plath, whose nature poems outstrip mirth. We are fluent in English not at the roots.

My doctor, Faruk S. Abuzzahab, is polite about Jamison, who renamed the illness bipolar disorder without taking a medical degree. I wonder how they corresponded. Depression appears in Kottke's trombone piece:

*(By the time I knew depression was free, and that I didn't have to play
trombone to be depressed, I'd imitated its "mood" for so long that I couldn't
refuse the Damned Cloud when it did arrive. If you've been imitating the
seeming cool, the detachment, and the languor, genuine depression won't be
noticed until you tire of your pose. Bored with oceanic despair, you reach for the
ladder back into the boat and you drown: no ladder.)*

My old dad died of cancer in 1992. He gave a grateful noise unto the
Lord. He trod the Earth's surface to file for me. He loved me, and I loved
him. "I did it with my dad. I did it wearing plaid and now I'm glad"—I
thought of quipping smartly, after one could, to Beauty in the Lounge.
Did it by avocation, not meaning sex—activities that clear the way to
Personality, such as fishing in the row boat on St. Alban's and near the
channel at Gray's—we tied a blue-and-black fly to plant a seed in Time.

Seven years after he died, I sat in A.A. at St. Luke Presbyterian,
where Reverend Hudnut had baptized me, a glad-tidings girl who grew
to belonging too soon to miss by ugly design. Cattle resembling my
grandmother's family rolled by meekly in a row, orienteers to a future past.
I said my father had died and rested in the cemetery near the church and
school. I wasn't healed, though the therapist in Houston had allotted one
session for grieving.

My dad was an Army Reservist stationed in the U.S.—New York
and Texas—the bugler in his corps. He golfed on summer weekends at
Hazeltine in the course of his career. I had seen houses water colored
prettily within the lines once on L.S.D. after noticing nothing in particular
twice. He called at nine on a Saturday morning to hear the review of the
picture. Wisconsin Synod and Episcopalian became hard of ringing part
of one day. Christa was from San Juan Capistrano. A story is a nest like a
small wooden boat set as a hymn in the slanting tree.

Whosoever befriends let friends believe free feeling. Christa would say,
"Offer it up!"

I drove once, not expected, to my boyfriend's house in Sugar Land.
Twenty-five miles. He acted amused when he opened the front door. I said,
"I'm not stalking you. I love you," and he said, "Come in. What are you
doing standing outside?"

This piece is crafted as an imaginary letter to the poet John Berryman, who died a grisly suicide in Minneapolis in 1972 at the age of fifty-seven after serving as lecturer in poetry at various universities, in particular at the University of Minnesota. During my own first hospitalization and diagnosis of bipolar in 1991, I learned that bipolar disorder is a newer term for manic-depression. "John Berryman," I said to the doctor then. My father who had been diagnosed with good prognosis with prostate cancer died about six months later. I completed my third degree in English at the University of Houston in 1994, a Master of Fine Arts degree in fiction. Afterward, I worked briefly as an adjunct teacher, for which I had been exceptionally well-trained, and since as a volunteer. The content of the imaginary letter has a basis in fact, though the telling is stylistically creative.

Alison Oatman

HOSPITAL CORNERS

How did you get in here?

It was a Saturday morning in late March when she was determined to jump off the concrete terrace of her parents' apartment. She rushed down the stairs towards the terrace when her mother stopped her. Her father, who had heard her mother screaming, spun out of nowhere and slapped his daughter across the face to get her to come to her senses. Afterwards, the morose young woman went up to the closet of her room to sob in a ball.

The following Monday afternoon, she and her parents met in a small, clean office for a family therapy session with Dr. S. They were all relatively calm. When Dr. S asked how the weekend was, however, her father piped up about the hysteria and said he wasn't sure if she was serious about jumping off the terrace. She said she was. Her mother told her later that she wasn't going to say anything so that her daughter would finally make it back to her junior year in college.

At this point, Dr. S insisted they go to the emergency room right away.

The emergency room was swarming with life. She and her parents waited for hours. Finally, a nurse led her into a dark room at the end of a long corridor and pulled back a curtain.

"Take a bed at the end," the nurse said, pointing.

Her eyes slowly adjusted to the dark. Shuffling forward, she nearly bumped into the guard, who watched her with narrow yellow eyes. She was able to make out about ten beds, five on each side, with various lumpy forms filling the greater part of them. A heavy snoring pervaded the room.

Taking off her sneakers (robbed of their dangerous laces), she tiptoed to the last bed and, thoroughly exhausted, she crawled in. Minutes passed. She must have fallen asleep because she was awakened by the following exchange:

Woman #1: Who be makin' that noise?
Silence.
Woman #1: I said, stop makin' so much damn noise!

Woman #2: You shut the hell up!

Woman #1: Listen, bitch…

Woman #2: Yeah, you listen!

Woman #1: No, you…you just want my man!

Woman #2: I don't need your fucking man, BITCH! I got my own man. What I need your man for? Bitch!

And so the volley continued for quite some time.

Sheltered by a towel she had centered across her face, she knew it would be impossible to get any more sleep when the bright lights were turned on and people were slamming the bathroom door right next to her head. What was she doing there? It felt as if she had been in the hospital for days.

The toilet, so close by, stank. Its flushing noises sounded unhealthy, as if signaling a clogged pipe. Fed up, she sought a walk down the hall for fresh air. The guard—a mustachioed white man of about thirty-five who was short and swinish-looking—was dozing in his chair. As she crept past him, his eyes fluttered open and his hand wrenched her shoulder back.

That was it. Or that was all it took.

She flew into a rage: foul-mouthing, kicking and punching. Attendants came out of the walls, holding her down and away from the guard who nursed his bruised shin. They left her soaking with sweat in her corner. Soon, she reached new heights of hysteria far removed from the room with the ten beds and the squabbling women and the filth and the stench.

They tried to stuff pills down her throat but they wouldn't go down. The pills were spat out somewhere in the tangle of the sheets. So she was given a shot in the arm and then tossed into a private room where she sat screaming her lungs out until her throat became sandy. So she spat up bile.

She wasn't exactly a child, but she certainly felt like one. A wronged little girl.

Finally, after two days in the emergency room, she made it upstairs. Two brawny attendants rolled her wheelchair to the third floor. They left her inside the locked doors of the psychiatric unit where the male nurse signed for her as if she were an express mail package. They took the empty wheelchair with them.

She sat in the dayroom (a large room with many tables, including one for ping-pong) where the television blared, unwatched. A nurse was supposed to come and admit her soon. While she was waiting, she surveyed the area. A few people dozed on couches. A woman in blue looked out the window at the miniature figures below on their way to work.

Shortly afterwards, there was a meeting with three doctors on staff.

"We're going to ask you some questions," one of them said. "Remember these three objects: a chair, a ball, and a tennis racquet. Now, count backwards by sevens from one hundred."

"One hundred, ninety-three, eighty-six, seventy-nine, seventy-two…"

"Who is the president of this country?"

"George W. Bush."

"Where are we?"

"The hospital."

"What are the three objects I named?"

"A ball, a chair, and a tennis racquet."

Next they asked her about the voices. She hated talking about the voices. *Auditory hallucinations.* They made her sound like someone with the makings of a serial killer. The voices never told her to do things. ("Kill so and so! Jump out the window!") They just droned on and on about what a truly horrible human being she was. ("You are disgusting and unforgivable!") Yes, she was "psychotic." Yes, she was "suicidal." She dug her nails into her palms to divert the pain the voices caused.

The winter before this hospitalization, she had seen a doctor who insisted she had to face up to her diagnosis, which at the time was schizophrenia. "You'll never hold a job," he had said. "You have to accept how ill you are."

All she wanted to do was walk down the street like a normal person: without sensing a presence chasing her or worrying that people could read her, or feeling on the verge of spouting obscenities like a street person. She felt like a character in a movie that suddenly discovers that the good guys are really bad guys and there's nowhere to turn, no one to trust.

After taking down a brief family history, they let her go. She was escorted to her room. Her roommates weren't there and she hadn't met them yet. She sank into the bare mattress of one bed, her only possessions a watch and a pair of laceless sneakers. Sun flooded the room crimson through half-closed blinds.

The television was on all day and evening, an excuse to sit and stare. One need not actually face the screen in the dayroom. Zoning out was a highly popular activity. There was always an odd sensation when they all started out the day with one of those chatty morning news programs that people watch as they piece themselves together on the way to work.

There they would sit in their hospital slippers after eating breakfast and lining up for meds. So Sue and Brad would be bantering about the weather or the hemlines for spring, while they sat there with nothing to look forward to but group therapy and more eating and then visiting hours. Real life, impossible to see from the windows, intruded through the television set.

Food was a common obsession. Filling out the menu card was an all-important event. It was one of the few areas in hospital life she had control over. The promise of plates to be uncovered two or three days down the road was like the anticipation of planning a trip abroad and of arriving at each future destination. Knowing she was going to get vanilla ice cream on Wednesday or Cheerios on Saturday was a consolation, a variation in the parade of identical days. At breakfast, she got her own tray with a thick plastic lid covering the contents so that *voila*! There was the cream of wheat and the orange juice and the roll with butter.

Her mother and father visited often. Visiting hours were spent playing games of Scrabble among sad cartons of Chinese food. The gifts of gossipy magazines, newspapers, and trashy paperbacks were distant voices from a distant world where, when it rained, you got wet. She would sit there with her parents who attempted to be lighthearted. They would all make self-conscious conversation and spy on the other patients and visitors.

There was one guy other patients called "Mr. Hollywood." He was a plastic surgeon who had responded well to shock therapy, but refused to join in any of the daily activities. During visiting hours, he sat with his two teenage sons and trophy wife looking a bit above it all. She was sure she was hearing him talk about her over most of one night. He made endless, awful fun of her the way Oscar Wilde may have teased a self-important dowager. The next day, she saw him and realized it wasn't him, though the look on his face said it was.

✳

She often requested to go into the quiet room. It was a small white soundproof chamber. If she heard voices while she was in there, she would know they weren't real. The same with an I-pod turned up high. At a certain volume, it was impossible to truly hear anything but music. Unfortunately, the voices never stopped.

Yet, suddenly, there was…Wilson!

Wilson was a *macho muchacho* from the Dominican Republic, and when the nurses weren't looking, they dove behind corners for kisses that were brief because they were scared of getting caught and sour because neither of them had toothbrushes during the first week in the hospital. His mouth tasted like a mixture of dog breath and gym socks and his tongue—as muscle-bound as the rest of him—did somersaults in her mouth like a fat acrobat.

He was handsome and she got a little carried away.

Wilson said he was *enamorado de ti como un loco* and that he wanted her love.

He ate like a Terminator, gobbling down Rice Crispies and pineapple juice and saltines and beef chunks and gobs of mashed potatoes—two plates full—and butter from the packet without bread or anything green. Then he crushed the packages before burying them in the garbage. She could tell he would be passionate in bed from the reckless way in which he ate.

They stole kisses in the hallway. The first morning after she had kissed him, he walked up to her in his black t-shirt and said, "You make me hot."

The way he said "hot" made her stomach crawl inside. She tried to explain to him that his kisses gave her vertigo, a falling feeling in her stomach, and then he told her what do you think I am, a stupid motherfucker, fist slamming down to the table, and she worried that perhaps he was very confused and not very smart. And then, it was sometimes that he just didn't understand English too well. She tried to tell him about vegetarianism and her love for animals, and he said, "That's just shit for women."

The carnal temptation between Wilson and her lurked behind every nursing station, under the dining room tables, or between the seats, as his hand touched hers or grazed her breast as he turned the pages of a magazine. She enjoyed the lust checked in place by the vigilant eyes of the nurses and doctors and attendants. It reminded her a little of Angelica and Tancredi from Di Lampedusa's *The Leopard*. They were two Italian lovers who spent their engagement chasing each other through the dusty corridors of a Sicilian mansion full of broken statues. They stole kisses in forgotten rooms. She pretended that the hospital was a dreamy Italian estate and Wilson and she, two noble lovers.

It took her a while to figure out why Wilson was in the hospital to begin with. She knew he had suffered some kind of head injury and was further victim to a battery of psychological tests. It turned out that he had been in a series of motorcycle accidents that had knocked a few screws loose and had left him with an aggressive streak. His family shunned him. The army wouldn't take him. Before his hospitalization, he tooled around part-time in a motorcycle shop.

Yet there was nothing they could share. Even her book of Octavio Paz poems showed what a distance there was between them.

She recited the poem *"Brindis"* ("Toast") from memory, and it ended with the lines *y el mantel se cubre / de miradas* (and the tablecloth's covered / with glances).

These two lines infuriated him. He saw no logic in a tablecloth being covered with glances and his frustration translated into aggression as he met his fist with the table.

At the same time, he painted nice scenes of the Dominican Republic in Art Therapy: beaches, boats, clear skies. He was very proud of his real artistic talent. Something inside of him fought for creative expression, when he really couldn't get his messages across verbally.

Art Therapy was enjoyable. This is what she liked: the greasy feel of pastels, munching through thick paper with scissors to create a collage, painting wooden boxes, and producing watercolors in which the paper puckered up and formed lakes in different places. Then there was the inevitable encouragement of the instructor, who accepted the patients' broken attempts at creating folk art masterpieces with the pride of a doting mother.

One day, about a week and a half after they had first met, she and Wilson robbed a kiss behind the nurses' station in front of her room. It was a long, thorough, searching kiss. She opened her eyes about midway through and saw that his eyes were open too and staring at her unnervingly. Edgy, she pulled away and backed into her room. Wilson followed her into the brightly lit bathroom. Just then, a male nurse crashed through the door.

"Get out!" he shouted at Wilson.

Wilson looked straight into his eyes, tossed his head back, and strolled out of the room as suavely as he could manage.

"And you!" The nurse was breathing hard now, attempting to stay calm. "You are to stay in the dayroom at all times—accompanied!"

She almost protested, but she had been caught in the act. She and Wilson were forbidden to speak to each other or stand fewer than ten feet together.

He wants to marry me, she thought.

"If I sleep with you, I'll never be afraid of anything," he said.

Several days later, a new overly made-up patient requested an apple juice from the nurse, her skin just clotted with the stuff of jars and bottles and spray cans and powder compresses. *God, Wilson is going to hit on her*, she thought with glee, though who knows why the idea pleased her. She just wanted him to betray his crush on her in her sight so that she would be able to ascertain whether he was honest or a dog.

A fellow patient named Lynn sat on her bed and revealed the truth about Wilson: he asked her to have children with him when he first walked in, he's lonely, he's sad, don't trust him, he hits on everyone except that little dumpling Lulu with the squishy limbs and braces...Lulu, who was there because her baby had died. She didn't look a day older than thirteen.

In the hallway, Wilson demonstrated his heart beating all night long for her by tugging on his t-shirt in a pinch over his chest. *Boom-boom.*

Wilson asked her if she would give him a pair of her used underwear. He said she needed to prove her love and trust in him so that he could honor and trust her. She felt a strong resistance to this unusual request. For one thing, her parents hadn't brought her anything but a supply of the most unattractive underwear to the hospital—large white cotton jobs with elastic that may have appealed to her granny, but not to her fireball of a Latin lover.

So when Wilson approached her the next day with an impassioned, "C'mon, I want them," she shied away and made some petty excuses.

*

Honestly, most of the time he disgusted and bored her. On the other hand, he was good-looking and he promised her the best time in bed ever. *Take me, Wilson, mi amor.*

Later on, she found out he used to deal cocaine. He told her that's why he had a fancy car that he'd park in front of a high school *donde estan todas las muchachas.* She also noticed how obnoxious he was when he stood criticizing everyone in Exercise and telling her how to play ping-pong. Hollering at her when she probably played better than him, anyway. Thank god she didn't give him a pair of her underpants. The passionate crush ended as quickly as it started.

She began to participate in group walks in the neighborhood. How strange it felt to be outside with a group of people so unaccustomed to fresh air and sunshine that they stumbled about in a cloud together, following the leader like a train of poodles and terriers and retrievers scrambling after an Upper East Side dog walker. What a sight they must have been walking down the street after days or weeks shut inside, navigating the sidewalks like geriatric tourists.

One woman—a fellow patient—stopped to buy a pretzel from one of those smoky stands with an umbrella near the park, and then she joined in and bought one of those giant dough-limbed yogis studded with huge grains of salt. Everything was in sharp focus, magnified by waves of anxiety kept at bay within the hospital walls. The trees looked like they were waving at her. The smell of the frigid city air was metallic and bracing. Passersby seemed to examine the group like bacteria under a microscope. She felt strangely porous and visible.

Group walks were little experiments to see if they could function in the real world. They all yearned for the walls at those times. Was what they experienced inside the walls something other than real life?

It must count as real life, even though there was no sense of time passing—no past, present, future—within the walls. Real life is something like a still life set in motion, the apples and pears and lemons ricocheting in all different directions like billiard balls. Hospital life is a painting set in a frame. Inside the hospital they were little waxy apples and moss-green pears and dimpled lemons contained within a bowl. Outside of the hospital, they were no longer part of a still life. They trespassed outside of the borders and life was fast and it constricted the lungs.

When she was depressed, there was no "real life." Just parallel universes. Little realities, little stories, everyone absorbed in the stuff of her own mess. Everyone feeling the lack of exactly the thing she needs.

Keeping her distance from Wilson, she wrote about the other people in the hospital—such as the skinhead who resisted treatment at first, shouting, "I don't want to be here with all of these Jews and Puerto Ricans!" Later on, he calmed down a bit. She caught him smooching with Wanda, the woman who sat down with one leg sticking out so that she could shake her flip-flop. Wanda's husband walked down the hallway during visiting hours, sucking on a lollypop. Apparently, as everyone learned in Women's Group, Wanda wanted a divorce from him and had for the last seven years. But he remained in love with her.

A guy named Jimmy grinned and chuckled as she walked by and sometimes he said, "Hi, honey," before collapsing into giggles. His popularity around people like Wanda and the skinhead had grown since he owned a box of Chips Ahoy cookies and was eager to share.

"Hey, Chinese man, want a cookie?" he asked.

Jean, who was Japanese, declined.

She and Jean had been having a conversation on animal rights.

"What gets me really pissed off about the animal rights movement is that they don't think about the consequences of their actions. I mean, what is going to happen to all of those cows and laboratory rats once they're freed? Who's going to take care of the cows?" Jean said.

She suggested an adopt-a-cow program or maybe partitioning off some land especially for the cows, but neither seemed like a completely satisfactory solution.

Jean asked her if she would protest the feeding of a kitten to a boa constrictor. She said yes, because kittens aren't their natural prey and Jean said too many people are taken by the cute ones, the furry animals.

We're like those cows, she thought. *Who is going to take care of us after we've been freed?*

*

She kept a diary during this stay. She would write late into the night, sitting on the floor next to the well-lit bathroom and scribbling in that piss-colored pool of light.

In her diary, she wrote: *This is my fourth hospitalization and the details of it will escape me just as those of the last three have. I just become fatter, thinner, more or less unhappy, and someday I'm going to really write…*

—ALISON OATMAN—

Since my first "nervous breakdown" at the age of eighteen—a harrowing experience of intense paranoia and unrelenting auditory hallucinations—I have been reluctant to share much about my personal history with mental illness. To tell a friend or a coworker or a potential romantic interest that I experience psychotic symptoms or that for many years my diagnosis was schizophrenia before it was renamed "anxiety and depression with psychotic features" would probably make them all run for the hills like victims in a horror movie. There is so much shame and secrecy that comes with a diagnosis that includes psychosis. People can allow for severe depression or even a bout of panic attacks, but voices? Only serial killers or other menaces to society share such scary symptoms. I wish I could explain that I have never tried to harm anyone or had thoughts that told me to. And the medications I have been taking for the last fifteen years have helped enormously. Even so, I am careful to hide the bottles.

Robert Fagan

CENSUS

I

I can try to count the creatures here. Perhaps a human or two. Surely myself as, well, not quite human. Neither fish nor fowl. The fish, the fowl, and the frog have a job here, sitting on these papers. But they hector, they lecture, they chide me for not writing the truth. The fowl is more like a baby bird, with a wide open mouth that chirps whenever I use the wrong word. Sometimes it ceases communication, suspecting I'm a human, though I am in my way a four-legged creature. And the fish is really a smooth dark stone and stares stony at me, knowing I can't say what I need to say. The frog moves by leaps and bounds whenever words start racing along, but I can't keep up with it, nor the rat, nor the cat chasing the rat. I'm silent and still, like the fellow at the side of my desk who leans over and reads every word. Or doesn't read every word, for most of the time his two light-bulb eyes are off. I can feel a twinge of pain from his bent wooden neck. But nothing compared to the lady behind him whose purple papier-mâché face is always pulled open in a scream. Or is it oral sex she wants? I have flirted a little I admit. But can I count her in my census? And the crowd behind her? And there's another painful her who's been somewhere about. Can I count her still? How many of us are here?

A bit of light from above sometimes flickers over the face of a rat, but usually they're too quick to count. The other group is the opposite of the rats, too slow to count. They surround me. They have no motors or muscles, so they shouldn't move, but they do. Or, no doubt, she moves them. But they're slower than chess pieces. The gentleman who's near my desk now, and is my reader, once stood near the door to the bedroom, as though he were the night watchman or Charon or somebody. How many years did it take him to cross this vast room just to read these words?

He's a strange creature, they all are. A little plastic and padding and a two-foot rubber penis is the best he can do for flesh. Yet he looks like a man and certainly seems akin to me. So I call such a creature a man-a-kin. In any case they're bad company, hiding in corners or staring at me from around columns, unwilling to be counted. What a terrible time Herod must have had.

Maybe they're ashamed of their spiky or inflated underwear that rarely covers their extra limbs, breasts, and genitals. They're encrusted with paint, newspapers, feathers, and God knows what, and weighed down with nuts and bolts, knives, stones, and light bulbs that sometimes flicker on as though one of them has had an idea. Like me, they fail to live in this dark room where high walls covered with big black paintings dwarf us, and a jungle of rusty pipes hovers above us, and countless closely spaced wooden columns are like a forest that we're lost in.

There's not a stick of furniture except this big Victorian desk and Gothic chair where I sit all day writing in the insufficient light of an ancient lamp that barely illuminates the page or the dirty floor or a stalking creature. Even more useless are the three little windows high above me, so dark now that they seem to be taking everything in the world into them like a black hole.

This enormous labyrinthine room is not what I wanted. I could settle for a corner, a closet, a cupboard, a coffin even. Any cranny where I can totter between desk and bed without agitation, agoraphobia, or exhaustion. Just lifting my crutches and puffing myself up has a certain cosmic excitement, like Archimedes' boast, "Give me a lever and I'll move the world." My boast, "Give me two crutches and I'll move myself enough to please Parmenides."

Until a few months or years ago, I lived in a little room in an SRO where getting from desk to bed didn't amount to more than falling into bed. In those days I was more nimble. Often I would stand on a corner with cap in hand, obstructing a hurrying public who sometimes paused when I splayed out my crutches, and sometimes even rewarded me with a curse or a quarter.

Not that I desperately needed the money. The government (SSI, SOS, OUT, MED) paid for my room with enough left over to purchase my yearly pair of socks, blue T-shirt, and Fruit of the Loom briefs, plus food stamps to provide many a portion of rice and beans, not to mention the occasional box of doughnuts. That was my biggest decision in life: sugared? brown? cinnamon? jellied? chocolate? glazed? I would peer at each obscene swelling circle with ever-growing gluttony, knowing full well my passion would be relieved, a consummation so unlike sexual cravings, when one dreams of an appropriate place for one's penis and then pokes and strokes and pulls and batters and squeezes the poor little thing thousands of times in transports of joy or rage. Or worse, when one has a rare real encounter with a woman or man or somebody of nondescript sex or a creature at least, when one is startled but otherwise disappointed and resolves to go back to one's solitary efforts, even though these are nothing compared to the satisfaction of a box of doughnuts.

Satisfaction? Never. Choosing one kind of doughnut and thus depriving oneself of the other kinds was always too painful. So I invariably chose the mixed assortment and arrived home full of gluttony and nibbled away at a sugar doughnut then cinnamon then sugar then cinnamon… until I always arrived at the same sorry place, staring at the rest of the assortment: four boring brown doughnuts.

I wonder if I had a choice in coming here. It wasn't entirely a kidnapping. There were various enticements after that fatal meeting in a bar. But who do I count now? Creatures? Manikins? Ghosts? How can I not count the woman I call the Ratcatcher? (When her face is streaked with colors I call her the Painter and when she brings me food I call her the Cook.) It's hard not to count the manikins, they are the only two-legged things here. But the rats may be the true majority. And must I count the cats? Or is it just one cat instead of many similar cats? I've never seen two cats romping with each other. And yet there have been times when I've heard a distant impassioned meow—as of a cat caught in a rat trap or making love to another cat or complaining of its existence or mourning its mistress—and then I've looked about and seen two angry eyes nearer to me than where the sound seemed to come from.

If only the cat were more docile, I could catch it and kill it, and then if I saw another cat I would know there had been more than one. However, if I killed the cat and never saw a cat again, I could never be sure there was not another or a band of cats or a coven or yowl or pack (that sounds right) wisely staying away from me in the next enormous room (her studio) or in the countless little rooms that attach themselves to the big rooms.

But I've omitted something, something important. I guess it will always now elude me, and thus elude you, reader. I'm wrong. You, having access to the printed page where this no doubt will appear—since strangely these vagrant thoughts often show up a year later in tiny magazines with tiny names such as Blurb or Blob—you can thumb your way back to prior pages and see exactly where I was going with my careful analysis or anguished revelation or patent subterfuge. While I cannot, since these tiny pages filled with strangely entwined miniscule creatures (oh's and I's and you's and why's) get thrown together into one big heap or ten big heaps, which are guarded by the fish, frog, and bird until they're carted away by the Ratcatcher—who no doubt carefully deciphers and types them and sends them off to wherever magazines exist. Though I have seen a shadow of a secretary, I don't doubt it is the Ratcatcher who performs most of this service, which may be just clerical or perhaps editorial or even authorial, I don't know, since when I finally see the words in print I can't remember whether they are the same or altered or entirely different. But I do presume that it is she who shuffles these papers around, since she performs every service for me, whether it be confronting me with a *maigret de canard* or a *daube de mouton*, or scrubbing my back and other bits of me in my weekly immersion in the big black bathtub, or placing my member carefully in what is apparently the appropriate place, or saying, "Do you love me?" and coaching me on the appropriate answer.

If only I could say how I got here and how many are here now. A few minutes ago I think I was close to saying something impossible that would free me. Oh, my God, yes I remember that I've forgotten to try to remember what I've forgotten. It must be…No, I can't. I'll put it this way: It must have been about a change in population here, or about what the cat knows. It must be…Reader, you're no help. You were supposed to go back to where I found out that if I killed the cat and no other cat appeared I would not be much the wiser. But in my hubris I insisted that if another cat did appear I would know there had been more than one. False, utterly false. There is no reason to think that the second cat was a simultaneous cat and not a replacement for the old one. Still, reader, we are making progress. Perhaps the census will work?

II

Maybe I can't bring myself to kill the cat. Lately he's been lonely and thus friendly. I've been giving him my meals. If the cat became my friend, I would never be able to kill him and then I would never see or not see a second cat. Unless, of course, I'm already seeing two cats. Perhaps one is my friend and one my enemy. Perhaps I feed my enemy and not my friend. And yet he stays my friend. The Ratcatcher fed me. But am I her enemy? My experience with women is piddling. I remember vividly only one. She was the, not wife, but what do they say now? I know, insignificant other, of an old, I almost said friend. Yes, he was definitely someone who walked with me at my tortoise pace from brick building to brick building in that institution I inhabited before my body and mind became more infirm or lazy or honest. It was a place of liar learning on a hill overlooking a city of shootings, knifings, or just injections with old bent needles, as I for a while was known to do.

But that stumble toward a career was several years, no, decades ago, when I declared property was thrift, no, theft, and sat with dangerous revolutionaries, no, graduate students, in one of the brick buildings, and then waited as one properteer after another was "elected" president of colleges, corporations, and above all, country, though I cannot make myself say the name, just as I can't say the name of the insignificant other though even now eli…enn…sometimes reaches my tongue and I have to bite down hard and try and forget to remember what I forgot, for it is a name not said since he said, "Why have you done this?" and I did not say "Because I'm a rat," or "Because I'm a psychopath," or "Because I needed to find an appropriate place for my penis," or even "Because I love her," the most convenient excuse. But I broke from her and ran out of that bedroom with a speed impossible for me. But too late, he now knew something about her, me, us, himself, humanity, so that she and he unleashed each other, but not to me, for I went to a place I never left, until the Ratcatcher rescued me, as her friends say. Such a euphemism.

But I'm getting off the track. I must find out whether I have a friend in the cat and how many cats and ghosts and other things are here or not here in this vast space. But you, reader, may know better, having access to Part I of this insidious scribble, for I remember that there I expatiated on what the cat remembers and what I will not remember. Though I'm not sure if you have a right to know these things, reader, raider of my mind.

In any case I'm stuck here crippled, crumpled, hand in cap, handicapped, disabled, unable to move significantly, as perhaps you, reader, even you, moving about blithely in your vast and varied world may sometimes hesitate a bit or even be unable to take a step. Do you ever stop suddenly and stay stopped? The R
atcatcher likes to make the manikins move, likes to make everything move, even me. I know there was a time when I was only driven to this loft for weekend bacchanals. And in those days I scratched and bit to keep myself free. But she hunted me, oh, she hunted me. I know I was a rat, but it didn't matter, she hunted me.

Yes, there was a time when I wasn't trapped here, was just a visitor, and knew the city or its suburbs, or at least glimpsed a few squat buildings from the grimy windows of her car. Maybe I even had an idea of what was outside this loft. She tells me many a tale of this. That there is a truck-loading platform or a bordello or a cathedral. But I have yet to hear the sound of a motor revving through these thick walls. There is a hum, a steady omnipresent hummm, which tells me I am in a city with its crowded thoroughfares or on a beach near an incessant ocean or in a deserted dynamo or that I hum to myself continuously. They say the universe has background noise too. It's all left over from the big bang. We're all left over.

It doesn't matter just so long as I can get to know this vast space and its inhabitants. But the terrain here is dangerous. One must make one's way through the manikins and the columns, always on the lookout for loose wires, outstretched arms, rat traps, creeping cats. Still, I could venture forth to corners and crannies or even other rooms. Slowly I would wend my way, head bent as always, over the sagging floor, past column after column, embraced here and there by manikins whose jutting nails and knives would wound me and whose light bulbs would flash blindingly in my face, forcing an intimacy with their ravaged faces. And then, though tired and bleeding, I might force myself even further and sneak into her studio, breaking every taboo of this spectral society of two strangers who somehow became hopelessly entangled.

Yes, we met or rather stumbled against each other and fell in a snarling snarl in a dark place of libations. It was my undoing. Man is a social creature and woman too. For many months I had resolved to have an outing. And one night I slid my way across my bed to my crutches and elevated myself into the air and slowly moved forward on the axle of my crutches and landed on the ground, solid terra firma, always a relief. This was only the first step, but I will spare the reader enumeration of the next ten thousand and only say that I hazarded myself again and again into the air and forward, always forward, only because I could not go backward, often as I tried I would only stay still like a stone, so forward to the door of my room, to the old cranky elevator, to the dark street, to the dark place of surprising assignation.

(I'm so tired of this sad snail of a narrator, so unlike my athletic optimistic self. Yet I need him. And the voice too. Not my voice, of course, but the voice of the old Irishman, the saddest voice I could find. Though perhaps I should try mimicking Hemingway or *Time Magazine* or the Census Taker being wonderfully objective. But it's useless, reader, for I will never be able to tell you, or me, what's important.)

The times we had, the two of us, she of the hefty hips and pendulous breasts in her black skimpy array and myself nude or wearing white athletic socks, ensconced in the little bed after a bottle of Medoc or Chateauneuf du Pape and a taste of pigeons with all their brittle little bones, watching the small but bright screen, reminiscing of those we knew of old, Bela and Boris and the lesser dark hooded figures, not to mention the ones in the sun, weathered by the wind, John Wayne and Randolph Scott and Gary Cooper, you see I know many a name, I have browsed through the flicks and the books, especially Myra Breckinridge and Geoffrey O'Brien, and can tell from afar the lanky frame of Rosalind Russell striding across the screen, or the naïve numinous smile of Ann Sheridan saying we're all human and thus should be happy even though we're not, and the other ancient women who inhabit our bed when she gets serious and snaps her bra at me or worse, insists that I need a massage and tries to unravel the question mark of my body, and then gets excited and grinds and grinds me into little pieces of muscle and inflamed skin, or twists me into every possible shape that fits in and around her, the two of us like protean pretzels, until finally she finishes thumping and shaking and milking me and I can go to sleep.

Sleep sometimes happens to me and I am grateful, though I always suspect I will not wake up, and that possibility makes me uneasy and expectant and hopeful and afraid, but never comfortable, for the mattress pushes against every inch of me, so that bits and pieces of me are almost trapped and it is an effort to turn to another side or onto my belly, the latter rarely, since the mattress smothers me, which is enticing, except that I know I will come UP for air.

But many a night I am lucky and fall asleep. Fall, what a fearful metaphorical use of an already frightening verb. Falling, not having to parade words into meaning, world into shape, myself into self, but swirling among the forgotten or the dead: my drowned brother still swimming over the ocean, my lost sister doing incredible things with her ten-thousandth trick, my drunk old dad undoing his belt for my fourth walloping of the day, then going off to war and certain doom, while back at home my old mom leans over my cradle watching for any sign of sinful tumescence. But not just people, oh no, things catch up with you, all the crinkled and shrunken images of every bed, table, broomstick, basketball or bush I have ever seen, now reappearing malevolently. Just as well I fall asleep never fully, always fitfully.

Fitfully, what a mad word. The sharp puff of the first syllable, and the sad hesitant fatness of the second, the foolish flutters of the Ps, disappearing in the endless echo of the final nautical syllable, leeeee. Is each word an aleph or only a few like *fitfully*? Like just now when the snow completely covered my three small windows and I reached out for the light and the light was there and I pulled the old metal cord and was illuminated. Just as when she shaves me with a malicious little electric razor, and I can feel a face appear. Just as when she presents me with some French thing to taste and I find I have not tasted anything like it ever. It is as though there is so much, so rich, so strange, so real. Sometimes I think that, yes, I would want to stay here, even alone in this vast space.

III

A rat is shamelessly scampering across the floor. But I won't even bang my crutches. I must stay immobile at my desk, working, not remembering what is not. There is a Borges-like story I must finish. It shows how the scriveners began to sneak fiction into the holy texts. And I haven't convincingly explained how the dwarf escaped from the circus to become Godiva's pimp. Perhaps these stories are less real than the cat. When he comes, the rats disappear. He likes to play with a little blue ball. He brings it tantalizingly near me, often near enough for me to reach down and grab at it and sometimes even manage to get it, which costs me a few scratches, for he never makes it easy, as delighted as he is to have me capture the ball and wave it around and throw it through the columns and the manikins to the furthest corners of the room where he disappears.

This is unlike his usual somnolent ways, when he crawls under the desk and immobilizes my feet for hours at a time, or worse, at night when he pushes his claws deep into the mattress, stapling himself into the bed, making himself an immovable object that my body must writhe around all night, often careening into the Ratcatcher's body, whose arms even in sleep are always ready to clamp around me, stiffing me and making it impossible for me to reach under the bed for the potty without waking them up and causing a caterwauling of complaints from both. So I'm better off at my desk, lost in these sentences, and always thinking of you, reader, rider of my words, for without you I might in fact feel lonely or useless or even sad.

But I have another audience. Several manikins are looking over my shoulder, grimacing at what I'm writing. They make me doubt the words. And they are always complaining about the vicissitudes of living. Right now they seem bowed down as if sadder than usual. Yesterday I had a long conversation with one who stands shamelessly before my desk. She has big pink balloon breasts and an emaciated metal body. She told me life is artificial and humans are a mistake, unlike her everlasting voluptuousness. I wanted to continue the conversation today and looked for her, but she was gone. Each day a manikin disappears. The population keeps decreasing here. Only the rats increase.

I must finish this pernicious piece. But the difficulties of keeping these papers on my desk are immense. My feckless paperweights, fish, frog, and fowl, often abandon me to gossip among themselves. And my breath is always stirring the papers, making them move across the desk and take off into the air and land far away, lost to me unless I lower my body out of my chair onto the splintery floor and pull myself every which way till I find a paper, usually not the one I am looking for but one that is ancient and strange, that does not fit in. There is one under the claw foot of the desk. By reaching down very carefully and putting my fingers against the...

> *Even though she is unwell she smiles often at me, somehow finding me amusing. And she says strange things like "You promised the worst, but you failed," or "You are my crooked angel, without you my paintings would be dark and the mannequins dead."*

I must bury this in a pile. And I must not let the piles blow away and give me more surprises. Frog, you must help me with this last heap of papers. Who do I care for most, the Eskimo bird, the Mexican frog, or the green stone that pretends to be a fish? It has marks on it, little lines that make letters. I spend hours staring at these even though I know I will never be able to read them, even though I know no one ever wrote them. Still, I can almost hear them, as I can almost hear the squeak of the baby bird chiding me in Aztec or Eskimo. And can I depend on the frog? It often rebels and jumps off and flies into the air and the papers fly into the air and I fly into the air to catch them and put them in the wrong order, and you, the reader, suffer. And even when the paperweights do their job, it is impossible to decide what makes a pile, what makes a paragraph, what makes a work of art.

(It doesn't matter just so long as it goes on, or another story begins, perhaps more suicides or deathbed soirees; no, better a story the opposite of this one, with a lively athletic optimist instead of the dreary cripple of this piece, who is so unlike me and so repugnant to me, yet who I needed to express the…no. The other story may help.)

Throughout a libidinous life, the athletic optimist seduces countless young women but ends up taking care of an old lady who he realizes he has been in love with all his life. He hadn't known it, this love, till it was too late. Oh, no, not too late, almost too late. He must have time, a bit of time, to prove himself to her. He can finally be happy in a world where man and woman and beast, oh yes, beast. The cat has been running madly from room to room, losing his struggle to keep down the population of rats, often getting sidetracked by sniffing at her paint rags, her potholders, her underwear. Now, suddenly, he's jumped up on the desk and is staring at me. He stares, she stares, for they were always confederates. I can't not finally end this endless prevarication and admit that in the census half the population is gone, if you look at it in human terms. I'm free now. I can go back to my little room soon. Meanwhile, there's been a hullabaloo and talk of wakes, elegies, retrospectives; and all kinds of slick characters intruding themselves, even with lights and cameras that make the space less vast and make the black paintings not at all black and make the manikins seem dead.

There was even some hullabaloo about me. The *New York Times* ended its obituary by saying she is survived by her longtime companion, the author of the collections of stories, *Lost Cities, Found Objects* and *Peaceable Kingdoms*. Worst of all there was talk about sending me to a nursing home, friends not of mine intimating in whispers and sympathetic murmurs that after twelve years with her I was no longer fit to live on my own, as though I were ever fit to live on my own, as though I could not be by myself finally, to be the self I am whoever that is, to sit at my tiny unVictorian desk and scribble, unbothered, unencumbered, and able easily enough to empty my own potty, merely by lowering myself to the ground and pulling myself across the floor, pushing it carefully ahead, not letting a drop spill, and carefully pouring it down the sink and cramming what little solid matter there is down the sink and carefully rinsing it out, not to mention crossing the street to the supermarket and buying boxes of doughnuts every time, for I am told now I can afford anything I want, I am the inheritor of a vast and varied artistic patrimony or matrimony, and a vast oeuvre of hers, to sort out they say, but I have things to sort out myself in my tiny room, even perhaps someday some versions of how I got trapped for so long in this vast space. A faded hand, the last remnant of a last manikin, is stuck to a pillar. Its stained wooden fingers are pointing the way out.

(I'm free now. I've finished with her, whoever she was. Now I can shuck the crippled narrator and write about the optimistic athlete and the lecherous dwarf and the blind ornithologist and the trapped pederast and the gothic novelist who leads a gothic life. I just have to be careful that the wrong words don't start running across the page.)

But the cat knows. The car mourns. He stares at me for hours. And when I rise and walk, he weaves around my crutches, trying to be my companion. And when we go to bed he stretches and stretches his legs, trying to fill the empty bed.

> *But the bed groans. Something has fallen forward upon her. It's him. She fell backward upon the floor, entangling him. And he groaned, moved, rolled, righted himself, sat gracefully in the sawdust and held out his hand. And said, "It's too crowded here, but have a drink with me. I know a passable rotgut, no, a deep and delightful Bordeaux (what am I saying?), for you are the best body in the world, you who fell backward under me and never got up. I touched your coldhard breasts. I even..."*

I've done it now. I've managed for a month to almost write so many colorful convoluted stories of how the hierophants outlawed the scriveners or how the athlete ravaged Melissa's dead bod, until just now I fell into the wrong story—and it may take all the years I have left to get out of it.

—ROBERT FAGAN—

I knew Robert Fagan for most of my adult life. He used crutches to get around after catching polio as a young man and spending a year or more in an iron lung. In his poem "My Life," he writes of this experience:

A psychiatrist put his finger
over the hole in my throat
and I discovered I could talk.
She and I whispered together
how I could die
without getting her in trouble
and then I started to get better.

The boy across from me had been there for years
never moving
                barely breathing
while I shot down the aisle
my wheelchair moving eighty miles an hour.
God, I was free
            I was a cripple.

Robert received his PHD in English from Columbia University and made his living as a freelance writer and scholar. He helped countless writers improve their works, He wrote poetry, fiction, and critical essays on topics as diverse as Paleolithic art to the world of Jorge Luis Borges. The poet and critic Geoffrey O'Brien writes: "Robert Fagan's writing has long been a secret resource for those lucky enough to encounter it…formally playful, compassionate, and clear-eyed, informed by an extraordinary range of traditions and histories, and suffused with a sublime humor that never shies from the harshest implications of human experience."

Robert died of complications of post-polio syndrome in 2009. His friends have never ceased to miss his extraordinary gifts as a conversationalist. As his obituary states: "Conversation with him was an unending delight, a voyage of discovery with a continual frisson of ideas and insights. The world will be a duller place without Robert to observe, comment, and make deeper sense of it for us." His writing—not as acknowledged as it deserves to be—is equally dazzling.

—Sheila Black

Lisa Gill

HOLDING ZENO'S SUITCASE
IN KANSAS, FLOWERING

Emma is standing on the side of the highway holding a postcard in one hand and one of her mother's old flowered suitcases in the other. The postcard is from her sister, shows a picture of the Grand Canyon, and is signed *Love, Carolyn*. Emma would have put the postcard in her suitcase, binding it with all the others, except that she almost forgot it, almost left the orange canyon decorating the white lace doily on her nightstand. She only remembered the card after she had already packed and sealed her bag. The zipper on the case is broken and so when she closes it, she uses duct tape. It isn't the ideal form of luggage and Emma tires sometimes of scrubbing sticky gray glue from the blue and yellow flowered vinyl. Emma is sure that her sister would not use such makeshift traveling gear. Carolyn has been many places across the country. She must pack and unpack frequently, in many hotels, in many states. Emma has in her bag some fifty odd picture postcards Carolyn has sent, all postmarked from different cities and towns.

Each time Emma receives a postcard from her sister, she puts it in her suitcase with the others, binding them with a length of yellow ribbon she wore in her hair to be confirmed. All afternoon, as she works the dough, hangs the wash to dry, cleans the three-bedroom house until there is nothing left to be cleaned, Emma thinks of what she will tell her sister in her letter:

> *Here, in Kansas, it has been the kind of wind that puts rats in your hair as soon as you walk outside, no matter how well you brushed it...And mother's canary, squawking up such a storm, that I covered the cage today just so I could hear myself read your postcard...And one of the slats on the barn door fell off, and I almost got another rusty nail in my foot like when I was ten... Garden is real pretty, have all these extra tomatoes...*

Thinking of what she will tell her sister when she sits down to write her, Emma's chores get done as if by somebody else. Postcard days always seem so much fuller than the other days.

Standing next to the highway now, Emma likes having postcards in her bag, the Grand Canyon in her hand. She can almost imagine the time her sister spends standing in front of a wire rack, looking amongst all those different pictures, some horizontal, some vertical, some with words over photos, some just pretty pictures. And Carolyn turning and turning the rack, saying, "Which one for my sister?" Emma wants to tell her sister: "Thank you for bringing me these places."

Sometimes, the postcards seem like an itinerary. After receiving a postcard, Emma used to pour over the pull-out maps inside *National Geographic.* The magazines were stacked on the coffee table until her mother decided to put them in a box in her closet. Emma would interrupt her darning to spread the map over the coffee table, to look for her sister, look for the lines that really go places, especially lines which lead right off the edge of the map.

Sometimes Emma would mark a point on one of the lines to show where she was. Even though the map usually wasn't labeled Kansas, she would pretend that she was at point A. Then she would put her sister some distance across the map at point B. Emma would take some of her thread, unwind it and place it on the line that leads from A to B. She would diligently make that thread follow every curve until she reached her sister and she would snip there. Holding the thread up, letting it hang down in a straight line, it inevitably seemed like such a long map distance. Emma would hold the two ends of the measured thread together and cut where the fold indicated half. She would take one of those halves, place it on the map to see how far half would get her, what the nearest town to the middle point would be. She would lift the thread again, fold and cut. Fold and cut. When the thread could no longer be folded, she would just cut. And, if her mother didn't interrupt and tell her to go back to her darning, Emma would cut that thread in half until there was nothing left but a stub of cotton no bigger than point A on the map. And then, her mother would say, "Clean up and do your darning."

When her mother took the maps away, Emma didn't really get angry because although she liked gaining a sense of distance and direction from the lines on the maps, she considered the places in the magazines far too exotic. Most of the maps didn't even show Kansas. The places on the postcards, however, Emma knows her sister has seen, so she knows that they exist and can therefore be reached.

Emma can practically see herself standing in the photographs, although at this point she is just standing on the gravely shoulder which marks the transition between corn and highway. Emma knows where she is and she knows she should start walking because standing on the side of a two-line highway in the middle of Kansas in the middle of the night isn't going to get her anywhere: no one will pick her up until the morning. She remains standing partly because she hasn't decided which direction on the road to follow, partly because she is leaving. She is leaving for good, leaving as Carolyn did so many years ago, as her sister left without telling anyone she was going, not even telling Emma good-bye. Carolyn wrote, of course, right away, sending letters to her parents and postcards to her sister.

Every time Emma receives a postcard from her sister, she reads it. She reads it over and over all day long until she knows it by heart, words and picture, then she binds it with the others. Sometimes, reading her sister's postcards, she feels older, has to sit in the rocker, drape a shawl over her legs. Those days, her mother ends up calling out for her tea, asks why the dinner is late, asks where the butter is that should have been placed on the table.

In the evenings of the days Emma has received postcards from her sister, she pulls out the fading cardboard box with her old school supplies. When Emma got pulled out of eighth grade, the box was relegated to the cellar where it remained dormant for more than a decade. Only a few years ago did she remember the supplies ever existed: paper and pencils, her fountain pen and readers. The day she rediscovered these belongings, the accumulation of dust and sallow discoloration of the paper seemed frightening, almost inaccurate, yet loving in the remembering.

These days, Emma sits down with this paper at the kitchen table to write to her sister:

> *Dear Carolyn,*
> *Thank you for the picture postcard. I have never been there.*

And that is as far as Emma gets. She sits at the table and looks at the space beneath that one ink line, and she doesn't know what to say to her sister. Fountain pen in hand, the beginning of a letter in front of her, Emma wonders why she can't put the pen on paper, put one word in front of the other, and get from the top of the page to the bottom. Carolyn fills many a postcard to Emma. Emma remembers how all day she thought of what she wanted to say to her sister, how she so much wanted to write a letter to her sister. She takes a new piece of paper, starts over:

Dear Carolyn,
    Thank you for the picture postcard. I have never been there.

Emma manages only one line, the same line. The paper is even ruled, not like the stationery of her mother's which is pastel-colored and doesn't have any lines. This paper, this old manila school paper, should make it easier for Emma to write to her sister, as if the green lines were obligated to show her where to go in her letter. Emma's handwriting is fair, and she should be able to stay on the line.

The line on the highway is yellow and leaves Kansas, just as Carolyn left, as Emma is leaving, streaking out in the middle of the night. Emma feels that she is leaving more than her sister left, if only because more time has passed, almost two decades. Only yesterday, her mother said, "You are not like Carolyn."

For a moment Emma tries to give herself memory of place, in hopes of being able to leave it, making a goodbye, creating a parting like creating gaps in memory. And she tries to think of the good things, to let them go, so she will not remain snagged as if on a tree, perhaps the willow by the stream where she carved her initials, E.R.M. That tree caught her up while she was playing tag with her sister. Calling out to Carolyn to wait up, she had pulled herself free of the tree's limbs and the brambles beneath it and had not realized how ensnared she was until she had already torn her blouse and cut her shoulder. How it had hurt as her sister came running, Emma sitting on the ground, tears streaking her dirty cheeks, and her sister laughing, taunting, "Catch me." And then, "What's wrong?"

Standing on the shoulder of the road, Emma knows that tree as well as if it were growing in front of her between the yellow lines on the highway, as if she could split it open, count and measure the rings, demarcate each drought and flood, the good years, the rough ones. This night she thinks of the tree, the one at the edge of the property and she knows that the tree refuses the darkness and maintains a pale shade of lime gray at night.

Emma purses her lips and readjusts the suitcase in her hand. She looks down the highway as far as the darkness will allow her but is pulled back to images of the house as if by gravity.

Earlier this evening, at the dinner table with its four place settings, her mother had looked at the empty chair, turned to Emma exasperated and said, "Emma, where is that sister of yours? She ought to know by now…"

Emma stopped her mother mid-sentence, "The Grand Canyon."

Her mother turned to stare at the plate and after a moment shook her head, "I was just saying, your sister ought to know by now to keep in better touch." Emma watched her mother butter a slice of bread. Her mother's lips tightened into two thin lines. She put her knife down and said, "The Grand Canyon? Did you receive a card from that sister of yours today? Emma Rae, don't you think your father and I might enjoy hearing how Carolyn is doing."

Emma lifted herself from the table, placed the stenciled cloth napkin next to her plate and went to get the card.

She showed her parents the picture of the Grand Canyon, but she didn't tell them that she was leaving or where she was going.

Emma is leaving her father to his diminishing land and the back wall of the barn pasted with pin-ups. She is leaving her mother to her family's silver set, all the medications, the chipped bone china and her aging canary. Because she is leaving, moving so drastically and finally, she has the right, Emma might even say, an obligation, to stand still—only yesterday her mother said, "You are not like Carolyn—ungrateful." Emma consciously stands still with her suitcase in her hand, offering a little of her time as one might offer a moment of silence for the dead.

For this moment she thinks she should survey the whole land, the scattered houses: her own with the paint peeling, the crooked porch, the wilting garden. Maybe she will tell her sister of all the changes, all the lack of changes. So these things she surveys in great detail and Emma absorbs everything despite the darkness, which prevents her from seeing anything except silhouettes and shadowy outlines. For almost forty years she has lived in this place. She has taken care of her mother and the house since her mother's first breakdown when Emma was eleven. She has darned her father's socks, made lunches for him to carry out of the house, stuffed him with potatoes and cornbread. She has avoided his drunken stupors, avoided the barn. She has made tea and baked sweet pastries for occasions when she covers the birdcage with a dark towel to hush the canary while the parson or doctor visits.

After all of this, Emma does not need to see anything in order to see everything. The images are embossed so heavily on her mind's eye that sometimes she doubts whether any other place would be different. But she has the postcards with pictures of all those places that do not look like Kansas, and the postcards are signed, *Love, Carolyn*, and the postmark on the back of each card proves that she is not in Kansas. Emma wants to tell her sister: "Thank you for bringing me places to look at."

Time has a way of getting by Emma, of slipping around her as she sits with her sister's postcards. Her mother asks, "Where is the butter?" Her mother asks this question knowing full well that in the fridge, sitting on the bottom shelf, is an oblong square of butter on a saucer that could have been picked up by anyone on their way to the dinner table.

Even the yellow dashes on the highway begin to look like butter to a person who is thinking about butter. Emma would like to tell her mother that all the butter a family can eat in a lifetime is lining the highway. She might even like to tell her mother that the forgotten butter is being eaten by Carolyn on the back of the postcard with the picture of the Statue of Liberty. All sorts of things are eaten or visited or seen and done on the backs of Carolyn's postcards. If Emma were just to read the words on the backs of her sister's cards, especially the cards from the East, if just anyone were to look at the backs of the cards like the one with the picture of the Statue of Liberty—

> *Dearest Emma,*
> *Today I saw the Statue of Liberty,*
> *Went to an art museum,*
> *Ate crayfish with butter sauce,*
> *Saw Les Miserables on stage,*
> *Bought you this postcard*
> *From an old woman*
> *Sitting on the pavement*
> *Outside of my Hotel.*
> *Love, Carolyn*

—the letters would resemble nothing greater than Emma's own list of things to do in Lawrence—

> *Things to do in town:*
> *Buy butter,*
> *Pick up black thread,*
> *Fill mother's prescriptions*
> *At the pharmacy on Main,*
> *Choose a better chamomile tea*
> *Than the last blend*
> *Which turned mother's*
> *Stomach.*

Emma knows that her sister's letters would not really help her with her errands in Lawrence. Sometimes though, as she stands next to the highway which leads there, she likes to imagine carrying a postcard instead of a shopping list to town, going to the art museum to buy butter, unweaving lengths of black thread from the tablecloth under the plate of crayfish, filling her mother's prescription at the theater, gathering leaves of chamomile from an old woman's hair. If Emma wasn't so pressed for time, if she didn't know how much she needed to get moving, she might laugh out loud. She might smile so wide that no one passing by on the highway could misunderstand the wealth of communication between Emma and her sister.

Feeling the Grand Canyon in her hand, Emma would like to be able to tell someone that her sister writes less impersonal letters when she is not writing from those places on the right side of the map where there are practically as many dots and lines as stars in the sky. If there was someone walking down the highway just now, Emma would hold out the card as proof:

> *Dearest Emma,*
> *I went to the Grand Canyon,*
> *Walked all the way down*
> *Bright Angel Trail.*
> *Mules carried my bags*
> *Kind of like that boy*
> *With freckles used to do*
> *When I was in fifth grade*
> *And you were in seventh.*
> *Love, Carolyn*

Emma knows that Carolyn, with the writing on the back of each postcard, is telling her more than what the words say, offering more than a list of what she is doing and where she is doing it. Reading is not a matter of simply deciphering the meaning of inky shapes on cardstock. Because Carolyn is her sister, Emma reads into and beyond the letters and tries to hear her sister's voice as it must sound in the place that is shown on the postcard. When Emma read today's postcard from the Grand Canyon, she imagined her sister standing, bare feet spread slightly for balance, standing at the very spot where the crack in the earth opens wide as a great mouth—her sister there, with her blond hair loose on the wind, her hands outstretched, her voice thick and rusty as the color of the canyons, etching into the rock walls a message to Emma, like letters written in dirt with a stick when they were girls, beginning when the sun rises with *Dearest Emma,* and not closing the letter until sunset with *Love, Carolyn.*

Every time Emma receives a postcard from her sister, her mother says, "Emma, don't you think your father and I might also enjoy hearing how Carolyn is doing?" Next to the highway, Emma thinks of all the times she has been asked to share her sister but doesn't feel she should have to. If Carolyn had wanted Emma to share the card, she would have written something between the *a* of Emma and the comma, like "Dear Emma and your parents," or "Dear Emma and Miranda and Bill." Emma could hug those commas.

The frame around Emma's window is shaped like a big postcard flipped on end. Sometimes in the winter Emma writes pretend letters in the frost on the window panes:

> *Carolyn,*
> *My Finger*
> *Is*
> *As Cold*
> *As*
> *I Miss*
> *You.*
> *Luv, Emma*

Paint is peeling from the yellow frame of the window, peeling in the places where Emma has crawled out at night, night after night, the places where she has crawled back in. Those bare patches on her window are hers: they belong to Emma. No one else, not even Carolyn, could look at the weathered window ledge and say: "That must be where Emma's fingers were, where she slid out on her butt, spreading the curtains carefully so her suitcase could break free of this house."

Now, standing a mile from the house, Emma knows those patches where the paint is especially barren. She thinks perhaps she could leave, leave her presence—or her absence—marked there permanently until the house should burn down or be repainted. Sometimes Emma thinks she will never be able to really leave until all the paint has finished peeling, so that the rectangular frame of the window is worn smooth as the glossy side of a postcard. Then, Emma might be able to slip out and go away for good.

She could do it once the window was all slicked up, as if the frame had been greased with butter like Emma had to grease those guardrails on the footbridge to get Carolyn's head unstuck. And then her mother had asked, "Emma, why are your sister's ears so red and why is she all greasy? Give her a bath." Then her mother had asked, "Emma, where is the butter?"

Emma rests her suitcase on the gravel. This is a spot she knows as well as the window frame. With her back to the house, the two ends of the road stretch in opposite directions like mirror images, the hills rolling flatly like sine waves. In order to move, Emma will have to choose a direction, a destination—the Grand Canyon maybe, or perhaps somewhere else, somewhere she has never seen, not even on a postcard. She thinks it doesn't matter where she goes, just so long as she gets away from this spot in Kansas. Still, she must choose west or east. Here to somewhere. Measure her progress in halves, and halfway to the half. Emma knows that you must get halfway to any destination before you can get any farther. She wonders if Topeka is halfway to somewhere.

Even when Emma can imagine getting somewhere, she doubts if she could stand on a street in Texas or next to the Statue of Liberty and see much of the new view without images of Kansas superimposed on top. Images of home, her mother's hair in a steel knot at the base of her neck, the pin-up on the barn of the girl who looks like Carolyn. All those socks, the mailbox, the land around the house. Emma figures that Kansas will follow her anywhere she might go, as certainly as *here* is contained in *there*.

She also knows that many other places, which could have stayed elsewhere, have come here to this house. All those postcards have trapped "there" in Kansas. Like her mother said, "If you can see it in a photo, why do you need to go anywhere?" Emma thinks of all the cards she has received in the mailbox.

If Emma were to go somewhere like the Grand Canyon and stand where her sister must have stood, then the Grand Canyon, that great orange crack in the earth, would look like nothing more than a flattened cardboard image resting on an oversized white doily. And the Statue of Liberty would have next to it, in the sky, a great wedge of butter because on the kitchen table the Statue of Liberty and the butter had the same dimensions that night her mother wanted to see the card. Like her mother always said, "A picture is worth a thousand words and not so expensive as taking the train." Emma wants to tell her sister, "Stop sending all those places here."

Emma looks up, away from the highway, as she often does such nights as these. She looks at the stars in the sky. She knows all those pinpricks of light have names, are supposed to form pictures, but to her, this night more than any other, each and every star looks like a hole, a hole in fabric, small pinpricked patches where the cloth is wearing thin. Like the cloth over the birdcage, daylight is seeping in, cloaked under another name: *star*. Emma thinks that whatever's been thrown over Kansas is wearing thin. More holes seem to arrive each time she does. She imagines the way the fabric drapes over hills, nestles on tips of trees, slopes down to graze the fields, rises with her house and the run of electric poles. The sky has taken its shape from the land in the same way as the cloth gains structure over the birdcage.

> *Carolyn,*
> *Mother's latest canary is getting old. Would be getting gray and*
> *hunched if that was how birds age. Even the cloth that I throw*
> *over the birdcage is fraying, making holes that must look like*
> *stars, new constellations to the bird. And Mother, she thinks it's*
> *the same canary you gave her all those years ago.*

It was Carolyn's idea to cover the cage, make the bird think it was time to sleep so it would be quiet. Emma has been doing what Carolyn suggested and her mother approved for years. She would like to tell the bird:

> *Canary,*
> *I lie to you. I make you think it is nighttime, make you think*
> *you can't fly or sing, just so Mother and her visitors can make*
> *the house dark and solemn with their words, their sermons and*
> *prescriptions.*

Emma knows that canaries can't comprehend such things. So she doesn't talk to the bird, just lets the cloth covering wear thin, thin as the fabric of her housecoat. The dress that she wears to clean and do chores needs patching, but the holes blend right in with the dark areas of the floral pattern. Emma's mother hasn't even noticed them yet. She hasn't said: "Emma, little holes always get bigger. Nip this in the bud like a good girl." A good girl for decade upon decade.

> *Carolyn,*
> *Mother says that if you have any mending to do you should*

send it here, to me. You never learned to sew, never mention
stitchwork in your postcards. Some things you shouldn't pay
strangers to do.

Emma looks at her hands, all rut and ridge. Even in the semi-light
of the highway, Emma's hands show bronze, but not the same kind of
darkness that her sister writes of when she says

I got a tan in Mexico,
Am all golden now.

Emma wouldn't want to tell Carolyn about her own darkness. Looking
at her palms, she can see where the hoe fits, where she holds clothespins, how
her knuckles must have been designed just to knead bread. Looking at her
hands in the kind of darkness that makes an old black and white photo of
everything, Emma sees that her fingers are meant to pick a single pill from a
bottle and offer it like a seed to her mother's mouth, make flowers grow.

If Emma could get somewhere to see her sister, if she met her sister at
the Golden Gate Bridge in San Francisco, if she offered her sister a bouquet
of wild flowers and her sister were to ask after their mother, Emma would
smile and say:

Mother is beautiful when she is hearing voices. Beautiful when she
sleeps and the lines on her face relax and become smooth as sheets
on the line or her hair. When I talk to Mother, I can see in her
eyes that she is listening to something else. Something wonderful
that flutters about my head like the wings of many birds.

Emma thinks that to talk of birds to her sister she will need to be more
specific, say something like "the wings of many small sparrows and robins,"
or she might be misunderstood. Once Carolyn sent a postcard with a
picture of an ostrich:

Dearest Emma,
Look at this bird.
Wings like dirty angels.
It can't even fly but runs
All gangly like you did.
In Kansas now I hear

There are farms of these birds.
Love, Carolyn

And Emma's mother asked, "Did you receive a postcard from that sister of yours?" Carolyn became Emma's sister on the day she left the state. Mother said, *"Your sister has run off."* Before that it was, *"My daughter Carolyn* is going to sing a duet at church on Sunday," *"My daughter* has the highest marks in her class," or *"My daughter* has been invited to go to a public speaking tournament in Topeka." Emma would like to say to her mother: "You made Carolyn my sister with fewer words than it takes to fill the back of a postcard picturing an ostrich."

Emma looks up, does not expect or find any birds flying, just lots of holes, bright holes. She calculates the number of patches required, the hours and hours of stitchwork that it would take to patch the places where fabric is worn. She can already hear her needle, clink, clink, as it passes into the fabric tapping the light bulb she has stretched the sock over in order to do her darning. The rhythm of dusk. Each night, light fades as quietly and unobtrusively as her father's socks regain heels and toes. All those socks. Socks enough for many more feet it seems than just her father's. But for Emma, the evening is always, "Emma, your father has some socks that need darning. Be a dear." Her mother brings Emma the stack without waiting for a response. *Certainly, Mother* has come out of Emma's mouth so many times over the years that speech has become gratuitous; echoes and memories replace language.

Emma's mother does rest an awful lot these days. Now, as Emma is standing on the highway, her mother can be nothing but asleep.

Carolyn,
Mother is resting now. I will show her your postcard with the picture
of the Peace Gardens later. Later when you have stopped bleeding
and crying after you have washed your face, I will tell Mommy that
you fell and scraped your knee on the highway but that it didn't
really hurt much, that everything is okay now, and that I have
already warned you not to roller-skate on the highway again.

Emma drops her suitcase on the gravel and drops the postcard with the picture of the Grand Canyon. Emma is not eleven or twelve and Carolyn cannot be a child any longer. She must have aged, could be in any number of places across the country.

There is so much Emma would like to say to her sister, but she also knows how much must remain unspoken, unwritten. If they met in Hershey's Chocolate Factories, Emma might admit:

Carolyn, I hate to cook.

If Emma found her sister still riding a mule in the Grand Canyon, she would be awfully tempted to tell Carolyn:

The boy who carried your bags, instead of mine, was called Jerry Davenport. And freckles were not his most distinguishing feature.

If Emma were to run across Carolyn in Graceland, she probably wouldn't say to her sister:

We don't go to church anymore. It has been so long that I can't even remember what the chapel where we were supposed to get married looks like. The pastor comes to us.

Emma knows that if she were to meet her sister at Yellowstone and her sister were to ask, "How's Mother," she would not be able to say:

Carolyn, you did not know Mother like this. You have not put the pills on her tongue which make her hands shake, make her tired, her stomach queasy. You have not put the pills on her tongue so that she can remember the day of the week, how to fix of cup of tea, who I am.

And if Carolyn were to ask, "How's Daddy?" Even if she were looking at Mount Rushmore, Emma knows she could not tell her sister:

Our father drinks more than before you left, less of his property remains. He leaves the house each day in overalls with a sack lunch and a bottle of JD. He says he is going to work. He doesn't tell mother what acreage he sells to pay the doctor's bills, to handle the recession. He doesn't tell her that there's not enough work to keep him busy, to keep him from sitting in the back of the barn, drinking and pasting pin-ups on the wall.

Emma knows that standing next to her sister in Las Vegas, she would not say:

Carolyn, there is a pin-up of a woman who looks like you did when you were fifteen. She was ripped out of a J.C. Penny catalogue, wears a blue bikini with flowers like that green one of yours that mother made you give to the thrift store. She has been there since you left, pasted against the back wall of the barn behind the tractor, next to naked women, in a dark corner where mother never goes. In the midst of shadows, this girl never stops smiling, swinging her blonde ponytail in the breeze, never ages, wrinkles only as paper does, blush fading, gaining a hint of yellow.

Emma knows that some things could not be said. Emma knows that she would be unable to lie to her sister. Emma feels lightheaded now and a wave of nausea passes through her body. The hills, which stretch out evenly from where Emma stands, begin to roll under her feet. The land undulates, as if the highway and the fields, even the house on its squared plot, as if all these coverings constitute some old rug in the process of being pulled from beneath her. A rug that is going to fly away without Emma, leaving her body in exactly the same spot but fallen.

Emma sits down on her suitcase and tries to collect herself. This has happened before. On other nights she has had to go back to the house, take a spoonful of Emetrol to calm her stomach, unpack the suitcase, replacing the vinyl bag under the bed, and try to sleep.

Carolyn,
Do you remember how I always won when we used to race, walking backwards between rows of corn?

Sitting on her suitcase next to the highway, Emma doesn't want this night to be another one of those nights where she goes in early, swallowing elixir from a spoon, telling herself as she has told her mother so many times before, "You shouldn't travel when you aren't feeling well." She doesn't want to lie in bed, in her own bed with its brass headboard. She doesn't want to lie in that bed wrapped round in the quilt her mother made for her when she was eight, the quilt with a single lavender flower in each square. She doesn't want to lie wrapped in that quilt and try to sleep. She doesn't want to count the number of times she has used illness as an excuse to go back to the house, to leave the highway, to abandon the dotted yellow line that leads like a fraying rope away from the house.

> *Carolyn,*
> *Lavender looks better on you. Even Mother knows that, giving*
> *you the purple dress to wear to the dance and making mine from*
> *navy knit. That dress I matched the tablecloth in.*

Emma wishes she felt better. In the middle of the night, she is beginning to sweat. She wishes a car would come by right now to pick her up. Or a bull would come charging towards her from the barn. Or the ghost of the woman in the pin-up who looks like her sister would shriek through the cornfield. Something, anything to make her move her tortoise body a little bit. Half the distance to the line in the center of the highway would do.

If her mother were to see Emma now, standing along the side of the highway, she would ask, "Did you receive a postcard from that sister of yours?"

Emma wishes she could throw her postcards down on the highway so they would get run over by a semi at dawn. She wishes she could throw down her postcards on the highway so that all those places with Carolyn's handwriting would spring up in front of her, sprout like pole beans.

From the valley rises light with a suddenness that is like a rip and Emma catches the brights of a semi in the face. Whiteness and noise pass her by, fall into a dent in the road beyond her. Her vision flashes with many white spots and her eyes carry the image of headlights to the hills, to the pavement in front of her, to her suitcase. As if that sudden light were a camera flash, Emma gains an image of herself, an image so honed and true she could be looking at a postcard. Picture a woman, brown hair already streaked with gray, calloused hands, a hardworking body showing a touch of strain, no high school diploma, no job training, money enough to fill a coffee canister, buy coffee, perhaps a train ticket, a night or two in a motel room. This woman is frozen on the side of a highway in the middle of Kansas in the middle of the night holding an old vinyl suitcase in one hand and a postcard of the Grand Canyon in the other.

Everything is glossy. In the afterglow of the semi, Emma understands that identical postcards get stacked in a rack that spins on an axis, how the same picture can be mailed over and over.

Watching the taillights rising on a distant hill, Emma thinks that perhaps there is only one postcard, one postcard which is written upon night after night, on many different dates, and all this desire for communication is layered in good handwriting, one night upon another, until the lines of the text pile on top of each other, drape over other lines, overlap and weave words together until the ink runs like water, until all the holes, the white places between letters are filled, until the postcard becomes unreadable and cannot be mailed.

Hundreds of one postcard, or one postcard written on hundreds of times—either way, Emma knows she still stands next to the highway in Kansas in the middle of the night with the Grand Canyon in one hand, flowered suitcase in the other.

—LISA GILL—

Reductio ad Absurdum—By my early twenties, when I wrote "Zeno's,"
I'd been frightening professors with odd feats of brain malfunction and
arguing literary theory on the psych ward. Wires spewed from my scalp
and doctors pulled out their hair. Connections in the brain slipped daily.
Fog I walked through in England reappeared in New Mexico desert. Fur
from the back of a wild boar in Germany was now felt on my fingertips.
Flashbacks rose in multiple languages and I did due diligence translating
them. Arms and legs came and went, the mouth dissolved, capacities
returned unheralded. I wrote what rose, what fell: I fell and "Zeno's" rose.
Fragment by fragment. After six months, I taped the pieces together and
color-coded the image lines so I could "read" what I'd written. 6,000 words
to traverse the length of a hallway and living room to the front door: I was
finally getting somewhere.

ALZHEIMER'S NOIR

It was about ten at night when I saw her walk out the door. Now they're telling me No, that's not what happened, she wasn't even there.

I don't buy it. The room was dark, the night was darker, but Dorothy was there. We were in bed and her curved back was against my chest. She wore the pale yellow nightgown I love, with its thin straps loose against the skin of her shoulders. My arm was around her, my hand cupped her breast, we were breathing to the same rhythm. Then she slipped from my grasp and I felt a chill where she'd left the sheets folded back. She drifted like a ghost over the floor, down the hall, and out the front door that's always supposed to be locked. I saw her fade into the foggy night.

They tell me I'm confused. What else is new? I'm also tired. And I have a nasty cough from forty-six years of Chesterfields, even after two decades without them. And I don't sleep worth a damn. That's how I know what I saw in the night. Confused, maybe, but the fact is that Dorothy is gone.

For three, four years now, Dorothy is the one who's been confused. That's what we're doing in this place, this "home." She has Alzheimer's. We had to move out of the place where we'd lived together around sixty years.

"Jimmy," she'd say to me, "you look so much like Charles."

Well, I *am* Charles. Jimmy's our son, gone now forty-two years since he went missing over in Cambodia, where he wasn't even supposed to be.

It broke my heart. Filled me with despair, all of it: Jimmy gone too soon, then Dorothy slowing leaving me, now Jimmy somehow back because of her confusion so I have to lose them both again, night after night.

I miss her. Where is my Dorothy? I saw her walk out the door that's supposed to be locked. Because Alzheimer's people wander. They try to get out of the prison they're in, who can blame them. I feel the same way, myself.

But at eighty-two I still have all my marbles. Thank God for that. Memory? Bush Jr, Clinton, Bush Sr, Reagan, Carter, then what's-his-name, then Nixon, Jackson, no, Johnson. Kennedy and I can go all the way back to Coolidge, but I don't want to show off. Or I could do 100 93 86 79 72 65 and so on.

✳

I saw her fade into the foggy night. The staff here can't remember to lock the front door, and I'm supposed to believe them when they say what I saw with my own eyes didn't happen? It's a crime, what they did. What they're doing. Negligence. It's like they're accomplices to a kidnapping. Anything happens to Dorothy, I hold them accountable.

Truth is, I'm not sure how long she's been gone. I thought it was only a few hours, but then I look outside and see the day's getting away from me. Dark, light, dark again. Makes me weary.

"Let me use the phone," I say to Milly, the big one, works day-shift.

"Sorry, Mr. Wade. I'm not authorized to do that."

Always the same thing. "Look, Dorothy wandered away! No one here's doing it, so I need to call the police and file a missing persons report."

"What you need is a rest."

"What I need is a detective."

Milly shakes her head. "We've been through this ten times today." The phone is in a locked closet. She tests the door on her way to the kitchen.

I saw Dorothy fade into the foggy night. They tell me that's not what happened, she wasn't there, but I don't buy it. Her curved back against my chest, the chill, her long white hair fading as she drifted like a ghost over the floor, down the hall, and out.

Well, okay then, it's up to me. I'll have to find her myself. Be the detective myself.

Why not? I'm used to hunting around, discovering lost old things. Forgotten old things. For fifty-plus years, I had my own antiques business here in southeast Portland, just a short walk from Oaks Bottom. Sellwood, the neighborhood's called, and that's just what I did: sold wood. Found my niche with bookcases—Italian walnut, mahogany, inlaid stuff with wavy glass doors—and then with other library furnishings, and rare books eventually. Always liked antiques. I just never planned on turning into one.

Wait a little while longer till it gets dark, till the other residents are in bed and the night staff is "resting" like they do. No doubt with a rum, a beer, whatever they drink. What I'll do is sit here in the old rocker, a perfect reading chair I found at an estate sale in Estacada, must have been '48. Dorothy wouldn't hear of me trying to sell this thing. Nursed Jimmy in it.

*

I find her at the Dance Pavilion. I knew she'd be there. With her long lean body and long blonde hair, she's easy to spot. Lights reflect off the polished wood floor that's marred by years of dancing feet. The low ceiling makes for good acoustics, and in the temporary silence I hear Dorothy laugh. I walk right over to her and take her hand.

No, that was 1945, just after the war. I'd met her two weeks before, and she told me where I could find her if I wanted to. Oaks Park, the Dance Pavilion, not far from the railroad tracks and the totem pole. I'm nineteen and it feels like it's happening right now. Like I'm at the Dance Pavilion with her hand in mine.

I wake up in the rocker, still eighty-two. Stiff in every joint, I creak louder than the old oak itself. What I need is a shot of good Scotch. The kind that's been aged twelve years, the last two years in port barrels, say, with a hint of chocolate and mint. Nothing peppery. Even when she was going away into Alzheimer's, Dorothy remembered her stuff about Scotch. I loved to kid her about it. The old dame knew her booze. How I'd love to toast her at this moment, to look across the room and see her gorgeous back exposed by one of those bold dresses she wore in the heyday, see her head turn so those green eyes twinkle at me, her hand rising to return my gesture, the amber liquid in her glass filled with light.

I find her tucked against the bluff in Oaks Bottom, looking up at wildly whirling lights. Discs, that's what they are, silvery and thin as nickels, and they're maybe forty fifty feet above the ground, spinning in circles, blazing with cold fire. Mesmerized, Dorothy doesn't see me yet. She can't take her eyes off them, these flying saucers. But I dare not risk calling out and alerting the figures moving toward her in the mist. Any luck, I'll get to her before they do. Before they can kidnap her and whisk her onto their ship.

No, that was 1947, when she was pregnant with Jimmy. Dozens of people down there in Oaks Bottom screaming, pointing toward the heavens, saying the aliens were landing. All over Portland they saw these things. Cops, World War II vets, pilots, everybody saw them.

I find her sitting with a half dozen women on the bluff overlooking Oaks Bottom. All their chaise loungues face north, upriver, with a clear view of Mt. St. Helens. It's twilight, but steam plumes are clearly visible and what feels like soft rain is really ash. St. Helens has been fixing to erupt for months now.

Dorothy waves me over. She spreads her legs, flexes her knees, smoothing her flowered dress down between them, making room for me to join her on the chaise. I sit there on the cotton material she's offered to me and it's still warm from her body. I lean back against her, waiting for the mountain to blow.

No, that was 1980, when she was thinking the world might come to an end. Hoping it would, I believe. We were tired of it then, so you can imagine how we feel now.

No, we're not watching the mountain. We're watching Fourth of July fireworks from Oaks Park like we do every year. Surrounded by kids, happy kids, full of life.

Ah, Jesus.

It's time to go find her. At least there's no rain. Always rains around here, often deep into June, and that would make it harder to track her. Not that a little rain would stop me. I have a warm jacket, a Seattle Mariners baseball cap, a flashlight. Nothing will stop me because I think this is it, the last chance. Because I don't know how long Dorothy's been gone. Floating down the hall. The dark. The night.

The only thing that makes sense is that she's lost somewhere in the woods again over in Oaks Bottom. That's her place, all right. One of the big reasons I decided to move into this "home" instead of some of the others we looked at was because it was in Sellwood and close to the bluff above Oaks Bottom. Clear days and nights, we can see across the wetlands and the little lake to the Ferris wheel and the roller coaster and the Dance Pavilion there at Oaks Park. Jimmy called it the musement center. Loved to ride the merry-go-round, spend a whole afternoon at the roller-skating rink. Sometimes now we hear the kids screaming as they spin or plunge on the rides. We hear the thunder of wheels on tracks. Lights flicker. I think Dorothy thinks it's him calling. Jimmy.

Even after Jimmy was gone, she liked to walk in Oaks Bottom. Not go over to the musement center, of course, but wander along the trails now that the city has turned all that land into a refuge. She'd stroll along the trail and name the trees: maple, cedar, fir, wild cherry, black cottonwood. I think maybe she was pretending to teach young Jimmy. Breaks my heart. She'd stroll along and smell the swampy odor, stumps sticking out of the shallow water, ducks with their ducklings. She'd. She. Then She.

✳

Then she started to get lost in there. One time I found her walking past
the huge sandy-hued wall of the mausoleum and crematorium, up at the
edge of the bluff. How she managed to climb there from the trail I never
understood. She was silhouetted against the eight-story building, its wings
spread like a giant vulture. Or like the great blue heron painted against a
field of blue on the building's center wall. She was drifting vaguely north,
and I hated to see her there, of all places. I had nightmares about that for
months afterwards. Another time I found her ankle-deep in water at the
lake's edge, swirling her left hand through algae then looking at it as though
she hoped her fingers had turned green. There were three little black snakes
slithering around and over her right hand where it braced her body on the
bank. One time I found her on the railroad tracks at the western end of the
wetland. Just standing there like she was waiting for the 4:15 to Seattle.

Dorothy has stamina. I can't be sure where she might have gotten to
this time. Or who might have found her and done something awful to her.
Those neighborhood kids in their souped up cars she always used to annoy,
telling them she'd call the cops.

I'm quiet leaving my room, quiet going down the hall, with its threadbare
carpet, its dim lighting, quiet opening and closing the unlocked front door.
But I don't have to be. No one is watching. I head off down the street like
I'm going to buy a carton of milk, don't turn to look at any cars hissing by,
just make my slow way toward the river and Oaks Bottom. It's not far.

On television, detectives always begin their investigations by going
door-to-door asking the neighbors if they've seen anything. But I can't risk
that. Start ringing doorbells around here, people will just call the "home"
and say another old loony is on the loose. Turn me in. I'd be finished before
I got started. Maybe when I get closer to Oaks Bottom itself I can find
someplace to ask questions.

But after a few blocks, I have to stop and rest. The weariness just keeps
getting worse. I think my only energy for the last few years came from
caring for Dorothy. It's what kept me going. Without that, I'd probably be
in the crypt by now, dead of exhaustion, locked away in the big mausoleum
there overlooking the musement park. Or I'd be technically still alive but
sitting in a chair all day while time comes and goes, comes and goes.

Now it's a few minutes later, I think. Could be more than a few. Truth is, I'm not sure exactly where I am. But that's because my eyes aren't any good in the dark, not because I'm lost. I'm right above Oaks Bottom, somewhere. It's just that the landmarks are hard to make out. But there's a tavern here. I don't remember seeing it before. But it's so old, I must have seen it without noticing. Or noticed without remembering. That's what getting old is, I tell you, nothing but solitary seconds adding up to nothing.

I don't know how long I've been standing here. Or why I'm at this new old building. Squat little windowless place looks like it's made out of tin, painted white and red, with a tall sign in the parking lot: Riverside Corral. Then I remember: I should drop in for a quick minute and find out if anyone's seen Dorothy. Could have happened. The old dame knew her booze. Maybe she dropped in to the Corral for a quick Scotch on her last rambling.

I take a deep breath. Which at my age is something of a miracle right there. And figure I have maybe another couple of hours before I have to head back to the "home," before they might start to miss me. So this can't take long.

I walk in, planning to sidle up to the bar and question the keeper. But the music, if that's what it is, is loud, and what I see stops me dead: two stages, one dark one light, and on the stage lit in flashing colors a naked woman with long light hair swirling as she gyrates above the money-filled hands of two men who look like twin brothers.

Is that? It's Dorothy! I'd know those broad shoulders anywhere. How could…No, wait…I blink and see now it's not her. Of course it's not. I'm confused. What else is new? But for a moment there.

I would give anything to see her again. To touch her again. To stand here near her again.

"What can I get you, old timer?" the bartender asks. He is twelve. Well, probably mid-twenties, pointy blonde hair and a hopeful scrub of moustache.

I'd forget where I am, forget why I'm here. Looking around, seeing the dancer again, I say "My wife."

He smiles. "I don't think so."

Then I'm walking through the parking lot, using my flashlight so I can access the trailhead and make my way down the steep bluff toward the trail. I'm too old for this, I know it. All the walking could kill me, even though I'm in pretty good shape. But I can feel through the soles of my feet that Dorothy has been here, and if it kills me I'm still going to find her.

A series of switchbacks gets me to the bottom, but I'm so turned around I'm not sure which way to walk. Time comes and goes like the wind, and I see the moon blown free of clouds as though God himself had turned a light on for me. It shines across the lake. Looking up through a lacing of tree tops, I see the now-moonlit mausoleum. So that's where Dorothy must be.

I begin walking north. Maple, cedar, fir, wild cherry, black cottonwood. The water makes a lapping noise just to my left. It sounds spent. Stumps sticking out of the shallows create eerie shadows that seem to reach for my ankles.

Rising out of the water, just beyond a jagged limb, I see a figure stretch and begin to move toward me. From the way it strides, I know it's my son, it's Jimmy. He wears some kind of harness that weighs him down, but still he seems to glide on the lake's surface, so light, so graceful.

Jimmy was never trouble, even when he got in trouble. That time, when the cops came to our door, it was only because he'd gone to protect his best friend, Frank. Johnny Frank. Or maybe Frankie John. I don't remember. A wonderful boy, just like my Jimmy, but a scrapper, and that one time he was surrounded by thugs and Jimmy went in there and—

Oh, Dorothy was so good with our son, all that time they spent at the musement park, and Jimmy lost all fear of the things he'd been so afraid of. Came to love the rides, the scarier the better. Of course, that's why he went into the service, why he ended up in flight school, why he ended up in a plane over Cambodia, shot down where he wasn't even supposed to be. Dorothy told me once it was all her fault. I took her in my arms, told her all that was her fault was how wonderful our son turned out to be. And now look, here he is, still wearing his parachute harness, coming home to us at last.

"Come on, Jimmy. Help me find your mother."

"Where is she this time?"

I point toward the mausoleum. He follows my finger and nods, and just then the clouds return, and the mausoleum fades into the night, its sandy face turning dark before my eyes.

Jimmy can see anyway. He leads me and I follow. The trail rises and dips, follows the contour of the bluff. For an old man, I think I'm doing well with the tricky footing. Then I realize Jimmy is carrying me.

No, he's stopped walking and now he's the one who's pointing. We're very close to the mausoleum. Up ahead, standing against the building where Jimmy's ashes are stored, where my ashes will be stored, where I remember now Dorothy's ashes are stored, I see my wife smiling. She is leaning back against the wall just under the legs of that giant blue-painted heron.

The wind rises. The clouds unveil the moon again and the building lights up. But no one is there after all. No one and nothing but a wall on which a hundred-foot-tall heron is preparing to fly toward heaven.

—FLOYD SKLOOT—

When I wrote "Alzheimer's Noir" in late spring 2008, the realities of living with a damaged brain had been on my mind for a long time. My mother had died a few years earlier following a long decline into Alzheimer's. And for two decades I'd been writing nonfiction about my experience after a viral attack on my brain left me disabled, with severe deficiencies to memory, abstract reasoning, word finding, sense of direction, structure-making, and other functions. So when the editor of an anthology called *Portland Noir* asked if I had something to contribute, I was struck by the idea of writing a mystery story from the viewpoint of a man with severely compromised memory. It was liberating and fun to turn to fiction. The voice and bits of plot emerged quickly one morning as my wife and I walked the trail at Portland's Oaks Bottom refuge area.

Candice Morrow

FOR THE LOVE OF HIM

Monday

The summer we believed in God was ending. On Maggie's calendar, stapled to the ceiling above her bed, seven white squares separated us from the first day of high school. If summer was life—a stumbling span of hot, green days, half of which we spent not knowing what to do, the other half wishing we'd done more—then high school was death. Purgatory, Maggie said. Hell, I said. Don't talk about it. I won't if you won't.

We told ourselves those seven empty squares fixed beneath a pile of sleeping kittens were only reminders that we didn't need reminders, that our time was our own. Calendars were paper, and paper had nothing on youth. No, our real concern was the early morning chill, which had, without permission, crept beneath our covers. Though we'd greeted June in a tangle of sweat and limb and sheet, we woke now in September fetal and warming our toes on each other's legs.

"For His sake," Maggie said. "I'm as cold as a witch's tit." Her skin was smooth, but I had yet to start shaving. She said my calves felt as soft as a rabbit's paw.

"A witch's tit. A rabbit's paw," I said. In search of a blanket, I rolled off and tiptoed over piles of clothes, some hers, some mine. When I opened her closet, a row of metal hangers clanged together. My mom called Maggie's mom cheap on occasion, and that's what I heard when I saw the hangers saved from trips to the cleaners—my mother's voice: *That woman is sooo cheap.*

I said, "A witch would have a tit like any other. *Or* she'd wave a wand to warm it. For that matter, why isn't it 'as cold as a witch's *tits*'? Is it me, or are we implying a witch has one tit?"

"That's fairy godmothers."

"With one tit?"

"No, fairy godmothers use a wand," Maggie said. "A witch uses a cauldron."

As I reached for a quilt on the top shelf, last year's binders spilled math problems and chapter summaries onto the floor. Unlike my own writing, which was scrunched and fraught with ink splotches, Maggie's sentences filled a page as effortlessly as water fills a cup. Subject, verb. Subject, verb.

Hearts punctuating i's. I envied her this, among other things, including the way her body filled a dress or her presence filled a room.

I balanced the quilt on my bad hand. With my good hand I mimed beating dust off it. I said, "It holds true, though, that a tit is a tit and probably the same temperature on a witch as on anyone else."

"Jesus fuck tit," Maggie said.

Words like tit or dick had something of the lingering magic of childhood. Abracadabra couldn't do shit to an empty hat, but we—we'd discovered how to turn a room full of heads with one crisp syllable. Fuck was a powerhouse with enough force to separate us from our teachers and from our mothers—Maggie's mom with her new love and my mom with her new grief, which came as bottomless as a basket of fries at the North Forty. All-you-can-eat grief, three meals a day, good for growing girls. Fuck.

"I'm *freezing*," Maggie said. "That better?"

I opened the blanket over us. I said, "For the love of Him, what would you do if I weren't here?"

"I don't know," she said with the same certainty she had when crossing her t's and hearting her i's. "I don't know what I do when you're not here."

Tuesday

We'd seen Him in tree bark and on water-stained windows and on water-stained walls. Water, we decided, was His favorite medium. Maggie had a knack for spotting Him, and the closer we got to school starting the more often He appeared.

She found Him in tire tracks near the post office, His features boxy and symmetrical.

She found Him in the creek behind Grandmother Sager's old cabin. His beard, disrupted mud. His eyes, smooth rocks. His mouth, a twitching trout—there and then not there, so like God.

She found Him in our chicken sandwich, ordered with no pickles and extra lettuce at the North Forty, a diner on the corner of Main and nowhere.

"It's the Lord who art in Heaven and also on my sandwich," Maggie said, lifting the toasted slice in both hands as if it carried the weight of the universe.

"*Our* sandwich," I said. I stuck my gum under the table, stuck it to all the gum we'd stuck there before.

Our booth, which had a view of both Main Street and the revolving pie case, was always available to us because of the gashes, like knife wounds on rosy cheeks, in its red vinyl seats. I liked nothing better than to sit back and massage out crumbs and cotton batting while taking stock of the day's pies. I ate most of my meals at the diner that summer. If not with Maggie, then with Mom, who preferred a corner booth the shape and size of our kitchen table.

"He's decidedly not handsome on bread," Maggie said. "What do you think? No, don't tell me. I'll be disappointed."

Sitting in the booth opposite us, old Grandmother Sager tented her novel over a saltshaker and squinted at us. "What're you talking about?" she said. "Mold? Is it mold?" She scooted out of her booth and, nudging my ribs with her bony elbow, slid in next to me. She smelled like cigar smoke and bacon.

"Excuse *you*," I said, presenting her with my best stare, bored and unwavering, a stare my dad once said could turn milk into butter.

Wrinkled, spotted, blue-veined and blue-haired, Miss Sager was famous for having lived alone in the woods for fifty years. She was, in fact, nobody's grandmother. She now lived by the library and, like me, ate most of her meals at the North Forty.

Using her forefinger and thumb as tweezers, she lifted a corner of the bread. "I don't see anything."

"We were *eating* that," I said. "Besides, I need you to move so I can get out. I have to *pee*." I didn't.

She examined my bad hand, and I followed her gaze as I always did when people looked. It was my hand, same as the day I'd been born, and it still caught me off guard.

She said, "Not now, girl." How did she do that? How did she make "girl" sound like a bad word?

"It's Jesus, Grandmother," Maggie said, sipping her lemonade. "On the other side."

"What's what?"

"The Lord and Savior. There's his beard."

Miss Sager tossed the slice back onto the plate and wagged a fry in Maggie's face. "When I was your age I didn't talk such nonsense. I talked about boys. In fact, I had me a different boyfriend for every day of the week. That gave me a lot to talk about. You could have a boyfriend, too. Maybe even three or four if you wanted." It was obvious she meant Maggie, not me. *You* could. She said, "Monday, Tuesday, Wednesday—"

"We know the days of the week," I said.

Miss Sager ate the fry and kissed the salt off her fingers. "Is she always like this?"

"Worse," Maggie said. "I can't take her anywhere."

"Mmm, Friday was like that. A regular junkyard bulldog." Miss Sager leaned forward and drew us toward her with a hushed voice. "Especially in the sack. He would get so stumbling drunk I was shocked he made it out to the cabin. He was sick for me. Even after he got married, which calmed most of my boys to the point they broke it off, well, he'd still come to me. I lost so many days, but I could count on Friday. He always made time for me, and he'd always put a hot bottle in his belly beforehand. Heck, he'd tell his wife—"

"I'm going to go ahead and pee on your leg now," I said.

"What happened to him? To Friday?" Maggie said.

"The piss is building," I said. "It's your call."

Miss Sager switched sides and pushed the plate toward my best friend. "Can I offer you sustenance…what's your name again?"

"Maggie," Maggie said.

"Well, *Mag-gie*, let Grandmother Sager tell you a thing or two about the less gentler sex."

The North Forty's bathroom had one toilet but a counter with two sinks and two oval mirrors. I washed my hands twice just to make sense of it. Then I leaned against the door, which felt cool on the backs of my legs. The knob jiggled.

"Beat it," I said. "Or I beat you."

If it was the summer of God, it was also the summer of anger, of rages small and potent like red hot candies I couldn't help popping into my mouth—never mind they burned my throat and left an aftertaste that was only sweet at first.

Anything could offend, and right now it was that I was young, and Miss Sager was old. Old things fell apart. Unlike my dad, who understood the merit in a quick goodbye, Miss Sager's gradual breaking was goddamn self-indulgent. As to her seven-day-lineup of boyfriends—what a crock of shit. At least that's what I thought then.

Now I think the more something breaks on the outside, the more pleasant it becomes on the inside. Who knows if that's true. I don't dare ask my children, who were born and remain perfectly assembled.

I was born with raised splotches like wine stains on my right arm and on my neck. The one on my neck resembles a duck, its purple tail feathers sweeping my breasts, its long neck rising with mine, and its flat beak pecking my cheek. I'd often thought that if this were all, I'd still have a chance. Small town boys weren't heartless, only ignorant. They could be taught to appreciate the duck. Thing is, I'd also been born without the last three fingers on my right hand, my missing parts.

"Well, not *missing,*" Dad used to say, "'cause it ain't like anyone's looking for them."

Some kids said my mom was to blame. I expect that she, with her highlights and low necklines, looked to them like a woman who had sinned before marriage. And, who're we kidding, she probably had.

Other kids said Dad was to blame because tweakers' babies shoot out real fucked up. But he wasn't a tweaker—a drunk, sure, and probably a pothead. But meth was pretty new—and scary in the way it swept through towns so fast it stripped the fat off people. If you weren't high on meth, you were high on the idea of meth.

I accepted all their reasons equally, at least for awhile, chewing on them until they lost flavor. All I wanted was for a boy to like me.

It helped to have Maggie, who never hesitated to look at me or touch me. She called my nubs the three little piggies and would tap each, saying things like, "This little piggy wants to have a sleepover, but this little piggy is too tired, so this little piggy punches the second little piggy 'til he gets his head out of his ass."

I loved Maggie—but not, I sometimes fear, as much as Maggie loved me.

I returned to find Grandmother Sager finishing the chicken sandwich by herself. On the cover of her novel, thick with dog-eared pages, a shirtless man dipped a farm girl back for a kiss.

"What's wrong with your friend?" she said first thing.

"Nothing's wrong with her. What'd you say to her?"

"Maybe *wrong* isn't the best word," Grandmother Sager said. "All I'm saying is you ain't the crippled one. You're her best friend, right? It's your responsibility to pay attention, to snoop around, to go through her drawers. Do whatever you have to do."

"Crippled seems worse a word than wrong."

Grandmother Sager rapped her knuckles on the table. "If you think that, then she's crippled, and you're stupid."

"Yeah, and you're an old bitch," I said and walked out.

✦

I jogged the three blocks to Maggie's house.

Her stepbrother, Calvin, answered the door. He was home for the summer, which meant Maggie's house since their parents married the previous fall. Though I spent half my time at Maggie's, all I knew about Calvin was that he was nineteen and the dusting of freckles on his cheeks reminded me of dandelion fuzz.

"Safrona, right?" he said, resting against the doorframe. On the floor behind him were Maggie's flip-flops, her old green ones with the soles that flapped up when she walked. She'd worn them that morning.

"You remembered your line," I said. "Maggie around?"

"What kind of name is that anyway? *Safrona.*"

I slipped the three piggies out of my pocket and let them hang at my side. In my head I heard my mother say, not unkindly, *Sweetie, you can't spring them on people like that.* But I liked to think it forced the other person's hand. To Calvin, I said, "I go by Frona."

He winced and said, "I wouldn't do that if I were you." He didn't look at my hand. He didn't not look at my hand. "Hey, that thing on your neck, what's the deal?" I told him it was a birthmark. He reached forward and touched the duck with the back of his knuckles. The veins in his forearm looked big, and I wondered if he had more blood than the average person. "What do you know," he said. "It looks like a bird."

"A duck," I said.

He dropped his arm. "Yeah, but if I were you, I'd tell people it's a swan. See, it's all about branding. I learned that in my business course. Maybe what you need is a nickname. Swan, Little Swan, Swany, or maybe—"

"Ducky?" I said.

"Ducks make people think about white bread and health warnings at lakes. You got to think about these things. You got to get psychological about it."

That sounded pretty smart to me.

"We'll come up with something," he said. Shutting the door, he told me he'd let Maggie know I stopped by.

First thing when I got home, I called Maggie's house. I decided I'd hang up if Calvin answered, but there was no answer. I tried again after lunch and again before Mom and I headed out for dinner.

With Dad gone, Mom didn't feel much like cooking. You could see when

245

she got off the couch that she was really pulling herself together. She'd roll up her sleeves, and it was like she was putting on her arms. She'd brush back her hair, and it was like she was screwing on her head. All this effort and for what? So she could mix a bowl of instant potatoes and fry a brick of spam?

At the North Forty, I scanned the booths for Grandmother Sager, but she wasn't there. Mom asked why I was quiet, and I told her about Maggie vanishing after breakfast.

Holding her menu like a shield, she said, "It's probably for the best, what with school starting. And Dad's severance is almost gone, so I'll be starting back at the pharmacy week after next. It would be good if we spent some time together."

"Just like that?"

"Mr. Peterson understands I only needed a little break. It's natural."

"I never criticized you for taking a break. I don't give a shit what you—"

"Of course you give a shit," she said. "I'm your mother. You give a lot of shit."

"You mean *get*," I said.

When we got home, I tried Maggie again, and this time she answered.

"I can't talk," she said all woozy sounding, but I knew she could talk because she *was* talking. I imagined her on her bed, lying on her stomach with her arms at her sides. She often talked on the phone like that, with her hands tucked under her thighs and the receiver lying by her mouth.

"Did I wake you?" I asked.

"Nuh-uh."

Now I felt dumb for even calling, but I said I'd been wondering how she was.

She said, "Grandmother Sager thinks we should check out her cabin."

I reminded her that we'd been there a billion times that summer.

"But now we can go inside. She gave me the key. Tomorrow?"

"Whatever," I said and ended the call like lovers do in movies—that is, without saying goodbye.

Wednesday

We met at noon behind the post office where a dirt trail veered off into the woods. Like me, Maggie wore jean shorts and a button-down shirt knotted at her waist. She smelled like an ashtray, and I told her as much.

"Nice to see you, too," she said, releasing me and running down the path. Over her shoulder, she called back, "What a lovely fucking day!"

When I caught up, perhaps twenty yards beyond the tree line, Maggie was squatting in the grass, inspecting something.

A dead possum, boney-skinny with wide open eyes, lay several feet off the trail in a bed of wild ferns. Its tail was caught in the iron jaws of an old trap that wore a powdering of rust like orange sugar around a mouth.

"Who would do such a thing?" Maggie said.

"Boys," I said.

She picked up a stick and poked at the trap and the chain connecting it to a stake in the ground. "'And the word became flesh and dwelt among us, full of grace and truth.'" She moved the tip of the stick toward the possum's pink belly—

"Don't," I said.

"Why not?"

I shrugged. I didn't have a good answer.

The possum's head snapped forward and clamped onto the stick. Maggie did a fast crab crawl backward, the ground coughing up dirt around her. The animal hissed and lunged, yelping as the movement tugged on its tail. I grabbed the back of Maggie's collar and tried to drag her away.

"Let go," she yelled. "Let go of me. Frona, stop. It's okay. Frona. Frona."

The front end of the possum folded over the back end of the possum. Its ribs stuck out like fingers in a fur glove. It gnawed on its own tail. It bit at ferns and at the ground. It coughed and spit and thrashed some more. Then it flopped down again and lay as still as surrounding plants. To finish the performance, its little tongue rolled out the corner of its mouth. It almost seemed rude not to clap.

Maggie stood and dusted off her clothes. "It's the squirrel all over again," she said.

I put my arm around her waist, and for a minute we stood there, giggling and comparing our goose bumps. "I didn't know they were so ugly," I said.

"Fuck yeah," she said and started to unbutton her shirt.

"What in His name are you doing?"

"I don't want it to bite off my fingers."

"Why not?" I said. "We could be twinsies."

She untied the knot in her shirt. She wasn't wearing a bra, and sunbathing in her bikini had created pale triangles over her tiny breasts.

"Shouldn't we get an adult?" I said lamely.

Maggie raised her eyebrows.

"I mean what if it's rabid?"

"I'll be careful." She then paused. "If anything happens, my mom is in Vegas. They're staying at the Rio until Saturday, but Calvin can get ahold of them. Just tell Calvin." She gripped the shirt in front of her and tiptoed toward the possum.

"You didn't tell me they were out of town," I said.

"It wasn't a big deal."

"If you wanted to keep it a secret, you could have."

She whispered, "That's it, little fucker, easy, easy, it's okay. Shhhh, Mama's here."

"I mean, rabies doesn't kill instantly, so you didn't need to—"

Maggie threw the shirt over the possum and collapsed to the ground in a fluid motion that reminded me of how my dad used to tuck me into bed. Throwing up the sheet, he'd drop to the floor as it fell. Poof, gone. For the longest time, it was his best disappearing trick.

"Feel free to help," Maggie said.

Beneath her hands, the possum thrashed in plaid. I tried to pry open the trap, but it was a job for ten fingers, not seven. We gingerly switched places, and I was amazed at how fast the creature's heart beat. When the trap opened, half its tail hung limp, matted with blood and dirt.

"You can loosen up now," Maggie said.

I gripped its neck with my good hand and crushed its body to my chest with both arms. The heat was startling and, oh, that smell—a combination of meat forgotten in the fridge and wet laundry forgotten in the washer. I gagged but held on.

In the drama of the rescue, we forgot to enjoy our first contact with the inside of the cabin. We got there and, as we'd done before, pressed our noses against the window panes. We saw the piles of grayish-brown dust molded into familiar shapes: a dismantled bed, a rocking chair, a few crumbling boxes. We'd been desperate to touch those things, things that hadn't been touched in so long it was almost as if they'd never been touched at all. Virgin things. But when Maggie, topless, unlocked the door and I followed with our squirming bundle, our touch was quick and brutal and operating under one concern: Where can we house this wild thing?

I could hear her singing from the path and paused at the window to watch as she twirled around the cabin with a rag and a bottle of Windex.

When she answered the door, I said, "Honey, I'm home."

"Thank Him you're here." She pulled me in. "I couldn't decide what to feed Princess Jasmine."

There were circles under her eyes, and her hair hung loose and greasy. Her shorts were the same from the day before, but it was okay, I thought, because the bloodstains had turned brown. Anyone else would assume she'd had a sloppy encounter with a fudgesicle.

I lifted the small bag of cat food I bought before heading over. I said, "I'm going to veto *Princess Jasmine*."

"You know, the second I said it aloud I didn't like it." Maggie locked the door and took the bag. "Whatever her name is, she can't eat this shit."

"I also brought alcohol and gauze."

The floor was swept, windows washed, and shelves wiped clean. She'd pushed the rocking chair and the cardboard box containing our patient to the front window. The bed frame was assembled in the back corner, and covering its grimy mattress were the same beach towels we'd spent our summer turning on. It was kind of livable.

She said, "What sort of booze did you bring?"

"What?"

"You said you got alcohol."

I pulled the travel-sized bottle of rubbing alcohol from my back pocket.

"Oh," she said. "You brought something we can't eat and something we can't drink." She grabbed her backpack from beside the door and dumped its contents on the bed. There were juice boxes, Twinkies and pop rocks, an opened box of Cinnamon Crunch and an opened package of bologna.

We decided to eat the Twinkies right away and slide a piece of bologna, like a red sun, under the edge of the possum's box. Maggie patted the top. "Eat up, girl."

The box wiggled.

"That's a good girl," she said. "There, there."

"How do you know it's a girl?" I asked.

"Duh," she said.

One of Maggie's little toenails was gone, a fresh black scab in its place. She said it was no big deal, she'd bumped it on her bed the night before, but I ordered her to the rocking chair. "Sit down," I said around half a Twinkie squishing in my mouth.

I got on my knees and slipped off her green flip-flop. Hands folded in her lap, she looked out the window while I poured alcohol over the toe.

"I love this place," she said. "Why do you think Grandmother Sager never had kids? If it were me, I'd raise a whole herd of babies here."

"Mom says talking to a childless woman is like going to a barbecue and finding the host's flowerbeds full of rocks."

"That doesn't explain *why*."

I blew on the toe to dry it. "Mom says she heard from Mr. Peterson's sister, whose husband's aunt was a nurse back then, that Miss Sager got raped right out of high school."

"You make it sound like she received her diploma, stepped off the stage and, *wham*, was raped."

"Whatever. I guess she got pregnant and miscarried. I guess that soured it for her."

"Can't you do a bow?" Maggie said because I'd forgotten to bring tape and was trying to tuck the gauze into place. While I tied a knot, which did sort of look like a bow, Maggie said, "Soured what? Having kids?"

"Yeah, or maybe the town or love or whatever."

"Your mom is full of shit," Maggie said. "I miss your dad."

I leaned over and tore the gauze with my teeth.

"Be him today, okay?" she said. "And I'll be my mom before she married Jim."

We performed our roles flawlessly, our adopted offspring rustling beneath its box on the floor. For years, we'd suspected my dad was sweet on Maggie's mom. He always brushed his teeth and changed his shirt before dropping me off. Even if it was a clean shirt. Then, with a hand on the doorframe, he'd lean forward and ask, "How's it going, Alice? How's work?" or "Did you change your hair, Alice?" He said her name a lot. You could tell he liked it coming out of his mouth.

"Alice, did you change your hair?" I said.

"Yes, Roger," Maggie said. "Do you love it?"

"Yes, Alice, I do love it."

I broke and folded the cereal box into two bowls. She picked wild flowers to garnish our lunch, and after we ate, I asked her to dance. I led, the piggies supporting the small of her back, while she talked about saving our paychecks for a new home, new appliances. If we lived frugally now, she said, we'd live like kings later.

"Works for me," I said, "because frankly, Alice, I can't do anything in moderation. Starve now, rule later. That's a plan I can follow. See, Alice, this is why we belong together."

"Starve now, rule later. I'll embroider it on a hand towel."

I twirled and dipped her, a maneuver that was harder than it looked on the cover of Miss Sager's novel. Panting a little, I said I didn't know she could do yarn crafts.

She let her head flop back. There was a tiny bruise almost in the shape of a heart on her collar bone. Closing her eyes, she murmured, "Mmm. I can do so many things, Roger."

We wet a beach towel in the creek and wiped down the walls and floor. "Cleanliness is next to Godliness," she said, ringing brown water over the front step.

"You religious?" I said.

For a moment she stared off into the trees. "I guess I'm not. I go to church, though."

"That's okay. It's just something people say."

"Right." She resumed her chore. "I never asked—Roger, are you religious?"

"Nah." I sat on the step, legs out and feet crossed, just like him. "Alice, am I the man you thought I was?"

"You are a better man than any other man."

"You know, I think it got to me when you married Jim."

"I thought we were going to do before I married Jim."

"I mean, Jesus, Alice. Jim? He's nearly bald. And fat, Alice. He's fat."

"I know. It really sucks."

"It's just..." I picked up a handful of dirt and let it run through my fingers. "I stopped doing stuff. I missed a lot of work."

"I know, but I thought we were going to do before. Let's do before."

"I wouldn't eat much but these cans of spam. About the time you married Jim, I got a hankering for spam. A can for lunch, a can for dinner. I got pale. My wife forgot how to cook anything else. I don't know, maybe it's all a coincidence."

"There are no coincidences. There is only fate."

"But do *you* believe that, Alice?"

"I don't know what I believe. Roger, I think I just go along with things. Isn't that sad? That is so sad."

"Well, you fucked up my life, Alice. You fucked it up real good. Everything is fucked."

She sat next to me, put her head on my shoulder and squeezed my arm. We stayed that way for a long time, and then she kissed my hair and said, "Where did you go, Roger? No one knows where you went."

I felt I was warmed up and ready to take on Daddy's poetic side. I said, "Naturally, Alice, I went to the place where high things go."

"High as a kite?" she said, and I could feel her sloppy grin through my sleeve.

"Don't try to be poetic, Alice. It doesn't suit you."

We were tired, exhausted by middle age, so we went inside and lay on the bed. After a while I remembered to fly a towel for her, matching its descent and vanishing before her very blue eyes.

But when I slept I didn't have my father's dreams, unless he'd dreamt about Calvin, about blowing freckles off Calvin's nose and watching them scatter and catch the last summer wind. I know Daddy couldn't have, though, and for so many reasons. To begin, he once told me that he'd only ever had the same dream.

Friday

Calvin's red Chevette was in the driveway, but when I knocked, no one answered.

I went through the back gate and tried the sliding glass door. The wooden stick was in place. Somewhere a TV, or maybe one of Calvin's cassettes, was playing something folksy and hopeful.

I returned to the cabin. The place was as settled as a body at rest.

I returned to her house and banged on the door.

I returned home and, into the ear of her answering machine, yelled, "Maggie, what the hell? Princess Jasmine needs to be fed."

Because it was Friday—date night, buy-one-get-one-half-off night—there was a group of high school boys whispering by the pinball machine and a group of high school girls whispering by the pie case. As usual, when they coupled off to their tables, it was always a handsome boy escorting a gorgeous girl. Or a fat boy escorting a mousy girl—as if their afflictions were somehow equal under teenage law.

"Just look at them," Mom said, and I thought she might actually spit.

"I can't say I'm surprised. The mountain has always been infested with the little assholes. What? You think because you're young you own words like asshole? Everyone's got an asshole, girl. I told your friend to use the cabin for making out. I said nothing about saving all of God's little creatures." Grandmother Sager took a long swig of iced tea and rapped her knuckles on the table. "Besides, I've got terrible arthritis."

"It's life or death," I said. "You can lean on me."

She pinched her bottom lip and stared at my hand. I looked away, waiting for her to finish.

On the path she pointed out the tall trees she'd known as saplings and the stumps she'd known as tall trees. "Cut down and for what?" she said. "Dreams of a perfect Christmas? Or wood for a fancy armoire?"

I assumed an armoire was a prosthetic arm. I based this on the fact that my presence seemed to incite conversations about prosthetics. How often did I hear sentences like *I got a cousin with a glass eye* or *My uncle gave his leg to 'Nam*. I don't give a shit about your cousin's wonky eye or your ignorant sense of what's giving and what's having had taken. I said to Miss Sager, "They make them all plastic now."

"Never were truer words spoken," she said. "It's all plastic. When you're my age, even trees will be *man*ufactured. It's the men, you see, who prefer plastic. I never knew a one of them who wanted the real thing.

"What thing?"

"Anything. When you're my age, you'll pick your tree out at the store. You'll have to choose between 'Now with thirty percent more' or 'Made from concentrate.'" Sweat made pale lines in her makeup.

"I'll never be your age," I said.

When we arrived at the cabin, she jiggled the door and then plucked a pebble from the ground and chucked it at the window where it sang *Ping!* and bounced off.

"You don't have a *key*?" I said. "Hello. Why did I bring you?" She threw a bigger rock, this time fracturing the pane. "*I* could have done that," I said.

"No you couldn't have," she said. "Or you would have."

I picked up a rock and threw it. It broke through one corner, glass flying in.

"Feels amazing, don't it?" she said. She handed me another, and I threw until most of the glass was gone. She stabbed off the remaining shards with a stick.

At the foot of the bed, still made up with Maggie's towels, were our cereal box bowls. Maggie's flowers had wilted inside them. Princess Jasmine was gone.

"It's not here," I shouted. "She took it." I unlocked the door.

"Oh my," Miss Sager said. "This place looks like—"

"It was ours and she took it, and she didn't tell me." I began to pace. "Can you believe that? I mean, *can you?*"

Miss Sager sat in the rocking chair, pushed hard, and lifted her feet like a child taking flight in a swing. "I've always loved this chair. It was a gift from Thursday. What a dreamboat, my Thursday."

I crumpled the cereal boxes and flowers and chucked them out the window.

"Hey now," Miss Sager said. "If you need to have yourself a tantrum, you can go outside."

But I must have looked pretty upset because she stood and steered me to the rocking chair. "Relax. I'll make a cup of tea." Then she saw the black pipe hanging down where the wood-burning stove had been. "Never mind," she said, patting my knee. "Tea never helped anyone. This chair, though, is pure magic. They moved it to town for me, but after a year I told them to move it back. Sitting in it only ever felt good here."

"But you're never here," I said. I was only half-listening anyway. I was thinking about running to Maggie's house and throwing rocks through her windows.

"You think you need to be in a place to be in a place?" Grandmother Sager said. She flicked pieces of glass off the window sill. "So what is it with you and Maggie? You two *close?*" She raised her eyebrows.

"She's my best friend."

"Damn, girl, I'm asking if you're sexual together."

"Gross, no."

She put her hands up. "I'm just making an observation. You're crying today, and she was crying the other day. I know teenage girls cry, but, shit, you two are a mess. I was telling her about Thursday and some of the things he liked to do, and—"

"You're a dirty old lady," I said.

"I'm at peace with that," she said. She leaned over and touched my hair. "You know, you've got some pretty in you, too." She let the hair fall through her fingers. "It's a shame about your hand and that rash."

"Shows what you know. It's not a rash."

"Will you let me finish? I was saying, it's a shame, but it won't matter when you're older. See, boys might care, but men don't." Again, she patted my knee. "Men don't care a thing about fingers. Probably better if you've got none!"

I didn't know what to say, but she seemed to be waiting, so I said, "Thank you." By the way she smiled, I could tell it was the right thing. I told her I had to go find Maggie. I said I'd return soon.

Calvin, wearing only red gym shorts and a thick triangle of orange chest hair, was padding out to his car. When he saw me coming up the sidewalk, he leaned back with his elbows against the Chevette's passenger door. Looking off over rooftops, he said, "Listen, Pidge—I can call you Pidge, can't I? See, I saw a movie once about two dogs, and one called the other Pidge and—"

"You mean *Lady and the Tramp*?"

"Hey, how'd you know that? Well, anyway, I've always wanted to call someone Pidge. And you need a nickname, as we previously established. *And* you *look* like a Pidge. Not a duck or a swan." He reached out and touched my neck, this time with his fingertips. "Yeah," he said. "Yeah, yeah, a pidgin. You belong in a city. Not here. Not like Maggie. You walk down Main Street, and you stand out real bad. But in a city, man, in a city, you'd be invisible, and that's the best feeling in the world. In a city, every person is…" He dropped his hand, and I felt a warmth run down my body as if he'd been applying pressure to keep me from bleeding out.

"What?" I said. "What is every person?"

"Why don't I show you sometime? I'm returning to school in a couple weeks. You could tell your parents you were staying with Maggie. That's what I'd say, and then—you ever buy a bus ticket?"

"No." I looked at my feet. I felt light-headed and spinny. Angry that I couldn't remember why I'd come. Oh, the possum. But I'd have to come back for that. I'd just have to come back.

"There's nothing easier," he said. "Don't say no yet. I know you want to say yes. You're a sweet girl. Heck, Pidge, I bet you never told a lie in your life. I'm only saying, if you want to see what life will be like when you grow up."

I nodded and retreated to the sidewalk. He waved, car keys jingling in the air, and I waved back, though it was little more than my good hand shuddering at my waist. My bad hand was firmly tucked in my pocket. I thought about what Miss Sager said: *men* don't care. Maybe it was true. I watched him out of the corner of my eye until my vision was filled with Mrs. Fisher's rose bushes, mottled from aphids.

Then he yelled, "Oh! Oh! Oh!"

I turned back, my thoughts momentarily blurred but for an impossible image of us old and married and laughing about that day he invited me to visit him at college and then slipped and fell on his ass. No, not an image, but a whole narrative, like how they say your life flashes before your eyes when you die. Well it was my life, my future life. I dated, married, raised babies, grew old and died with Calvin. In a flash, it was a good life.

Naturally, when I reached him, I brought with me our fifty years of marriage.

He hadn't fallen, but he was standing by the trunk of the car, bent over and vomiting. I cupped his forehead with my good hand the way Mom did when I was sick, the way a wife does for her husband. A putrid smell filled my nose and mouth, and at first I thought the stench came from the rivulets of puke running down the driveway—my mind already revising my future memory to the time he invited me to visit him at college and was then suddenly stricken by food poisoning.

He pointed to the passenger door, hanging ajar. Inside the glove box, two milky marbles bulged out of blood-matted fur. The tongue was blue and fat enough to choke open the mouth.

All I could think to say was, "Her teeth are all broken."

"I think from biting the trap," Maggie said. Like magic, she was on the porch, propping open the screen door with her foot. "I'm sorry you had to see this," she said to me.

Calvin wiped his mouth and charged toward her.

"Sweetheart," I called and reached for him. Fuck, it just slipped out, what my mom called my dad. What my dad called me. For a second, Calvin glanced back, confused and maybe even disgusted. Then he was on the step with her, pinning her against the side of the house with his hands on her pelvis. The screen door swung shut.

"You did this?" he said.

"Scene of the crime, Baby," she said.

"You little bitch. When I'm done with you—"

"What?" She grabbed his chin like a mother leading a fussy child out of the candy aisle. "When you're done, *what?*"

I turned and ran up the sidewalk—dragging my arm through rose bushes and relishing the stings. I thought of the aphids and on impulse put a few leaves in my mouth. I suppose I wanted to taste what they tasted. Chewing on rose leaves, I wept the rest of the way home. I thought, Oh God, oh wow, how embarrassing. Oh wow. Oh my God. It wasn't just the thing with calling him Sweetheart. Or with seeing Princess Jasmine dead and stuffed in a glove box. Worst of all was this part of me—a part that longed to be slapped around, just a tiny bit, just enough—that liked Calvin even more now.

Mom was bent over the stove. "You got mail," she said, taking a postcard out of her robe pocket.

On the front, a mouse was standing on a cat standing on a dog standing on a man on his knees on the sand. *Miami, Florida,* it said. Who did I know in Florida? On the back, it said: *Sweetheart, have a great first week. Love, Dad*

Mom wrapped an arm around my waist, and together we watched three pieces of spam sizzle in the pan.

Sunday

It occurred to me that I'd abandoned Grandmother Sager in the cabin just as Mom, gripping the steering wheel with her knees, dragged coral lipstick across her mouth. Her black church skirt was bunched up in her lap, exposing dimpled, ghost-white thighs. It was out of my hands, I decided. I'd have to fetch the old lady later. Besides, she still had cereal.

Maggie wasn't in service, but her mom and stepdad were. After half an hour, I excused myself and hunted around until I found Maggie outside by the dumpster. She was smoking a cigarette. Her hair was loosely pinned up with strands falling across her face.

"So Calvin gives you cigarettes," I said. "That's low."

"Some things are just mine," she said. "He hides them for me in his car. He was getting me one yesterday." She slipped the butt under a black pump I recognized as her mother's and then sat on her hands as if that alone could calm their bad habits.

"How's it going in there?" she said.

"With every sentence, he's like, *I relate to you. Watch me as I relate to you.* Then Zack passed a dumb note, and Audrey looked at him like he was the second coming."

"Or like in that second she was coming?"

I pulled a weed from a crack in the pavement and ripped off the leaves. They were fuzzy on top and prickly on the bottom, very different from rose leaves. I said, "I can't believe you did that to Princess Jasmine."

"She was going to die anyway. Besides, that wasn't her official name. You vetoed it."

I wanted to say, *Touché,* but the word escaped me. I kept thinking, Toupee, Toupee. I noticed then that her hair was not actually pinned up. It was shorter, cut severely at her jaw line. I said, "I don't like it. You'll go back to school looking like a bug."

The stem was bare. We tossed it aside and picked another.

Finally I asked, "With Calvin, I mean I guess you two…What is"—I didn't know what to call *it* and moved my hand as if waving steam off hot food—"like?"

"You mean…?" She raised her eyebrows.

I nodded.

"His chest hair is like an orange Shroud of Turin. I wanted to tell you about it all summer."

Anger reverberated up my body like a force enacted upon a taut rope. It made a ringing in my ears that sounded like the church bell. No, that *was* the church bell. *Ding-dong,* it said, *Good bye.* Or maybe *Sor-ry* or *So long* or *You're wrong* or *Hur-ry.*

Out came the congregation. My mom and Maggie's mom walked shoulder-to-shoulder as they chatted and laughed. Behind them, Jim carried Alice's purse. A remnant of my dad, my cabin-pretend version anyway, whispered, *He looks like a goddamn homosexual. She deserves a real man.* The three of them caught sight of the three of us and headed our way.

"Your parents appear rested," I said, knowing she'd flinch at my use of "parents."

"You're not going to tattle, are you?" Maggie said. "You are, aren't you? I knew it. Jesus, some friend. At least give me a minute to compose myself."

I realized then that Maggie wanted me to tell. Maybe she hadn't always, but she did now. She'd been trying to get my attention. When I couldn't see what she was going through, she'd stuffed Princess Jasmine into a glove box.

I lifted my bad hand like a gun to her head. All the piggies were in agreement. Someone had to be made to feel sorry. For the secrets, for Calvin's unfettered freckles, for my mother's grief, for Maggie's body, for my body, for every body, even my dad's body. How hard it must have been yearning for Alice. For his absence and His absence.

It was so easy. I didn't even have to curl my fingers—fingers that weren't there, that would never be there. For a moment I thought— wildly—I thought I'd been born for this one thing, to avenge Maggie. Only, it seemed pretty clear that Maggie had to die to be avenged. I was calm. My heart was racing. You know what really irked me? That someone might cut off her own hair to be noticed. Sweat beaded at my temples and slipped down, water off a duck's back.

"How does it feel?" I asked. "To be dealt a bad hand?"

Maggie doubled over her knees, laughing. When she saw I was serious despite the finger gun hovering between us, she started to weep. She said, "It wasn't what you think. He's not a good person."

I pushed the barrel into her temple, and to shut her pretty mouth, I pulled the trigger. "Bang," I whispered.

She flew, reaching to cup her head as it hit the sidewalk. One leg fell open and one splayed out forward, Alice's black pump pointing up like an arrow.

"*Girls*," Mom said, taking my elbow. "Explain yourselves."

"Honey, are you alright?" Alice knelt next to Maggie and brushed the bug hair out of her face. Jim remained on the grass. His expression seemed to say, Best to let the women handle this. *What a pussy*, my dad thought.

"It's only a game," I said, shrugging. "She's fine."

"Is that true?" Alice lifted her daughter's chin to look into her eyes, windows, they say, into the soul.

I guess Maggie's soul said, "Yes."

That night I slipped out and bought a bus ticket to Miami. I chose the seat with tears in it, there's always one, and held my backpack in my lap. I spent hours like that, riding on adrenaline and on fantasies about what people would say at school. Would anyone notice the missing girl with her missing parts? Nah, I decided. Would they send a search party? Nah. That's the thing about missing stuff—what separates it from lost or taken—no one hardly ever goes looking for it. They would be too busy settling into their new classrooms and writing their little essays, "What I did this Summer" and shit like that.

As if there was more to say beyond it was summer, and it was hot.

When I was a little girl, before I met Maggie, I used to stand in front of the bathroom mirror and talk to the duck.

How are you today, Ducky?

Quack, quack-quack, my dad would say. He'd be shaving or brushing his teeth, his eyes bloodshot but always happy to see me. *Quack, quack-quack. Quack?*

Oh I agree, Ducky! The park!

I got as far as Fayetteville before I remembered, again, that I'd left Grandmother Sager in the cabin. Had she hobbled back to town or was she reliving her glory days? What if she broke a hip? Wasn't that something old people were always doing, along with bingo and meddling?

I went back and forth between leaving it be and alerting someone but also between Arkansas and Florida. My thoughts, contrary as they were, sped and ricocheted so that by the time I stepped off the bus in Little Rock and shielded my eyes from the station's lights, I could phantom-feel both pine needles and sand in my shoes. I could smell a basket of North Forty fries and the ocean at high tide. It was all one sleepy, sifting, greasy, fishy, salty moment, and when it passed, I felt I understood the real meaning of full and the real meaning of empty.

I dialed Mom on a payphone. I was only going to tell her about Grandmother Sager, but then a skinny hobo with pieces of cardboard tied to his feet padded loose from the dark. His eyes were so wide and drugged they gave the impression of goggles. When Mom answered—sounding half-awake as she said, "Roger, is that you?"—I wondered if it were all planned.

Maybe she'd watched me leave and then hired this man, who did somewhat resemble Mr. Peterson from the pharmacy, to follow me. Had filth turned his palms black, or was it Mom's eye shadow that she, herself, had generously applied?

Roger, is that *you?*

It was sneaky and mean, and she was capable of it. Her love, I realized, wasn't confused by affection, by who I was or even by who she was. It was blind and unbreakable. She would cheat, steal, and kill to bring me home, but all she really had to do was give me doubts about how I'd find Daddy, about what shape his life had taken.

What I know now about motherhood, what I know for certain, is that we are all only illusionists. So, sure, I was probably wrong then, but I wasn't that far off right.

Knowing I'd call, she rehearsed her line. She readied her man. Stare hard, she directed hobo Mr. Peterson, and open your arms as if to say, Welcome. Because that's how you scare this girl.

✳

When I gave birth to my son—a hard, natural labor because I insisted I could handle the pain, even after the doctor said there was no shame in taking the edge off—the nurse placed the baby on my chest, and I touched him quickly all over. I rolled each toe and finger. I stretched his arms. He wailed and sputtered as I rotated his pink head. He was perfect. A little messy, but perfect in every way. Despite having found adulthood to be, if not evenhanded, at least kinder toward my body, I'd spent my pregnancy imagining—to the point of making myself cry, to the point of getting high—that my child would somehow be deformed, birth-defective, and that he would need me to protect him. *I'll do that*, I'd whispered to my ballooning belly. *God give me strength, I'll never let anyone hurt you.* Now that he was flawless, a part of me wondered what I could even offer and recognized him not as the hurt but as the hurter. Wait for it, I told myself. "Shh shh shh," I told my son as his daddy, my first husband, kissed us both. "Shh shh. Mommy's here. Mommy loves you." Just wait, I told my son in my head, a habit of pregnancy not so easily pushed out. You'll fuck up like everybody fucks up, and I'll be there to see it, to catalog it, to count it against you. That's what I'll do for you. I'll see everything. And in the end you'll need me, and my love will be there, stronger than ten strong men. Then, in your weakness and in my strength, we'll be of a kind.

—CANDICE MORROW—

Maggie's hand was inspired by Dickinson's poem, "My Life had stood—a Loaded Gun," which I encountered as a young, still hopeful writing student. My first thought after reading it was, Holy shit, I know that feeling. I've *owned* that feeling. Much of my childhood was spent fretting over the timing—sometimes inconvenient, sometimes brilliant—of the next seizure. Even my doctor called them "electrical misfires in the brain." Like all young, still hopeful, writing students, I recorded the poem in a notebook, along with any other bits that begged to be picked off the world. Years later, while revisiting old writings—I should mention I'm afflicted with chronic nostalgia, a truer disability than epilepsy in my mind—I rediscovered the poem. I couldn't stop thinking about it, so I set about creating a character who was, like me, a loaded gun. I felt that if I wanted to convey my experience, I couldn't write about epilepsy. Rather, I had to write *of* it. Then, for kicks, I took a few fingers.

Kristen Harmon

WHAT LAY AHEAD
(Three Linked Short Stories)

Wrestling Daddy: Lucas

Someone's hearing aid whistled, and Lucas blinked. The two white boys standing next to him in the well-lit kitchen automatically reached up to make sure it wasn't either one of theirs. As they turned to a place inside themselves, concentrating, they looked like broadcasters with a breaking news report—a hand pressing the ear—waiting. Risa, the only girl in the group and the only one not wearing aids, smiled for the first time all evening, probably at the sudden, synchronized movement.

They were all graduating seniors at the state school for the deaf, and Lucas would not have minded a little news about where to go from here. He tapped his aid and barely heard the shallow thump. The battery must be dying.

"Mine," said Shane, turning down the volume on his behind-the-ear aid, a color that used to be called flesh. Lucas' first aids—a loaner pair—had been that Ken doll color, crescents behind his ears until his own arrived.

Only one more month here, Lucas thought. And then?

In the kitchen of this old house near the school, Lucas crossed his arms and watched Shane toss back the rest of his beer. Shane continued signing and voicing his story about Mrs. Fulton, the school's speech and language pathologist. From experience, Lucas knew Mrs. Fulton seemed too fond of pressing reluctant fingers into her neck. She had just changed her hairstyle after her divorce and wore bright red lipstick, too, and so jokes about her ran wild over the school, in corners, wherever the administration couldn't see.

Feel here, she always said. Shane mimicked her over-enunciation, the way she angled herself so that you had to see her lips, no matter how hard you tried to look away. Watch my lips. Learn to listen. See the train leave. Hiss out the "s," like an arrow. S-s-s-s. Shane spit when he hissed.

Expelled from the mainstreaming programs at the public schools, Shane had started as a senior at the institution. Lucas could tell he loved being there, loved using his new signs. They'd become friends even though

Lucas refused to use the deaf and dumb signs, as his dad called them, waving his hands and twisting his face like a gargoyle. Plus, as his uncle Gene had made sure he understood, get into the wrong place at the wrong time and you might get hurt. It happens, Gene said, and put his hand on Lucas' shoulder. Be careful. You know?

That afternoon, before the party, Lucas had been in a speech session. When Mrs. Fulton became exasperated with his mistakes, she pressed his hand harder into his own throat.

Shane mimicked her prissy manner. "You sound like a cartoon character." Shane shook his head back and forth and placed his hands on his hips.

Lucas wondered if Mrs. Fulton meant the hero, villain, or sidekick. Who would hire a sidekick? He vowed to work harder with his speech, work to get his father's deep glass muffler rumble.

"You know my girl, Becka, right?" Shane signed and asked around the kitchen. His wild blonde curls wavered above his questioning face. His eyes widened, and Lucas could see the two differently colored eyes, one greenish-brown, and one green-gray. Shane paused when he looked at Lucas, and he knew that Shane waited, out of habit, for a response from Lucas. Sometimes this constant checking annoyed Lucas, especially since it meant that he had to get involved.

Lucas nodded: gotcha.

Sure, Lucas remembered Becka, the hearing white girl who came to the school from the nearby university's speech pathology program. But when had she become *Shane's* girl? Every time Lucas and Shane went to the mall, girls trailed out of The Gap and Victoria's Secret, trying to fingerspell their own names. After shaping each letter like a fist, those skinny girls nearly fell over laughing.

Becoming deaf had been, in the beginning, the best thing Lucas could have done for his budding love life. Girls fought over holding his hand. At first, after getting sick with spinal meningitis at the age of eight, he had not been glad that he'd survived, with the sudden deafness dropped around him. But then girls either thought he was sweet or romantically aloof.

At home, though, his mother was always so worn out from her job as a paralegal in training that she couldn't pay much attention. Every day, after the small, endless demands of her workday, she gave Lucas a drooping hug, her forearms heavy on his shoulders, her hands wilting from her wrists.

While his mother took care of dinner, his daddy spent just as much time out in the garage—really an aluminum overhang that used to rattle with the rain, Lucas remembered—with his friends, slid up under cars and listening to the radio.

Lucas tried and tried to understand his father, but he was too hard to lipread, too quick in exchanging one-liners with Russ and Mack and 'Dolphus and Uncle Gene. Lucas got his hair cut close to the skin like Gene and even got a tattoo of a flaming arrow and still no response from the men, just a quiet inspection from Russ.

"Who you putting the show on for over there at the special school?" he asked. Lucas shrugged, embarrassed by Russ's grin and wink. Russ laughed and said something, his mouth shaping an unrecognizable message.

Rather than show that he didn't understand, Lucas slapped the question off his face and practiced blankness, followed here and there with a causal, I-hear-you, tell-it hand clap on somebody's back. He almost never gave himself away. That way, no one could wince at his mistakes, least of all his dad.

One thing Lucas couldn't quite adjust to was how easy so many of his classmates were with their voices, how they didn't care what they sounded like to the waitresses, grocery store clerks, all the hearing people in the town with their suspicious eyes and deaf-mute jokes.

"I asked Mrs. Fulton to teach me to say 'I like the way you giggle at me,' so I can try it out on Becka, right?" Shane said. Shane had begun to sign only the nouns, relying more on his voice, and this telegraphic signing was hard to follow. Lucas saw that Risa had dropped out of their circle. She looked instead out the doorway to the porch and her cousin, Marjie.

"Well, I practice saying it, and Mrs. Fulton swats my hand." Shane lifted his hand, and with an effeminate downswing, tapped Risa's arm. Startled, she looked up at Shane.

"She left and the counselor comes in, all worried because she thinks I came on to Mrs. Fulton." Another holding-back pause, working the room. "I say, 'So, what're you saying?' to the counselor, who says, 'You mean, you didn't make inappropriate advances on Mrs. Fulton?'"

Shane ducked his head, laughing. "Turns out, what I accidentally said to that old fart: 'I like the way you jiggle at me.'" He cupped his hands in front of his chest. Shane and the other boys burst out laughing, and Lucas slipped out of the room, embarrassed.

Rocco and Marjie, two of the "smooth" signers, stood out on the front porch under the one weak light, rehearsing the school play.

As usual, Rocco and Marjie seemed unnecessarily intense to Lucas, moving from tight comment about history to angry signed explanations to getting choked up to some sob story the teacher, Mr. Woods, told. Lucas had a hard time following all of their signs and facial expressions, but he usually got the gist of things. He didn't understand why they felt so oppressed. They were white. Rocco's family ran a restaurant in town, so they had money. And everyone knew Marjie. She never had to prove herself. Lucas knew the type from before: even though her family didn't have a lot of money, Marjie was the head cheerleader, the student body president, and she walked around with either a laugh or a frown, depending on who you were. Her parents often showed up after school to watch the varsity football practices, and Lucas wondered about that. One or both of them usually had a huge 7-11 cup of Coke, the kind that almost required two hands to hold.

In the deaf history and culture class he had with Marjie, he kept to himself. Every once in awhile, Woods put a hand on Lucas' shoulder and asked him to stay after class. Lucas didn't want another father, and so he acted like he didn't understand Woods' signing.

Feeling comfortably invisible, Lucas sat on a folding chair in the dark side of the porch. Past the street and below, he could see the Mississippi River, a slow unwinding flash. Rocco and Marjie ignored him.

Marjie wanted to go on to be a deaf actress or something, so she argued with Rocco about the play's translation.

Thinking, Rocco twisted off his ball cap, flattened the brim, and slapped it back on.

He used the name sign, *H-Prince*, for the main character, and signed something about how he was pissed off at the world. Lucas remembered the flyers advertising the upcoming school play, an American Sign Language version of *Hamlet*.

No, no. Marjie shook her head at Rocco. Always tan and smooth-looking, with long straight light brown hair, a long nose, and narrowed eyes, she looked good on the stage.

Being. She stood taller and swept a hand over her figure, presenting herself. She paused and then, with slumped shoulders and a firm shake of her head, swept her hand before herself again and crumbled a decaying body between her hands, *Not being.*

She stepped forward toward an imagined audience in the dark yard, the

Mississippi River curving the horizon, and with raised eyebrows, balanced her hands: *Which?*

Rocco shook his head. *No, not that.*

Marjie saw Lucas watching. She glared at him and then turned so that he couldn't see her face. He saw her shoulders shrug in a comment she made to Rocco.

With a dry feeling in his throat, Lucas pushed forward and stood between them. Rocco reached for Lucas' arm, but Marjie stepped between them. They stared at each other, waiting.

"Say it," Lucas yelled into Marjie's tight face. "Go ahead. To my FACE."

Marjie, with a slow, deliberate movement: *Stop. Stop talk, talk, talk. No one understands what you say.* But then she paused and looked like maybe she felt sorry for him. *Wake up!*

She turned away from him again, and Rocco copied her movement, with an extra head toss and *so-there* flair. But this time, they stood so that Lucas could see their faces.

Lucas watched to see what they would say about him, like he had once when his daddy had been listening to the radio while he worked on the car. His father had turned, looked at Lucas with an open face, shouted, and danced Lucas around the garage.

Turned inside out with joy and fear, Lucas had waited for an explanation. But then, they turned away from him and life went on as usual, without breaking news, no directions on whether to come closer or to just go on. Cut your losses.

Lucas got on her nerves, just standing around the porch like that.

No fight, just like her character, Ophelia. Waiting for something to happen. She couldn't respect that.

Jim Woods, the teacher of her Deaf Culture class, always opened class by pointing to images of different groups of activists waving banners and walking a protest line. She wanted to rush right down into those photographs and wave placards mounted on two-by-fours and kick some butt. She couldn't wait to get there, wherever it was.

When Jim first came to the school, she had made up her mind that he didn't have much to teach her. He had graduated from the oral deaf school in the same state, a school where ASL was forbidden in the classroom but the students still signed, on the sly, in the dorms. He signed like he came from a hearing family.

But at the beginning of that first class, Woods had told them that too many people in the hearing world thought that deaf people could only be poster children or factory workers. He then pointed to all of them.

Are you a victim? he signed. Most shook their heads with energy. *No? Then what do you plan to do?*

Nobody had asked her that before.

She had even taken one of his many inspirational sayings as her e-mail sign-off: "Go and have adventures. You'll live longer." She wondered what that would mean, though.

Rocco sat down on the edge of the porch. *Can't stand him.* He made a claw of his hand in Lucas' direction.

She shrugged and sat next to him. She dangled her legs off the porch.

Holding her hand out for a cigarette, she angled herself, making sure they could still see each other in the flickering light of the porch. Rocco was okay, as long as he didn't go on and on about how he would become famous after he left the school.

The way she saw it, the best thing you could do is to go get your education and then come back to where you began, do something where it matters, at home. When so many of the school's students left for larger deaf communities in the cities and better jobs on the coasts, the decision to return to this small river town was no piece of cake. She'd show them, those townies who thought deaf people were dumb.

Like Woods, she wanted to get her degree and then teach at the deaf school. Before Woods had come to the school, there had been no deaf people in the faculty, just a lot of blank-faced hearing people with smoker's mouths who thought they signed better than they did. It was cool, having him there.

Rocco shook his head with disgust. He stubbed out the cigarette he'd been smoking, shook his pack like a pro, and lit a new one. Like a flare, his cigarette burned traces on the air. An expensive brand. He took a long luxurious puff.

Show-off, she thought.

But then Marjie sighed. She did care, because he was cute, and girls outnumbered boys three to one at the school. Most of the boys she'd started with had dropped out, frustrated, bored, or restless, ready to get on with *something*. Some of them had moved to the nearby city, and she saw them when she and her cousin Risa took off to go there on Saturdays. Lately, though, Risa had been disappearing for whole days, coming back reeking of smoke and grinning like she'd had more beers than she could handle.

Hate this P O V E R T Y town. Today, at Pizza Barn, an idiot refused my note-order. He talked-twisted his lips at me. Said, if you're deaf, then lip-read me. Come on, lip-read me. Rocco squeezed his hands into a choke-hold in front of him and made a frustrated face.

I am deaf and do not read lips. I want one medium, pepperoni pizza and a large Coke. Why can't YOU read, asshole? He held out a hand, miming the scene and his note.

Marjie laughed and nodded. Once, when she'd gone to a jeans store and tried on a pair in the dressing room, the security cops broke down the door. All because the saleslady thought she was shoplifting when she didn't answer some dumb "How's everything in there?"

Should have taken Lucas, he can interpret, she told Rocco. *But then they might think he's stealing something.* She looked over at Lucas and mock-grimaced an *oops.*

She figured he wouldn't understand anyway.

But then Lucas moved forward into the circle of porch light and waved at her, flagging her attention.

Again? he signed. *What did you say?* He tapped his lips, a slow challenge in his walk.

Here it comes, she thought. She stood up slowly and put on her bitch face.

She'd be damned if she let Lucas look down on her just because she signed and he spoke. She would not be pressured into becoming something she wasn't.

Her dad said that when you got worn out from kicking and being mad about the world, that's when your soul got tested. That's where faith comes in, he said, but she wasn't quite sure how that worked, how that kept you from getting knocked around, how that kept you from getting rug burn on your chin.

She liked her father, but sometimes he got too wrapped up in his own theories. Before getting religion, he'd collected newspaper clippings about unbelievable events, alien abductions, brain implants, and joined twin separations. Lately, he'd gotten involved with petitions, going door-to-door to get signatures to protect American jobs.

Rocco sighed for her benefit, stood, crossed his arms, and turned to face Lucas, his careful fingers holding out the cigarette away from his elbow. Lucas clenched his fists, and as clear as anything, Marjie saw that Rocco waited for Lucas to knock the cigarette out of his hand. Rocco wanted the fight, she saw, but he wanted Lucas to start it. Such a stupid guy thing. At least she wasn't the focus anymore. They stared at each other, not her.

But if that security cop hadn't been twice her size, she'd have fought him all the way to the police station. Instead, when the cop showed up and wrestled her to the floor, she had screamed just as hard as she could.

But this time, the fight wasn't with some hearing dickhead. She knew that Woods sometimes had to stop fights in the dorms. What would Woods do with Lucas and Rocco?

One day, in class, they had been shouting in sign about being minorities in a hearing world, and Woods said that if he were a hearing person and there was an operation to make him deaf, he would be the first in line.

True biz, he had told them. *First in line.*

That hit her. *True biz.*

What if everybody had that chance, to choose?

Maybe that's what it came down to, in this yard, at this party just above the Mississippi River.

You have to choose something that meant something. That's how you move forward, to the next thing, and the next, no matter where you are.

Maybe she didn't need to worry about working at the warehouse or the greenhouse just because there was nothing else and state VR had been cut. Maybe she didn't need to feel the ache in her stomach whenever her mom said she didn't like how Marjie and Risa's school had changed—not like it used to be—and that they should move to Indiana or even as far as Maryland. Maybe she wasn't stuck after all in somebody else's world.

Living your life and getting on with something that was real, that you made happen. Nobody else but you. Having some fun every now and then.

Fun, she thought.

And then: *I'm tired.*

Maybe she should just leave, and forget everything else. She sighed. She expertly twisted off the black rubber band on her wrist, held it in her mouth, and pulled her hair into a ponytail. Both boys looked at her, caught up in the small personal ritual. She twisted and tightened the ponytail, and then smiled at them, a tight, *let's-just-forget-it* smile.

She walked into the house. At the doorway, she looked back, and sure enough, both boys stared at her.

Your life. She shrugged.

Rocco shrugged at her and took a drag on his cigarette. He looked at Lucas, ready to keep going. Lucas watched Marjie, a surprised look on his face. Looking at Lucas, Rocco relaxed his shoulders.

Of course, she thought, pleased.

Come on. Doesn't matter. Not your fault. Want a beer? she asked them.

Lucas nodded.

Rocco flicked his cigarette out into the dirt yard, a small red light spinning outwards.

Look—a UFO, she pointed and told Rocco, grinning. They had their own joke about UFOs and crop circles, stuff her dad used to go around photographing.

Lucas frowned.

She held her first fingers together in a circle and imitated a round disk hovering and zipping through the sky. *The cigarette—he flicked it out— spinning—it looked like a UFO.*

He looked at her for a long moment. Then: *you're weird.* He grinned.

They smiled at each other. Rocco shifted next to her, not sure what was happening.

Anyway, she slapped her hands together. *Imagine. Night. A small earth—closer—go to sky—saucer flying.* She smiled at her audience. *Then, a tree. Saucer circles slow, and slower, and pauses, behind a branch. Like a strange bird perching.*

I like that, Lucas signed. *Nice. Clear. Beautiful.* He nodded at her. *You should do that again, sometime. A play.*

True, beautiful, she told Lucas. *I saw one time. True biz. With a red ring, arrows shooting out. But not dangerous.*

She saw her life: not an alien abduction, and not a falling star, burning up, but a letting go, fiery like living, watery like faith.

When Rocco swaggered into the kitchen from the porch, Marjie and Lucas behind him, Risa thought *Marjie, so typical, she captured a new conquest*, and then looked away from the trio. She focused instead on Shane, seated across the card table from her. Marjie, Lucas, and Rocco nodded as they passed. They made their way into the steamy living room, warm with old yellow lamps and too many people.

When she made sure it was just her and Shane left in the kitchen—for once—no one in the kitchen—she waved her hand at Shane, told him, *Watch, ok?*, and when he focused his beer goggles on her, she asked, *Why did Rocco put condoms in his ears?*

Shane tilted forward on his toes and shook his head. Shane grinned with the same waiting anticipation Rick had when she tried her voice with him and told her joke.

Because he didn't want to get—she paused and fingerspelled and said—AIDS. *AIDS. Hearing aids. Get it?*

Judging from how Shane paused and looked over at Rocco, standing with his back to them in the doorway of the living room, Shane must have heard something from Rocco about her.

All she'd done was spend one night out in the woods with him, watching him gripe. Nothing happened, not really. Not anything important. Eventually, they had stretched out beside the bonfire, pretending to sleep.

The next day, when Risa and Shane were sitting and waiting for math class to start, he'd taken her underwear out of his backpack and thrown it at her, laughing, but with a face like maybe he was disgusted with her. She had thrown them under her desk into her bag. I don't care, she had thought. You're just a boy, anyway.

With a wishing so deep that it felt like nausea, she wished that Rick could drive up right then in his truck and take her away somewhere.

Risa crossed her arms on the table and rested her chin on her stacked hands. Heavy-lidded and sweaty, Shane lounged back in the kitchen chair. His gray-green eye opened wider than the other, and his hands formed fragments of thoughts.

Her chest pressed against the table, Risa felt her heartbeat rattling the flimsy table. She wondered if anyone else could see how she had a secret, how she was loved by someone none of them knew, not a single one of them.

Rick was the first hearing man she'd ever met who seemed not to need anything from her, who liked Risa for herself, and not simply because everyone knew who she was. He was older, twenty-four, divorced, with a daughter he saw when he could get away.

They'd met at a pool hall. He'd come up to her and her friends and fingerspelled, H-O-W A-R-E, then laughed and pointed at Risa's chest, bringing the slurred question to her.

In spite of herself, she'd fallen in love with his awkward, thick-fingered fingerspelling. He'd shown her a picture of a blonde, startled-looking little girl holding a Barbie doll by her hair, and told her how much he loved his little girl and how he wanted more kids. Her friends had laughed at the same old story of a guy like that with a girl like them, but something about him had caught her attention.

She sighed, a heavy one, halfway hoping that someone would see and ask her what was wrong. Somebody turned on the music in the next room and the table rattled and shook with the heavy bass.

When she went to the dance club with Rick, she never wore her hearing aids, and the bass jarred her vision, in pulses. The music pressed thumbs into her eye sockets, ba bump, ba bump.

Before meeting Rick, she'd never opened up when a strange hearing man sat down next to her. She just nodded and smiled, then looked away and talked with her friends whenever his mouth moved. But then she'd met Rick. He had a funny little blonde soul patch under his lip. She smiled back. He listened to her, even though she wondered just how much he understood of her excruciating, slow signs and fingerspelling. He'd nod and smile, and watch her hands.

Her cousin Marjie walked into the kitchen and held up her wrist under the kitchen light so she could see the time better. Their fathers were brothers and had gone to the school together twenty years ago. Risa's dad had left for the city while her uncle stayed and started up a deaf Holiness church, called Tenderly and Sweetly Jesus, with a sign showing hands holding a dove. He talked a lot about *Jesus Time*. She didn't think that the ministry had lasted.

Marjie nodded her head at Risa. *Bored-me. You do do?*

Shane stared up at Marjie, trying to figure out who she was and what she was doing there. He squinted at her and burped. Marjie grimaced and fanned her face.

How's W O O D S? Risa asked Marjie. She grinned in a way that meant: *How's your crush on somebody totally inappropriate, and I know something you are trying to keep a secret.*

Why you ask? She'd caught Marjie off-balance but she recovered quickly. *Not interested—gossip.*

So something has happened, Risa thought. She smirked at Marjie.

What are you doing? Marjie told her. Risa thought she looked excited and angry at the same time, like she did have something she needed to protect.

Lucas walked into the kitchen and put a hand on Risa's shoulder. She looked up at him and saw he now had an empty red plastic cup in one hand, ringed with suds.

"Ladies," she saw on his lips. He windmilled his other hand in Marjie's direction, motioning her toward him. He must have a crush on Marjie. Risa shrugged his hand off her shoulder.

As if he were on TV, Lucas put his hands together in a prayer. "You two—family," he said and signed, his eyes on Marjie. Rocco walked into the kitchen, fist-bumped Shane, and picked through the pockets of the jean jacket on the back of Shane's chair.

No, Risa signed slowly for Lucas' understanding. *Family not always mean friends.* Marjie frowned.

Rocco pulled a crinkled, empty condom packet out of Shane's jacket pocket. He snorted and tossed it at Risa.

Risa jumped out of her chair as if he'd thrown a match at her. She stood and pointed at everyone. *You—you—you, I don't need. One month, we graduate, but you are all stuck.* She lingered on the v-shape, the fork in the throat.

Ten years later, what will change? Marjie, teacher at the school but dream dream dream something different. Rocco, mooch off his family. Lucas, sit alone all day at a computer. All alone.

A sharp movement from Rocco: *Peabrain talk.*

From Marjie: *Think yourself. You negative, negative.*

Lucas looked puzzled. "What?" he asked.

Marjie shaped the signs a beat too slow, emphasizing the sarcasm. *And yourself? You win L O T T E R Y?*

Take care of myself, can. Risa told her cousin.

Marjie just looked at her, like she was a stranger.

Risa leaned forward and grabbed Marjie's arm. *Look at me. Know I can. Believe me.*

As far back as Risa could remember, Marjie had always been lucky. She just was, and it had nothing to do with looks or personality because as everybody knew, Risa was the sweet, friendly one. Marjie rubbed people the wrong way. But people didn't dare try to walk all over her.

I'm leaving, she finally signed.

Ok. Tell me. Marjie pointed at her chest, held the point for a moment, and then waved Risa forward, but with a movement that could mean, come here, or it could mean, confess. Or it could mean, come on, a challenge.

Risa sighed.

The last time things had been calm and easy was a few years ago, when she and Marjie, their brothers and sisters, and their fathers drove downriver one summer day. On the way home, their dads sat up front, and the kids stretched out in the back of the pick-up, looking up at the stars scrolling by, the wind blowing over their bodies. She wanted that feeling again, of leaving and returning, comfortable, sweaty, full, tired, and close.

Risa paused. How to tell her family about Rick? She wanted to know things her family didn't know. They wouldn't understand.

Her pulse raced at the thought of meeting Rick next month at the Greyhound station in the next town over and then leaving in his truck. It was difficult to lip-read him, but she always put her hands on his shoulders and moved him so the light fell on his face. When she did, he seemed so touched, he put a hand over hers, and she knew that had to be a starting place.

They wrote e-mails back and forth. He'd talk about the sign language class he was taking, and sign it, luv u, Rick. Rick and Risa, she wrote in her notebook, with fancy handwriting, taking care that no one saw the scribblings. She wasn't yet eighteen, and so she had to keep it quiet.

In the school's computer lab, she made sure to get a terminal over in a corner, and day after day, they made plans about the kind of house they would buy, what kind of furniture they would get once they figured out where to live, where he'd get a better job. He had learned the deaf's language for her, he wrote.

Nothing, she told her cousin. *Good L U C K college.*

OK, fine, Marjie told her. *Don't tell me. Your decision.*

But then Marjie reached out and squeezed her cousin's arm.

Risa nodded, feeling strong enough already, for what lay ahead.

"What Lay Ahead" is actually a series of three interlinked short-short stories. The characters of one story show up in another story, and what changes is the point of view, who is telling that particular section of the overall story. I started writing this story in my twenties, when I was just beginning to learn American Sign Language and to "come out" as a deaf person. During part of that time, I visited Washington, D.C. and worked one summer as a writer for the "History Through Deaf Eyes" exhibition at Gallaudet University. I met a wide variety of Deaf people, some from Deaf families and Deaf schools and others with backgrounds more like mine. Some started signing early, some later.

Each person has his or her own sense of what it means to be deaf, with some focusing more on how identity arises from a Deaf-centered, ASL-focused context, and others, on identities that come out of contact, or even conflict, between hearing and deaf, signing contexts. And along with this comes other important individual identities such as race, ethnicity, sexuality, socio-economic status, and additional disabilities. There isn't one way to be deaf; there are many, and I wanted to look at that aspect of being deaf, but to do this in a Deaf-centered, signing context with Deaf, deaf, hard of hearing, and hearing people all mixed in together.

The connections we make as deaf individuals with each other may be fragmented or temporary or they may be deep and long-lasting. Or maybe those connections will always be flawed or hurtful because of the ways in which members of communities face and deal with racism, sexism, linguicism, audism, and ableism. But in small communities like the one in this story, there's bound to be some kind of contact and with that, the possibility of some kind of connection. And to top it all off, all of the characters in this story series are still young, still deciding who they will be, trying to figure out how to deal with the mixed messages about who they are perceived to be.

This story came out of a moment at a party I attended in the mid '90's, a party where many different kinds of deaf people were in attendance. A couple there—who would later go on to break up—were arguing with each other about the best way to sign Hamlet's "to be or not to be" speech. That was the genesis of the entire story series. And while writing, I visited one midwestern Deaf school and some observations from that visit mixed in with some of my own experiences in a small town set on a bluff above the Mississippi River.

Michael Northen

THE DISABLING OF SHORT FICTION

An Afterword

"I ain't goina do it. I don't need no shoe when I got ways of getting my own."

When Rufus Johnson utters these words in Flannery O'Connor's "The Lame Shall Enter First" in response to an attempt to normalize him by getting him to wear a specially created shoe, O'Connor may have created the first short story to have disability sensibility.

Sixty years have passed since O'Connor's story was published and to date, despite a handful of remarkable single-author collections, there have been no anthologies of disability short fiction. This contrasts markedly with African American, Latino and Feminist writing.

This is not to say that there was no fiction before O'Connor that included characters with physical disabilities, but they were those like Dickens' Tiny Tim or Klara of *Heidi* fame, characters calculated to inspire pity or worse, those whose bodies were metaphors for their moral disability. None were created by writers who knew what it was like to live with a disability themselves. After O'Connor, there was a long hiatus until 1984 when Anne Finger broke out with her story "Like the Hully Gully But Not So Slow." It featured the cynical, sassy narrator who refused to be marginalized that became Finger's trademark. Finger followed in 1988 with *Basic Skills*, the first—and one of the few short story collections to date—in which every story featured a character with a disability. It was a landmark book in disability literature and one that short story writers today can still use as a baseline.

In the early 1990's, two short stories appeared that put male characters who were in wheelchairs on the map. The first was Thom Jones' acerbic Vietnam Vet in "The Pugilist at Rest," first published in the *New Yorker*. The second was Andre Dubus' Drew, of "Dancing After Hours," possibly the most widely anthologized piece of short fiction about a person with a physical disability. Both of these stories demonstrated that making a character with a disability the focal point of a story did not preclude the story also being a literary work of art. Jones and Dubus both followed up these efforts with short story collections named after their previously successful work, but, as good as each of these collections were, both had their limitations. In Dubus' case, "Dancing After Hours" was the only piece in the book to feature a main character with a disability. Jones' powerful stories, on the other hand, were so disturbing that they left one wondering whether with all of their psychological issues, it wasn't safer to keep people with disabilities marginalized. Moreover, both Dubus' and Jones' disabilities were acquired. Unlike Finger, neither of them were able to portray what it was like to grow up in a society that refused to accept them as "normal." It was not until 2002 that a collection of short stories focused solely on disability appeared—Noria Jablonski's *Human Oddities*.

Despite the work of writers like O'Connor, Finger, Jones and Dubus, and the fact that such literature represented the lives of the largest minority in the United States, even at the turn of the century the disability short story was slow to gain recognition. A case in point is *The Columbia Companion to the Twentieth-Century American Short Story* edited by Blanche Gelfant in 2001 and intended as a contemporary perspective on the fiction the past one hundred years had to offer. While the book includes introductory essays that reflect the literature of nine minority groups including gay/lesbian, the working class and holocaust victims, it makes no mention of the work of writers with disabilities.

Nevertheless short stories by writers with disabilities were being written. They were seeping out slowly into small magazines. Kenny Fries seminal anthology *Staring Back* (1997), subtitled *The Disability Experience from the Inside Out* included short fiction by Finger and Dubus. Even today, however, fifteen years after Gelfant's volume, in an age when an increasing number of universities across the country have degree programs in disability studies, there is no anthology that collects the short stories of writers with disabilities into one place. It is about time.

The need for *The Right Way to Be Crippled & Naked* would seem obvious: America's largest and most permeable minority should receive representation on the bookshelves of the country. Beyond this democratic consideration, however, two other considerations are in play. Fiction is arguably the literary genre in which our imaginations are freest to take flight. Few would argue that a writer who has never been to Nebraska should not be free to write about Nebraska, that Stephen Crane should not have written *The Red Badge of Courage* without ever having fought in the American Civil War or that a person who is sighted should not be able to include a blind protagonist in her work, but disability activist Simi Linton's mantra, "Nothing About Us Without Us" still holds. The stereotypes and negative attitudes towards disability that have accreted through our literary history and helped to form public perceptions can only be authentically transformed by moving marginalized voices to the center. As Finger writes in "Our Ned": "In this story, the fools come out of the attic."

The second consideration is more subtle. As disabilities scholar Leonard Davis has pointed out, the novel and, to an even greater extent, the short story is a modern middle-class invention. Readers are familiar with the traditional narrative arc in which a problem jolts the protagonist out of stasis and the entire point of the story is to return the situation to the status quo. When a disability is involved, the "problem" to be solved is frequently the character's disability, and the solving of the problem becomes what David Mitchell and Sharon Snyder have coined narrative prosthesis. The traditional short story offers three forms of narrative prosthesis: cure, overcoming or epiphany. What they all have in common is the assumption that there is something wrong with disability, that a person with a disability is in a less-than status that must be remediated. Avoiding this trap is the real challenge to writers with disabilities. What alternative structures for short fiction can writers come up with? One of the tasks the writers in this volume faced was coming up with such alternatives—to not only write fiction about disability but to disable the fictions about disability as well.

"Accessibility," that buzzword of the ADA era, is not merely about building concrete ramps where there are now stairs. It is also about putting disability culture into the public eye in a way that frees it from its banishment to the margins. Our hope is that *The Right Way to Be Crippled & Naked*, by drawing together work that has up until now been unknown and inaccessible to most readers, provides a literary ramp to a body of work that has for too long been neglected. This anthology provides a microcosm of the literary world that the disability short story has to offer. Readers encounter the artist losing his vision in Raymond Luczak's "Winter Eyes," Nisi Shawl's neurodiverse prisoner, Anne Finger's resurrected Rosa Luxemburg and the conflicted perspectives of young deaf adults in Kristen Harmon's "What Lay Ahead." These short stories provide fuller, more complex views of disability and, at the same time, prove that disability fiction can be an engaging, enjoyable and intellectually satisfying experience.

CONTRIBUTORS

TANTRA BENSKO teaches fiction writing. Her psychological suspense series—The Agents of the Nevermind—begins with a novel called *Glossolalia* (www.insubordinatebooks.com). She lives in Berkeley.

SHEILA BLACK is the author of several books of poetry, most recently *Iron, Ardent* (Educe Press). With Jennifer Bartlett and Michael Northen, she co-edited *Beauty is a Verb: The New Poetry of Disability*. In 2012 she received a Witter Bynner Fellowship from the Library of Congress. She lives in San Antonio, Texas, where she directs Gemini Ink.

ANN BOGLE's work consists of short stories, prose poems, poetry, essays, flash fictions and notations given online and in print. Her weblog Ana Verse and Fictionaut are the best sources for learning more about it. She lives near Minneapolis, Minnesota.

PAUL DE ANGUERA is a retired systems analyst. He's volunteered for over 12 years at a large west coast retirement home. His other interests include wilderness sports, photography and, of course, writing. This is his second published story.

KARA DORRIS earned a PhD in English from the University of North Texas, as well as an MFA in poetry from New Mexico State University. Her two chapbooks are *Elective Affinities* (Dancing Girl Press) and *Night Ride Home* (Finishing Line Press).

ROBERT FAGAN (1935-2009) received his Ph.D. in English Literature from Columbia University. His poetry and fiction have been published in many literary journals. His publications include a collection of his poetry, *Stepping Out* (Red Moon Press, 2007). He contracted chronic Guillian-Barre syndrome as a young man.

ANNE FINGER is a writer of fiction and nonfiction, as well as a teacher, social justice activist, and a lover of movies and chocolate. Her most recent short story collection is *Call Me Ahab* (University of Nebraska Press).

ANA GARZA G'z has an M. F. A. from California State University, Fresno, where she teaches part-time. Over sixty of her poems have appeared in various journals and anthologies. She also works as a community interpreter and translator.

DAGOBERTO GILB is the author of, among others, *The Magic of Blood, Woodcuts of Women,* and most recently, *Before the End, After the Beginning,* all with Grove Press. He lives in Austin.

LISA GILL is the recipient of an NEA Fellowship and author of five books, including the poetry collections *Red as Lotus, Mortar & Pestle, Dark Enough*; as well as a verse play, *The Relenting*; and the hybrid memoir *Caput Nili*. Delayed diagnoses of PTSD and porphyria finally made sense of Gill's chronic health challenges. She lives in the high desert near Moriarty, New Mexico with her dog.

MEGAN GRANATA is a second-year MFA candidate in fiction at Arizona State University. She lives and teaches in Tempe, Arizona, and is at work on her first novel, also about disability. "The Sitting" is her first publication.

KRISTEN HARMON is a professor of English at Gallaudet University in Washington, D.C. In addition to fiction, she has published creative non-fiction and academic essays.

LAURA HERSHEY (1962-2010) was a Colorado-based poet and writer, activist and mother with spinal muscular atrophy. She held an M.F.A. in Creative Writing from Antioch University Los Angeles. *Spark Before Dark,* her last poetry chapbook, was published by Finishing Line Press.

CHRISTOPHER JON HEUER is the author *of Bug: Deaf Identity and Internal Revolution* and *All Your Parts Intact: Poems.* His short stories and poetry have appeared in many anthologies and periodicals. He is a professor of English at Gallaudet University.

NORIA JABLONSKI is the author of the story collection *Human Oddities* (Counterpoint). Her stories have appeared in several magazines and the anthology *Who Can Save Us Now?: Brand-New Superheroes and Their Amazing (Short) Stories.*

LIESL JOBSON is a writer, photographer and musician, who loves rowing her single scull and playing her bassoon. She works in enterprise development, in Cape Town, and is a contributing editor to *Books LIVE,* an online portal to South African literature.

THOM JONES (1945-2016) was the author of three short-story collections. He said of writing: "I think fiction is a way of approaching the truth. A good fiction writer is the hardest thing to be. You can go to medical school and learn neurosurgery, but anybody can do that who's got the IQ. When you create something out of thin air you have to know the human heart."

STEPHEN KUUSISTO teaches at Syracuse University and is the author of numerous books of nonfiction and poetry.

RAYMOND LUCZAK is the author and editor of 18 books. His latest titles include *QDA: A Queer Disability Anthology* and *The Kiss of Walt Whitman Still on My Lips.* He lives in Minneapolis, Minnesota, and online at raymondluczak.com.

BOBBI LURIE has worked as an occupational therapist, crisis counselor, medical researcher, muralist, etcher, essayist and poet. She is the author of four poetry collections, most recently *the morphine poems.*

JONATHAN MACK was raised on a family farm in New Hampshire, but has spent most of his adult life in India and Japan. His stories and essays have appeared in many journals. He was a 2016 Lambda Literary Fellow in Fiction. He blogs at Guttersnipe Das.

KOBUS MOOLMAN was born with spina bifida. He is a South African poet and playwright who teaches creative writing at the University of the Western Cape. He has published seven volumes of poetry and two collections of plays.

CANDICE MORROW received her MFA from New Mexico State University. "For the Love of Him" is dedicated to her dear friend, Gina, who provided the spark (in her beauty and wit and tendencies toward superstition) for the character of Maggie.

MICHAEL NORTHEN moderated the Inglis House Poetry Workshop for writers with disabilities in Philadelphia for thirteen years. He is the editor of *Wordgathering*, an online journal of disability and literature, and is one of the editors of *Beauty is a Verb: The New Poetry of Disability*.

ALISON OATMAN holds a master's degree in Medieval Studies from Columbia University. She is a recent transplant to Santa Fe, where she teaches "Italian for Opera Lovers." Finally, she has almost finished a memoir about food and sexuality called *My Mother's Body*.

NISI SHAWL is coauthor of *Writing the Other: A Practical Approach*, and a founder of the pro-inclusivity organization the Carl Brandon Society. Her Belgian Congo steampunk novel *Everfair* was recently published by Tor.

FLOYD SKLOOT's 20 books include his most recently published novel *The Phantom of Thomas Hardy* (University of Wisconsin Press), the poetry collection *Approaching Winter* (LSU Press) and the memoir *In the Shadow of Memory* (University of Nebraska Press).

ELLEN McGRATH SMITH teaches at the University of Pittsburgh. Her chapbook *Scatter, Feed* was published by Seven Kitchens Press and her book of poetry, *Nobody's Jackknife*, was published by West End Press.

JOE VASTANO started writing at sixteen. He traced Jim Morrison to Kerouac and Rimbaud, took them at their words and deranged his senses on the road for twenty years. Now he's sorting through it all.

ACKNOWLEDGMENTS

Laura Hershey's "Getting Comfortable" was originally published in *Beauty is a Verb* (Cinco Puntos Press, 2011).

Tantra Bensko's "Virus on Fire" was first published on January 26, 2015 in *Everyday Genius*.

Noria Jabonski's "Solo in the Spotlight" was originally published in her story collection *Human Oddities* (Counterpoint, 2005).

Stephen Kuusisto's "Plato Again" was originally published in *Telling Stories Out of Court* (Cornell University Press 2008).

Liesl Jobson's "Still Life in the Art Room" is from her short story collection *Ride the Tortoise* (Jacana Press, 2013).

Joe Vastano's "Twinning" won a first place prize in *Glimmer Train*'s Family Matters contest in late 2011, and was published in *Gimmer Train* #86.

Ellen McGrath Smith's "Two Really Different Things" was originally published in *Wordgathering* (September 2012).

Anne Finger's Story "Comrade Luxemburg and Comrade Gramsci Pass Each Other at a Congress of the Second International in Switzerland on the 10th of March, 1912" was originally published in *Ploughshares* in Spring 1995, and is included in her collection *Call Me Ahab* (University of Nebraska Press, 2009).

Nisi Shawl's "Deep End" was originally published in 2004 in *So Long Been Dreaming: Postcolonial Science Fiction and Fantasy* (Arsenal Pulp Press). It has been reprinted in *Filter House* (Aqueduct Press, 2008) and in *WisCon Chronicles 7* (Aqueduct Press, 2013).

Dagoberto Gilb's "please, thank you" was originally published in *Harper's Magazine* on June 2010.

Thom Jones' "Bomb Shelter Noel " originally appeared in *Playboy* in January 2011.

Christopher Jon Heuer's "Trauma" was originally published in *The Tactile Mind Quarterly* (Tactile Mind Press, 2004). It has been republished several times, most recently in *Deaf Lit Extravaganza* (Handtype Press, 2013).

Ann Bogle's "Letter to John Berryman" originally appeared in *Fictionaut* on February 26, 2013, and then as part of a longer essay in *Wordgathering* (September 2014).

Lisa Gill's "Holding Zeno's Suitcase in Kansas, Flowering" was originally published in *American Fiction: The Best Unpublished Short Stories by Emerging Writers Volume 7* (New Rivers Press, 1995).

A different version of Floyd Skloot's "Alzheimer's Noir" appeared in *Portland Noir* (Akashic Books, 2009).

Kristen Harmon's "What Lay Ahead," was originally published in *The Tactile Mind Quarterly*. It was later revised and reprinted in *Wordgathering*.

OUR THANKS

As always, I'm grateful for the support of my wife Lora and children Eli, Maya, Maura, Melissa, and Pat, and to my brother Ed, my constant reader. I'd particularly like to dedicate this book to the next generation, my grandchildren Amelia, Connor, Jack, Andrew, Liam, Maggie, Owen and Daisie. Special thanks to the Inglis House Poetry Workshop with whom my journey in disability writing began as well as to the editors of *Kaleidoscope* and *Breath and Shadow*, Gail Wilmott and Chris Kuell, whose journals were among the first to give a home to short disability fiction. I'm also thankful for those who have helped keep *Wordgathering* going over the years including Eliot Spindel, Linda Cronin, Sean Mahoney, Jill Khoury, Emily Michael and, of course, Sheila Black.

—*Michael Northen*

For support with the creation of this book, I thank my husband Duncan, children Walker and Eliza, and daughter Annabelle Hayse who provided intense material support with the shaping and editing of this book. Also, the writers of disability who have provided such steadfast friendship and support—most especially Jennifer Bartlett, Kathi Wolfe, John Lee Clark, Jim Ferris, Denise Leto, Amber DiPietra, Jillian Weise, Laurie Clements Lambeth, Kara Dorris, Meg Day, Ona Gitz, and Dan Simpson. For her steadfast friendship and unerring editorial eye, I would also like to thank Connie Voisine. Last but not least, this book is for my first family—my parents Clay and Moira Black, and my wonderful sisters Samantha and Sarah.

—*Sheila Black*

Thank you to my friends Keith, Andra, Nikki, Haley May, and, most especially, Jon. Also thanks to my sister Eliza and brother Walker.

—*Annabelle Hayse*